THE CELESTIALS
BOOK 1

BIANCA K. GRAY

For MY DAD AND 엄마, THANK YOU FOR CULTIVATING MY VAST AND NEVER-ENDING IMAGINATION.

MY FIANCÉ, THANK YOU FOR SUPPORTING AND LOVING ME.

THIS BOOK IS DEDICATED TO YOU ALL.

1

Before the Celestials were killed, they had been born. Birthed by creatures of Asynithis, the Gods would choose the Celestial body that fit them best and the God of Death was no exception. His choice was very deliberate. Whether he made the best choice or not remains to be seen.

———

The wind blew hard as Ralnor made his way back home. His feet could not move fast enough as the harsh air pushed him back with every step. The electricity in the air was unfamiliar as was the intense darkness caused by the overcast and the cover of night, but Ralnor didn't think twice about it despite it never being this dark in Aureum. His mind was racing with thoughts of his wife and the words that he heard at the tavern that night.

"Hurry home, Ralnor! Your wife is in labor," a coworker had told him after bursting into the tavern in a hurry. Sweat rolled down his forehead as he forced his way through the woods in order to get to his cabin, not from exertion but from his heart pounding loudly in his chest. Louder and louder did it pound and harder and harder was it getting for him to breathe. Ralnor didn't know what a father was supposed to be. He never had one that would be called a father and he never experienced fatherhood himself. A memory flashed in his mind. White hair and unforgiving green eyes. Bruises everywhere. And the distinct sound of wood on bone. Of flesh on flesh. No, Ralnor didn't know what a father was supposed to be.

Ralnor stood in the doorway, his clothes sticking to his cold, clammy skin. His long, snow white hair, the sign of a pure elf, was tangled and windswept. It looked orange as it reflected the light of the fire. His green eyes, that echoed the father that he never got to know, never wanted to know, swept across the room and fell upon his wife. Lying in the one room cabin on the floor in front of him, lay his wife, belly swollen. Red filled his eyes as he saw her lying there, brown eyes staring into nothing. Her copper hair was a sign of impurity and yet he had never loved a person as much as he loved Ava. Heart twisted inside of his chest, pounding louder and louder than before, he walked over to where the love of his life lay. The birth-witch sat beside her, hair knotted in a tight black bun. Her face echoing her hair. Her hands moved quickly around his wife and not a word was being spoken. The firelight led up to her eyes and stayed there, not letting her eyes go. But the firelight avoided Ava's eyes, avoided her face completely. Ralnor stood there, just above his love's face and held her features in his heart, as one would cradle a baby in their arms. He could not move, her gaping mouth and faded eyes holding him there like a timber head holding a boat to the docks as waves crash against the side of it. He could not move and did not dare to. His normally warm green eyes now echoed that of his father's. Unforgiving. Cruel. Broken.

A cry of a baby filled the otherwise tiny, empty cabin. The birth-witch's hands shook as she took the baby into her arms. This wasn't normal. Something was wrong. Of course something was wrong, Ava was dead. The light reflected the color of the baby's hair, flashing the color into Ralnor's eyes. Copper. A dark copper brown. Ralnor's thoughts stayed fixated on Ava. *How could she be dead?* Ralnor turned to the child that favored the mother that it had just killed. Childbirth was perfected by magic. No one dies from something as simple as childbirth in Asynithis. Ava's eyes held a mysterious scream, as though horrified by the last thing she saw. The baby's hair flashed in Ralnor's eyes again as it struggled and cried against the birth-witch's arms. Dark copper brown. Impurity. The sign of a muddled elf. Ava, exactly like Ava. What happened, Ralnor wanted to scream, what happened? Just this morning, Ralnor saw her toothy grin before heading off to work. Just this morning, Ralnor heard her excitedly tell about the coming birth of their first child. Just this morning, they were trading names back and forth across the kitchen table. Just this morning.

As Ralnor took a step forward, red filling his vision, the cries of the baby stopped mid-scream, as if knowing what Ralnor's possible intentions were. His eyes moved upward, locking with the birth-witch's. Terrified. No, horrified. The same expression in Ava's eyes.

"Mr. Norovir," the birth-witch finally spoke. Her voice was tired, heavy, exhausted. It was without strength and didn't hold the words above a whisper that well. If Ralnor was not paying attention, her voice would have disappeared into the roaring winds crashing against the side of the stone cabin. Ralnor took another step forward, the baby as silent as can be as if waiting for Ralnor to make a decision. He couldn't think straight; he couldn't see straight. Looking back at Ava, red covered her like it covered the floor. Her copper brown hair was splayed out above her head on the ground as if she were underwater. He looked back at the birth-witch as she took the blanket off from the child that caused this bloody scene. It screamed from the cold hitting its skin as if it were the worst feeling, as if grief didn't touch it, remorse didn't touch it. And Ralnor's knees hit the pool of blood with a thud as he stared at the back of the child, *his* child. No one could mistake the marks that ran down the spine of his baby. Black intricate lines up and down the spine. Guilt bubbled up from his chest to his throat as he recalled what he was about to do to this child. The child's eyes opened, brown like Ava's. Ava, exactly like Ava. And just like that, those eyes held Ralnor there, on the floor in the blood of his love.

"Her name is Rhea," the birth-witch's voice said, with a bit more strength, though her hands shook as they wrapped the child back up, away from the harsh cold.

Ralnor did not speak, could not speak. He had no more ties to this child anymore. Her name was Rhea, just Rhea. The name that Ava gave her, though a name that would only be considered her birth name and nothing more.

"Your daughter is a Celestial, Mr. Norovir," the birth-witch whispered. Not any Celestial, Ralnor knew. His daughter was the God of Death.

2

Khalon strapped on a leather vest, covering the almost black red scales that were embedded in his naturally tan skin. The scales had no pattern, no rhyme or reason, besides the ones on his back. They were scattered in clusters beautifully all over his body; though they didn't cover him completely, not in the slightest. Scales were a characteristic of the people of Draconia, but the colors of the scales were normally a pale or faded red. Some were so faded that their scales were almost white, though Khalon's scales were different from most draconians. His showed his status in society. His showed his bloodline.

He patted down the vest that covered his broad shoulders and grabbed the sword that lay against the gray stone wall next to him. The sword flashed black-red for a moment, reflecting the color of the scales that ran up the side of his neck and branched out a little onto his face, like phantom scratches from a claw. Khalon gripped the handle hard as he jumped up and down. Shaking his limbs and stretching, he looked around the little room that he had learned to call home. The room wasn't wider than the length of Khalon's arms stretched all the way out from both sides of his body. It was a square room, made completely of stone. There was one little barred window where the wall met the ceiling and if Khalon stood up straight, he could see the dirt ground of the arena that waited for him. The only extravagant thing that he owned was this sword. It was forged in the boiled blood of a dragon and the handle was wrapped with the skin of one, with a large, curved ivory tooth as the pommel at the end of the handle that extended past the end of the fist that gripped it. The blade was made of white glass, a glass that was indestructible, and only a handful were ever made. It was originally a stone that was found in the den of a dragon that, when heated by the blood of one, turned white – almost translucent – and reflective. The last dragon gifted these weapons to the first Draconians. This sword was one of a kind in look and was one of the most powerful weapons to ever grace Asynithis.

"Khalon," said a man at the opening of Khalon's, essentially, cell. Khalon looked up and smiled at the familiar face.

"Liam," Khalon spoke the man's name, and the man flashed a smile, revealing his pointed teeth. Liam's scales were pink and there were not quite as many of them, only on his hands that Liam always had on display. They were never covered in any way, not even by gloves in the colder months. He was very proud of his draconian bloodline, even if it was only a couple of drops.

Liam ran his hand through his sandy hair and smiled as if to challenge Khalon. Though, Liam thought, he would never get to be in the arena with Khalon for if he did, he knew it would be his last. He was grateful but at the same time was disheartened, for a battle with Khalon could maybe prove his strength, his true raw power (if he were to win) and that was Liam's purpose in life. He loved his strength, he flaunted it, but he could never do just that in front of Khalon. Liam frowned quickly and then:

"You're up." Khalon nodded. Liam eyed his sword, enviously. If he were to have that, he would win hands down. Khalon followed Liam's eyes to his sword and didn't say what he wanted: *Even if you had my sword, you don't have my strength. You wouldn't have a chance.* But, Khalon said nothing, walking past Liam through the doorway and down the hallway towards the arena. Khalon thought of Liam's sharpened teeth that he had flashed at him. He knew what Liam did with those blindingly white teeth just hours before and for a moment, Khalon was relieved that he would probably never meet Liam in the arena. For if he let his guard down, even for a moment, he knew Liam would lunge toward his throat, like a predator in hunt, and rip the life out of him. Those teeth were the only things Khalon was afraid of. Those teeth weren't the predictability of humanity or the wisdom of dragons. Those teeth were the chaos and need of an animal. Khalon shuddered. He had many a nightmare with Liam's teeth cutting through the flesh of his neck, but he would never tell a soul. He would never show Liam how much those teeth scared him. He would never show fear to anyone. For he had to leave, he had to escape. And showing fear would have him dead. And he couldn't die, for he was meant for something greater. He was not just Khalon.

"Ladies and gentlemen, Khalon Draconia," the announcer boomed, his voice bouncing off the stone walls that surrounded Khalon as he walked uphill, the large arch in front of him showing the middle of the arena. No, he was not just Khalon.

He was Khalon Draconia, son of the Dragon King.

• • •

Well, bastard son of the Dragon King. That's an emphasis that Queen Aoife wanted creatures to keep in their minds when they thought of Khalon Draconia. To remember that he was *just* a bastard son and nothing more. But she knew better than that, as she watched him walk across the arena to stand in front of his opponent. She knew, as she looked at the cheering crowd, yelling, screaming louder than they have for any other Champion. Oh, Queen Aoife knew all too well what the public thought of Khalon Draconia and the first thing that came to their minds was not "bastard".

Her bright red scales bristled against her skin as her eyes caught the color of his, such dark red that glistened black, or sometimes, endless black that somehow glistened red. And when she looked at the color of those scales, she knew, as did everyone else, what noble bloodline he had hailed from. He was a bastard child, but his mother was of royalty. And the people who were behind his mother were now behind him, even if he didn't know it. Even if he was locked away to battle others until his death, there were still people who wanted him to ascend the throne. People who believed the spirit of the dragon lay inside of his soul. Her eyebrows furrowed as she watched him plunge the sword that his father, her husband, gave to him when he was just a boy into the heart of his opponent. Just a boy, Queen Aoife thought, and yet, *somehow*, he survived this long.

"He's a good fighter," the Dragon King, King Vien, spoke, almost proudly. He hardly spoke to her now. Her beauty was fading and his spirit was dying. He was not as enthusiastic anymore and he could feel how cruel she was becoming. How bitter. But, for some reason that he could not explain, she had a hold over him that he couldn't quite shake off. It was the only reason keeping him from disposing of her.

The crowd was screaming as the announcer revealed the results of the match. Screaming like madmen, mindlessly, while Khalon lifted his hands in victory. He smiled at the crowd that spurred him on while his eyes avoided the body that lay next to him. His sweat was intermingled with hot, sticky blood, but it wasn't his. He didn't have a scratch on him.

"Quite," Queen Aoife said through gritted teeth, though she feigned a smile at her husband. How badly she wanted that bastard child to be dead. And then, she smiled genuinely at King Vien, and he could feel that an idea was forming behind those lifeless eyes of hers.

"Since Khalon is *such* a good fighter, and since the public *loves* to see him fight so tremendously, wouldn't it be grand if he were to have another fight? An encore." King Vien looked at her for a moment, but he didn't have the backbone to fight her, he knew this. There was something that always kept him from disagreeing with her. Yet, he tried.

"But fight who? All the fights are over for today. All that's left are the Champions for tomorrow," King Vien almost pleaded with her. He begged her with the same half-moon shaped eyes that graced the face of Khalon. Her jaw tightened. How much that bastard child looked like the King. She shook her head and looked back at the arena from underneath the shaded thrones in which they both sat.

"Nonsense. He should fight Liam," she said, her smile filled with joy at the thought of Liam ripping the throat of Khalon. Liam and Khalon were in different classes. Liam was a mutt, so he was on the lower rung of the fighting ladder while Khalon was a pure Draconian, through and through, so he was considered more of a noble fighter, not a dirty one. But, Liam, despite being seen as simply an animal, was a crowd favorite. People wanted Liam to win. He wasn't quite as big of a public celebrity as Khalon was, but a celebrity in his own right.

"People would *love* to see Khalon and Liam fight," Queen Aoife stated, smiling down at the bastard walking back to his cell. He had taken off his vest, revealing the birthmark on his back that marked him as part of the royal family of Draconia: a dragon shaped by scales down the spine of his back. Queen Aoife pressed her lips together tightly, gripping the arms of the throne that she sat on.

"Yes," she said through gritted teeth, "The people would love that."

———

Khalon dragged his sword and his vest on both sides of his body as he left the screaming crowd behind. The doors of the archway began to close and Khalon looked over his shoulder to see the bloodied body of his opponent on the ground lying twisted like a lifeless puppet, and it took everything in him not to throw up right there. He stood, frozen, until the doors finally closed, shielding him from the horror that he just created. It wasn't the first body that he had taken life from and yet every single time he felt the same pain and disgust as the first life he had taken. *I'm just trying to survive*, Khalon thought as he continued down the narrow hallway that led back down to his cell. But wasn't that man just trying to survive too? Weren't we all trying to survive in this violent hellscape? Waiting for the day that we could leave, unscathed; for the day where we could have a taste of freedom?

He shook his head as he wiped the sweat off of his nose, leaving a trail of blood across his face. He couldn't think like this. If he did, he wouldn't be able to take the life of the next one, and if he couldn't do that, he would die. Turning the corner to enter his cell, a guard stood in the doorway preventing Khalon from entering.

"Move it," said Khalon, trying to push past the guard. The guard stood still and stared down Khalon with his beady eyes, the only feature on his face that Khalon could see.

"My fight is over," Khalon explained. *God*, he thought, *these guards could be so stupid.* Though what did he expect from brainwashed, brain dead guards?

"No," the guard said, "Your fight is beginning." Khalon frowned as his eyes narrowed. But before he could let his anger bubble in his chest, Liam walked by him with guards flanked in front and behind him. Liam's eyes flashed with fear for a second before he smiled at Khalon, revealing his pointed teeth. Khalon's face remained expressionless as he watched Liam walk away, but his heart had started to race. The one thing in his short, sheltered life that Khalon was afraid of was what he had to face next.

"Let's go," the guard said. There was only one of them. They knew that Khalon wouldn't try to run. Not only because he never has, but Khalon had something at stake, and they knew that. Everyone knew that.

Khalon wanted to scream. He wanted to run. He knew he could take down every person who tried to stop him. But, if he did that, he would be considered a terror to the country. He would be a fugitive, a criminal. And he would never get to take his place next to his father. A fight that crossed classes was unheard of. It wasn't something his father would've thought of. King Vien was a stickler for the rules. Queen Aoife, on the other hand... Khalon saw the way that Queen Aoife looked at him while he was in his first fight. He had felt her glare, even from where she was sitting, yards away from him. He had felt her hatred for him grow as he continued to win. He knew she wanted him dead, she didn't make that fact hidden. And

Khalon's anger grew during the fight as he felt her stare on him. So much so that he wanted to provoke her, wanted to remind her just who exactly he was. So he took off his vest, revealing the birthmark of a Draconia that went down the spine of his back with the colors of both families. Both Draconia families. The Red Dragon and the Black Dragon. He wanted to remind her that he was a direct descendant of both.

He was arrogant, he realized, in doing that. For she had the power, not him. She was up there making the rules and his father and everyone else were her pawns, her puppets. He made her angry. So angry that she wanted him dead sooner, rather than later.

The doors opened up, revealing the arena once again. He went to put on his vest, but the guard stopped him. Khalon bit his tongue as his jaw smashed against his teeth. Yes, Queen Aoife wanted him dead so badly, they were not only crossing classes in this fight, but also fighting by the rules of the lower rung. They were fighting dirty. There were no rules, only one: no protection. Only pure strength and power would win in a fight like this, which is why Liam had always won.

"I'm guessing I can't have my sword either?" Khalon more said than asked but the guard grunted in answer. Khalon handed the guard the sword his father gave him and stared out into the middle of the field through the arch. He could already hear the roaring crowd, though he could sense their confusion as the announcer revealed the participants of the next fight. Liam and Khalon? Khalon could almost hear the whispers that were running through the audience sitting in the amphitheater. Aren't those two in different classes?

He took a deep breath and closed his eyes, shaking out his limbs. He didn't even have the chance to wash the blood out from his skin or hair. But he walked out into the arena with his head held high. His chest glistened in the setting sunlight, his scales flashing black. With an overconfident smile, Liam stood in the middle of the arena, ready for what was to come. Khalon suppressed the urge to shudder and crouched down into the stance of the lower rung. He kept his center of gravity low to the ground and analyzed Liam's stance. *All I have to do is keep those teeth away from my neck*, thought Khalon. With that, the fire around the arena was lit by the breath of King Vien, and the fight began. Liam lunged towards Khalon and knocked him over. Khalon quickly rolled to the side before Liam could hold him down and then backed away. He didn't know what to do. He had never fought hand to hand combat before, besides in training when he was young. As Khalon tried to think of his next move, Liam's fist hit Khalon's jaw, whipping Khalon's head to the right. Khalon backed up a couple of steps as the crowd simultaneously cheered and booed. Khalon wiped the blood from his mouth and glared at Liam.

"Not so much of a hotshot now without that little sword of yours, huh?" Liam taunted. Khalon's jaw tightened. That's it. Anger bubbled up inside of Khalon, anger that he had been suppressing for eleven years. A punch for his father, and Liam fell to the ground. A kick to the ribs for Queen Aoife, and Liam grunted in pain. Khalon straddled Liam as he lay on the ground, struggling against the true strength of a Royal Draconian. Another punch across the face for the master of arms who always beat Khalon as a child. A punch from the left hand that connected with the jaw for his half brother Khai who got to live the life that Khalon desired. A flurry of punches that were meant for people other than Liam were being bestowed to his face. One after the other, but Khalon was so caught up in his unbridled anger that he didn't notice Liam hooking his leg with Khalon's. Liam twisted himself and slammed Khalon into the hard ground. There was a ringing in Khalon's ear as he looked up at Liam. He should've seen it coming. He had seen

Liam's battles for the few years that Liam was contained in the Ring of Fire and yet he missed Liam's signature move. Liam's lips were enlarged from a wound and one of his eyes was swollen shut, but he still pulled back a smile, baring those sharp teeth of his. Khalon struggled against Liam's grip, but Liam also knew exactly where to put pressure to keep someone down. It was just like Khalon's nightmares, but come true. He looked over at the thrones that held his father. His father's eyes were downcast but Queen Aoife was standing in anticipation. Khalon closed his eyes and waited for those teeth to sink into his skin and rip the life away from him. But instead, all he heard was the sound of cracking bone and the gasp from the audience.

He opened his eyes to see Liam holding his mouth in pain and rolling off of Khalon. Khalon got up in confusion and then looked down at his skin. Where there used to be tan, smooth skin were black scales that glittered red in the sunlight. And it wasn't just in the places where they usually were, but rather, all over his body. He looked over at Liam and then at the ground where he was just laying and saw the shattered remains of Liam's sharp teeth. The crowd was silent as he stood in the middle of the arena, in confusion and with adrenaline still pumping through his veins. The only sound that could be heard was the groan of pain that was escaping from Liam's lips. And then someone from the crowd called out, "The spirit of the dragon!" and suddenly rows of people were dropping to their knees, bowing to the young bastard prince.

"Long live the dragon!" they exclaimed. Khalon stood in shock as the scales started to disappear, revealing his skin once again. He looked over at his father who looked like he had seen a ghost.

No one was able to cover their whole body in scales. No one

could breathe fire or walk through it. No one except the one who inhabits the spirit of the dragon.

Khalon's black brown eyes met his father's and he knew in that second that any love that his father might have had for him was gone. Khalon was now the enemy. Khalon was now a threat to the throne.

3

The night hid Rhea's face almost as well as her black cloak that was draped around her shoulders. She glided through the woods towards the glowing bright lights of the capital city of Aureum. Rhea passed by people like a shadow, moving faster than any creature could possibly move, until she reached Regium. The city that held all the most important people of Aureum. She didn't take off the hood of her cloak as she walked into the blinding lights of the city.

Regium was a city of grandeur. It held all the past architectural types as well as new age architecture. A mixture of old and new was intertwined throughout the city. Metal blocks with marble columns or Gothic cathedrals with orange metal rings surrounding it as if it were Saturn. It was an interesting city filled with the most corrupt but seemingly upstanding people.

Rhea's black cloak stood out in a city like Regium where everyone had snow white hair, light eyes, while wearing light pastel clothing. Stares followed her as she glided through the streets but Rhea didn't pay them any mind. She knew what they were seeing if they looked underneath the cloak and into her face. They were seeing whoever they cared about most who had already passed or they were seeing what they themselves thought death looked like, but never her herself. Sometimes she wondered what it would feel like if loss touched her. She could vaguely understand it, somewhere deep within her, but the God of Death made sure no one could ever be around her. Not in this lifetime, nor her previous ones.

She fixed her gaze upwards past the hover cars that were zipping around in the air above her like shooting stars. Focusing her eyes on the horizon, she saw her destination.

The castle that held the royal family of Aureum was unlike the city of Regium. It was old, classic, and it stood tall as it loomed over the city. A reminder that the past is always a part of us. Rhea blew her hair out of her face as she looked up at the castle, causing the hood of her cloak to fall around her shoulders. She heard gasps, guttural cries, and a scream as people saw her face. She didn't know what face everyone was seeing, but she quickly put her hood back on and disappeared into the shadows so that they couldn't rush towards her. She saw them run towards the spot where she was, some falling to the ground in the agony of grief. It is what she carried around with her always without feeling it or without realizing it: their grief.

Rhea rushed up to the palace gates and slipped through them. The inside of the palace was just as grand as the outside, made completely of gold and marble. She glided up the stairs and entered the room where the King of Aureum was lying in a large, circular, crimson bed with gold trims. Rhea stood next to the bed and revealed herself, startling the four princes and their partners.

"God of Death," the prince next to her exclaimed, breathlessly. Rhea pulled the hood of her cloak down, letting it fall around her small shoulders. She didn't know what they were seeing but a look of sadness fell upon their faces.

"You are as beautiful as ever," the prince said, kissing Rhea's hand.

"I look like your mother," Rhea guessed, taking her hand away from him slowly. He looked up with tears clouding his light blue eyes.

"Yes," Adamar said, as if he were far away in thought. Rhea looked him up and down in quiet disgust, and then turned her attention to King Elkhazel. He was gasping for breath and his eyes were closed as tight as they could, wincing from the pain of death. Rhea lay a hand over his wrinkled forehead and he breathed deeply, the skin around his eyes relaxing.

"Is there any way that we can save him? Anything that we can give you to save the king?" asked Prince Adamar's wife Essaerae in an almost desperate but not quite there manner. Rhea looked her in the eyes and she looked away almost immediately.

"The only way to save a soul like King Elkhazel's would be a life that is worth the same as his soul," Rhea said, in an almost monotone voice. She knew that these people didn't want to save King Elkhazel. They were circling around his deathbed, waiting for him to decide who was going to become king in his place. Those desperate clutches around their necklaces were just the wives praying to An in hopes that their husband could become, in their eyes, the king of the most powerful country in all of Asynithis. Rhea couldn't hear their prayers, but she could feel them. It was almost enough to make her gag at the falsity of it all.

"What soul would be equivalent to my father's?" asked the youngest prince, Prince Elion. His soul was young, burning brightly as Rhea looked at him. He was about the same age as the body that she resided in. She then heard his prayer, sincerely asking to save his father. *Please spare his life. He's all that I have left.* Rhea's face softened, but she was unable to tell him the truth.

"Prince Adamar, as he is the oldest and the rightful heir to the throne. Do I assume correctly?" Rhea lied through her teeth as she looked at Adamar. He put his head down in false modesty.

"Yes, I will assume the throne when my father passes. It is his dying wish," Adamar said in a sad tone that didn't necessarily ring true.

"According to you," muttered Prince Edwyrd under his breath. Rhea glanced over at him and then looked back at King Elkhazel. The light in his soul was dimming. It was time for her to snatch it.

"Will you sacrifice your soul for your father's?" asked Rhea, in the same monotone voice. Adamar looked shocked that she asked him outright but then composed himself quickly.

"I think it's only right that I honor our father's last wish. He wants to be taken from this world. He has lived for far too long already," the last sentence was said with a touch of bitterness.

"Your decision has been made," Rhea said and before they could say another word, she reached her hand into the chest of the king and pulled out his soul. His soul grew brighter as it was pulled out of his body. It always amazed her how alive souls were when they left their decaying shells. It was almost as if the soul was saying "Ah, I can finally breathe." But all that the princes and their partners saw was the last breath of King Elkhazel and the eventual stillness of his chest, indicating that breath and life was gone. Corpses always looked strange without their souls, Rhea felt. They would look like the person, but not quite. There's something you can't place your finger on that's different, when one looks at a corpse, but something is definitely different. Something is not right.

Rhea disappeared into the shadows, putting the glowing soul of King Elkhazel into the container that held them. It looked crystalline in nature and distorted the light of the soul inside. She placed it inside her cloak and as she looked up, she saw Prince Elion wipe a tear from his face.

"The only son who cried," Elkhazel's distant voice muttered sadly. The soul dimmed for a second.

"You were a good person, Elkhazel," Rhea assured him, "You were a good king. Your sons just have greed." She stared at the soul of Adamar. Something wasn't right. It was like she was looking at a corpse without a soul. There was something wrong with his soul, but she couldn't quite put her finger on it.

"Did I choose the right son?" Elkhazel's voice echoed around her as the ground opened up to reveal stairs leading down into darkness. No one else could see the passage into the underworld. It was only for the eyes of Rhea and the dead.

"I hope so," Rhea answered as she walked down the stairs, the ground closing up behind her. Though there was a part of her that knew the answer. A part that she couldn't quite access, like it was on the tip of her tongue. Fire lit up the lanterns that hung on the wall as she walked down. It was a long walk into the underworld, but eventually the area around her got lighter and opened up to reveal a very busy room.

"God of Death," a reaper on standby said, bowing as he did. Rhea handed him the soul of the king. Reapers just look like death. Not what people think looks like death, but death itself. A soulless body, rotting body. It startled Rhea every time even though her own soul had seen it since time began.

"King Elkhazel. His soul is golden so he gets his paradise," Rhea said. The reaper took Elkhazel's soul and scurried down a hallway.

"Don't forget to put him in the same paradise as his wife!" Rhea called after him. The reaper waved an arm in acknowledgment but didn't look back. Rhea took off her cloak to reveal a long sleeved black dress. She wasn't sure why she liked to dress in black, it just seemed fitting.

"My goddess," said Farrah, bowing. Rhea scrunched up her nose and motioned for her to stand up.

"Farrah, can you stop doing that? I don't need you to greet me like that," Rhea muttered.

"I apologize," Farrah said. She held a big red book that scheduled every death that was supposed to happen that day. Everyday the names and times would change in the book. No one knew who's name was going to be on there before the day of that person's death. Although, depending on the day, names that weren't on the list can end up in the underworld as well. It depended on how Rhea was feeling on the surface that day.

"We need one million three hundred and fifty four thousand one hundred and two reapers up on the surface today," Farrah said as she walked quickly beside Rhea. Farrah was much older but she was incredibly short and her legs had to move twice as fast to keep up with Rhea's long strides.

"All right, so do we have one million three hundred and fifty four thousand one hundred and two reapers up on the surface taking souls on time?" asked Rhea. She looked around at the large room that held reapers lining up to get to the surface and the reapers who had just come back. Already she had a headache from managing the underworld for the day, even though the day had just begun.

"*Well*, we're missing one," Farrah said quietly. Rhea blinked and stopped in her tracks.

"We're...missing one?" asked Rhea, turning to face Farrah. Farrah's blue eyes blinked quickly upon looking at the face of Rhea. In the underworld, people can see the true form of Rhea which meant she didn't look quite as menacing, but hellfire still flickered in her eyes occasionally.

"Yes, see, this morning we were tallying up the reapers that were supposed to go up onto the surface today and they were lining up, but then Felicity forgot that she told one of them we had on the list that he can have a day off today and we didn't know and we're trying to find him as we speak but unfortunately, we don't know where he is and—" Rhea held up a hand as Farrah took a long breath.

"Are you telling me that *Felicity* told a *reaper* that he can have a day off?" Rhea asked as she burned with anger and frustration. She closed her eyes and took a deep breath before looking at Farrah once more. Farrah twisted her long, blonde hair around a finger as she looked down at the ground. She nodded slowly. *That Felicity...* Rhea pivoted quickly and walked in a fit of anger towards the room that held the strings of life. Once she opened it, Rhea found Felicity and Francine cutting the strings one by one, in a blur, as they looked at the time and their copy of the red book.

"Felicity," Rhea said. Felicity didn't look up from the string that she was cutting.

"Yeah?" Felicity asked as she looked back up at the time to make sure that the next string she cut was on time. It was awkward for reapers to just stand there over a body, unable to get the soul that they need, for a long period of time. Plus, if they waited too long, the soul was lost, forced to wander Asynithis and to never reach the afterlife. It was better to be on time. Rhea understood this, but it still annoyed her that Felicity wasn't looking at her.

"Did you tell a reaper that he can have a day off?" asked Rhea with practiced control over the volume of her voice, in order not to reveal the anger bubbling underneath.

"Oh, yeah. I told Jeff that he could have off today," said

Felicity, tucking a brown curl behind her small ears. Rhea's fists balled up and then relaxed.

"Felicity, you *do* know what a reaper *is*, right?" asked Rhea, taking a step closer to one of the three women who raised her. Felicity nodded as she carefully cut another string.

"A reaper is a terribly evil soul that is forced to serve until their soul rots to oblivion in which all they experience is nothingness for the rest of eternity," Rhea clarified. Felicity nodded as if she's always known this.

"I know," Felicity said, reassuring Rhea's belief that she had always known this.

"Then *why* in the *world* would you let a *terribly evil* soul that is forced to serve until they disappear into oblivion have a *day off?*" asked Rhea, clenching her jaw.

"Well, Jeff said that his great, great granddaughter was dying today and he wanted to make sure that her soul went to the right place," Felicity explained.

"Oh, so he took the job of someone else?" Rhea asked.

"Oh no, he's just waiting for her soul to come down," said Felicity finally looking over at Rhea. She cowered as she looked at the fire blazing in Rhea's eyes and quickly redirected her attention back to the strings that she was cutting, in silence.

"Right. Okay, Farrah?"

"Yes?" Farrah came up right beside Rhea.

"Can you please find Jeff in the waiting area and tell him that he doesn't get a day off and that he will work until the skin falls from his bones and his bones crumble into dust?" Rhea snapped.

"Yes, I'll do that right away." Rhea sighed and put a hand on her forehead as Farrah turned towards the door. She, then, paused and turned back towards Rhea.

"Also, there's someone waiting for you at the temple."

"Who?"

"Khalon, the Draconian King's bastard son." Rhea rolled her eyes. She knew what this was for, as all the Gods knew about the battle that Draconia had started. *Alator must've said no*, Rhea thought to herself as no one really asked the God of Death for help in anything.

"All right, I'm on my way." Rhea walked over to the stairs that led to her temple and scurried up them, the ground opening behind her "throne". She appeared from behind it and saw a boy standing with his back towards her.

He had black hair that was cut very close to his scalp. His arms were exposed revealing scars and bronze skin. He wasn't bursting at the seams with muscles, but you could tell that he could break someone's bones very easily, despite his lean stature. He definitely looked like a Champion.

"Khalon?" Rhea gingerly asked. He turned around, in surprise. His face was very angular, with his high cheeks and his sharp jawline. Black-red scales went up the side of his face, as if someone clawed at it, revealing scales underneath his skin. His eyes were almost black as they seemed to stare into the very soul of Rhea. She felt weird, almost exposed in some way. She shook the thought out of her head and sat down on the seat behind her. It was a very fitting seat for someone called the God of Death. Made of obsidian, it showcased creatures dying with skulls resting at the end of the armrests. It was overly dramatic in Rhea's opinion but the first God of Death was very over dramatic.

"My goddess," Khalon said, bowing at her feet. His voice was deep; not so deep that it rumbled through the earth but rather it felt warm, as if the sunlight was washing over her. Rhea motioned for him to stand up straight

"What brings you here, Prince of Draconia?" Rhea asked, though she already suspected the answer. Khalon seemed surprised that she didn't know. Rhea laughed at his facial expression.

"I can't see the future, you know. I just take souls."

"Oh," Khalon laughed a little, "I didn't realize that. I've never met a God before."

"I don't think you've been outside the Ring of Fire before," Rhea responded, an eyebrow raised. Khalon laughed a bit more freely now as he looked up at her with eyes wide open. He seemed...vulnerable, somehow.

"Yes, that's very true."

"So?" Rhea prompted. He rubbed the back of his head with his hand.

"Ah, right. I am here on behalf of my father, King Vien of Draconia. As you may know, we are in battle with the beast-oids tribe and are losing men on the daily—"

"The beastoids?" Rhea said, sitting up in her seat a little. She frowned as her gaze unfocused in thought.

"If it's battle that you are in, why are you here and not at Alator's temple? I'm sure that would have been a much quicker journey for you," Rhea said, refocusing her gaze on Khalon's eyes. She hid the teasing smile that threatened to grace her face, and her eyes unconsciously glanced over at the faint scar running down his left eye.

"The God of War is backing the beastoids, my goddess," Khalon said politely. His gaze didn't meet Rhea's. Her frown deepened for a moment and then she burst out laughing.

"Well, isn't that like Alator?" she said more to herself than to Khalon, smiling like a kid. *He really did say no*, she thought glee-fully. Alator's temple was held on the side of Dragon Mountain that resided above the kingdom of Draconia. He usually sided with Draconia on whatever battle they went on, considering he was the God that the citizens of Draconia primarily worshiped. It was interesting for him not to. The draconians must have done something that he was disappointed with. Rhea thought to check in on Alator to ask in order to sate her own curiosity. She knew not to ask about the Goddess of War. Draconia didn't associate with Neith. They weren't as welcoming of female warriors as other countries.

"So, why are you here?" Rhea asked after a moment. Khalon looked up and blinked before looking away from her gaze again.

"Um, we are in battle so my father, King Vien, sent me here to ask if you would—"

"No, Khalon, why are *you* here?" Rhea interrupted, sitting back in her seat.

"I'm sorry?"

"What are you doing here? Why did your father send *you*?"

"I..." Khalon drifted off and searched for the answer in the ground with his eyes. Then, he breathed in deeply, nodded to himself, and then looked into Rhea's eyes, straight into the flaming eyes of a God.

"I am here... as sacrifice." Rhea's face broke out into a smile as she tapped her finger against the head of the obsidian skull that graced the end of the armrest.

"I see," she muttered, trying to hide her smile, "However, it is not your time yet."

4

Khalon knew the moment that he entered his cell what was going to happen. He couldn't explain what had gone on during his fight with Liam, but he knew the consequences that went with it. His hands were covered in skin now, but Khalon remembered what they had looked like a few minutes ago. He remembered what it felt like for his skin to turn inward in order to reveal the scales that, seemingly, lied underneath all this time. Turning his hands over to reveal his palms, he thought about the look that his father had given him from a distance. Yes, Khalon thought, he definitely knew what was going to come next.

He had never been more afraid than he had been in the moment that a guard came to the front of his cell. Khalon had learned to repress fear, to get rid of it or to not acknowledge it. But in this moment, fear bubbled up and Khalon couldn't swallow it down. He didn't know what to make of that moment in the Ring of Fire. He didn't understand what was going on. Spirit of the dragon? But his father wasn't dead yet.

"The king wants to see you," the guard said, opening the

door to his cell. The guard didn't reveal any emotion which disappointed Khalon as he was hoping that he would see what mood his father was in before going to see him. But what did he expect of guards who had been brainwashed?

"Let me get dressed," said Khalon. The guard turned around and Khalon quickly took his armor and put it on, hiding his handheld sword in the chest of his armor by making the retractable blade go back into the handle. Using the water that was left in his room, he quickly wiped the blood off of his face and then walked out of his cell with his head held high, though his heart was pounding. The guard led him down the corridor. There was fear and excitement lingering in Khalon's heart. He had not left the Ring of Fire since he was five years old, or seen his father up close for the same amount of time. But, he felt as though this would be the last time he would be in the Ring of Fire as well as the last time he would be able to leave it.

———

Khalon thought about the moment that he left the cell earlier to see his father as the guard pushed him forward on the dirt path that they were walking along.

"Keep walking," he said. Khalon did what he was told. He always did what he was told. He had never left the Ring of Fire and for that matter, never left Draconia and seeing the world around him was kind of exciting. The temple of the God of Death was in No Man's Land, a sliver of land between the countries of Draconia and Aureum. It was decided that the temple resided there under no one's rule because the God of Death was not a patron God to any country due to the fact that death was something everyone experienced. The dark crea-tures of the night who resided in Caedoxia were the only creatures in Asynithis that tended to pray to the God of Death more so than others, considering their way of living, but they didn't pray to or see the Celestial often. The God of Death, Khalon's stomach grew uneasy just thinking about it. He had never met the Death God but he had heard stories, as all kids of Asynithis did. You didn't meet the God of Death unless you were meeting your demise. Khalon knew that the moment that his eyes glanced upon the face of Death that would be the end of him. It was a choice that he didn't get to make himself.

"Well, I guess this will be the last time I see you, buddy," Khalon said over his shoulder at the guard that was walking behind him. The guard just grunted in response. He was in charge of making sure that Khalon got to the temple without running.

"You know, aren't sacrifices supposed to go willingly? Shouldn't you untie me?" Khalon shouted over his shoulder again. The guard didn't waver in his step and glared at the back of Khalon. Or rather, Khalon imagined that the guard glared at him, but knew that his face was probably as blank as it usually was.

"Are you going willingly?" the guard asked. Khalon didn't answer because they both knew the answer to that. The king told him he needed to go to the God of Death's temple, so Khalon was going to the God of Death's temple. He didn't have a choice. Khalon just hoped and prayed to Alator that the God of Death would spare him. It was the second day of their journey and Khalon continuously tried to talk to the guard as his nervousness grew.

"Have you met the Death God?" Khalon asked, as his bound hands hit the side of his body while walking. The silence between the guard and Khalon was palpable and stretched out for a long period of time.

"It took my sister," the guard said, with the littlest bit of emotion peeking through. Khalon's eyebrows raised. Maybe they weren't as brain dead as he thought.

"What did it look like?" Khalon asked, quietly.

"It looked like him," the guard said. "The man I killed. The reason I am who I am now." Khalon glanced back at the guard to look at his face, hoping for some kind of emotion to flicker across it. It was blank, as usual.

"Who did you kill?"

"Your grandfather, on your mother's side. At the behest of King Archion of course," the guard said, almost quietly. Goosebumps puckered up along Khalon's arm at the mention of King Archion.

"They tried to take the memory," the guard said. "But seeing the God of Death, it all came back." Khalon didn't know what to say. He wondered if the men that he had killed in the Ring of Fire would come back to haunt him in the face of the Death God. Swallowing, Khalon quietly prayed that they wouldn't. The silence continued while they walked. And eventually, the guard and Khalon ended up at their destination.

The temple loomed over Khalon as he stared up at it. It definitely looked like the kind of temple the God of Death would have. The guard stopped at the foot of the black marble steps that led to the larger temple in the distance. The architecture was ancient Greek mixed with Gothic architecture of the past, as Khalon remembered the secret lessons that Khai, his half brother, would give him when they were younger. Khalon looked at the guard and it was the first time that he had seen emotion flicker across the brain dead guard's face. It was fear. The guard looked downright terrified, not wanting to see the horrors of his past once again.

"This is as far as I go," the guard said, his voice wavering slightly. "I'll wait here to make sure you uphold your promise to the king." The guard released Khalon's hands and tucked the restraints into his pocket. Then, he turned around, refusing to look at the temple any longer. On the other hand, Khalon couldn't stop looking at it. It glittered in the sunlight and was incredibly unique that he couldn't bear to look away. Khalon started to walk up the steps and saw a glimpse of the Pond of Tears in the near distance. It was a pond of silver, thick blood, the blood of the Celestials, and Khalon stopped for a moment, staring at it. He knew the story of how it got there but it was a gut wrenching feeling, looking at it. The story was sad, a memory personal to the God of Death, but staring at it in person made it somehow more disturbing. Khalon couldn't lift his feet in order to go on as his gaze fixated on the pond. He closed his eyes and thought about his promise to his father— the *forced* promise to his father. He took a deep breath and started to walk forward up the steps to his doom and as he walked, he thought about the last conversation that he had with King Vien.

———

Khalon kneeled down before King Vien, casting his eyes downwards in respect.

"What was *that*, boy?" King Vien snarled. Khalon could feel the anger radiating off of his father, but Khalon answered the way that he did, despite the fear that was making a home in Khalon's chest.

"Can you be a bit more specific?" Khalon asked. King Vien stood up from his throne suddenly and barreled towards Khalon, standing in front of him. The king took Khalon's head in one hand and lifted it up so that he could look at the face that mirrored his own. He leaned down so that Khalon had nowhere to look but his father's eyes.

"That trick that you did in the Ring, *boy*," the king spat out the word, making Khalon wince slightly. He had never said Khalon's name out loud and that wasn't going to change now.

"Please, your highness, sit down. You must think about your health," Queen Aoife pleaded, lightly grabbing King Vien's arm. He glared at Khalon once more and then dropped Khalon's head, turning around to sit back in his throne. Khalon kept his head down but wished he had the nerve to glare at Queen Aoife. She was always playing the nice guy but Khalon knew that she was the driving force behind the misery of Khalon's life and his banishment from the palace. King Vien took a swig from the cup that rested on the arm of his throne. Khalon eyed it, suspiciously. He was pretty sure the queen was poisoning his father causing him to slowly go insane as he got more and more paranoid throughout the years. This wasn't his father. This angry, stomping, paranoid man that sat in front of him, glaring at his own son was not his father. No, his father was the one who read to him before bed, before banishing him from the palace; who would give Khalon anything that he asked for, would give him the moon and the stars if he could. This wasn't the man that Khalon remembered from his child-hood, but it was the only version of his father that he had seen since. The king slammed the cup down and Khalon quickly lowered his eyes once more.

"Let me ask you a question, boy. Do you think that *you* have the spirit of the dragon living within you?" King Vien asked, venom in his words.

"No, sir," Khalon said with a clear voice. He didn't even know what happened in that Ring. He barely had time to think about it, let alone confirm it to be true. Was it a fluke? The spirit of the dragon just looking out for him?

"You think that you can just start a revolution, huh?" King Vien said, standing up with the cup in one hand. "You think that you can dispose of me and become king, huh?"

"No, sir," Khalon repeated, looking at the feet of his father.

"You think that you can just take the throne from your brother, Khai, don't you?" King Vien continued, as if his rage was blocking out anything that Khalon was saying to him. "You, a bastard child, think you can become king? Think the dragon spirit chose *you*?"

"No, sir, I would never betray you like—"

"Sir? I am your *king*, Khalon. You should address me as such," King Vien exploded.

"I'm sorry, your highness," Khalon choked out. It was the first time that his father addressed him by name, but it was to show that they were strangers not to demonstrate familial closeness.

"*Look at me when I'm talking to you*," King Vien ordered. "Look at what a true king looks like. A true Draconian with the spirit of the dragon within them." Khalon slowly looked up from his father's feet to his head, watching as the exposed skin turned into bright red scales. As the scales encased the face of his father, King Vien's eyes turned just as red as the scales on his body. He stood up, opening his mouth, revealing the sharp teeth of a dragon. The teeth were stained red, as if they had just bitten into fresh human flesh, though Khalon assumed the color was from the wine in his father's cup. Fire billowed out of King Vien's mouth, narrowly missing Khalon's head but slightly singing the tips of his hair. Khalon could feel the unbearable heat that the flames radiated. When Khalon opened his eyes to see the red eyes of his father staring back at him, flickering in realization for a second before returning to hatred, Khalon realized he made a mistake. He closed his eyes, wincing. He showed the fear that he had so carefully hidden from others for so long. And he knew his father saw it, that Queen Aoife saw it. *Damn it.*

The scales covering King Vien's body slowly turned back to

skin, and his eyes went from red back to their almost black color. And then King Vien looked like the father that Khalon knew in face.

"*That* is what a true king looks like," King Vien said, almost smug over the superficial performance that he had just given. Then, his black eyes grew cold.

"Your trick today in the Ring was treasonous." Khalon knew that his father needed a reason to kill him or get rid of him, but treason? He couldn't hide the shock from his face.

"It wasn't a trick, fa—your highness," Khalon stammered, "It just sort of... it just happened. I didn't even... I didn't mean to... I would never try to undermine your authority." Khalon stumbled over his words. He mentally kicked himself over revealing his emotions once again. He felt like a little boy in the presence of his father. The little boy who only ever wanted the approval of his father; to be the son that he always wanted. And Khalon could never hide that.

"Treason is punishable by death. You will be put on display for everyone to see and mocked for two days. The citizens of Draconia will beat you and throw things at you. And on the third day, you will be torn limb by limb and thrown to the dogs, if you do not die from the two days being paraded around the capital Furvus, as is the punishment for traitors," King Vien ordered, sitting back down in his throne. He motioned for the guards to take Khalon away, but Queen Aoife suddenly stepped forward. She had been silent for most of this conversation, but she knew better than King Vien did. She knew that the people weren't going to stand to see Khalon get a traitor's sentence, especially since the public saw what he did in the Ring. She knew if King Vien pulled a stunt like that, her family would get killed as Khalon usurped the throne. She couldn't let that happen. She would die before she let that happen.

"Your highness," she interjected, bowing before the king,

"On behalf of Khalon, I don't believe that he should get a traitor's death, though he *does* deserve it." King Vien stared at her with his black eyes, anger building behind them. Queen Aoife had seen this look a few times, but she knew she had him under her control.

"The boy says that he didn't mean to make a mockery of you, your highness, didn't mean to commit treason. He says that he is loyal to you, my king. In order to prove that loyalty, he should do a task that will benefit you. Don't let his death go to waste," Queen Aoife said, her eyes twinkling as she thought of her plan. King Vien paused to think about this as Khalon glared at the back of Queen Aoife's head. All Khalon could think was: *What was she up to?*

"What did you have in mind?" the king finally asked after a long pause.

"The battle with the beastoids has been going poorly, as you know—" The king stood up in protest.

"We have only lost two battles. We have more creatures than those savages. We will—"

"But of course, your highness. However, the God of War has proved to favor the beastoids, as he has denied our sacrifice. Perhaps, instead of seeking help from the God of War, we should seek help from another," Queen Aoife suggested. King Vien turned his head to look at her better and that's when she knew she got him.

"You're suggesting to offer the boy up as a sacrifice," King Vien followed her line of thinking.

"Yes. A more noble death for a bastard of a king and would make you look merciful."

"A sacrifice can only be accepted if they are willing," the King replied. Queen Aoife turned to look at Khalon, unable to hide a smile from her face. Khalon knew he didn't have a choice, despite the idea that sacrifices could only go of free will.

"Well, are you not loyal to your king?" asked Queen Aoife. She got him, Khalon knew. She had him in her clutches for so long and it all led up to this. This was her favorite fantasy and it was all coming true. The king was ordering Khalon to die.

"I am loyal to you, your highness, and willingly offer myself up to a God of your choosing as sacrifice," Khalon said, lowering his head. He didn't show his fear this time and lifted his head up high to stare into the eyes of his father that he inherited. The king narrowed them and then looked Khalon up and down as if asking where this bravery had come from.

"The God of Death," ordered the king, "Promise me you'll go willingly to the God of Death." The king's face softened and he looked away for a moment, as if he was sorry for what he had done, sending his son to his death. But it was almost as if the king was trying to say that the God of Death was Khalon's best chance. Best chance at a better death? Khalon couldn't figure out what his father was trying to say to him.

"I promise," Khalon said, standing up straight. The king couldn't look at Khalon as he left the throne room, a guard following him out.

———

Khalon thought about this as he reached the entrance of the temple. In front of him, behind black marble columns that lined the entrance, was a single chair. It was terrifying, with images of death carved into it. It was also a giant black chair which made Khalon wonder how big Gods were. He turned around to look down the steps and saw that the guard was no longer there. *I guess he decided he fulfilled his duty,* Khalon thought.

"Khalon?" a high pitched voice uttered, almost as if part of the breeze itself but slightly more distinct. He turned around to discover a face that wouldn't stand still. It was a girl, that he was sure of. But the face kept changing from a corpse to a beautiful girl with golden hair and bright blue eyes to the image of his mother with a tan face, black eyes, and long flowing black hair. He knew that the God of Death would take on the image of what one thought the face of death was, but the quick changes of images made him feel dizzy. But then he started to see an image behind the flickering mask. A girl's face, but different from the other faces. It was as if the other faces were encasing her own.

"My goddess," Khalon said, unsure of what to really call her. Was it rude to call her the God of Death? As she motioned for him to stand up straight from his bow, it slapped him in the face. The conflicting images were gone. Not gone, necessarily, but he could see through it. He could see through them as if they weren't there, and as he stared more intensely at her, he could see the God of Death's true face.

"What brings you here, Prince of Draconia?" she asked. Khalon raised his eyebrows. She didn't already know? He supposed she wasn't all knowing, considering she wasn't An, the God of All. She laughed at his facial expression. The laugh made her features gather up towards the middle of her face. She was... underwhelming for a God, Khalon thought. She had too big of ears for her face, though he could tell that she was mixed. Elf, but not pure elf. He suspected there was some human in her. Her eyes were small and the color of copper and she had red brown hair that was not thick but that wasn't thin either and didn't frame her face all that nicely because of it. Her face was round, not that she was overweight, but if one were to look at her face without skin, he supposed the skull would still be round. Freckles dotted her nose and she had some scarring on her cheeks where the war between skin and adolescence had made its mark. She was also small, the giant seat engulfing her and she wore a formless black cloak that hid her body. No, she wasn't pretty in the slightest. But she wasn't absolutely horrific either. She was just... underwhelming. She finished laughing. Her laughter was nice, though. Warm.

"I can't see the future, you know," she said. "I just take souls."

"Oh," Khalon said, thinking about how he was right about her not being like An, "I didn't realize that. I've never met a God before."

"I don't think you've ever left the Ring of Fire before," she said softly, but a twinkle appeared in her eyes. It wasn't like the twinkle that would appear in Queen Aoife's eyes. It was softer and kinder, somehow. Almost as if she wanted Khalon to be surprised that she knew so much about him, which he admittedly was. Khalon laughed.

"Yes, that's very true," he said, confirming her knowledge of him.

"So?" she asked, indicating to him to tell her why he had come. So he did. He told her that he was there in hopes that she will take Draconia's side in the war with the beastoids. She didn't know that Alator, the God of War, had sided with the beastoids to Khalon's surprise. He thought that she would know somehow. She found it funny. Even though she wasn't pretty at all, Khalon felt like smiling when she smiled. This was the God of Death? She wasn't as terrifying as they make her out to be.

"What are you doing here? Why did your father send you?" she finally asked. Khalon felt his heart pound in his ears. Here it was, the moment of truth. It was time for him to die.

"I..." Khalon started. He took a deep breath and just accepted that it was his time, "I am here as sacrifice." He looked back up at her and just saw this knowing smile on her face as she stared right back at him. It looked like flames were flickering in her eyes, but in a mischievous way.

"I see," she said, pausing slightly as she looked at him, "However, it is not your time to die." Khalon held his breath, waiting for her to take it back and admit that it was a joke. But, she said nothing more. Inside, Khalon was jumping for joy, though slightly confused. On the outside, his face gave away nothing.

5

K halon walked closely behind Rhea as she led the way down the steps from her temple. He didn't respond when she said it wasn't his time. *Was he just not curious?* She wondered what he was thinking. His face was stoic and angular, making it look more like stone, due to the lack of emotion. Perhaps he just didn't want to tempt chance, to ruin this second chance at life. She shrugged at her mental monologue. Rhea was always monologuing.

"I haven't been to Draconia in a while," Rhea said, making conversation once they got to the bottom of the stairs, "And never in this body." Rhea looked at him for some sort of reaction but there was none. There could've been slight confusion in Khalon's face, but whether Rhea was imagining it or not, she decided to explain.

"The Gods are just in creatures' bodies. They pick a creature as their Celestial body and just kind of attach themselves to their soul, so I've been reincarnated a good handful of times," Rhea said, nodding to herself. She smiled up at Khalon, but he looked past her at the fading horizon.

"It's getting dark," is all he said.

"Ri-ight," Rhea said, dragging the word out into two syllables. She rolled her eyes. This was going to be a fun trip. He was walking beside her now, if not slightly ahead of her in order to lead the way. Rhea knew the way, even if it was a bit hazy, from another lifetime that she could sometimes remember and sometimes could not.

"So, you're a Champion then? Of the Ring of Fire?" Rhea asked, again trying to make conversation. *Even the dead are more talkative than this guy.*

"Yeah," he said, curtly. Rhea's lips thinned to a line.

"Dangerous business," Rhea said. Khalon nodded. She frowned up at him. He was tall, a head taller than she was. He looked taller than he was from where she was standing due to the slight slant of the ground, and his gaze was a bit intimidating. Rhea shook her head. What was she thinking? She's the God of Death. What's more intimidating than Death?

"Are you not curious about anything?" Rhea finally asked, evidently annoyed. He raised his eyebrows at her tone and finally looked down at her.

"About what?"

"You know. About how it's not your time yet," said Rhea.

"I just figure it's not my time," Khalon said. "I mean, you *are* the God of Death aren't you? So there's no reason for me to doubt you." Khalon looked around. The woods around the temple were vast and were full of relics from the past. Rhea looked at what Khalon was looking at and immediately recognized the shape that was sprouting moss all over it. It was rusted and broken down, but Rhea still could recognize it.

"It's called a car," Rhea said proudly. "The humans used to travel all around the world in them. They would power themselves and be controlled by these pedals." Khalon didn't look the least bit impressed by Rhea's knowledge and turned his attention elsewhere. Rhea bit the inside of her cheek. *This guy...*

"We should stop here for the night," Khalon ordered, looking around for firewood. *...is frustrating.*

"Right," Rhea said. She was disappointed. She thought the bastard Prince of Draconia, who had been cooped up in the Ring of Fire for most of his life, who was a fighting machine, would be more exciting than this. She sat down and leaned on her elbow, which was resting on her knee.

"Listen, Khalon, even though it's not your time yet, you're still a sacrifice," said Rhea. Khalon looked up from his foraging, wide-eyed. *That got his attention.* Rhea smirked.

"What do you mean?" he asked, trying to keep his voice stable but failing.

"You're still a sacrifice, which means you're not free."

"Oka-ay, I'm not following," he said, picking up the piece of firewood that he dropped previously. He brought it over to the pile that he had created and then began trying to start a fire.

"You belong to me," Rhea said, matter-of-factly. "You have offered yourself up for sacrifice. Usually, the God of Death doesn't take temple servants, but since it's not your time yet..." Rhea let herself drift off as she gauged his reaction. His jaw clenched as his teeth grinded together in frustration.

"So, I'm in another prison," he muttered. "Thanks dad."

"Right, prison, tell me more about that," Rhea said, leaning forward, excited to finally hear something out of him. He looked at her incredulously.

"I was stuck in the Ring of Fire. Don't know if you know this, but criminals get stuck in the Ring of Fire," Khalon stated, patronizingly. Rhea rolled her eyes. Khalon furrowed his eyebrows in concentration as he tried to make sparks hit the pile of sticks that he had just collected.

"There's an easier way to do that," Rhea said. Khalon

looked at her with the same stoic, expressionless, yet somehow terrifying, face.

"And that is?" he said, obviously impatient with the way that Rhea tended to speak.

"Watch," she said, smiling. She closed her eyes and felt the underworld underneath the earth. Then, she moved her hand upwards, feeling the eternal fire that only she could control, and concentrated that feeling onto the pile of sticks that Khalon had gathered. Soon, the sticks were engulfed by a purple-blue flame, which faded out to the regular orange-red color of fire. Rhea opened her eyes, blue fire flashing in them for a moment. For a second, Khalon looked frightened, but it only flashed across his face for a moment. Rhea's smile faded as she recognized the expression. Even the stoic bastard dragon was scared of her.

"Hellfire," Rhea said, quietly, "It's what the humans call it."

"Yeah," Khalon whispered, staring at it. A moment of silence filled the air between them. The orange glow of the fire made Khalon's tan skin look like it was being engulfed by flames. He was mesmerizing, as his intense stare focused on the crackling fire. The scar over his left eye looked more prominent in this light and his black-red scales that crept up on the side of his face, that were like scratches left over from a claw, glistened and glittered. Rhea looked away, as if looking at him any longer would make her spontaneously combust.

"Were *you* a criminal?" Rhea asked, after a moment. Khalon looked at her from across the fire, confusion on his usually expressionless face.

"You said only criminals end up at the Ring of Fire," Rhea clarified. Khalon nodded slowly.

"No, I don't think I was," said Khalon, turning his intense stare back on the flames of the fire. "I was put in there when I was five years old. Had my first fight when I was ten. If I did commit some kind of crime at the age of five, it was only that of my bloodline. Crimes of my father, I suppose."

"Right, the bastard prince," Rhea said. Khalon snorted.

"If you can even call me a prince. I don't think I even hold that title," Khalon said. His black eyes looked unbelievably sad. The urge to reach out and hug him engulfed every part of Rhea's being that she had to hug her knees to her chest in order to stop herself.

"What made you decide to be a sacrifice?" Rhea asked. He laughed, but it wasn't filled with any kind of joy. His eyes were dead as his smile reached them.

"Does anyone really truly decide to be a sacrifice?" Khalon asked, the ghost of his smile still on his lips. Rhea blinked.

"A sacrifice can only be accepted if only they are willing," Rhea said.

"Yeah, and they're only willing because the alternative is worse," said Khalon. "At least being a sacrifice to a God is a more noble death." He scoffed and turned his attention to the fire. Rhea looked at the fire, as if to ask it for some kind of answer. She opened her mouth to say something, anything, about how cruel creatures are and how the world has recently been going back to the dark ages, but before she could say anything that could possibly comfort this beautiful creature that sat before her, the flames spurted and spitted as it turned blue and purple. Then, suddenly, a face manifested itself in the flames.

"Morrigan," said a familiar voice, ominously. Rhea rolled her eyes as she recognized the face that was attached to the voice. Poseidon was the only person who never called her by the name that she had chosen.

"That's not my name," Rhea responded.

"Who is this?" Poseidon asked, his voice normal again. He

looked Khalon up and down and smiled as his flame eyes somehow glittered.

"My new temple servant and also none of your business," Rhea said, crossing her arms across her chest.

"A temple servant? Are you even allowed a temple servant?" Poseidon exclaimed. Before Rhea could even say anything, Poseidon continued, "You missed the meeting. An was really upset about it."

"No one told me about a meeting," Rhea said.

"It was an important one," Poseidon said.

"Okay? No one told me about it," Rhea said, with some attitude. She liked Poseidon but at the same time he really pissed her off.

"The Seer is spouting off some nonsense," said Poseidon. "Anyways, be careful. Especially if you're outside of your temple."

"What nonsense?" Rhea asked, frowning slightly. *Be careful?*

"Oh," Poseidon's face looked back at the darkness behind the fire, as if he was looking at something, "I gotta go." And before Rhea could say another word, his face disappeared. The fire sputtered purple and blue and then turned back to its yellow-orange color. Rhea frowned to herself as she looked up at Khalon's face. He looked genuinely frightened that she couldn't help herself let out a chuckle. He looked up at her, surprised.

"What? You haven't seen a face in hellfire before?" she laughed. He looked at her confused.

"Is this a normal occurrence?" he asked seriously. Her smile faded as she stared back into the fire, defeated.

"No," she said, dejectedly, "No, it's not."

6

Khalon didn't understand her humor as her face fell. It was easier to see her true face now. The ever-changing images that encased her true face were almost invisible to him the longer he was around her. He wondered if that was normal, since he was now her temple servant. Or if she even knew that he could see her true face. He wondered if she would strike him down to the underworld if he told her.

"Who was that? In the flames?" Khalon asked, changing the subject from her weird failed attempt at a joke.

"Oh that? That was Poseidon," she muttered, holding her knees closer to her chest. Her face looked conflicted. Her nose was slightly scrunched and her lips were twisted to the side as she thought. She was kind of cute. Cute in the same way that a shih-tzu dog was cute. Khalon shook the thought out of his head. *You can't call a God cute, especially cute in an ugly dog kind of way.*

"Poseidon is the..." Khalon hurried to think back on his knowledge about the Gods. The Gods' reincarnations take a different name for each reincarnation so sometimes it was hard to remember all the names that the humans named their Gods before. Luckily, he remembered what Khai taught him when they were younger, before he was afraid of his older brother. But before Khalon could show off his knowledge to Rhea, she cut in.

"The God of the Sea, yes," she muttered. She looked so lost in thought that the faded faces of hers were changing faster than before.

"What are you thinking about?" Khalon finally asked.

"What?" she asked, looking up. The flames flickered in front of her face, casting an orange glow over her pale white skin. The glow made it look like there was some life in her face. Khalon had seen many corpses in his life, and no matter how much he tried to shake the thought out of his head, her skin was as pale as one.

"Oh," she said after a while, "Something he said bothered me."

"He called you Morrigan," pointed out Khalon. She waved her hand as if she were waving the words away from her face.

"That doesn't matter right now. What matters is that he said to be careful. Why do we need to be careful?" asked Rhea, but Khalon didn't really feel like she was asking him. She groaned loudly as she threw herself down to the ground, laying down harshly.

"I shouldn't have missed that meeting with An. This is like the third meeting that I missed. I'm surprised he didn't show up in the hellfire to scold me," she whined. Khalon was shocked. It was weird to see someone that you thought of as a God to be whining and groaning like a child who was afraid of being scolded by the knowledge master for not knowing the right answer. He decided not to respond. It felt like she wasn't really talking to him anyways. She looked over at him, her head turning to face him as she continued to lay down, flat on her back.

"Khalon, if you had to give up your life for me, would you?" she asked.

"I *am* here as a sacrifice so I guess," Khalon muttered, unhappily. If he didn't try to save the God of Death, he knew he would be *put* to death by the other Gods, probably. He leaned his back against a tree trunk behind him.

"I think you might have to, eventually," she said, looking back up at the sky.

"Aren't you a God?" Khalon asked, his tone a little harsh. She smiled slightly.

"I guess technically I am. But, I am not, at the same time," she turned on her side and rested her head on her elbow. "Didn't I tell you? The God of Death's soul is more like a parasite. My soul is in here, somewhere. My real soul..." She turned on her back to stare up into the sky.

"That's why I go by Rhea. Because I know I am not just the God of Death. I am Rhea, too." She smiled to herself. Her smile looked so genuine that Khalon's heart skipped for a second. She seemed so pure, somehow.

As the flames flickered and faded, the moonlight shone on her face. Her round face looked so white, almost blue, making the freckles on her face stand out more. Khalon wasn't quite sure what she meant. She looked just like an awkward mixed blood elf in her teenage years. But, her skin was that of a corpse. One would mistake her as a corpse if she were sleeping, he would think, except that the slight blood in her cheeks might give her away. That skin definitely screamed the God of Death to him.

"You know," she continued, almost carefully, "It looks like there's something preying on your soul, too." She didn't look at him as she said this. Something preying on his soul? Like how the God of Death was with hers? It felt like she wasn't really looking for him to respond, but her brown eyes glanced his way as he closed his.

It was a long day for him. A long journey of almost dying, of his father trying to get him to die, and now being told that he was a prisoner once more. Temple servant? Was this what his father wanted from him? *Perhaps dying for the God of Death wouldn't be so bad,* Khalon thought as his consciousness started to drift, *at least I would be put out of my misery.*

———

Sunlight stained the inside of his eyelids orange as Khalon uncomfortably woke up. The wood that fueled the fire last night had turned white. Khalon rubbed the sleep from his eyes as he blinked and stretched his sore neck a bit. He had a nightmare last night; he was sure of it by the pounding of his head. Something about... water and blood. So much thick, black blood like those of sea creatures, with some silver, the blood of a God. Khalon shook his head as birds were chirping loudly in his ear making his head hurt slightly more. There wasn't any use trying to make sense of it. He looked around as his eyes adjusted to the sunlight pouring in through the canopy of leaves above him. Then, he looked around more urgently.

"Rhea??" Khalon stood up. Where Rhea was before, she was gone. He walked around the fire pit that they had created and looked around the trees.

"Rhea??" he called more urgently and more loudly, "Goddess!" His voice shook a bit. *Great, I lost the God of Death? How in the world did I lose the God of Death??* Khalon looked a bit further from the area that they were in and then when he didn't see her, he sat down on the ground, pulling his muscular legs up to his chest, the words of Poseidon echoing in his head: *"Be careful. Especially if you're outside of your temple."*

Khalon hit the back of his head against the tree trunk that was behind him and looked up past the glowing green canopy into the sky. *Gods*, he thought, *I really must be cursed.*

7

"I assume your coronation went well. Apologies that I couldn't attend," a low voice that sounded like a hundred voices spoke from the shadows. Adamar jumped, almost dropping the crown that made him the new King of Aureum. With shaking hands, he carefully gathered himself and put the crown back into its glass case. Turning around, he looked at the cloaked figure that towered over Adamar.

"Your holiness," Adamar barely choked out, as he bowed down. The cloaked figure waved a hand, gesturing for him to stand up.

"I take it no one suspects a thing?" the voice of a thousand rumbled. Adamar nodded.

"Good, let's keep it that way," the voice said. The figure moved like a shadow across the room, closer to Adamar. It took everything in his power to keep his legs from moving backwards, away from the figure.

"Be careful, young one. My creatures are coming soon,

however the Seer suspects our plan," a thousand whispers came from the figure, filling the room.

"I promise that they won't know it came from us," Adamar said. The cloaked figure stood still, sensing the insecurity in his words as it stared in the direction of Adamar. Adamar couldn't tell if the figure was looking at him or not as he looked up at it, its face covered by darkness.

"For yours and your son's sake, I hope that is true," the whispers threatened before the figure disappeared in a black smoke. Adamar's knees buckled from underneath him, but his arms caught his body before hitting the floor.

"This is necessary," Adamar whispered to himself. But the more he dealt with the cloaked figure, the more he wasn't sure if he was the one controlling the fire or burning with it.

8

Rhea woke up to her name being screamed by Khalon, who was shouting into the sky. She felt her nose scrunch up in frustration as she glared at him.

"I'm right here, you knucklehead," she called, throwing a whitened stick in his direction. He moved his head down from the sky and stared at her, shell shocked.

"No, no no no," he said quickly, barreling towards her. She backed up on her arms as she got up before he could tower over her. But, to her dismay, he was still towering over her slightly.

"You were not there before," he said, pointing at the ground where she was just sleeping. Rhea made a face and Khalon scoffed at it. He backed up, turning around with his arms raised before turning back to face her.

"I am *not* stupid, Rhea. You might think I'm stupid because I got hit in the head a few too many times," Rhea wasn't sure how he knew what she was thinking, "but you were *not* there this morning, okay? You had disappeared and I thought I was dead, for sure. I thought all the Gods were going to strike me down for getting the God of *Death*, for Gods' sake, *killed*." Rhea was pretty sure this was the most Khalon had said to her in one sitting, *and my Gods is he talking fast*, she thought.

"I don't know how you're so comfortable saying my name like that," Rhea muttered. Khalon narrowed his half-moon shaped eyes at her, his scar on his left eye looking more prominent. Then, he relaxed his face and sighed, staring up at the sky. She could see his prayer to Alator, and it looked desperate. Rhea felt her face twist in annoyance.

"Just," Khalon said, pointing a finger in her face, "Don't disappear like that again." Rhea moved his finger and glared up at him.

"I didn't," she insisted. Khalon clenched his jaw in frustration and walked away from her.

"Where are you going?" Rhea called after him.

"To Draconia," he yelled, angrily, back.

"Without me?" she said, a hand on her hip. Khalon looked at her, his face the epitome of disbelief.

"Look, I'm your temple servant or sacrifice or whatever because of the war happening in Draconia. You say you didn't disappear, fine. I'm not blind but whatever, fine. Let's say you didn't disappear. And let's just pretend this didn't happen. So, can we please head towards Draconia so my father doesn't try to kill me for not honoring his wishes?" Khalon said, sighing as he talked. He looked fed up. This was the most emotion Rhea had seen coming from his ice, cold face. She kind of found it enjoyable.

"Fine, but you're really disrespectful," she said, waving a finger at him as she started walking in the direction towards Draconia. She heard another sigh from him and then his heavy footsteps following after her a couple of seconds later. As she walked towards Draconia, she wondered what he meant by her disappearing. It was a while since she fell asleep on the surface. Perhaps she went back into the underworld while she was sleeping? She made a mental note to ask the Fates later.

Just as she thought about the Fates, she heard their prayer. Prayers are ways that creatures of Asynithis can communicate to the Gods. Only the God that the prayer is for can hear it. And it was an easy way for the Fates to contact Rhea when they needed her. Francine's voice came loud and clear, interrupting any thought that Rhea had in her mind.

"Rhea," Francine's voice echoed in Rhea's mind, "An is here. And he doesn't seem happy." Her voice drifted out of Rhea's head as Rhea winced and sighed, stopping in her tracks. She turned around to look at a surprised Khalon.

"I'm sorry, Khalon," Rhea started. He raised an eyebrow, "I'm going to have to disappear again."

"*What?*" Khalon asked, a bit ferociously. He looked up, past her head, as his eyes searched the horizon before looking at her again.

"Listen, wherever you're going, I'm coming with you. I have to make sure you get to Draconia," Khalon said. Rhea rolled her eyes.

"I made a promise, Khalon. I'm a God. We honor our promises," Rhea said. Khalon scoffed.

"What? Like Alator promised to protect Draconia but now is siding with the beastoids who are trying to take territory from us?" Khalon laughed without feeling. He crossed his arms and shook his head.

"Yeah, like how the Gods heard my dad's prayer to protect my mom, only to ignore it and rip the life away from her?" Khalon asked, stepping away from Rhea. "Gods honor *nothing.*" The bitter smile that was on his lips faded, his jaw clenching in anger. Rhea looked down at his feet and then back up at his face. He wasn't looking at her. Rhea reached up and grabbed his face and pulled it down towards her, so they were eye to eye. His stony expression became a mix of surprise and obvious discomfort as Rhea noticed the tips of his ears turning red. Rhea swallowed the lump of embarrassment down her throat and softened the grip that she had on both sides of his head.

"I'm not going to argue with you about your experiences with the Gods, Khalon. But Alator has his reasons for turning his back on the draconians. And... I don't know what happened to your mom... But, I promise that I honor my word. Other Gods might not. But I do because that's kind of part of my job description. Nothing is more honest than death. Just trust me," Rhea almost whispered. His eyes were more brown than black when looked at up close. A swirling galaxy of dark brown. He just stared into her eyes, and she felt like he could really see her. Like *really* see her. Rhea blinked and then let go of his face, taking a couple of steps back while holding the side of her arm, awkwardly.

"I just... I have to go into the underworld and I can't take someone who's living with me," Rhea muttered. Khalon blinked and rubbed the top of his head with his hand. He looked confused.

"I can't go into the underworld with you," he repeated slowly, and Rhea nodded in response.

"If a living soul goes into the underworld, they won't be able to come back to the surface. I've never had a temple servant. And truth be told, I'm not even sure if I'm even allowed one. So, I don't want to risk taking you with me. Not when I told you it's not your time yet," Rhea explained, staring at the ground as her feet moved the dirt underneath her. He put his hands up.

"I don't want to go into the underworld anyways," Khalon said. And then more quietly: "Fine, I trust you." Rhea looked up at him and he was looking at her, his head bowed a little, but his eyes were looking at her through his eyelashes. Rhea wasn't sure why, but her heart started to beat a little faster in her chest. No, she knew why. It was because he was a damned beautiful creature, and that was the only reason for her heart's betrayal.

"Okay, I'll meet you back here," Rhea said. Khalon grunted.

"Why don't we just meet at the entrance of Draconia? It's obvious you have a different way of traveling," he pointed out. She felt her mouth twist in frustration. She wanted to go with him on this journey together, but he had a point. And she didn't feel like it was fair to argue with him about it.

"If I'm done before you make it to Draconia, I'll find you, okay?" Rhea said. He looked at her and nodded, not questioning how she was going to find him. Rhea nodded back, turned around, and took a deep breath. Her hand waved over the ground, causing the ground to open up and reveal the steps into the underworld. As she walked down, she looked over her shoulder to look at Khalon's face before the ground closed completely. He stared straight at her. *Can he see the path to the underworld?*

Rhea shook her head. There was no way. He was a living soul. But, there *was* something in his soul, and it was growing bigger by the hour. *Perhaps that was making him be able to see.* Rhea quickly started walking down the steps. An was not a happy person when he was kept waiting.

The stairs opened up to show the busy room. Reapers were walking everywhere, but there was a wide berth around An. His back was towards Rhea but even his back looked angry. His black hair was longer than the last time she saw him, and it looked like the body that he resided in had gotten a little older as well, slightly more taller. He was almost the same height as Rhea, now. Rhea quickly took long strides in order to get to An's side as quickly as possible. As she arrived, she reached out a hand to touch his shoulder when he grabbed it before she could, turning around and flashing his ice gray eyes at her. Damn, he was definitely angry.

"Where have you been?" An asked. His voice sounded mature for the body that he was in. His current reincarnation was only around thirteen years old. Rhea snatched her hand out from his grip and glared at him.

"I've been busy. Sorry that life and death is so pressing. What have *you* been up to exactly?" she snarled. Rhea blinked and took a step back. The God of Death's soul that was in her always acted up more when around An's soul. There was a universe of bitterness that resided in the God of Death's soul over the God of All. An blinked and then motioned for her to follow him. She couldn't help the bubble of annoyance that spread over her face. But, she followed him.

"Not here," he whispered as they walked. They walked in silence, as the rotting reapers kept away from An, until they reached the room that held the strings of life. The Fates were sitting there, cutting strings while referring to the big red book of death, but they glanced up as An and Rhea entered. Francine stared Rhea down in desperation as she walked in. Her brown eyes flashed with fear, and her thick curly hair was tied up in a puff at the top of her head, which she only did when she was stressed or concerned.

"What's going on?" Rhea asked as An closed the door. There was a huge one way window that looked out at the large lobby of the underworld.

"You've missed the last few meetings," An said. Rhea nodded her head and waved the words away from her.

"Yeah, we all know. I've been busy. What's going on that's so pressing that you had to come visit me in person?" An looked out the window and then turned around to look at Rhea. His icy eyes were dead.

"The Seer has told me some disturbing news. A future that none of us have expected would happen so soon," An said, "And Francine alerted me that it has begun."

"What future? Stop talking so cryptically. We all hate it, An. Can you please just talk straight to me?" Rhea said, frustrated, as she ran a hand through her hair. An was the oldest of all the Gods and had created them long ago, and Rhea felt he was always trying to flaunt how all-knowing he was. She quickly glared at Francine. A look that alerted her that she should have told Rhea before she told An. Francine cowered at the flames that flashed in Rhea's eyes.

"Don't be angry at the Fate, Rhea," An said.

"What is it, An? Your stay here is limited. This isn't your territory and I can kick you out if I wanted to," Rhea said, almost growling. The God of Death's anger towards the God of All was beginning to get unchecked and it was hard for Rhea to contain him.

"Francine, show her the string of life," An said, dejectedly. Francine carefully got up and moved towards the black onyx cabinet that held the golden strings of life. The golden strings of life were connected to the Gods. They were the only strings that the Fates couldn't cut with their scissors. She carefully opened it and revealed the strings. Rhea's blood turned ice cold as she stepped slowly towards the cabinet. One of the golden strings was snapped, cut. She stared at it as a thousand thoughts raced through her head. It's true that the Gods' reincarnations were not immortal, that they could wither away and die, but a God's soul...

"It's white," Rhea whispered. The string had turned from what was supposed to be gold to white. The soul was gone. Rhea turned around, scared but mostly angry.

"An, what is this?" she whispered, holding the string tight in her hands. She could feel it, the imprint of the faded soul.

The soul of Belenus, the name that she had chosen for this reincarnation. The God of Healing. Tears burned her eyes.

"What *is* this?" she repeated louder.

"The Seer told us someone is going to start killing us, the Gods," An said, carefully, "And not just our reincarnations, Rhea, *us*." Rhea looked into An's eyes, and for the first time saw an emotion in those ice eyes of his. Fear.

"Someone is killing the Gods."

9

Khalon had been wandering around for a while by himself, following the path towards Draconia. He was alone, once again. Kicking a rock in his way, he watched it jump across the dirt into the grass while thinking about how nice it was to travel with someone. He looked up at the blue sky and at the nature around him. It was nice to be outside of the Ring of Fire. A guard wasn't with him, watching him. He felt almost free. The flames of Rhea's eyes flashed across his mind. Almost.

Despite feeling like a prisoner of the God of Death's, he couldn't deny that he enjoyed her presence. Even though she *was* the God of Death, she was as warm as sunshine. Her voice was like wind chimes dancing with the wind. She was as just a part of nature as a tree or a plant. Full of life. Khalon smiled to himself as he thought about her. She was such a weird looking creature, with her round face and impure elven features. He told her he would trust her. *Trust her? Trust a God?* Could Khalon do that? He looked up at the sky as he stopped in his tracks, soaking up the feeling of warmth on his skin. For Rhea? Yeah, even though he had only known her for a day, he could trust a God as long as it was her.

Just then, a scream cut through his thoughts. Khalon looked around himself, frantically. He heard a scream like this before. A scream of a child who was about to die. He knew it because he had heard it escape from his own lips when he was first in the Ring of Fire. Before Khalon could think, his body took over, running towards the sound. He ran through the trees, looking for the source of the scream. Hearing it again, Khalon ran faster until he found it. It was definitely a child, but it looked like a weird mutated bear cub. A beastoid. Goosebumps rose up all over Khalon's skin as he looked at the unnatural being. Circling it were beings that were unmistakable. Tall and bony, with their fangs glistening in the sunlight. Vampires.

"Someone! Please help me!" the beastoid cub cried, its voice warbled by its mutated voice box. Tears were staining the fur around its eyes.

"No one is coming for you," one of the vampires hissed. His skin was dark and his face was gaunt from hunger. It was odd to see vampires out during the day, unless they were crazed from hunger.

"No one is going to help a beastoid child," another vampire hissed. Her bony white fingers reached towards the child, and the child screamed again. Its bear-like face was twisted in fear. *Unnatural*, Khalon couldn't help but think. It was on its back but Khalon was sure that it walked on two paws, like a human would. He unconsciously made a face of disgust. The vampire's eyes glanced around the child, desperately. He recognized the expression: fear. Khalon blinked. They were too weak to fight a grown beastoid. They were making sure the mother wasn't around. Khalon glanced back down at the child whose face was soaked with tears and snot. Its brown and strangely human-like eyes looked around quickly for an escape. Khalon recognized those eyes. He slowly closed his as he came to a decision, breathed in deeply and then breathed out. *Fine*, he thought. *I can't just let it die.*

Khalon grabbed the sword that he had hidden in his chest armor. With a flick of his wrist, the white translucent blade made from dragon stone came out from the handle of the sword, almost like magic. Gripping the handle and long tooth that jutted out of the end, he ran out in front of the beastoid cub, holding the sword up in front of him. He quickly saw the look of shock from the cub's face before staring at the three vampires in front of him. They cowered from the blade and snarled at him.

"A draconian?" one of them hissed. The girl laughed, her eyes looking like they were going to fall out of her face. She glanced at the scales that were glistening in the sun.

"Do you *know* what this creature is?" she said, waving her bony hand at the child. The other vampire moved slowly around Khalon. Khalon quickly moved, facing him, and brandished the sword at him. He hissed and moved backwards from it.

"You guys are weak. Do you really feel like fighting a Champion?" Khalon asked, staring them in the eyes. He saw the fear that he hoped he would see.

"A Champion?" the dark one whispered.

"Champion or not! No one cares for these creatures. They're free real estate, *Champion*," the woman vampire snarled, her mousy brown hair sticking to her face from sweat. Khalon kept his stance.

"I don't care, vampire. Get lost, or I'll take your life myself," Khalon clenched his jaw and stood up straighter. They were taller than him, as vampires usually were, but they backed up still.

"Champions are traitors anyways," the other male vampire hissed, poised for an attack. The woman vampire grabbed his arm and pulled him back.

"Let's just find something else to eat," she whispered, not taking her eyes off Khalon. They all backed up keeping their eyes on him until they were far enough away, and then they disappeared in a blur. Khalon sighed and put down his sword, turning around to face the creature. His stomach still turned looking at the beastoid cub, but it turned for a different reason. The cub looked at him with horror. Those eyes glanced down at the scales that covered parts of Khalon; the scales that he usually was proud of but that he felt suddenly ashamed of at this moment. Khalon swallowed his shock and held out a hand towards the cub.

"C'mon," said Khalon, "You're safe now." Khalon paused and then said softly, "I promise I won't hurt you." The cub looked at Khalon's hand and then back up at his face. It blinked and then gingerly grabbed onto his hand. The paw looked like a paw but also like it had fingers. It disturbed Khalon, but he kept his face stoic as he lifted the cub to its feet. Like he suspected, the cub walked on two paws. It eyed him suspiciously, but the look of fear had almost disappeared, replaced by a look of curiosity. Khalon felt like he could breathe a little bit more.

"Thank you," the cub muttered. Khalon pushed the blade back into the handle of his sword and then put it in his chest armor. The cub's eyes widened at the action and Khalon smiled a little. Despite the cub looking so unnatural, the emotions that flickered across its animated face was familiar. The look of wonder reminded him of Khai when he was younger. Khalon shook the thought out of his head.

"What's your name? Or... do you have a name?" Khalon asked, feeling a bit awkward at the thought of a bear cub having a name. The cub looked at him strangely and then gave a little sigh.

"Yes, we have names. We are *not* animals," the cub said quietly. Khalon was startled at that response because the cub looked like a bear cub. *Was it not an animal? Weren't that what beastoids were though? A humanoid animal?* Khalon rubbed the back of his head.

"Yeah, of course," he laughed awkwardly.

"It's Luke. My name is Luke," said the cub.

"I'm Khalon," Khalon replied. Luke looked at Khalon desperately.

"I'm sorry to ask you this, after you have just saved me," Luke said, his voice garbled as if the words were not familiar to him. Though, this was how all beastoids sounded, as if they had just started learning how to talk with voice boxes that won't let them shape the words that they wanted to make.

"Yeah?" Khalon asked. Luke rubbed his paws together and then looked up at Khalon.

"Will you take me back to my camp? I've gotten lost and I don't... I just want to go home," Luke said, quietly. *Home?* Khalon thought. The beastoids didn't really have a home. That's what they were fighting for. Khalon's face twisted together. He needed to get to Draconia in order to take the God of Death to his father. Then, Rhea's voice echoed in his head: *"I'll find you, okay?"* Khalon looked at the desperation in Luke's eyes and sighed.

"I don't know..." his voice drifted off. Luke pressed the pads of his paw against Khalon's arm.

"Please, sir. I don't... You can protect me and once I get home I won't make you stay long and you don't have to see anyone," the child pleaded. Luke knew. Khalon could tell that

Luke knew what would happen if a bunch of beastoids saw a draconian. *And yet, he was trusting me?* As if hearing Khalon's thoughts, Luke said, quietly, "You saved me. I know you won't hurt me."

"Ah..." Khalon groaned and then thinking about Rhea's words again he nodded, "Fine. I'll take you to your camp. Do you know what direction it was in?" Luke pointed in a general direction.

"I came from that way," he said.

"Didn't anyone teach you how to track animal tracks?" Khalon asked. Luke glared up at him.

"I'm *not* an animal," he said, more defiantly. Khalon raised his eyebrows and nodded.

"I'm sorry, Luke. No, you're not an animal," he said. Luke smiled, or at least Khalon thought that Luke was trying to smile. It was hard to tell whether the cub was just baring its teeth or smiling. But since the eyes were trying to squint, Khalon decided that he was just trying to smile. Khalon tried to swallow his disgust and smile back.

Luke's paw reached up and Khalon looked at it in confusion. In response, Luke just reached and grabbed Khalon's hand. His fur tickled the back of Khalon's fingers, which made his stomach turn a little. But, when he looked down at Luke, he felt his heart warm a little. It was just a child. A child that was scared and needed to be protected. It might be disgusting to look at, disturbing even, but that didn't mean that it didn't deserve to live like everyone else.

"This direction?" Khalon asked. Luke nodded. Khalon felt his heart start to open up a little more to the beastoids. Or rather, he started to understand where they were coming from. Didn't Queen Aoife look at Khalon like that? With disgust? With eyes that said that he shouldn't be alive? It's not Luke's fault that he was created. It wasn't their fault how the creatures of Asynithis reacted to them being created. It wasn't any of the beastoids' faults.

Khalon looked out for animal tracks as they walked. Despite Luke telling him that they weren't animals, they still made tracks like animals. Though, slightly different. Their paws were feet-like. Khalon followed the tracks that Luke had made previously in the ground. As he concentrated on the ground, Luke tugged on his arm.

"Yeah?"

"Why do your people hate us?" he asked. Khalon blinked as he stared at the faded print in the ground.

"My people?" Khalon asked, his throat slightly dry.

"Your people. *All* creatures," Luke clarified. Khalon looked at Luke as they walked.

"Well, have you heard of humans?" Khalon asked. Luke nodded.

"Yes, humans look like everyone else. But they're different," said Luke.

"Right, they look like me but without scales, right? They look like vampires but without fangs. They look like elves but without the ears. But, even though they *look* like the magical creatures of Asynithis, they are without magic," Khalon said. Luke nodded along. It was something that he had heard before.

"Some humans are born with magic and they become witches. But witches aren't really human, it's a little confusing," Khalon muttered. "But anyways, when humans started popping up in Asynithis, we all were disgusted by them as well. We said they were without souls because they were without magic. But, they were smart on their own. They were creative and innovative and eventually drove the magical creatures of Asynithis into hiding. Into a deep sleep. They deluded themselves into thinking they were the rightful owners of the planet even though they were not connected to Asynithis by magic in any way. When they started to destroy Asynithis, we came back and put them in their rightful place. It was bad, for a while, for humans. It still is bad sometimes. But, the magical creatures of Asynithis were disgusted by them. How they moved around without any care in their actions. They felt like humans were just clay puppets."

"The War," Luke said. Khalon nodded.

"Right, we came back with The War. Took back Asynithis. But, just like how we were disgusted by humans, we—or rather some of us—are disgusted by beastoids," Khalon said quietly. He watched Luke's reaction to see whether he understood or not.

"We are different from you," Luke said slowly.

"Yes, in a way. You are like humans. Without magic," Khalon said. "And you are new. So just like with all new and different things, the creatures of old are scared and disgusted by it."

"Are you a creature of old?" Luke asked.

"I..." Khalon stopped. *Was he considered a creature of old?* "Some draconians feel that way, because we are descended from dragons. But, we are relatively new, too," Khalon whispered the last part. They were, weren't they? Almost as new as humans.

"So were the creatures of old disgusted by you as well?" Luke asked. *Good question*, Khalon muttered in his thoughts.

"I don't know," Khalon said, after a moment. "Draconians don't talk about it. So I don't know. Maybe they were."

"Don't you have a knowledge master to teach you these things anyways?" Khalon asked, a little annoyed. He didn't learn much besides what he told Luke. Khai had stopped coming to teach Khalon secretly about what the knowledge master taught him long ago. Luke shook his head no.

"We don't have knowledge masters," Luke warbled, his voice having trouble forming the words "knowledge masters".

"Oh," Khalon muttered. Of course they didn't have knowledge masters. They were too busy trying to survive.

"But, my mom told me the stories about The War," Luke said, proudly. He beamed up at Khalon, or tried to at least. Khalon awkwardly smiled back at him. Then, Luke pointed at the smoke that was rising from the horizon.

"That's where my mom is!" he exclaimed, excitedly. His brown eyes twinkled.

"Let's go," Khalon said. Luke pulled him along and then Khalon stopped when he was a little a ways from the camp. He saw maybe a hundred tents in the clearing. Beastoids were walking around, chatting, or eating near campfires. Khalon's belly rumbled like an earthquake as he watched the beastoids eat. He didn't know how long it had been since he had eaten. Luke didn't notice, or if he did, he pretended not to.

"Mom!" he shouted. A bear-looking humanoid that resembled Luke but in a bigger fashion looked over in their direction. Her eyes got big but Luke ran towards her as Khalon stayed back in the shadows of the trees. She stared hard at Khalon but hugged her son as he ran up to her. He was quickly talking to the point where Khalon couldn't understand anything he was saying. She looked back up at Khalon and from a distance, signed thank you. Liam had taught Khalon a little of the beastoids' signing when they were at the Ring of Fire together. Liam was part beastoid, it was where he inherited his teeth from. They would sign with their paw-like hands to one another because they couldn't communicate with other species of beastoids very well. Their voice boxes are all so different from one another and some beastoids can voice words in different ways and others can't shape them, which is why a lot of them just sign to each other. It was how they were so good at battle

as well, since they could communicate with one another
without saying anything.

Khalon nodded in response and then backed away into the
woods more. She turned her attention back onto her son and
hugged him tightly. Khalon's eyes suddenly burned, and he
turned away. He never got to feel the warmth of a mother
missing him or loving him. Queen Aoife had never wanted him
near.

"Get away from me, you bastard," her voice echoed in his
head. She was always pushing him away, hating him for existing, when all he wanted was a mother who would love him.
Now, he wasn't sure how he was going to bring the God of
Death to his father in order to destroy the beastoids. They just
wanted a home. A place where they felt like they belonged.
Isn't that what Khalon had always wanted as well? Khalon
rubbed his eyes with one hand and sighed as he started
walking in the direction of Draconia. Maybe he could convince
Rhea to reject him as sacrifice. Then, she wouldn't have to
support his father in the war against the beastoids. But, that
just meant that he would die, just by the hands of his father
instead of by a God.

Khalon groaned loudly as he put his head in his hands.
Wasn't that a noble death as well? To die for a group of people?
For creatures that deserve the same rights as everyone else?

"Why do I have to think about this?" Khalon groaned.

"Think about what?" a voice said from behind him. He
jumped and turned around to see a man who was slightly
taller than him. He had short brown hair in tight curls close to
his head and skin the color of deep wet sand. The man smiled
crookedly.

"Are you Khalon?" he asked. Khalon nodded. Khalon felt
like he had seen this face before. *Right*, he thought, *the face in
the hellfire.*

"Hi, I'm Poseidon," he smiled brightly at Khalon. While Rhea's eyes would flash with fire, his looked like there were waves crashing in his hazel eyes. He looked around Khalon, in confusion.

"So, where's Hades, temple servant?"

10

Rhea brushed her hair back from her forehead with both hands as she walked An out of the Fates' room.

"How is this possible, An?" she asked in a hushed tone. An held up a hand to quiet her. The God of Death's soul bristled within her at the movement.

"We can't talk about it in a realm like this," An whispered. His gray eyes looked up at Rhea, lifeless once again.

"Gods can't..." she let the sentence drift away. "Can they?" An's face looked ten times older than the thirteen-year-old body he resided in.

"We are still trying to figure out how this happened," An muttered. "The reason why I came to you, specifically, Rhea is because you have eyes and ears everywhere. Whoever is doing this, is moving in ways that I cannot see." His words said one thing, but his eyes studied Rhea intensely. She frowned. The God of All asking for the God of Death's help in something? Almost unheard of.

"I'm a bit *busy*," Rhea snapped, in unbridled annoyance.

She waved a hand towards the bustling rotting corpses running around in the underworld's lobby.

"Too busy handling the whole of the universe. Life and death pretty much hangs in the balance every day and *who* has to manage that balance?" Rhea put a finger to her head as if she were thinking, "Oh right. Yeah, that's *me*. Because you didn't want to — how did you put it eons ago? Deal with death? I think those were your exact words, right?"

"Brother," An's voice changed slightly, deepening, "Your hatred of me needs to be put aside. Our family is dying."

"By whose hands?" The God of Death was unbearable. Rhea put a hand to her aching head as her eyes glared at the boy in front of her. "Why do *you* get all the glory while *I* get leered at? I get isolation and you get all the prayers and praise when I do everything that *you* should be doing. Your pride, *your ego*, is what has killed our family. Gods?" Rhea felt herself laugh, "*You* are the God. We all just divvy up the work meant for *you*." Rhea felt the simultaneous cold and hot wave pass through her, settling back into her chest. She wiped sweat off of her forehead, exertion from trying to keep the God of Death at bay.

"He's said what he wanted," Rhea gasped. "He's gone now." An's eyes still showed that the God of All was present there, but slowly they turned to a dull gray once more.

"It is hard for us to meet," An said, more to himself than to her. For An it was different than it was for Rhea. While Rhea had access to the God of Death in parts, An had the God of All coursing through him continuously. The soul attached to the body that the God of All decided to live in was barely there. Rhea put a hand on An's shoulder, though the kind gesture towards him innately sickened her.

"I'll ask the Fates to tell me if the reapers see anything

weird," Rhea reassured him. He patted her hand, his hand smaller than hers, and nodded.

"Hope we don't need to meet again for a while," An confessed. "He's a bit more lively than usual." Rhea didn't know what to say to that as, for her, the God of Death was always lively around An. She just couldn't handle it as well this time.

"We've been stressed, I guess," Rhea muttered. "A war happening and all." An nodded. He walked forward towards a set of stairs that led back to the surface. Turning around, he gave a friendly wave before disappearing up the stairs. Just like Rhea, An moved quickly but through light or air.

Rhea felt someone standing next to her. Turning her head, Rhea looked at Francine whose brown eyes looked frightened as she stared into Rhea's.

"Francine, I'm going to need you to be in charge of this," Rhea sighed. Francine nodded.

"Better me than Farrah or Felicity," she agreed, the fear disappearing from her eyes. She was right. Farrah was a bit of a worrywart while Felicity was as scatterbrained as ever. The only thing that kept her mind from straying was cutting the strings of life. Francine chewed on her bottom lip.

"I *am* worried for you, though, Rhea," Francine admitted.

"Don't worry. I'll be fine," Rhea reassured.

"A," Francine's voice lowered as she looked around, "*God-killer* is on the loose and you're not able to stay in this realm. Plus, you're away from your temple."

"Again, I'm fine. Anyone can die, apparently, and I'm," Rhea gestured towards herself while giving Francine a reassuring smile, "literally death so, I'll be fine." Francine squinted her eyes and made a face before breathing out a sigh.

"Fine. But I'm going to have the reapers keep an eye on you too, if they're nearby," Francine ordered. Rhea rolled her eyes.

"Let them do their work, Francine. I'll be *fine*, I promise."
Francine angrily scribbled something in her notebook.

"Let me do what I want, Rhea," Francine muttered, turning
away. Rhea chuckled a little. Francine was not someone who
liked to be told what to do. Imagine her dismay when she was
told that she was supposed to serve the God of Death for the
rest of her life as a reincarnated Fate. Rhea wasn't alive when
the revelation was brought to her, but she wished she could've
seen Francine's face.

"Oh," Rhea remembered the conversation that she had
with Khalon that morning, "Francine!" Francine turned
around.

"By any chance, did I sleep down here last night?" Rhea
asked. Francine frowned.

"No, I didn't see you," Francine mused. "But, this place is
massive, as you know." It *was* the underworld and it's possible
that she could've ended up anywhere throughout it. Rhea's lips
twisted in thought.

"Why?" Francine asked. Rhea shook her head.

"Oh, no reason." *Khalon is probably just blind*, Rhea thought
to herself. Speaking of Khalon, Rhea figured he must be close to
the border of Draconia by now. Her temple wasn't too far away
from the famed Dragon country.

Rhea scurried up the stairs to the surface, the ground
opening up to a large valley in a field. She climbed out of the
hole in the ground, groaning at the face that stared at her.

"Osiris!" Poseidon exclaimed happily. His lanky arms were
opened into a possible hug. Rhea felt extreme annoyance
washing over her, ignoring the hug.

"Poseidon," Rhea muttered politely. Khalon's face just
looked shocked. It was hard not to laugh at the sight of
emotion on his face. He followed behind Poseidon absent-

mindedly as Rhea glared up at him, but a shadow of a smile was still on her lips.

"We were *just* talking about you," Poseidon exclaimed.

"Did you have to run into him of all people?" Rhea asked Khalon, completely ignoring Poseidon. Khalon held his scarred hands up in defense.

"Are you serious? Don't talk to me, I didn't purposely run into him," Khalon muttered. Obviously he was still annoyed about her disappearance this morning. Rhea smiled slightly. It was funny, seeing him upset.

"Don't talk to *me*," Rhea said back, turning away.

"Am I interrupting something here?" Poseidon asked, leaning back. Rhea's smile was wiped from her face as she glared at the tall, lanky man.

"*Why* are you here, Poseidon? Shouldn't you be on the shores of Argenti at—I don't know—your temple?" His eyebrows raised at Rhea's tone.

"Someone's feisty today. I'm guessing you got the message from An," he said. His normally teasing tone was a bit more subdued.

"More like he gave me the message himself," Rhea mumbled. Poseidon's eyes widened.

"An came to see you? He never does that. He knows how much the God of Death hates—"

"I know."

"So, this is serious. What exactly is going on? He hasn't really given the rest of us the memo yet," Poseidon sounded uncharacteristically bitter. Rhea smirked as she put a hand on her hip.

"Is someone upset that the golden child didn't entrust sacred information to their favorite Brother?" the God of Death was really not giving Rhea any rest today. She blew the hair out from her eyes as Poseidon rolled his hazel ones.

"You're *really* in a mood today. I already know a God has died, Kali. But I don't understand the Seer's message of doom. We can die, our vessels *are* creature after all." Khalon was just standing in the middle of them, his head whipping back and forth as if watching a starfire game, which was a common game among witches where they use a big piece of a fallen star, starfire, to hit back and forth towards each other with just their power. If you miss, the starfire burns the other into oblivion. It was more a game of natural selection than a game for entertainment.

"Yeah-h-h," Rhea drew out the word, "about that. Turns out, our souls *can* die." While she said that nonchalantly, the blood in her body ran cold. The Gods dying? For good? It was a frightening thought. Poseidon and Khalon stared at her in disbelief. Khalon's mouth was gaping a bit.

"What?" Khalon said. "Is this why you were asking if I would sacrifice my life for you?" Rhea shrugged. Poseidon sharply turned to him, as if just realizing that he was there. He pointed at Khalon as Khalon frowned at the gesture.

"Is it okay for him to be hearing this?" Poseidon lowered his voice. "What if he's a spy?" Rhea wished her eyes and ears could turn inside out so she could neither hear nor see Poseidon.

"He's my temple servant and he's been with me the whole time. Including the time where Belenus," the breath hitched in her throat. Poseidon's eyes softened.

"I heard about her," he said softly. "So, she's gone forever?" Rhea nodded her head. The God of Healing was no more, she wanted to say but couldn't bring herself to. Poseidon nodded his head in understanding.

"So, that's why everyone should stay at their temples, like you told me to last night," Rhea pointed out. "*You* should be there, not seeking me out for some idle gossip." Poseidon laughed.

"While I do *love* a bit of gossip," he admitted, "I'm not here for that." His face hardened, revealing his true age. His body, or vessel as he liked to call it, was only twenty-six years of age but with his light-hearted nature it always looked much younger. Now, the twenty-six years were clearly shown in his smooth face.

"The temples aren't safe, as I have discovered," Poseidon chuckled a little, but without feeling. Rhea's stomach dropped. She had a feeling she knew what he was about to say.

"They didn't just go after Belenus last night, my dear Ah Puch. They also came after me," his jaw tightened as he patted down his tightly curled brown hair on the top of his head.

"You saw who it was?" Poseidon shook his head, his eyes wet from the memory.

"They came to me wearing a hood, after brutally murdering all of my temple servants. They didn't stand a chance. The way he fought with me showed he was a trained killer. The odd thing was his choice of weapon," Poseidon said. Rhea gestured for him to go on.

"He was holding a tooth. It wasn't a big tooth, maybe like a medium sized tooth. He was trying to stab me with it, but I was able to get away and..." his voice trailed off. He shrugged, "My temple is now a part of the Argenti Sea, and hopefully so is he." A tooth?

"So there were two assassins, then," Rhea said to herself.

"Someone hired them," Khalon's voice cut through the air. Rhea looked up at him, studying his face. He thinks someone was hiring assassins to kill the Gods?

"What do you mean?"

"I don't think this is just an organization of people who want to kill the Gods," Khalon said, "An organization—I probably would've heard mutterings about it at the Ring of Fire. We hear everything that goes on in Asynithis as the Champions are pretty much from all over."

"An organization trying to kill the Gods wouldn't be some rumor that would be spread around," Poseidon dismissed. Khalon's jaw clenched in anger.

"An organization trying to kill the Gods would *definitely* be trying to recruit Champions for it. We are highly skilled fighters who don't really trust the Gods anymore, or even want them to be deciding the future of the world. Since I didn't hear anything about it, I don't think it's an organization," Khalon snapped. *He really hated being undermined.*

"You think someone just thought of how to kill the Gods all on their own and then hired people to do it?" Poseidon doubted Khalon's thoughts.

"Assassins would do anything for money," Khalon argued. "And maybe they didn't decide all on their own but there's definitely someone pulling the strings. I'm sure the information on how to permanently kill a God is out there. Either in old books or maybe even in folk tales. Information is everywhere if you really look for it." It was something his dad used to say to him. Khalon felt his heart fall at the thought of how his father used to be towards him. Poseidon raised his eyebrows at the mention of folk tales.

"I do wonder..." he muttered to himself. Khalon's face relaxed and he leaned back slightly, obviously proud at finally convincing the Sea God. Rhea couldn't hide a smile at Khalon's obvious facial expressions. When he did show an emotion, it was written all over his face, like an open book. Though it was clear he was always trying to contain them.

"Folk tales," Rhea said to Poseidon, a twinkle in her eye. Poseidon nodded in agreement.

"If there is information about how to kill a God, it *would* be in myths, legends, or folk tales," Poseidon said. Rhea didn't think Khalon was really thinking about what he was saying earlier when he mentioned folk tales, by the look on his face, but he still nodded along as if it was his original thought from the beginning.

"The problem is," Poseidon said, "we weren't raised on folk tales or legends." He was right. While Rhea was raised by the Fates when they were only eleven, the other Gods were given to their respective temples as babies. Temple servants would help the Gods in their baby form get what they needed in order to survive, but truly the soul of the God that the baby had within them would raise them. It was why the reincarnations of the Gods were so connected to the God's soul. Their soul was ever present within the body. Due to the nature of the God of Death, Rhea, and the reincarnations before her, were not raised by the God's soul but rather by the reincarnated Fates instead. The God of Death lying dormant within the body for most of the time was the best course of action, the God of All had decided many centuries ago.

"Felicity used to tell me stories growing up, but knowing her—"

"They're probably made up, of course. How *is* my dear Felicity? I love her energy, you know," Poseidon gushed. Rhea rolled her eyes.

"*Please*, she's a mess," she huffed, thinking back to the reaper with the day off.

"Who's Felicity?" Khalon piped up.

"Oh, she's one of the Fates. The ones who cut the string of life. It unties the soul from the body so that we can grab it," Rhea explained. Khalon had a look of disgust on his face.

"You just...pull the soul out from the body? Is it like... gooey or slimy or something?" Khalon asked. Rhea never thought about how people must think of souls and it made her laugh a little.

"No," she shook her head, amused, "the souls are more like balls of light that I or a reaper pull out from the corpse and then take it into the underworld."

"Humans had such grand ideas about the underworld but it's not all that interesting really," Poseidon said, answering a question that no one asked. Rhea's eyebrows lowered towards her eyes as she stared at him. Poseidon glanced over at her and then said, "It's really more just like a big building with a bunch of rooms."

"*Okay*, thank you for your judgment, Poseidon," Rhea said sarcastically as Poseidon winked at Khalon. Khalon's face was once again stony at the exchange.

"Khalon, have you heard of any folk tales or legends about the Gods growing up?" Rhea asked him in order to change the subject. Khalon's eyebrows knitted together as he concentrated.

"We have legends about the dragons," Khalon said slowly, "But I don't really remember much of them. I was five when I was put into the Ring of Fire, so not a lot of storytelling days from my childhood." Rhea nodded slowly.

"Sorry my temple servant can't do his one job of being the expert of societal matters in Asynithis," Rhea apologized to Poseidon. "He's defective." Poseidon put a hand over his heart as Khalon looked at her with mouth agape.

"Don't talk to me," Khalon muttered as Rhea stuck her tongue out at him.

"It's perfectly fine, Brother. You can get a new temple servant." Rhea put a hand to her chin as she seriously thought about the offer.

"I have thought about returning him and getting a new one. It would be most advantageous to our journey to get one who knows about life in Asynithis, don't you think?" Poseidon exuberantly nodded in agreement.

"Yes, yes, quite."

"Okay, guys, I get it," Khalon said, his hands up defensively. He sighed as Rhea burst out into laughter. Poseidon's eyes twinkled with amusement.

"I do have someone we might be able to pick the brain of," Poseidon said after Rhea continuously smacked Khalon's arm while laughing. Khalon looked at her like she was a mad woman. At Poseidon's words, Rhea looked over at him, her hand sliding off of Khalon's arm to his relief.

"We have to go to Draconia. I have a promise to keep," Rhea stated seriously.

"The person I know is in Draconia. He owns a little bar in one of the towns. Should be on the way to the battlefield," Poseidon mused. Rhea's jaw dropped.

"How did you—"

"Gossiping among us isn't necessarily a bad thing, dear Brother," he chastised. Rhea rolled her eyes.

"Besides, I've been meaning to see this human of mine. He also *does* love a good story," Poseidon smiled.

11

On the way to the bar called "Dragon's Blood," which Khalon felt didn't sound appealing whatsoever, Poseidon and Rhea refused to stop bickering. Khalon couldn't help but wonder if he and Khai would've argued similarly.

"Just so you know, the underworld is not just this giant building with a bunch of rooms," Rhea stomped as she walked in her long, black robe. Khalon was surprised that she hadn't tripped over it yet. While Rhea was taller than the average girl, the cloak obviously hadn't been tailored from the last God of Death as it was still a bit big on her.

"When you get to the underworld, you're greeted by a white corporate looking room," Poseidon disagreed, "I'm surprised the reapers haven't converted to suits yet."

"Oh yeah," Rhea had responded sarcastically, "Because the person who's dying would *love* to be greeted by a rotting corpse in a suit. The suit makes the prospect *so* much better."

"I'm just saying the suit is part of the corporation fantasy that you're going for," Poseidon shrugged.

"I'm not going for a corporation fantasy, Poseidon," Rhea huffed. "Besides, that's just the lobby of the underworld. The other parts are more creative than you can imagine."

"Not as creative as the humans had thought of. Humans were so...inventive, you know. The River Styx? Circles of Hell? I mean, where did they think of this stuff? They must've been so incredibly disappointed when they finally met their doom," Poseidon cried.

"I don't want to talk to you anymore," she responded, walking away in a huff. Khalon wasn't sure what a corporation was, but whatever it meant Rhea was insulted by it.

Another argument they had while they were traveling to the "Dragon's Blood" bar had to do with Khalon, which made him a little uncomfortable.

"The *little* bar in the *little* town is actually in the capital city of Furvus, where the *King* of Draconia lives, and you didn't think that was something that *needed to be mentioned?*" Rhea fumed. She had stopped in her tracks after Poseidon had mentioned that the bar was in Furvus.

"Furvus isn't *that* big of a city compared to Amnis Lux. To me, it's just a tiny town," Poseidon dismissed. Khalon watched as Rhea threw a silent fit behind Poseidon's back, trying to hide a smile as she did so. She was enjoyable to watch sometimes. Even though she was the God of Death, and her skin *was* as white-gray as a corpse so it was hard to believe that she might have a heartbeat, she seemed to wear her heart on her sleeve. She was a very animated person with big facial expressions. When she frowned, her whole face frowned with her. When she spoke, it was as if her eyes and cheeks spoke as well.

"It's a pretty important detail considering we have the *banished* son of the king traveling with us," Rhea pushed her hair out of her face in frustration. Poseidon had glanced over at

Khalon, looking him up and down, before continuing their argument.

"No one will recognize him," he had declared. Rhea looked at him with eyes wide and her mouth slightly open.

"Are you an idiot, Poseidon? I didn't know that you got reincarnated into a body with the lowest IQ I've ever seen," she berated him. Poseidon rolled his eyes.

"If it's *that* much of a big deal to you, why don't you *disguise* him?" Poseidon said, anger slightly peeking through. His normally twinkling hazel eyes turned stormy.

"He's a Champion, Poseidon. It'd be kind of hard to disguise him to be unrecognizable with nothing at our disposal," Rhea criticized.

"I don't know, Pluto, maybe think about the resources you *have* at your disposal?" Poseidon snapped. If Rhea was taken aback by his anger, she didn't show it.

"The only resources I have are the cloaks that reapers wear and we don't know what that might do to a living soul!" Rhea argued. Poseidon stopped walking as he stared at her head on. She looked up at him, her face comically angry.

"I know you see what I feel emanating from his soul, Shinigami. He'll be fine," Poseidon ended the argument.

"Besides, I don't think it'll do anything to a living soul," Poseidon muttered to himself. Rhea made a face of confusion as she tried to make out what he said and then started to grumble to herself in response. She waved her hand, making the ground open up and reveal never-ending stairs. Turning into a shadow, she disappeared down them. Just as suddenly as the ground opened, it closed, as if a big, gaping hole with stairs was never there in the first place.

"You'll be fine," Poseidon had said to Khalon in reassurance. Khalon felt that Poseidon was sure of himself but Khalon wanted to know why. He felt like he and Rhea were being studied by the Sea God and he wasn't sure what they were talking about when it came to his soul. Rhea had mentioned seeing something attached to his soul a few times, and it was some change in him that even Poseidon could feel, without being able to see it. It made him frightened to know that something was attached to him without knowing, but he would never admit to that.

But, that was how Khalon ended up standing in the capital city of Draconia wearing a long, black cloak with the hood covering his face. People walking around them looked at the group of three with weird looks. Two of them were wearing shapeless black cloaks and the other was wearing swimsuit bottoms with a T-shirt on top that read "Amnis Lux! Best crab-cakes around!" They definitely stood out in the traditional city of Furvus.

"Dragon's Blood" was a bar that was architecturally similar to the rest of Furvus. It was a city that was quite opposite from Regium. While Aureum loved to take the inventions of humans (claiming them as their own) and incorporate them into their everyday lives, Draconia valued tradition over everything. The architecture was reminiscent of ancient times of the past, before the age where humans were completely in control of Asynithis. There were many columns, stone buildings, but also swooped roofs and intricate wooden structures. The roads were made of stone with beautiful patterns that showed dragon serpents on the sides of the roads. Their eyes held little jewels that no one dared to steal or bad fortune would come for you. Considering Khalon felt that he already had bad fortune, he sneakily tapped some of the more loose jewels out along the way, pocketing them.

Furvus was a beautifully simple and elegant city, unlike the chaos of Regium. Khalon had only seen the city of Furvus once when he was a young child. His father had taken him to some of the local shops in order to get something for the birth of his younger brother. It was still possibly the best day of Khalon's life.

The bar that they stood in front of also had the characteristic swooped shingled roofs and was made of wood with blue painted columns in the front. A giant sea dragon's head stuck out from the front of the roof, glaring at anyone who entered.

"This is the place," Poseidon marveled. He opened the door, revealing the sea-themed structures inside. The bar very much looked as if the place was underwater in Argentiunda, the country that spread across the ocean floors.

"Dragon's Blood? More like Dragon's Ocean," Khalon muttered to himself. When he heard the name of the bar, he was thinking that it would look something a little more similar to the Ring of Fire. However, he was a little relieved that it was completely different.

An old man was sitting behind the bar shaped like the body of a blue sea dragon. The sun was starting to set, and the light glittered off the different surfaces inside the bar, resembling how the sunlight glitters underwater. The old man's eyes brightened in recognition. He was human; it was apparent by the smell emanating off of him. There were many humans in Draconia, but few owned shops within the capital city. His glasses slipped slightly off of his tall nose.

"Tefnut, is that you?" the man's weak voice called out. He was incredibly old, and as he got up, Poseidon gestured for him to continue sitting.

"I go by Poseidon in this life, my dear," he said. Khalon's eyes widened at the exchange. My dear? He had heard that the Gods sometimes took lovers but didn't realize that the reincarnations would continue the relationship with the lover of the last reincarnation, even as friends. Poseidon sat down on one of the bar stools, while the old man smiled brightly at him. They held each other's hands tightly.

"You remembered," he croaked out, choking on the tears bubbling up in his throat. Khalon looked around, still shocked, as Rhea looked over at Poseidon, annoyed.

"Of course I remembered, Tiege. This body is twenty-six years old now," Poseidon said, his voice soft. Tiege wiped a tear that slipped out from his eyes. He smiled warmly.

"The same age as when we met," he whispered. Poseidon smiled back at him.

"On the day we first met, my dear," he said. They stared at each other for a long while, remembering the past life that they shared.

"You took us on a highly dangerous journey just to visit an old flame?" Rhea muttered. Poseidon glared at her and then his eyes softened looking back at Tiege.

"I apologize for my Brother, Tiege," Poseidon patted his hand before withdrawing it. "She is a bit annoyed today. Long day."

"The longest," Rhea agreed. Tiege seemed to finally recognize that Rhea was standing there, his face going through many emotions at once.

"I—" he choked back a sob, "I saw you die." His voice was barely above a whisper. Rhea sighed. Khalon noticed that the face that encased her own was stuck on a gruesome image of a man dead.

"I'm so sorry I couldn't save you," Tiege muttered, holding his hands together. He looked horrified, but unable to look away from Rhea. Rhea held a hand up, stopping him from his speech.

"I am not the person that you see. Apologies," she said coldly. Unlike before, there was no emotion emitting from her. Normally, Rhea seemed to have a cascade of emotions emanating through her, but now... Khalon wondered why she shut down like that. Was it because creatures looked at her with that expression? Horrified but also full of guilt and grief? *I can kind of relate to that*, Khalon thought as he thought about his father. Poseidon patted the table.

"It's bygones, my dear Tiege, bygones. Don't be too hung up on the past. I am alive and well right here in front of you," he said, spreading his arms. He smiled at Tiege as Tiege finally tore his eyes away from the sight of Rhea.

"Considering you came with guests, I'm guessing I am not the only reason why you have come," Tiege said. There was a hint of sadness in his voice, but it was clear that whatever love that Tiege and Poseidon had once shared, it was lifetimes ago. What remained was respect and care for one another, so while Tiege seemed slightly disappointed, he understood.

"Well, I happened to run into my little Brother here—"

"We were all created at the same time *basically*," Rhea interrupted.

"—And we are on a great search for stories. Specifically stories about the Gods. See, Hine-nui-te-pō here," his pronunciation was impeccable, "unfortunately hasn't completed her studies about the history of the Gods and since her God's soul remains dormant, for very good reason I might add, she has no one to teach her."

"I go by Rhea, just by the way," Rhea crossed her arms. Tiege glanced over at Rhea and then quickly looked away. Khalon noticed that Tiege wasn't able to see the face behind the image in front and wondered why he seemed to be the only one who could see her true face. He glanced over at her, her face still like stone.

"Why don't *you* tell her the history of the Celestials?" Tiege asked, using the term that described what the creatures of Asynithis called the bodies of those that inhabited the Gods.

He was slowly washing the cups that were about to be used for drinking once the sun had fully set and draconians were ready to celebrate the night.

"I have but we're at the part about the myths of Gods and legends that are told to us as children. Like bedtime stories or folk tales. And unfortunately, I've never heard of any," Poseidon feigned disappointment. Tiege thought for a moment while washing the cups.

"Let me think," he said. "A bedtime story about the Gods..." Khalon looked around the place as Tiege thought in quiet. There were pictures at the far wall and upon closer look, Khalon could see a younger version of Tiege with a man who was a draconian. The scales in the picture were clearly visible. He was smiling a crooked smile similar to the one Poseidon frequently donned.

"It's a former reincarnation," Rhea said, appearing next to him. Khalon was startled at her sudden appearance but tried to not show it. She gave him a knowing look.

"We're not supposed to take pictures of our reincarnations," Rhea said. "It's because we might not look as godly as the creatures might think we should. It breaks the illusion, you know?" Khalon hoped that Rhea couldn't read thoughts. The fear that she was describing was similar to the feeling that Khalon had when looking at her at first. She was underwhelming as the God of Death, but what did he expect her to look like? Like a giant skeleton with a skull head and sharp teeth? What exactly was Death supposed to take the form of?

"People should lower their expectations," Khalon replied. Rhea frowned slightly, obviously disagreeing with what he said.

"Or they should just realize that we're taking over a creature body that looks like them," she refuted. Khalon could feel his ears turn red at her reply. She was right. Not lowering expectations but instead changing them to meet reality. A God wasn't going to look like a God on Asynithis. Their true form wouldn't be able to really be looked at by creature eyes. He stared at her as she tucked a copper lock of hair behind her large elven ears. Her side profile was pretty, he unconsciously started to think. She had a swooped nose and her cheeks protruded from her face slightly. Her chin was just under her lips and her bottom lip jutted out a little more than her top. Her eyes rested on top of her cheeks and were like polished andalusite.

"Poseidon was a draconian," Khalon tore his eyes away from her and changed the subject. Rhea squinted and then nodded.

"Yes, it does look that way," she said. Khalon looked back at Poseidon as he intently stared at Tiege who was still thinking to himself. Poseidon sighed in frustration. If Tiege noticed, he didn't make any acknowledgment of it.

"This reincarnation is human," Khalon pointed out. Rhea shrugged.

"Yeah, so?"

"From my understanding," Khalon thought back to the materials that his brother used to bring, "the Gods don't really reincarnate as humans, not after the first time." Rhea frowned at this new information.

"And Poseidon is human, and you're at least part human," Khalon pointed out.

"What's your point?" Rhea asked. Khalon wasn't sure *what* his point was. But there was an odd feeling washing over him, knowing that the Gods were reincarnating as humans.

"It's just interesting, is all," Khalon muttered. Rhea stared at him for a moment longer, as if trying to read his mind.

"It *is* interesting," she said, barely above a whisper, mostly to herself. Her eyebrows scrunched together in thought.

Khalon wasn't sure what she was thinking about, but he
guessed she was thinking about the other Gods' reincarnations
that were currently still on Asynithis. By the look on her face,
he wondered if they were all human or part human. And if they
were, what did it mean for the future? There was a reason why
the Gods refused to take the form of humans. There has to be a
reason why the Gods suddenly shifted away from that.

"Ah," Tiege finally said. Khalon and Rhea glanced at each
other for a moment and then walked back to the bar. Creatures
had started to come into the establishment and Khalon pulled
the hood down further to mask his face.

"It's okay," Rhea put a hand on his arm. "Your face is
completely shrouded by this kind of cloak. It's to keep creatures from being afraid when death comes to them. A rotting
corpse appearing suddenly in front of you is a bit..." She made a
face to demonstrate what she meant. Khalon understood what
she was trying to say.

"I see," he said, taking his hand away from the hood of his
cloak.

"Did you hear?" a draconian girl said to the human next to
her as she walked into the establishment.

"King Vien banished his son—you know, the Champion
one—to be a sacrifice to the Death God," the girl whispered.
Khalon felt his body straighten. Rhea stiffened next to him and
tried to make herself look smaller. The creatures in the room
knew who he was, and probably knew what he looked like.

"He's been killing those who talk about the prince. I would
be careful talking about this in public," the human whispered
back. The draconian shook her head.

"He's becoming more and more like King Archion every
day." *King Archion.* He was Khalon's grandfather, and the one
who successfully ended the Black Dragon bloodline. Known for
going crazy, at the end of his reign, he was killing anyone who

spoke ill of him, including his other son, Khalon's uncle Khoi. When he died, he was eating the flesh off of those he killed as a way of punishment towards their dead bodies. Khalon froze thinking about his father. This wasn't the man that he knew, but Khalon barely knew King Vien, only holding onto memories from before he was five. Rhea tugged on the sleeve of his cloak, motioning with her head and eyes for him to pay attention.

"It isn't really a folk tale about the Gods, but they are Gods in their own right, I suppose. Or a monster," Tiege mused.

"Just tell us any story that you know," Poseidon encouraged.

"It's an old bedtime story that we used to tell the kids growing up. It's about these monsters called the Mortiferis," Tiege spoke slowly, coughing as he talked. "They are the ultimate judgment of the state of the world. Without thought or feeling, they come to worlds and destroy them, if they feel like it. So if you don't want the Mortiferis to come, then you must be a good little boy or girl." Cheers and some groans erupted from behind Khalon. He turned slightly to look at the hologram that the bar patrons were looking at. The bar was starting to fill up. It was a Champion fight from inside of the Ring of Fire. Khalon would recognize that arena anywhere. On the ground, Mateo lay, blood pooling around his head.

"Here," a draconian man shoved money towards the bald man next to him. His scales covered the top of his head.

"I told you Mateo wouldn't stand a chance," the man said, happiness in his voice. Khalon's stomach turned at the sight of Mateo. He knew the child. They had spoken a couple of times. He was just a kid, younger than Khalon. He was arrested for killing his abusive parents. Khalon remembered that today was his first fight in the Ring. His first fight, and he was dead. Mateo's lifeless holographic eyes stared up at the sky as the hologram zoomed in on him. Around the hologram, Khalon could see laughing, smiling faces and playful jabs towards one another as they looked upon the lifeless Mateo. He felt his fists ball up. *There was one thing that humans had over magical creatures,* Khalon thought. *At least their form of entertainment wasn't just violence and death.*

"What do you mean they come to worlds and destroy them?" Rhea said, leaning in towards Tiege. Tiege shrugged. Khalon noticed that Poseidon eyed her as he took a sip of his drink. *What does he want from her?*

"The story says they just destroy worlds," Tiege said.

"Could I get a glass of mermaid's tears on the rocks?" a bar patron interrupted. Tiege nodded in acknowledgment and started to make the drink.

"By explosion or a nuclear war? How were they able to destroy a whole world?" Poseidon asked. Tiege shrugged again as he slowly took the ice out of the ice machine.

"They ate it," Tiege said. Poseidon made a face.

"Is this the only story that you could think of? It doesn't even have to do with Gods," Poseidon said exasperatedly. But there was a note of desperation in his voice.

"Oh," Tiege said, pausing as he thought, "The part with the Gods. My mother used to say that the Mortiferis had the ability to kill the Gods as well. No one could stop the Mortiferis once they started. Mortiferis. Mortiferi?" Tiege thought about the plural term of the monster he was talking about. Rhea and Poseidon shared a knowing look, though Poseidon looked more doubtful.

"There's only one of these creatures?" Rhea asked. Tiege shook his head.

"No, there's an army of them. That's how they're able to eat the whole world into oblivion," Tiege handed the drink to the bar patron who was paying more attention to the

Champion fights than to the three strange creatures at the bar.

"But, it is just a story of course. A unique one though," Tiege wagged his finger at Rhea. "You won't hear that one from the youngsters anymore. Hopefully this helps your studies." He refused to look Rhea in the face, and instead opted for looking at her neck when talking to her. Rhea feigned a brilliant smile, though Tiege didn't see it.

"Yes, thank you! What a unique story, truly. Thank you so much for telling it to us," Rhea said. Tiege smiled at her words as Poseidon patted his hand.

"Yes thank you, my love," Poseidon said. Tiege kissed the top of Poseidon's hand and then patted it afterwards.

"Of course, my old friend," Tiege smiled. "If you need a place to stay tonight, the inn down the street should be open for guests. She's a good friend of mine. A draconian named Alina."

"Thank you, Tiege," Poseidon said, gratefully. He got up from the bar.

"Let's go, kids," Poseidon said, stretching his arms up and cracking his back audibly. Rhea pulled her hood down more and ducked her head as she walked out the door. Considering it seemed that no one ever saw the real face beneath the carousel of faces, she didn't want to cause anyone unnecessary grief or fear. Khalon wondered how Rhea would respond to him being able to see her true face. He shook his head. It would be better for her not to know.

Outside the "Dragon's Blood" bar, the streets were relatively empty. The streetlights were aglow and cheers once again erupted from inside the bar, though muffled.

"How much time do you think he has?" Poseidon asked Rhea, staring up at the cloudless sky.

"Not long," Rhea said quietly. Tears welled up in Poseidon's eyes as he looked down at Rhea. The corners of his lips turned up slightly.

"I want to be there, when he goes. Promise to let me know when it's his time," he told Rhea. Rhea chewed the inside of her cheek before finally nodding.

"Fine, I'll let you know," she said dejectedly. "By the way, he has a picture of your reincarnation in there."

"It's okay," Poseidon said, "He wouldn't dare say it was me anyways."

12

Prince Elion was the only son of the late King Elkhazel to mourn his father's death. He continued to wear the black robes even after Adamar's coronation, the event that officially made Adamar the King of Aureum. Was Elion trying to make a statement on Adamar becoming king? Mourning the Aureum that once was? Perhaps, though Elion tried to convince himself otherwise.

"Did you see her?" a servant said to another as they cleaned the great halls of the palace. The halls were adorned in gold, an addition that Elion's great grandfather had ordered. It is said that he sat on his throne lamenting on how Aureum was the richest country in all of Asynithis and yet their palace was the same as any other.

"Yes, she truly exudes beauty and grace, even in that human fairy mixed body of hers," the other servant replied, dreamily. Elion's ears pricked up. Adamar must've called upon the God of Love and Fertility to check on Essarae, his wife. Turning on his heel, he headed towards the throne room. It wasn't every day that a God came to the palace, though he had already met the Death God, an unnerving experience for him. She had said that she looked just like his mother, but to Elion she looked...

He shook his head, not wanting to remember the sight, as he continued to walk quickly towards the throne room. Before the guards could stop him, Elion slipped through the larger-than-life doors into the throne room. The throne room had gold and white themed decoration and moldings, with large marble columns lining the walls. The throne itself was made of pure gold, the top of the seat shaped like the sun. Adamar was standing up, bowing slightly towards his guest. Essarae, her stomach swollen with child, stood next to him, wearing a deep blue dress. Her tanned hand was holding her stomach. Adamar's light blue eyes glanced up at the intrusion. They squinted slightly before smiling with the rest of his face.

"I apologize, your holiness," Adamar said, straightening up out of his bow. "My youngest brother seems to be curious about your arrival." The girl in front of him turned around and it took everything in Elion not to fall to the ground from her beauty. Her skin was as dark as night and her hair was short, close to her head, framing her face with waves of somehow blacker hair. Her pink-brown lips smiled slightly at him.

"He looks a lot like you, your highness," she said, her brown eyes twinkling at Elion. He stood there, frozen. Her lips revealed brilliantly white teeth as she smiled fully at him, as if recognizing he was struck to nothing by her beauty. She gazed at him for a moment longer before tearing her eyes away to look back at his brother standing in front of her. Elion felt the air come back into his lungs and he took a couple of steps back, as if his soul was just pushed back into his body. Being in the presence of the God of Love was truly the hypnotizing experience that the stories proclaimed.

"I just wanted to make sure that the Queen is doing all

right," Adamar said, with an expression of fear and anxiety that Elion had never seen before. He watched the back of the Love God's head nod and then a small hand with long fingers beckoned for Essarae to come to her. Essarae looked annoyed by the order but came forward anyway. Elion walked closer to the God of Love, walking towards his brother's side, just to get another glimpse at her face.

She had her head bowed with her hands on Essarae's stomach. Even her side profile was mesmerizing. The softness of her side profile tugged at the heart. She was intoxicatingly beautiful, and Elion felt himself not wanting to ever leave her presence. Her eyes opened, long black eyelashes fluttering. They then glanced over at Elion, as if she felt his stare. He ducked his head quickly.

"The child seems to be growing fine. Is there another concern that you had?" the Love God spoke, her voice melodic. Hearing her speak was an experience similar to looking at a thousand diamonds glittering in the sunlight. There was no other way to describe her otherworldly tone. Elion felt Adamar glance over at him, but his eyes were fixated on the God. *Get it together, Elion,* he said to himself, trying to shake the hypnotic feeling that washed over him. *You need to pay attention.*

"It *is* a boy, yes?" Adamar almost demanded. Elion noticed that he was wringing out his hands, and he wasn't the only one who noticed. Adamar realized that the God was staring at his hands and quickly put them behind his back.

"It is," she said, dragging out the last word. She stared at Adamar, as if trying to figure out what he wanted from her.

"He is healthy and most definitely elf-like," she finally said. Adamar unconsciously blew out a sigh of relief. Essarae quickly glared at the action. *Elf-like? What else would the kid look like?*

"If that is all, I *really* must be going," the God said, apologetically. Adamar nodded quickly. As she turned, she looked back at Adamar.

"Your highness," she said, her voice slightly venomous, "Now that you know your answer, do not call upon me for trivial matters such as this." Adamar's eyes flashed, angry at her words, but then relaxed. He smiled, but it didn't quite reach his eyes.

"Of course, your holiness," he said politely enough. She bristled, unsatisfied by his tone, and then glanced over at Elion once more, as if asking him to follow her.

"If you don't mind, your highness," Elion said, his eyes not leaving her as she walked towards the doors of the throne room, "I would like a few words with the God of Love." Adamar chuckled, believing that his younger brother was just enthralled by the presence of her, as all were.

"It *is* a marvelous feeling, being in her presence. Go on," he said. Elion bowed deeply towards his brother and then bounded out of the throne room, as he heard his brother settle back into his throne, speaking in hushed tones to his wife.

The doors to the throne room closed and she was waiting there, resting against the wall. A short girl was beside her wearing the white gown of a temple servant. She was obviously a fairy as her height and small frame suggested. The Love God's eyes roved over him as she kicked herself off of the wall.

"Elion, correct?" she asked. A finger motioned for him to come hither. Elion nervously walked over to her, walking beside her confident strides. He wiped his sweaty hands down the side of his funeral robes. She glanced at the action.

"Still in mourning?" she asked. Elion nodded his head. She sighed wistfully.

"King Elkhazel, one of the good ones I've seen," she said, "I can count on one hand the number of good kings I've come across." Elion felt his throat close up at the mention of his father.

"You wanted to speak to me," he changed the subject. Her eyes glanced up at him. She was a couple of heads shorter than he was, her human side giving her more height than a normal fairy's.

"Yes," she said, "You picked up on that." She eyed him appraisingly. Sighing once more as she flitted down the halls of the palace, her fairy temple servant barely being able to keep up with her long strides, she looked around the area of the castle.

"Your brother is a *bit* of a paranoid creature," she muttered, moving her finger indicating Elion should keep following her.

"If you could walk me out," she said, absentmindedly. Elion bowed his head slightly.

"Of course," he barely whispered. Once outside the palace, she continued to move quickly until almost reaching the castle gates. Then, she seemed to relax. In the sunlight, her skin glittered slightly. Elion had seen a few fairies in his lifetime, but was still hypnotized by their skin.

"You must be careful, little one," she said. *Little one?* Elion thought. She looked like she was the same age as him.

"Your brother's child, there is something wrong with it. Considering that your brother wanted me to confirm that it did look like an elf, I'm curious about the child's origins. It is not normal. I would be careful when that child is born," she said.

"Your holiness—" Elion started. She held up her hand.

"Freya, please," she said. Elion's eyes widened and swallowed hard.

"Freya," using the chosen name of a Celestial was unnatural to him, "What do you mean there's something wrong with it?" Freya looked at him exasperatedly.

"That child is *not* an elf. It will take the form of it, but it is not what it looks like. There's something sinister about the conception of that child," she muttered. She waved her hand, dismissing the conversation. Elion bowed his head, recognizing that she was done talking. Her hand lifted his chin slightly, as she smiled pityingly at him.

"You remind me of him, you know," she said. Elion knew who she was referring to. Anyone who knew King Elkhazel always said that, even though Elion looked more like his mother than his father.

"I hope you live, Prince Elion," she said before disappearing into her carriage. The carriage flew up towards the sky and disappeared from sight. *What did she mean?* Elion pondered over her words as he headed back up into the palace. He stopped as he looked back up at the sky. *Did she know about Adamar?*

13

The inn wasn't anything special. It was a little bit on the outskirts of Furvus and looked like it received outsiders as visitors mostly. Furvus was already at the edge of Draconia, facing No Man's Land, but this little town was even closer to Rhea's home. When entering the inn, Rhea turned up her nose at the heavy smell of alcohol. There was a bar in the rundown lobby and many different creatures from all over were partaking in the spirit of the night. Rhea watched as Poseidon's eyes lit up at the sight of the woman greeting them; the innkeeper. She was draconian, her hair black and straight, falling over her shoulders. Her eyes were upturned like a fox's, with short eyelashes surrounding them. Her small button nose scrunched up at the smell, slightly, and then her lips smiled brilliantly for her customers. Her eyes also became a bit more alive at the sight of Poseidon.

"Welcome to Alina's Guesthouse, I'm Alina," Alina greeted, her eyes not straying from Poseidon's face. Rhea knew the look that Poseidon was giving her and sighed, disgusted.

"Hello Alina," Poseidon's voice was like butter, "We need

three rooms for three people." He smiled that crooked smile of his at her and her ears flushed red. She busied herself, looking for three keys for three rooms, but her face looked up, disappointed.

"Unfortunately," she said, "there's only one room available for tonight." Poseidon feigned disappointment. She gave him the key slowly. Rhea looked at Khalon to see if he realized what was happening but he just looked terrified. *Probably about sharing a room.*

"Here," Poseidon said, handing Rhea the key, "I'll meet you guys up there in a minute."

"More like in the morning," Rhea muttered. Alina finally glanced over at Rhea's face, her own contorting into a mixture of horror and sadness. Rhea sighed loudly as Poseidon stepped in front of her. He smiled at Alina as she tried to get another glimpse at the Death God. With his hand, Poseidon motioned for Rhea and Khalon to leave and tried to change the subject, though to his credit, it was a smooth segue. Rhea pulled the hood of her cloak down over her face once more and led the way to the room. Still wearing the reaper's cloak, Khalon dragged his feet behind him. They stopped in front of room 1031, and Rhea turned the bronze key to unlock the door. Opening it, there was one small bed in the corner, a door to a bathroom, and the floor made more noise than the ghouls in the underworld. Rhea's face scrunched up in disgust.

"Great," she muttered. Khalon's eyes were fixated on the bed. Considering she didn't really have to sleep on a mattress, Rhea waved her hand towards the bed.

"You can sleep there if you want. I don't think Poseidon is coming back tonight," she said. Khalon gave her a look of confusion.

"What do you mean? He said he'll be up here in a minute," he pointed out. Rhea snorted.

"Yeah-h-h," she said, dragging out the word, "He's trying to get with the innkeeper. I doubt he'll be up here at all." Rhea turned around, locked the door to the room, and then took one of her shoes to jam it underneath the door.

"There," she said. Khalon gave her another confused look, glancing down at the shoe.

"There's a killer out there, remember? And unlike Poseidon and the others, I can't really walk around like I'm a normal creature," Rhea said, a note of sadness in her voice. Khalon's eyebrows scrunched together as he went and sat on the bed. He took off the reaper's cloak, revealing his draconian armor underneath. Leaning back on his arms, he caused the veins in them to pop out. Rhea's eyes widened at the sight and then she forced her eyes to look away quickly.

"Why *can't* you walk around like a normal creature?" he asked and just as he asked this, his eyes widened and he quickly started to busy his hands by folding the reaper's cloak.

"Sorry?" Rhea asked after a moment. Her mind was racing through what he could've meant by that question. *Could he... No, there's no way. But...* Rhea paced back and forth for a second and then walked up close to where Khalon was sitting. She lowered her head so that they were eye level. Up close, his eyes were the color of brown moonstone. She watched as his pupils dilated, pushing back the strings of brown in his eyes.

"What do you see when you look at me?" she asked. Khalon stared at her, his eyes panicked.

"Uh," he said loudly as he looked away, his ears turning red. Then he looked back at her.

"A corpse," he said quickly.

"What corpse?" Rhea asked, pointedly.

"Um..." he struggled to think about what he could say.

"You can see me, can't you?" Rhea asked, her voice small. She leaned back, away from him. She never had a living creature, who wasn't the Fates or the Gods, be able to see her true face before. There was a feeling of fear washing over her. What did it mean if this bastard prince could see her real face? But, somehow even more importantly to her, was he disappointed when he saw her? She tucked her copper-brown hair behind her too-large elven ears and Khalon's eyes softened at the gesture. It was as if he could pick up on her insecurity, which made Rhea feel even more embarrassed.

"No," he lied, but Rhea wasn't able to pick up on the tone of falseness, "I just don't see *one* face." Relief washed over her.

"What do you mean?" she asked, straightening up and sitting down on a chair in the room. She had never heard of someone seeing more than one face before. Khalon sat up straighter, as she did.

"Your face flickers between a lot of different faces for me," Khalon said. "It's not just one face. Sometimes, it's my mom," he squinted at Rhea like he had to look really hard at her to be able to tell what she looked like. "Sometimes, it's a corpse of someone I've killed, and other times it's this lady with blonde hair." Rhea put a hand to her chin as she concentrated on what he said.

"I've never heard of someone seeing many different faces before," she said. She looked back at Khalon and smiled, sadly. "It must be really difficult to look at me for a long period of time." Khalon nodded ferociously.

"Yeah, you know, sometimes it does give me whiplash but I'm getting used to it," he said, obviously relieved. Though, Rhea wasn't sure what he was relieved about.

"Though," Khalon said, "I will say that I *do* see when you disappear." *Well, that was new.*

"Oh, you mean when I go into the underworld?" Rhea clarified.

"Yeah," he nodded. "The ground opens up and there's a

bunch of stairs leading into darkness." His eyes looked faraway as he thought about the memory. Rhea bit the inside of her lip. *Yeah, he definitely wasn't a normal creature.*

"Khalon..." Rhea started, wanting to tell him what she could see in his soul, though it would shatter his dreams about his father. But he interrupted her while he felt the mattress, as if he could feel the disappointment that he was about to experience and wanted to prolong it for as long as possible.

"You know, I've never slept on a mattress in a bed in a really long time," he said softly. Rhea looked at him as he continued to press his hands into the mattress. It wasn't a nice mattress, she could tell, but by the look in his eyes, it was clearly a very nice mattress to him. Khalon looked up at Rhea, his face almost vulnerable.

"We slept on mats on the floor in the cells of the Ring of Fire," Khalon muttered. "I haven't slept on a mattress since I was five." A pain throbbed in Rhea's chest as he spoke. She couldn't imagine what life must have been like for him. To be caged up like that and to be forced to kill for his life. And now, he was forced to be a God's sacrifice. *What did that make me?*

"I hope you don't think it's rude of me to claim this mattress for myself tonight," Khalon said, looking up at Rhea through his eyelashes. He smiled slightly, and it only made the pain in her chest get worse. She shook her head, smiling back at him.

"No, I don't really need to sleep much anyways," she said quietly. *Plus, this ordeal is more exciting for you than for me.* Her eyes lingered on Khalon as he tried laying on the bed, smiling over at her as he did. *What am I doing?*

Accepting him as sacrifice was just putting him in another cage. Granted, probably a better cage than the one that he had before, but still a cage nonetheless. He never had a moment in his life where he could live for himself, she knew, and yet she was going to make him live out the rest of his days serving her? Forcing him to be a prisoner just because she knew the alternative was worse? She couldn't do that to him. Her hand grabbed her chest. The pain was getting unbearable. It was a feeling that she never experienced before. Though it was a familiar feeling for the God of Death, and she could feel him start to stir in anger.

She couldn't let him be a sacrifice, a temple servant, for the rest of his days. But she didn't want to let him go either. She wanted him to stay by her side.

Damn it, Rhea thought. The little part of humanity within her was making her go insane. She couldn't think about this now. It wasn't good for her body's elven-human heart. The sound of snoring interrupted her thoughts, easing the pain in her chest. She looked over at Khalon who seemed to fall asleep the moment his head hit the pillow. His mouth was wide open and his head was almost falling off of the bed. She giggled to herself at the sight of this giant draconian boy sprawled across the small mattress. Grabbing a blanket from the closet, she draped it over him as she felt a prayer coming her way. Rhea didn't get many prayers. The creatures of Asynithis were stuck in their ways. Usually their patron God was who they prayed to. Draconians tended to pray to Alator, while Argentiundans prayed to Poseidon. No one really bothered with the God of Death, so whenever a prayer came Rhea's way, it usually was one of three people.

"An has called a meeting of the Gods," Felicity's high toned voice echoed in Rhea's mind. Rhea sighed, annoyed. *Of course An picks the most inconvenient times.* The part of her soul that absolutely despised the God of All was rustling back into her head. She shook it, trying to keep that part of her at bay.

"I'll be right there," she replied, out loud, though Felicity probably didn't hear her. She looked over at Khalon's snoring body. There was so much noise emanating from him that people from miles away could probably hear him sleeping. She threw the cloak over his body, in hopes that it would conceal him if someone broke in, checked the lock on the door, and made sure the shoe jammed beneath it was not going anywhere.

"I'll be right back," she said to the sleeping boy as the door to the underworld opened up. She looked back at him as the ground closed shut, before slipping down the stairs into the underworld.

"He's been waiting for you," Felicity said, her wavy brown hair pushed back by a red headband. A bow was on the side of it, making her look like a doll.

"Aren't you a little old for ribbons?" Rhea heard Farrah's voice say from behind her. Farrah's blonde hair was pulled back into a tight bun on the top of her head. Though she was short, her aura made her seem taller somehow. However, both Rhea and Farrah had to stare up at the towering Felicity.

"It's cute," Felicity replied, a pout on her face.

"You're twenty-seven," Farrah pointed out. Felicity rolled her eyes.

"Just because I'm twenty-seven doesn't mean I can't enjoy beautiful things," she retorted.

"Guys, Rhea needs to get to her meeting," Francine exclaimed from across the lobby, her hair tied into mini buns dotting her head. She had a hand on the door that Rhea used for the meetings of the Gods. No one could enter it, apart from her.

"I think it looks nice Felicity," Rhea told her as she ran towards the room. She heard Felicity say, "See? Even Rhea likes it." To which Farrah responded, "Rhea's sixteen, of course *she* likes it!"

Rhea entered the room, closing the door behind her. In

front of her were the holograms of all the current living reincarnations of the Gods. Not all the Gods lived on Asynithis at
all times. Sometimes they took breaks that could last hundreds
of years before reincarnating. Which, in these times, was probably a good decision in hindsight.

The holograms were all sitting around in a circle in the
room that looked like the inside of a stone cabin. Rhea
modeled it after the home her mother had died in, and the
home she herself was born in. It made her feel connected to her
birth mother, somehow. She knew her father Ralnor Norovir
was still alive, but she had heard terrible things about him.
After the death of her mother, he went into a downward spiral.

"Took you long enough," Freya rolled her eyes as she sat
back in her seat. She gave Rhea a onceover and then sighed.

"Didn't the Fates teach you how to do your hair, my dear
Brother?" Freya said exasperatedly. Her hands gestured at her
head in frustration. Her hair fell in perfect black waves that
went past her small shoulders. If she were truly in front of
Rhea, she knew Freya would definitely be trying to do something with her thin hair. Rhea took a lock of her copper-brown
hair and stared at it before tucking it behind her ear.

"You are a *girl* in this life, Brother, please I beg of you,
change up your hairstyle and if you have any love for *me*,
change your uniform," Freya criticized. "Even as a man, I
dressed better than *this*."

"We are genderless beings," Rhea retorted, "So it doesn't
really matter if I'm in the body of a girl or boy." Freya made an
inhuman sound.

"I swear to An, Rhea," she said, "Think of the choices you
could make with your uniform. I mean the cloak? It's so
outdated. Look at Neith." She gestured at another God sitting
in the circle. She was wearing light gray armor with intricate
blue designs carved into it.

"Neith loves to wear armor but look what she's done with it! Made it beautiful!" Neith was the Goddess of War. While they were genderless beings, Neith and Alator being twins made their reincarnations pretty much the same gender every time. They didn't necessarily look like twins since their reincarnations were born to different parents, as Neith was pale with bright red hair cut at the base of her chin and Alator was tanned with straight black hair, but they were still considered twins, being born on the same day every time. She was the Goddess of War while he was the God of War. Without one, the other was unbalanced, crazed. She was also considered the God of Weaving for some reason, so seamstresses loved her.

"Thank you Freya," Neith smiled at the Love God. Freya shook her head as if the compliment were truly no big deal, putting a hand over her heart, and smiled back.

"I don't really feel like changing it," Rhea muttered looking at the shapeless cloak that swallowed her body. Maybe it would feel nice to wear something different... She shook the thought out from her head.

"We're just waiting on Poseidon, it looks like," An said, his hologram looking at a clipboard in his hand. An always brought notes on what he wanted to talk about in the meeting. Alator leaned back and waved at Rhea. He was a big guy, a lot older than Rhea was, though he didn't look much older than her. Neith, on the other hand, looked her age with gray hair starting to adorn the red.

"I hear we're going to war very soon," Alator said, smiling a toothy grin at Rhea. Rhea shrugged.

"We might not," Rhea muttered. Alator's eyes widened as he leaned forward in his chair.

"I heard you accepted the bastard son as sacrifice. I've been told he's your temple servant now," Alator remarked.

"Where did you hear this? Poseidon?" Rhea snapped. Alator's down-turned eyes looked amused.

"Don't tell me you feel *bad* for the boy," Alator said, surprisingly intuitive in his answer. Rhea felt her face burn at the remark.

"Ah," Alator said knowingly, "I was looking forward to a good fight. You never busy yourself with war."

"Why didn't the king ask me for help with the war against the beastoids?" Neith mused. Alator's laugh boomed.

"Would you have even helped him? Gone to war against me?"

"We've been on opposite sides before," she pointed out. Alator nodded.

"Yes, but this war is different," he said, seriously. She nodded.

"He must've known I wouldn't have sided with him on this," she said. Alator chuckled.

"Or he knew you wouldn't hesitate in killing his son as a sacrifice," he said. They both laughed.

"Oh that's so true. I never let the sacrifice live unless they're useful to me," Neith replied. Alator nodded.

"Such truth in your words, Sister. Maybe the bastard prince is useful to Rhea," Alator said.

"It's just not his time," Rhea muttered. Alator laughed his incredibly loud laugh once again.

"Don't you dictate when his time is or isn't?" Alator and Neith continued laughing along with each other as Rhea's annoyance was starting to build. Poseidon's hologram finally started to shimmer into existence, appearing in his seat.

"Did you really have to call a meeting at this inopportune time?" Poseidon said, uncharacteristically upset. An raised an eyebrow and looked over at Rhea for some kind of answer.

"He was with the innkeeper," Rhea gave as an explanation.

An's lips tightened into a thin line and then looked back down at his clipboard.

"A gorgeous draconian innkeeper, mind you," Poseidon said, smiling over at Alator as Alator looked over at him appraisingly.

"Well first, I must tell you the immediate news. As you can see, Belenus is no longer with us," An said. The rest of the Gods didn't look fazed at the news.

"Do you think she'll take a longer time to be reincarnated this time?" Hotei, the God of Good Cheer and Alcohol asked. An put down his clipboard, sighing as he ran a hand through his hair.

"Belenus will not be returning to this world," he said carefully. "Belenus is dead. The God of Healing is no more." Silence followed his announcement.

"I'm sorry, what?" Freya said in disbelief.

"What do you mean that she is no more?" Ganesha, the God of Knowledge, asked. Her brown eyes were wide open as her lips were held in a tight, thin line.

"She is dead. She won't be returning. Her string of life has snapped," An said plainly. The rest of the Gods stared at him and then back at Rhea for confirmation. She held her hands together nervously.

"Um, yes, her string has turned white and is cut. The Fates don't have the power to cut the string of life of a God's, of course, but we found this morning that it was. She cannot return because her soul is no more," Rhea explained.

"And a God's soul doesn't come to the underworld, so we can't find her and ask how this happened," An concluded, though Rhea knew he was just assuming. A God's soul just disappeared, it seemed like. No one really knew what would happen to a God's soul before this incident but afterwards, it was clear they didn't seem to go anywhere.

"You're telling us that we can... die?" Alator said. "For good? Just gone? Zip zap we're dead?" An nodded. He and Neith exchanged looks with one another.

"And there's someone out there that has the ability to just kill us, to make us disappear forever?" Freya asked. The Gods were bewildered. In all their time existing, no one had ever tried to kill *them* before and succeeded in doing so. Killing their Celestial bodies, of course. But *them*? Their souls?

"They came after me last night, too," Poseidon piped up. The Gods looked over at him in horror. "The assassin is hopefully at the bottom of the Argenti Sea now, but he came after me with a tooth. Bigger than an average creature's tooth but not the biggest around. I'm sure werewolves have bigger teeth than that."

"A tooth?" Neith asked incredulously.

"Yes," Rhea interrupted, "And we've done some digging, Poseidon and I—"

"You two are traveling together?" Freya interjected. "Well, that's simply unfair. Of course you two would be safe since there's two of you and Rhea could kill anyone with the wave of her hand."

"I can kill anyone with a wave too, Sister," Poseidon bristled. Though Freya was genderless, she preferred to be called Sister rather than the usual Brother. She waved his words away.

"It simply isn't fair," she grumbled.

"You *can* travel with us," Poseidon pointed out. Rhea looked over at him, her eyes wide in order to tell him to shut up. Freya leaned back as she thought about it, not noticing the interaction.

"I might," she concluded.

"Anyways," Rhea said, continuing her thought, "we came upon a story about the Mortiferis. Apparently, they're mythical

monsters that are able to destroy worlds. They eat them up."
Poseidon's head whipped around to look at her at the mention
of Mortiferis. His expression was unreadable, while Ganesha's
eyebrows furrowed together.

"But Rhea," she said, "You already knew this story." Rhea
looked over at her, confused.

"No, I never heard it before," Rhea said slowly. Ganesha
shook her head, the wrinkles around her eyes crinkled together
as she thought, slowly.

"Yes, it *was* you. You had asked me when you were younger
about different worlds, whether they existed or not. You also
wanted to know if those worlds had Gods too. Did each world
have their own set of Gods or were we the ruler of all worlds. I
answered it with the story of the Mortiferis," Ganesha said.
There was a time in Rhea's childhood that the God of Death
was more prevalent, but no... *It couldn't be...*

"There are multiple different realms, worlds that are like
ours but with different names. Our world is called Asynithis. In
a different realm, our world is called Earth, or Terra as An likes
to call it, and so on. The Mortiferis are creatures that were
created to destroy these realms. They go realm to realm
through reflections in mirrors or rivers. And they have the
ability to make the entire realm, the universe as we know it,
disappear, including the Gods, if they so wanted to." Ganesha's
lips tightened into a thin line.

"I mean, you should already know that considering..." An
gave Ganesha a pointed look which rendered her speechless.
She looked away as Rhea stared at Ganesha for a long while.

"I already knew all that?" Rhea asked, holding her breath.
Ganesha nodded, slowly, her eyes on An.

"Yes."

14

Khalon woke up after feeling the ground shake around him as the door to the underworld closed. If Rhea wanted to leave quietly, he realized that it was impossible to do so the way that she traveled. He rolled over, facing the wall. *That was a close one*, he thought, his mind drifting back to seeing Rhea's face close up. Her freckles that dotted her cheeks and nose were more noticeable when her face was a few inches away from his. And her eyes were a light, golden brown that flashed the same color as her hair in the dim, yellow light of the room. He put his hands on his head. It was a good thing that he still was able to see the carousel of faces that encased her own, otherwise he wouldn't have known what to say.

"*You can see me, can't you?*" Rhea's words echoed in his mind. Khalon couldn't help but stare into her eyes as she said it. Insecurity clouded her usually confident golden copper eyes. "*We might not look as godly as the creatures might think we should look.*" Did she know how her true face would look to others? Khalon closed his eyes, trying to chase Rhea's voice out of his head. He tried to focus, instead, on the mattress that he was laying on.

Wanting to burn the memory and feeling of laying on a mattress into his mind, he ran his hand over the side of the mattress, as if he were petting it. It had been such a long time since he had laid on one. He remembered the shock his half brother Khai had after seeing how Khalon was sleeping in the Ring of Fire.

Khai must have only been six or seven years old at the time, while Khalon was eight or nine. He came to the bars outside of Khalon's cell, the ones that looked out into the arena. Khalon remembered thinking how impressed he was that Khai was able to get into the Ring of Fire without being noticed.

"I'm small," Khai had whispered, guessing at what Khalon was thinking at the time. His face was smushed against the bars, looking around Khalon's living area. "I can fit in anywhere." His half brother looked more like Queen Aoife than their father. His hair was a light brown, and his eyes were similar to Khalon's but they were deeper set. His skin was also slightly lighter than Khalon's.

"Where's your bed?" Khai had asked him. Khalon felt embarrassed at how he was living compared to the palace. It had been a few years since he saw Khai and was curious why he suddenly came to visit him.

"They don't give us a bed," Khalon had mumbled, gesturing towards the mat on the ground. "That's where I sleep." Khai's face was thoughtful as he stared at the mat.

"I'm sorry mom is acting this way," Khai had said, showing more maturity at his age than one would've thought. Khalon shook his head at the time.

"It's cool that you'll be a Champion though," Khai had said excitedly. "I heard mom and dad talking about your first fight.

It's coming up soon!" He was so excited, Khalon remembered. So excited for him to kill someone.

"Not for a few more years," Khalon had mumbled. He was too young at the time to fight, and so full of fear.

"Everyone I know thinks it's so cool that my brother is going to become a Champion," Khai had gushed. He was so excited that it was almost infectious. But Khalon's stomach had started to turn.

"Although," Khai had said, a familiar look in his eyes that Khalon had seen before in Queen Aoife's, "There's a rumor about you." Khalon stared at Khai, encouraging him to continue.

"They say that you're part of the Black Dragon family *and* the Red Dragon," Khai said slowly as chills went down Khalon's back. "But that can't be right because we're brothers, right?" Khalon had shrugged at the comment, afraid that Khai would find out the truth and disown him as well so he changed the subject. Since that night, Khai had kept coming back to tell Khalon about his day and to teach him about what he learned from his knowledge master. It was something that Khalon looked forward to. Once he had his first fight, though, Khai stopped coming. Khalon was never sure why.

Khalon felt his heart hurt at the thought of his little brother. He wondered what Khai was doing and how he was now. But just as his mind started to wander again, he heard a slight movement in the air. Quickly, Khalon's arm shot out just as he started to sit up, grabbing the assailant's wrist. The face of the creature was shrouded by the black cloak he was wearing. *Wait a minute...* It looked like the cloak that Khalon was wearing earlier. In his hand was a tooth. Khalon frowned as the creature struggled out of his grip. Grabbing his sword and flicking his wrist so the blade came out, Khalon got to his feet, getting into a familiar stance. The assailant was shorter than he was but in his other hand was a knife. He slashed at Khalon, as Khalon backed up onto the bed. With another swish of the man's knife, he stabbed forward with the tooth. Khalon dodged, and just as he did, the tooth made contact with the wall that was behind him. Suddenly, the wall turned light gray and disintegrated into nothing. Wind came through where the wall once was. Khalon looked at the man incredulously.

"What the—" he started to say but then the man came barreling towards him again. Before Khalon had time to process, he blocked the man's attack with the knife, dodged the tooth, and then used all his strength to sink his sword into the man's stomach. Red blood came bursting out of the wound after Khalon quickly took the sword back out. Red blood. The assailant was human.

The man's cries became garbled by the blood filling his lungs and he eventually hit the floor. Khalon took the cloak's hood off of the head of the assailant, revealing a woman with long blonde hair and blue eyes. A face he had seen before on Rhea's ever changing mask of faces. Frowning, he removed the cloak further from the corpse, revealing makeshift clothes.

"She's from Sylva," Khalon muttered to himself. Just as he did, he felt the air behind him move, and looked at the assailant's face. His face contorted into shock as he recognized that she wasn't dead, as he previously believed her to be. Her eyes glared at him, and she cried out as her hand came down towards him. Khalon turned around and watched as the tooth came towards his face. As if by instinct, he felt his skin turn inside out to reveal the scales that lay hidden underneath, and his chest filled with a burning feeling. Opening his mouth, fire erupted from his throat, burning the woman's arms. She cried out in more pain. The tooth that she was holding fell to the ground. Khalon quickly got up, away from the tooth, and watched as the woman's eyes slowly started to glaze over. A gray film replaced the life that was once in her eyes. Khalon looked down at his hands, black scales glittering red in the moonlight. They still weren't turning back to his normal skin.

The ground rumbled as the door to the underworld opened up. In the opening, Rhea's head popped out. She stared at him with wide eyes, seeing the form that Khalon was unable to get out of. Her eyes glanced over at the wall that disappeared and at the woman dead on the floor, lying in her own blood. Those copper-golden eyes of hers then stopped at the sight of the tooth on the floor. Pulling herself out from the door to the underworld, it then rumbled shut as she wiped her hands on the front of her black cloak. She looked up at Khalon, who was still covered in scales.

"Well," she said, "Someone had an eventful night."

15

Prince Khai watched as another prisoner was dragged towards the throne room. He stopped, his stewards stopping behind him as he watched the throne room doors slide open, a glimpse of his father pacing back and forth, stopping to glare at the prisoner. The doors slid shut. *It was starting to get out of hand.*

Quickly, he walked towards his mother's quarters of the palace. The steps of his and his attendees echoing against the polished wooden flooring. Once outside her door, one of the Queen's handmaidens announced his presence. The doors slid open and his mother sat behind a small table, writing something on parchment. She glanced up at him and waved her servants away. They scurried out of the room, like mice who didn't want to be seen, quickly sliding the doors shut behind them.

"Khai," Queen Aoife said. She was always a disconnected mother to Khai. There wasn't a feeling of warmth that came from her. She wasn't a maternal being, but this was something Khai had accepted a long time ago.

"You need to stop him," Khai said. His mother glanced up from her parchment and then slowly folded it closed.

"Stop who?" she asked, her eyes innocently doe-like. She looked up at Khai as she waited for his answer. He clenched his jaw shut in response.

"It sounds like you're questioning the king," she tutted as she took out another parchment.

"Mother," Khai pleaded, "He's starting to act like King Archion. And I'm sure it's being noticed by those in the capital at least." She pursed her lips as she continued to write whatever it was she was writing. *Probably palace menus for tomorrow,* Khai thought bitterly.

"Your father has it under control," she said, absentmindedly.

"He just now brought in another person to, I don't know, kill? Eat? Is he *eating* those who talk about Khalon now?" His mother's eyes flashed at him.

"*Don't talk about Khalon,*" she hissed through her teeth. The parchment in her hands crumpled up. Khai felt himself shrink from his mother's anger. There was a side of her that only he knew, and he didn't want to be on the other end.

"You care more about Khalon than you do for me," Khai muttered. Aoife stared at Khai for a moment, and then pushed herself off of the ground, taking Khai's hands into her face.

"Look at me," she said. Khai stared at the floor until Aoife moved his face to look at her.

"I love you, my son," she said. "I want you to become King of Draconia and I want no one to question it. That's why I've done all of this, for you." She gestured around her.

"Sending Khalon away to his death? All you did was make him more popular with the creatures of Draconia. You put him on center stage, there for everyone in the nation to watch and fall in love with as he killed creature after creature. You didn't do that for me," Khai cried, "No one knows anything about me. I'm cooped up in this palace, watched twenty-four seven for what? I'm not going to become king and if I do, the creatures out there will drag me down from that throne waiting for Khalon." He gestured towards the window that oversaw the city of Furvus.

"I didn't think Khalon would survive a day in that Ring," Aoife muttered, stepping away from her son. Her eyes lit up as she walked back to him.

"But, he is with the Death God now. Whether he dies as sacrifice or becomes a temple servant doesn't matter. Temple servants cannot become king," Aoife pointed out. "They are the property of the God they serve."

"As long as he lives, Mother, my reign is questioned," Khai said. She stared at him for a moment.

"Do not worry, my son. No one will question your reign as long as you have the spirit of the dragon within you," she cooed.

"But I don't—" She shushed him.

"Your father doesn't either, but that hasn't stopped him from taking the throne." Khai stared at her for a long while.

"What do you mean he doesn't have the spirit of the dragon?" Khai asked. He thought back to when Khalon won his last battle. His skin suddenly was covered in scales, his head elongated slightly into a dragon's head. A tail had sprouted from behind him. He had even grown maybe a foot taller, and then it slowly started to fade as Khalon looked at himself shocked. A fluke, Aoife had told Khai when she got back from the Ring. "A little bit of witch's magic."

"Don't tell me that he—" Aoife glared at him into silence.

"No," she said. "The spirit of the dragon has laid dormant for a long while. He doesn't have it. It wouldn't have chosen him." It sounded like she was trying to convince herself more than Khai.

"How is father able to fake it?" Khai asked, "Because of you?" Aoife laughed a little.

"No," she said. "I've done things to keep you in his favor, of course, but I don't have the power to fake that." Khai stared at her. He lied to her about Khalon. If she wasn't able to feign the spirit of the dragon with her power, then no one was able to. He knew then that the rumors going around the capital were right, and that's why his father was so hellbent on making sure each and every creature who rallied for Khalon's reign was dead. Because if Khalon truly had the spirit of the dragon, it would make his father obsolete.

"Tell me," Khai said after a while, "Show me how to fake the spirit of the dragon." Aoife smiled slightly at him.

"You hate him, don't you?" Aoife said after a while. Khai knew who she was referring to and he wasn't sure how to answer the question. He was raised to hate him. Everything Khalon did, the creatures in Draconia praised him for it. Khalon would win every battle within the Ring of Fire. He was the nation's number one favorite Champion, and it was merely because he was also the son of the king. It was unheard of. A prince fighting in the Ring of Fire. It was scandalous, something that creatures ate up and who doesn't love an underdog? He was also the child of a concubine. Not just any concubine either, but the daughter of the Black Dragon. The creatures of Draconia adored him. If anything, it wasn't necessarily Khalon that he hated. It was the life he was given. Khai could've proved himself in the Ring of Fire, if given the chance. Then the creatures would be able to see that Khai was just as strong as his older half brother. *The dragon spirit would've been able to see that too...* he thought.

His mother was too greedy. She wanted Khalon dead when

she could've just kept him hidden. If she just kept him hidden...
Khai realized he had been glaring at his mother for far too long.
She narrowed her eyes at him as he looked away, clearing his
throat.

"Yes, I do," Khai answered. But it wasn't really his half
brother he hated, it was his mother for ruining the life that
Khai could've had. Aoife smiled, satisfied by the answer.

"Come with me," she said. They walked out of her quarters,
Aoife waving the servants away. It had been a while since Khai
was able to just walk without an army of people following his
every step, his every movement. It was a bit freeing.

He followed his mother down the palace hallways, past the
throne room where he could hear the ravings of his father
speaking to his advisors.

"Is he dead?" he could hear his father shouting, "*Is Khalon
dead yet?*" It was unbelievable that the whole capital couldn't
hear him. His mother quickly walked past the throne room, not
wanting to see the work that she had done on the man she
proclaimed to love. Once getting to a far wall, his mother said a
chant under her breath, causing the wall in front of them to
open up. It revealed a staircase that led into darkness.

"Come," she ordered, hurrying down the steps. Khai stared
at it in wonder, not knowing that the palace had a secret basement. He gingerly stepped onto the first step, causing the wall
behind him to close shut, dust spewing from the action. He
coughed into his arm as he started down the steps, desperate
not to lose his mother in the darkness. She led the way, a
glowing ball of light in front of her that she held above her
hand. It still amazed Khai to see his mother using magic. He
sometimes wondered if he inherited that part of her as well, as
he looked so much like her.

At the bottom of the stairs, Khai squinted into the darkness
to see what was in front of him. He felt heat radiating off of

something and a breeze hitting him periodically, as if a giant creature was taking a breath of air and blowing it at him.

"How does this help me fake having the spirit of the dragon?" Khai asked, staring into darkness, annoyed. Aoife chuckled at her son's ignorance and then released the light into the darkness. The light lit up all the torches in the room, revealing a giant red dragon laying on the ground in front of them. The cavern they were in was massive. Perhaps three times bigger than the palace that was up on the surface. And the dragon... Khai took a couple of steps back as he stared at it.

The red dragon was the biggest creature he had ever seen. It was hooked up to a bunch of machines that looked tiny next to it. Its eyes were closed and every once in a while the dragon's mouth twitched upwards, revealing a giant fanged tooth. Khai stared at his mother in horror.

"The dragons still live?" Khai barely squeaked out as he stared at Aoife. He had heard his whole life that the dragons went into hiding when the humans took over Asynithis. In order to completely go into hiding, they took on the form of humans. By the time that the humans had gained power, only the black-scaled and red-scaled dragons were still living and were the only clans to be able to turn into humanoid creatures to continue living among humans. But there was a full and *alive* red-scaled dragon in front of him. He stared at it in shock.

"This one is the only one left," Aoife muttered, "That we know of." She walked over to the dragon, petting the scales and checking the machines that it was hooked up to.

"Your father's family hunted down the rest, desperate for power against the Black Dragon family," she explained. "They were in hiding, sleeping for thousands of years as the humans had their fun. And when the draconians were finally able to step out of hiding, they just wouldn't wake up." Khai took a small step forward.

"The spirit of the dragon is truly the soul of a dragon. If it latches onto a draconian, they are able to have all the strength and power of a dragon. It was how Draconia decided to choose their kings," Aoife explained. "The direct descendants, the *pure bloods* if you will," she said the word with distaste, "wanted to make sure that the Red Dragon family stayed in power. But, the only other way to mimic as if you had a dragon's soul within you is if you drink the blood of a dragon."

"You see, there were two clans. The black-scaled dragons and the red-scaled dragons. Draconians who descended from the leaders of these two clans were the only ones with the marks on their backs," she gestured towards Khai's. He stiffened in response, knowing that she envied the mark of the dragon that he had.

"They felt that the power of the dragon only belonged to those with that mark. But sometimes, the soul of a dragon would attach to someone else, maybe an impure draconian. It didn't matter if you had the mark or not, you could get the power as long as you were a draconian. But if that were the case, then anyone could become king, right?" she said, walking down the length of the sleeping dragon, admiring it.

"So your father's family, and really my clan as well since I *am* a descendant of the Red Dragon family, hunted down these sleeping dragons so that they could drink their blood," she glanced over at Khai. He felt like was going to be sick. "These creatures, our great ancestors. They were stupid with it though. They would suck them dry, like filthy vampires, until the dragon was dead. Soon they were running out of the source of their power."

"How is it still alive?" Khai asked, his voice quivering. His mother glanced over at his weakness and scoffed.

"Your father wouldn't have survived as king this long without me. I told him that instead of sucking them dry and then leaving them for dead, to continue to replenish the blood supply. Make it healthy. Humans created all sorts of machines and inventions which were great for health. Use those, keep the beast alive so that way his power could grow," she said. Glaring at the floor, she continued, "But your father had other ideas. He felt that the best way to strengthen the family was to unite the two clans. The 'spirit of the dragon' would choose the descendants of the two dragon clans coming together. Hah!" She looked up at Khai angrily, taking a needle that was hanging from a container in the wall. She stomped up to the sleeping dragon and sunk the needle through a part of the skin that had the scales ripped off. Khai felt the room start spinning as she pulled the crimson almost black blood from the creature.

"Of course he truly only wanted that because he thought he was in love with the girl. I took care of that, for your grandfather. I didn't realize that she bore Vien's *child*, however," her face was contorted in disgust and anger. She took the needle of blood and poured it into a crystal cup.

"It took years to master witchcraft. I had to go to my wretched mother's side just to learn it but I succeeded. All so that the king would finally look at me, touch me. I *had* to bear him a son, a better son," her hand balled up into a fist as she forcefully handed Khai the glass.

"Now the king is under my control and what? The Gods decide to grace Dal's child with a dragon's soul? Instead of mine?" She motioned for Khai to drink the blood. He looked at her incredulously.

"Mother, I can't," he said softly. She glared at him.

"Your father is fine and he's been drinking it his whole life in order to keep the throne," she stated. "You want the throne, don't you?"

"Yes, but I can't just—" He couldn't drink the blood of a

clearly suffering creature in front of him. Especially a creature as great as a dragon, something that many creatures in Asynithis thought were to be dead for thousands of years. His mother made a guttural cry of unhappiness and grabbed her son's head.

"You *will* be the next King of Draconia," she said, forcing his mouth open with the twirl of her hand. Khai tried to force it closed but felt some invisible force holding it open. She took the cup of blood into her own hands and as Khai glanced apologetically at the dragon sleeping next to him, she poured the blood down his throat.

"I don't care if the blood drives you crazy in the end," she muttered as her son choked on the blood of the dragon.

16

Khalon inhaled the soup that was placed in front of him as Rhea looked on with an expression of mild disgust on her face. His eyes watched hers as she watched every spoonful that was shoveled into his mouth. It was unnerving, watching her watch him.

"Do you want something?" Khalon asked as he picked the bowl up with both hands and started drinking the broth of the soup. She waited silently until he had downed its contents. Khalon wiped his mouth with the back of his hand as she squinted at the action.

"What?" Khalon asked. "It's been a while since we've gotten to eat, you know." Rhea held up a hand.

"Don't talk to me," she said, closing her eyes. Khalon eyed her as she looked over at the other people in the restaurant, sighing. Her forehead was covered by the hood of her cloak, but her eyebrows were tensed, to the point where Khalon could slightly see the tendons sticking out of her temples. She stared at the humans who were mindlessly eating their food, and Khalon wished in that moment he was able to read her mind in some way. They were in a small town in Draconia, heading towards the most recent battle with the beastoids.

"You're thinking about what happened the other night," Khalon pointed out, guessing at her thoughts. Her eyes flashed at him.

"And you're not?" she whispered, taking a sip from her soup. The town that they were in was run by humans, so the patrons were eyeing the two of them suspiciously. Khalon paid no mind to them. Though it was obvious he was a draconian due to his scales, he knew the humans weren't sure exactly who he was. It was such a small town that they didn't even have the funds for hologram technology. He doubted they ever watched a Ring of Fire fight before in their lives.

"I mean, someone tried to kill me but it's not the first time that happened," Khalon answered. "First time with a tooth — actually, that's not true. Liam tried to kill me with his teeth." He waved down the waiter as Rhea stared at him incredulously.

"Could I get another bowl of this soondubu?" Khalon asked. The waiter nodded and took the empty bowl away as Khalon smiled brilliantly at Rhea. She narrowed her eyes at the action. The truth was he couldn't stop thinking about the other night. He was stuck in the form of a dragon for longer than he ever had been that night and it unnerved him. One thing was clear to him, somehow he had the spirit of the dragon within him. And it wasn't something that he celebrated, especially when he was about to see his father again. Though, he tried to convince himself that it was still somehow a fluke. A mistake. He couldn't possibly have the spirit of the dragon within him, could he?

Rhea shook her head after a while and Khalon could see her feeling around in her cloak for the tooth that she pocketed that night.

"Do you still have it?" Khalon asked. Rhea's head whipped up to look at him.

"Of course I still have it. Why wouldn't I?" she asked, defensively. He raised his hands up as the waiter returned and put down his bowl of soondubu, the tofu bits floating up to the surface of the soup.

"Is the battle near here?" Rhea asked the waiter. The waiter frowned his sparse black eyebrows.

"The one with the beastoids, ma'am?" he asked, his eyes not threatening to look into hers that hid beneath the hood of the cloak.

"Yes," Rhea said, impatiently.

"You have to cross the Longwei Desert," the waiter said, quietly. "The battle is being had near the oasis there."

"Thank you," Rhea said, giving the waiter a little bow as he bowed back.

"That's a couple of days' trek," Khalon pointed out, digging into his meal. Rhea watched on, this time with less judgment on her face.

"We must go," she said.

"Even with a God-killer on the loose," Khalon muttered. Rhea smiled as she put her head into her hands.

"You did promise to sacrifice your life to protect me, didn't you? It's perfectly safe," she teased. Khalon stared at the life that was held in Rhea's brown eyes. It was so different from this morning. He remembered that he had looked over at her bed that morning to find that she wasn't there. And, only a few moments later, the door to the underworld had opened with Rhea walking up the steps. Khalon had pretended to sleep, but he saw her eyes through the reflection. Lifeless. Khalon pushed the tofu around in the broth with his spoon.

"Did you ever ask the Fates about where you went that one night?" Khalon asked, his eyes glancing up at her through his eyelashes. She frowned at the question until recognition clouded her face.

"Oh, you mean when you were shouting that one night? Yes, I asked them about it," Rhea said, leaning back in her chair.

"And?" Khalon asked. She shrugged.

"They said they didn't see me. But the underworld is a vast place. I could've been anywhere in there. It had been a long time since I had slept on the surface," Rhea pointed out. She smiled and then her smile faded slightly as a thought came to her mind.

"Why?" she asked. "Is it still happening?" Khalon shook his head and smiled slightly, though the smile didn't quite reach his eyes.

"No," he said. "No, I was just curious."

———

As Rhea asked someone for directions and gathered some supplies for their long trip, Khalon made his own inquiries. He walked over to a witch's shop in town and stepped in, looking at the different herbs that were drying from the ceiling.

"Can I help you?" asked an old woman sitting in the back of the store. Her black eyes were shrewd and she glared up at Khalon as he swallowed his nerves back down his throat.

"The Seer," Khalon said, "They're alive?" The old woman laughed slightly.

"Of course the Seer is alive," she said. "What would a draconian want with the Seer?" Khalon shook his head.

"I just have some questions that I want to ask them," he muttered. A little louder, he said, "Do you know where I can find them?"

"Ustrina," she said. "The city of Invenire. You'd find her there."

"Thank you," Khalon said. The old woman studied him for a moment.

"You don't think you'll live long, due to who your father is," Khalon felt himself stiffen as he stared at the woman. She recognized him.

"I'm sorry, I think you have me mis—"

"You will, though," she interrupted. "You'll live a long, but miserable life." Khalon stared at her for a moment, and then the jingle of the store door broke the silence.

"I've been looking everywhere for you," Rhea hissed as she grabbed her arm. She stared at the old woman who looked slightly frightened at the face that donned Rhea's. Rhea pulled on Khalon's arm and he quickly followed her out of the store.

"What are you doing in a witch's store?" Rhea asked. Khalon shrugged, unable to look her in the eyes.

"I was curious," Khalon muttered. Rhea sighed as she put some things into a bag and then motioned for Khalon to lean down. He did as he was told and she put the strap over his head.

"I thought you ran off on me," Rhea whispered, slightly teasing before patting him on the back to stand up straight. He did. *You'll live a long, but miserable life.* Khalon shook the witch's words from his head. It was an answer to a question he didn't want to know. He watched as Rhea led the way towards Longwei Desert. At least he knew one thing. They weren't going to die on this journey.

"Khalon," Rhea said, slowing down her strides so that they were walking side by side.

"Yes?" Khalon asked.

"How did your mother die?" Rhea asked. He stared at her

for a moment and then sighed. Why was she asking this question?

"Shouldn't you already know?" Khalon asked. Rhea squinted up at him, the sun hitting her face.

"A lot of people die. I don't remember them all," she merely said. Ouch.

"Uh, she was chased out of Draconia all the way into Aureum. She had just had me a month prior, I think, and she took me with her, afraid that my scales would cause them to kill me," Khalon explained, repeating what he had heard about his mother's death.

"Because they're not bright red," Rhea pointed out. Khalon nodded.

"Yes, they're not. And one night there was this... terrible storm," Khalon's mind wandered as he said this. It was a memory that he had but not quite a memory. Almost a dream. Rain pouring down his mother's face as she looked down at him. He remembered her lips moving, words of reassurance. And then... fire. Khalon shook his head.

"They say the storm killed her," he finished quickly. Rhea stared at him, her eyes wide slightly and then she looked away.

"I see," she said. "The storm that happened in Aureum." Khalon nodded. She then nodded, a little more slowly.

"When I was reincarnated, a terrible storm came to Aureum," Rhea whispered. She smiled, a bit. "I killed my mother. I probably killed yours, too." Khalon stared at her for a long while, the memory of fire setting his mother's face aglow.

"I don't know if the storm truly killed her," he said, eventually. "That's just what is said." Rhea kept nodding her head and then she started walking faster so that she was ahead of Khalon again. The urge to reach out and grab her hand was immense. It pumped through Khalon's veins as he watched her walk faster, getting further and further away from him. He folded his long fingers towards his hands, into a fist. He refused to hold her hand. To get too close to her. Not until he knew what was going on. He didn't understand why she kept disappearing. Or why he kept having dreams of this dark cloaked creature... He shook the thought from his head. If he did survive this ordeal with his father, he would just have to seek out the Seer. She would have answers.

17

Prince Elion watched as Essarae, the Queen of Aureum, complained to a drunken Lady next to her as his brother Adamar continued to laugh and speak with the nobles of Aureum. The celebration was taking place due to Adamar's recent coronation, this being the first instance where he could wine and dine the nobles. He had to get them to be on his side, woo them, in order for the large country of Aureum to run smoothly and, more importantly, run by his command.

"She beckoned for me to come over to her, with her hand, as if I were a mere commoner. Can you *believe* that?" her hand was on her belly as she spoke bitterly. Her white elven hair was parted in little braids that framed her face, the rest of her hair was tied up into a bun on the top of her head. It had been a couple of days since the God of Love and Fertility had graced the halls of the palace of Aureum, but Queen Essarae was still making noise about it. Elion bit his tongue as he took a sip of the wine.

"Gods believe they are the authority in this world," Essarae continued her rant, "but really all they are a bunch of old souls that cling on to their power, when their power is not needed anymore." The Lady next to her laughed loudly and nodded.

"So true, my Queen," she said, which wet Essarae's appetite of praise. Elion ignored the rest of Essarae's conversation. The blasphemy that he was overhearing was not one that he wanted to partake in. Didn't she feel the aura of the Love God? The presence of the Death God? They were not ordinary creatures with simple power. They were the first beings that breathed life into the universe. Elion shook his head. No, he would not hear the ravings of a power hungry mad woman. Especially one whose child was not even an elf. What was it that the God of Love said? *There's something sinister about the conception of that child.* For all of Aureum, he had to figure out what she meant.

"The God of Love really riled up her highness," Prince Edwyrd muttered next to Elion. Elion glanced over at his brother. Prince Edwyrd was known for being a great general and his looks showed it. His characteristic elven white hair was cut short and spiked. Even in the androgynous robes of royal court, he couldn't hide his broad shoulders and muscular figure. He was much taller than his siblings, even taller than Adamar. Unlike Edwyrd, Adamar was lanky and lean. His hair was long, the way most elves chose to wear their hair. There was a gentle nature about his face, while Edwyrd's was marred with faint, puckered scars. Adamar had the look of grace that a king should have, but Edwyrd had more the manner of a king. He was brave, experienced in battle, and a charismatic guy. The creatures of Aureum adored Edwyrd. Most lamented the fact that he was not the first born of King Elkhazel's.

"Essarae must *always* be given the highest respect," Prince Ardryll teased, sipping on his mug of beer. Elion's third older brother's hair was a bit longer than Edwyrd's, cut at his chin. His white hair was wavy, like Elion's, a trait that their mother had. Ardryll was much more reserved than Elion's other brothers. It might have been due to where he fell in the order of birth. As the third prince, there wasn't much that Ardryll really needed to do. He didn't have much desire, either, besides living a grand life. Adamar trusted Ardryll only because of his lack of ambition. So much so, that he recently gifted Ardryll with a lordship, which brought with it land, a small army, and ruling over the land. Edwyrd was understandably angry at Adamar for doing this for Ardryll and not for him.

"Now that she's queen, she believes she should be treated better than the Gods," chuckled Ardryll's husband Crispin. Ardryll took Crispin's dark-skinned hand into his as they glanced over at each other in amusement.

"She's also pregnant with a son, I've heard," Lady Batula, Edwyrd's wife, remarked. She picked at the quail in front of her with her fork. Her thick white hair was in a singular braid that rested on her right shoulder. Edwyrd silently comforted his wife. Batula had recently lost a child before it could ever see the light of day. She refused the action from Edwyrd, eating in silence.

"How *was* being in the presence of the Love God, Elion?" Ardryll asked, changing the subject. His familiar blue eyes glanced at Elion as he ate gingerly.

"You *saw* the God of Love?" Edwyrd boomed, his face full of shock. Elion shied away from the conversation. Ardryll leaned forward in order to be able to see Edwyrd's face.

"Adamar has told that Elion was *so* taken with the Love God that he followed her out of the palace," he exclaimed gleefully.

"Never showing any interest in anyone but you show interest in the God of Love. Go big or go home, my brother," Edwyrd teased. Elion didn't say anything. What Edwyrd said wasn't necessarily true. Elion *had* loved someone before. A girl's face appeared in his mind. Heart shaped face framed with curly brown hair. He watched as the life went from her dark brown eyes, a smile fading from her lips as she had looked down in horror. Elion choked on the memory, finding himself glaring up at Adamar, who was blissfully unaware.

"Oh careful there," Edwyrd said, clapping Elion on his back. "You gotta chew slowly so big pieces don't get caught in your throat."

"You would know," Lady Batula teased, her gray eyes smiling at her husband. Edwyrd nodded.

"I ate so much and so quickly at his age," Edwyrd mused. Batula giggled and shook her head in agreement.

"Do you remember when my father and I came to visit the palace and you were eating this giant turkey leg?" she said, her eyes lit up from the memory. Edwyrd looked thoughtful and then smiled.

"Yes, and I choked on a piece of it when I saw you for the first time," he said, putting his hand on her chin. Her olive-toned skin flushed red. They continued reminiscing in gag-worthy conversation as Elion watched as Adamar excused himself from the drunken Lords. He looked... nervous.

"Excuse me," Elion said to his brothers and their partners before getting up from the table. They didn't acknowledge his leaving, enthralled in conversation with one another. Elion slipped out of the gold adorned room and peeked his head around the corner to watch his brother disappear down the maze of palace halls. He followed silently behind, trying to catch a glimpse of where Adamar disappeared to. Elion's mind wandered, an image blinding him.

"Elion?" she had asked as she looked down at the red blood spilling out of her. She looked up, her dark brown eyes big and frightened. She had looked like she wanted to say something to him, one last thing, but her eyes glazed over. Elion knew she was gone, her body slumped over the sword that had run through her. Then, the sword was pulled out of her, making her body almost drop to the ground. Elion reached out for her, falling to the ground with her body in his arms. He looked up at his brother who wiped the blood off from his sword using the blanket from the chair next to the door. His brother looked disgusted, and not the least bit fazed by his action.

"Why?" Elion asked him, tears running down his face. Adamar stared at him coldly, his long white hair slightly covering his face and dotted with human blood.

"Why? *I* should be the one to ask that, Elion," Adamar said, angrily. He gestured towards the girl that Elion held close. "A *human*, Elion? You would ruin this family by falling in love with a *human?*" Elion's face was covered in hot tears, blurring his vision. All he could see was red blood, her blood, all over him, all over the place.

"She didn't even know, Adamar," Elion barely got out.

"What?" Adamar asked, leaning forward. Elion stared at her, not being able to take his eyes from her beautifully imperfect face.

"I never told Pilar how I felt," Elion said, regret washing over him. Adamar straightened up.

"Well," he had said, "Then it's good I got here just when I did." He then left the room, leaving Elion with the corpse of the girl he once loved. He petted her face, blood smearing over it as he did. Her blood. Elion didn't part with the corpse of her for days; calling out her name until his voice was gone. She was only fourteen. *He* was only fourteen. It wasn't a serious love affair, but Elion felt so much guilt for letting her get killed. It was his fault for showing interest in her.

Elion shook the memory out from his head, his eyes wet. Only their father and Elion knew about the true bloodthirsty nature of Adamar. The others didn't know, Adamar hid it so well. But he was an angry man, a violent man, who killed anyone who looked at his wife in a way that he didn't like. Essarae didn't want to marry Adamar at first, but he had murdered every man who was the least bit interested that eventually she had no choice. But, Elion believed, she wasn't any better than his brother.

He wandered the halls, haunted by the memory of Pilar and how they grew up. She was a servant's child, running around the halls with him. He watched as the ghosts of their younger selves played throughout the hallways of the palace as he walked through them. She was the only child that was his age in the palace. His father thought it would be good for Elion to have a friend and Elion *adored* Pilar. Her humanity was so interesting. She was curious and liked to make up stories. She called it playing pretend. They would pretend they were married and that he was the King of Aureum. They would pretend they both had magic, like witches. One time, he heard Pilar speaking a strange language with her mother and he wanted to know what it was.

"Oh, I speak Spanish," she said. She explained that it was an old human language. Humans spoke in different languages to one another, unlike the one language of the magical creatures. She told Elion of the different cultures that humans had from one another.

"Do all humans speak the different languages?" Elion had asked in wonder. Pilar had thrown her head back laughing with her whole body.

"No," she said, "Some can speak a few different ones. But I speak Spanish because my family came from an old country that spoke Spanish." She scrunched her dark eyebrows together in thought.

"I think they said that we're from Columbia," she said slowly as she tried to remember. She shrugged. "There were a lot of different Spanish-speaking countries thousands of years ago. Before the War."

Elion watched as the memory of the younger Pilar laughed and then ran away, calling for Elion to catch her. He followed the ghost of her, wondering what happened to her family after she was murdered. He never saw them again in the palace after her death. It was as if they had never existed.

Pilar's ghost smiled up at him and then disappeared in front of a door. The door was to Adamar's bed chambers. Elion slowly walked up to it, hearing voices from behind the large marble door that was slightly ajar. Not just one voice, but a thousand voices whispered the same message. Elion's eyes widened. He tried to get a closer look, but the space between the door and the door frame was almost nonexistent. He was unable to see anything that was going on inside the room.

"You stupid, *insolent* creature," the voices hissed.

"Your holiness, I—"

"To attack a mere Champion," the voices continued to scold, "a *Champion*."

"The information given to me was that Poseidon was at that inn..." *The Sea God?*

"He *was* there," the voices said in unison. "A meeting called him away. You have sent two assassins now in pursuit of him. If she had just *waited*..."

"Yes, he has evaded their attacks twice," Adamar's voice quivered, "But, the Sea God wasn't there, in the room. It was only the—" Adamar's voice was cut off with a whimper.

"Poseidon is *not* that strong of a God. Isn't An your goal? Having the world at your fingertips with no one to answer to? You must try harder... for the sake of your son," the voices cooed. There was silence for a long while.

"You did well with Belenus," the voices praised. *Belenus?* Elion thought. *The God of Healing.* He had heard that the God of

Healing's body had been killed. It wasn't abnormal for the Gods' reincarnations to be killed or murdered. But there were some murmurings that this time was different, that the corpse had looked odd. Part of it was missing, and the rest had turned the color gray, much like a stone.

"The God of Healing is no more," Adamar said, a bit more confidently.

"Yes," the voices sounded far away now, "soon they will all never return." Elion felt a cold chill course through his body. Quickly, he backed away from the door, running down the hallways back to the celebration that was happening within the palace. *Celebration?* Elion felt his heart pounding in his ears. It felt wrong, somehow, to be celebrating. He never thought Adamar would go this far. *Could he really be killing the Gods?*

He stopped in front of the doors to the Great Hall, his hand hovering over the handle. Freya's bewitching face entered the forefront of his mind. He couldn't let Adamar kill her like he did with Pilar. Backing away from the doors, he ran towards the front of the palace.

I have to warn her, Elion's voice screamed within his head. Determined to protect her, he started towards the country of Sylva.

18

Rhea marched ahead of Khalon, leading the way towards the most recent battle between the beastoids and the draconians. She had heard rumors, on their journey there, that the king himself was going to show up in order to scare the beastoids into submission. The power of the dragon is something that is revered and feared throughout Asynithis, and perhaps reminding the beastoids of that would put the draconians at an advantage. Except, Rhea glanced back at Khalon who was sweating profusely from the walk, the king didn't have the true power of the dragon. His bastard son did.

"Do you think we could take a break?" Khalon shouted towards Rhea. Rhea stopped in her tracks, thinking about how weak creatures were and then realized her body also needed a little bit of rest. She rolled her eyes, annoyed momentarily about the body she was in.

"All right," she said, turning around and walking over to Khalon who was guzzling down the water from a crystal cup. He looked up at her, panting a little.

"Don't Gods get like, I don't know, special rides to get to different places?" he asked, sweat dripping into his eye. He quickly wiped the bead of sweat away as Rhea's eyes lingered on his scar.

"Don't talk to me. I'm not a God that creatures want to see as fast as they can, so I don't get any free services and *I'm sure* you don't have any more money," she said absentmindedly. Khalon pursed his lips and then shrugged a shoulder, agreeing with her statement as he drank some more water. She sat down next to him and gingerly touched the scar over his eye. He flinched from her touch and stared at her in annoyance before taking another sip of the endless water.

———

"Your journey is going to be long and you can't travel in the shadows with this guy," Poseidon had said before he departed. Handing Rhea a crystal container, he said, "This will give you endless water. It'll fill itself back up once it's gone. Pretty neat, huh?" Poseidon had separated from them, deciding to meet them in Sylva. He was going to look for answers while they were meeting with the King of Draconia.

———

Rhea stared at the puckered skin that went down vertically on the side of his left eye.

"How did you get that?" Rhea asked, gesturing towards Khalon's scar. Khalon looked at her confused, and then his face lit up with recognition.

"Oh, this?" he said, his thin fingers tracing the scar over his eye. "I got this in a fight." He then took out a bag that was

attached to his waist and pulled out some bread. Handing one
to Rhea, he took a bite out of his. It was clear he was done with
the conversation. Rhea's lips tightened into a line of annoyance. *Such a way with words, this one.*

"What fight?" she pressed on. He wasn't much of a
converser, but she hated the silence. There was also a nagging
bit in her that wanted to get to know his past and who he was
as a person. It was clear he wasn't someone that was afraid of
death. Which meant he wasn't afraid of who she was, and...
everyone was afraid of her. He took another mouthful of bread.

"Uh," he said loudly. He said that a lot when he was unsure
of what to say and it was always obnoxiously loud. "I think it
was maybe my third fight? I fight with weapons, it's the class
that I'm in. The other dude was an elf, a big one. I'm not sure
how he got into trouble in Draconia, since elves usually stay in
Aureum. But he had one of those crystal knives, the ones that
elves make out of unicorn bone. Good stuff. And it, uh, nicked
my eye." He pointed at his eye absentmindedly and then
continued to eat his bread.

"Did it hurt?" Rhea asked, staring at the other scars on his
body. There were a lot on his arm, as his armor didn't protect
them. Many Champions in the Ring of Fire liked to show off
their scales, the sign that they descended from the dragons
long past. His armor also represented that, showing off the
patches of scales covering his arm. She took in his face as he
looked at her incredulously.

"Yeah, *of course* it hurt," he said, "But mostly afterwards.
During it, there's just a lot of adrenaline going. It wasn't until
after the elf was... defeated did I really notice that I couldn't see
out of my left eye." He paused for a moment, "I can see from it
now. It was just because it was swollen and there was a lot of
blood." The claw mark that went up the side of his face was an

unusual scale pattern for draconians. Rhea realized that the spirit of the dragon had probably been with him for a while, making a mark on him, probably before he was even born.

"You never sprouted a tail or been covered with scales before this? To protect yourself?" Rhea asked, referring to the other night when Khalon stood over the body of an assassin.

———

"*I'm not turning back to normal,*" Khalon had started to panic as Rhea surveyed the scene. She grabbed the tooth, gingerly, with the sleeve of her cloak, putting it in her pocket.

"It's okay," Rhea had said, distracted by the cloak that the woman wore, "You'll turn back eventually."

"When?!" Khalon's voice had gotten uncharacteristically shrill. His normally black eyes were a yellow-gold color and his face was distorted into a short snout. His teeth were long and pointed and his whole body was covered in scales. He looked like a werewolf in half creature half werewolf form. Not quite at his full form, but not quite his normal self either.

"Soon," she said, picking up the cloak that the woman wore. There was no doubt about it; it was a reaper's cloak.

"It shrouded her face," Khalon said, his eyes focused on what Rhea was holding. *Way to state the obvious*, Rhea couldn't help but think. She folded the cloak quickly and then tucked it into her own.

"Poseidon probably knows as well," Khalon said quietly. "I've noticed he's been watching you, carefully." *Poseidon was watching me?* Rhea shook her head. She had nothing to do with this. The distraction was causing him to turn back to normal, his scales turning to his normal tan, copper colored skin. His face reverting back into its angular self and his eyes returning to those dark brown, almost black eyes of his.

"I don't know how they got this," Rhea said, quietly. She wracked her brain of any mention of one of her reapers getting attacked, but no one but her and anyone dead could see reapers, normally. She was wrong about living creatures being able to utilize the reaper cloak. And whoever was killing the Gods was also able to access her reapers and their clothing. From all accounts about the Mortiferis, they didn't seem like they had a thought in their mind. So someone must be controlling them, but who?

"I know," Khalon had reassured her at the time. Poseidon had come in a moment later, and they came up with a plan. Rhea couldn't ignore the king's sacrifice. She *had* to meet with him on the battlefield. So Poseidon would go and try to find out who the assassin was and where she had gotten the tooth.

———

Khalon shook his head, his answer of "No" bringing Rhea back to the present.

"It's only happened once before, but only for a second," Khalon said.

"In the Ring of Fire?" Rhea asked. He nodded, his crescent shaped eyes lowered.

"My father, the king, said I committed treason," he whispered. He looked back up at her, looking like a puppy dog that had lost their way home. The pang in Rhea's heart sounded once more. She looked away.

"You have the spirit of the dragon in your soul," she said, "And it's becoming more and more intertwined with yours." Khalon shook his head.

"I know you said that but it's impossible."

"It's the only reason you're able to have the power of the dragon," Rhea argued.

"The king is still alive and has the power of the dragon. You can't have the power of a dragon without the spirit of one," Khalon retorted, but his lips twisted and his eyes darted away.

"I know you don't believe that," Rhea muttered. She sighed and pushed herself off the ground.

"C'mon," she said, "We have to go meet your father anyways."

"Do you want some water?" he asked, handing her the crystal cup. She realized she hadn't even taken a bite out of the bread he gave her, but her mouth felt dry. She traded the bread for the cup and watched as it filled itself up with water. She drank all of it and then wiped her mouth, handing it back to Khalon.

"Thanks," she said. He put it away in his little bag and he stared at her for a moment, as if he were studying her with those piercing eyes of his.

"What?" Rhea asked, as she started walking forwards. She didn't want to look at his face. A face that casted doubt on her and who she was.

"Nothing, Rhea. I'm just a little worried about you." Rhea could barely make out the words.

"You don't need to worry about me," Rhea said, her head held high. "I'm a God. I've lived a million lifetimes before this one." She turned around to look at him and he just stared at her. She couldn't tell what was going on behind that stone face of his.

"I think I'll always worry about you," he muttered after a while, staring at her for a moment longer before darting his eyes away. He silently got himself off of the ground and then started walking forward. Before he could get to her, Rhea started on their path once again. His words echoed in her brain for the longest time. For some reason, his words made her heart beat a little faster. Ears burning, she picked up the pace.

They traveled further, stopping near a rock in the desert-like area. There weren't many villages around this part of Draconia. Mostly due to the desert atmosphere, but anyone who was living in Longwei Desert moved out due to the ongoing conflict with the beastoids.

"Let's rest here for the night," Rhea said. She dropped to the ground and then rested her back and head against the side of the rock, cooling her skin down. Walking like a normal creature made her back incredibly sore. She wished she could just travel in the shadows like usual and glared at Khalon for making her have to walk so much. Khalon laughed.

"What's that look for?" Khalon asked. She looked away quickly.

"I just hate walking," she grumbled. Khalon laughed some more as he came and sat next to her. The heat of his body next to hers was almost electrifying. She cleared her throat and scooted herself over a little.

"No one likes walking, I don't think," Khalon said. "Except maybe centaurs." Rhea scoffed.

"Have you met a centaur? They love laying about and not moving," she said. Khalon looked at her surprised.

"Oh," he said, "I wouldn't have guessed that."

"Don't you have a special way of traveling, besides going into the underworld? I've heard — I mean, read — that the big three Gods are able to travel in a special way," Khalon said after a while. Rhea thought to herself. Big three? Were they called that? Well, they were the first ones who existed before the rest of her annoying family.

"I do. I travel through the shadows. But it's not exactly that accurate if I'm bringing someone along with me. Also, traveling in the shadows will give a living creature some issues. It's hard on the body," Rhea explained. Khalon mouthed "Oh," and they sat in silence. But it wasn't an uncomfortable silence.

Rhea had gotten used to the softness of quiet that seemed to surround Khalon. It was peaceful, sitting with him, without words to pierce the air. They stared at the crackling fire that Rhea had brought up from the underworld.

"If this person wanted to bring the Mortiferis here to destroy the Gods," Khalon started. Rhea had already told him everything that Ganesha had said about the Mortiferis. She left out the part where Ganesha told her that she had asked previously about it, which she had no memory of.

"Yes," Rhea encouraged him to continue.

"Wouldn't the Mortiferis not stop at just the Gods? Wouldn't they destroy the whole realm?" Khalon asked. Rhea nodded her head slowly.

"Yes, I don't think you'd be able to stop the Mortiferis once they start. But," she pointed at him, "I don't think the Mortiferis *are* in this realm." His thick black eyebrows knitted together.

"What do you mean? You think someone just got one of their teeth by chance?" he asked.

"Ganesha said you're able to go to realms through reflections in water or mirrors. Perhaps this person went through a reflection to a realm that was being destroyed by the Mortiferis, plucked one of their teeth out, and..." her voice drifted off, realizing how incredulous it sounded. Khalon looked at her with an eyebrow raised. She knew that people could go to different realms through reflections, as she herself had done it multiple times before. But... her mind wandered. *When did I travel to different realms?* **Why** *was I?* Rhea's eyebrows tensed in concentration for a moment and then she mentally waved the thought away. It wasn't important.

"Anyways," she said indignantly, "It's possible that the Mortiferis as a whole aren't here in this realm. Maybe only one is here, and whoever wants the Gods dead is just using that one in order to get their goal completed."

"Maybe," Khalon said, eyeing her carefully, "But I don't know how they were able to capture a Mortiferis from another realm and then bring them back here without being killed themselves." Rhea shrugged.

"I just have a feeling that they're not all here, yet," she muttered. Khalon stared into the fire. He was quiet for a moment. Rhea noticed that there was something on his mind, and it had been on his mind for a while. She sighed inwardly.

"Are you going to tell Poseidon that the cloak was a reaper's cloak?" he asked after a while. She knew he was going to ask about it. He'd be stupid not to. Rhea looked over at him as he stared at the flickering flames. She watched as his jaw twitched, knowing that he felt her gaze on him.

"No," she said after a while, turning back to face the fire, "If what you said is true, he already knows anyways."

"Are you going to tell the God of All?" Khalon asked. The mention of his name made Rhea's blood boil.

"Never," she snapped. Khalon looked at her in surprise and she closed her eyes to try and calm herself down.

"Sorry," she muttered, "Don't mention him to me. The God of Death really despises him."

"Why?" Khalon asked. Rhea shrugged.

"I think we feel that we have the most work to do out of the rest of the Gods. Plus, no creature really appreciates the work that we do either," she toed at a pebble near her feet. "We rarely get any prayers, we're no one's patron God, no one really cares for us. All they see, when they look at us, is horror."

"Not everyone sees that," Khalon said quietly, looking into Rhea's eyes. Once again, she had that gnawing feeling that he could *really* see her. Her true face. She cleared her throat and looked away.

"That woman," Khalon changed the subject, "I've seen her before." Rhea looked at him in surprise.

"Who? The assassin?" she asked. He nodded.

"I've seen her on your face before," he said. Rhea stared at him for a moment. He had seen her on her face?

"What do those faces mean? That creatures see?"

"When they look at me, they see what they think death is. It could be a loved one of theirs that's passed away, or someone they've killed. Just what they think death looks like," Rhea explained.

"Have you met the faces of the creatures that others see?" It was an odd question. Rhea looked at him weirdly.

"I mean," she said, thinking seriously, "considering they've all died, I probably have met them in a way. I know every soul that comes into the underworld."

"But I saw her face on yours," Khalon pointed out, "And she hadn't died yet." Rhea bristled.

"Perhaps what you saw was your *own* death. She could've killed you. You were very close to death in her presence if it weren't for the other soul attached to yours. Maybe *that's* why you saw her face," Rhea said, frustrated. "I don't know." Khalon stayed quiet for a moment.

"Yeah," he said, agreeing with her, "that's probably it." Rhea laid down on the sandy ground, turning away from Khalon. She used her elbow as a pillow to rest her head. She didn't want to be having this conversation. Khalon was a weird creature. She didn't know why he saw a face that she's never seen before on hers. He sees a bunch of different faces, which was already weird enough. Plus, Rhea thought, he might be able to see her true face. Which... her thoughts wandered. Did she *want* him to be able to see her true face? If he could see it, why would he lie about it unless... She closed her eyes in horror. He probably thought she was ugly and didn't want her to feel embarrassed about it. That was the only reason why he would lie about not being able to see her face. She stared at the flat ground of the desert plains, the dark sky in the horizon. *Maybe Freya was right,* was the last thought she had before she drifted off to sleep.

When she awoke, she quickly sat up and looked over at Khalon still heavily sleeping. She never really had dreams, mostly because the God of Death kept her soul from dreaming much as he never slept. But last night she had a dream that Khalon was staring at her in disgust as Freya taunted Rhea over and over again about the condition of her thin hair. It was horrible.

She didn't really know how to do her hair. It wasn't like the Fates didn't try to teach her. They used to do her hair in cute little pigtails and buns all the time when she was younger. But Rhea was never really interested in doing her own hair, opting to let it hang limp. She normally had her hair tucked behind her pointed ears. It wasn't that she didn't care, it was more that she didn't really know how to do it herself. And honestly, Rhea thought, what was the point if no one could see her? But... She looked over at Khalon and made up her mind. Thinking back to the headband that Felicity was wearing the last time she saw her, Rhea quickly ripped a part of the bottom of her too-long cloak and tried to wrap the fabric around her head into a makeshift headband, making it so that a bow was on the side of it. *I don't have a mirror,* she groaned inwardly. Frantically she looked around for something to see her reflection in. Then it came to her, the crystal cup. It wasn't going to be a *great* surface to see herself in, but it's possible she'll be able to see herself faintly in the water.

Carefully, she walked over to where Khalon was lightly snoring, but it seemed different than the usual sounds he made. His face was contorted, as if he was frightened or concerned about whatever he was dreaming about. He had placed his bag next to him, and in his crossed arms was his Dragon sword. She quickly nabbed the bag and slowly opened it up, careful not to make a sound. *Why am I doing this?* She asked herself as she pulled out the cup. *It's a test,* she tried to convince herself. It filled up with water and she moved it around in order to faintly see herself. Her hair was pulled back by the black makeshift ribbon and her face looked rounder than ever. *This is ridiculous.* Sighing, she reached up to pull the ribbon out of her hair, but froze when she heard a rustling sound. She looked over at Khalon in horror as he stared at her in confusion. His eyes glanced up at the ribbon in her hair and then back at her.

"Why—" he started to say but then Rhea started theatrically laughing.

"Ha!" she said, completely embarrassed but trying not to show it, "I knew it. You *can* see my face." Khalon stared at her for a moment as his ears turned bright red. She caught him. Her heart fell.

"You...can see me," she said slowly. He stared at her, expressionless for a moment and then his eyes glanced away.

"Yeah," he admitted, "I can see your real face. There is a carousel of faces that encase your real face and if I'm paying attention to it, I can see that. But, I can also see past it." He looked up at me.

"Is that why you're wearing a ribbon in your hair?" he asked. It was Rhea's turn for the blood to rush up to her cheeks.

"Yeah, I just wanted to know if you noticed or not," she said, reaching up to take it out again.

"It looks nice," Khalon said, a smile playing on his lips. Rhea froze as she felt her face heat up even more. She tucked her hands into her cloak and stood up from the bag.

"Don't talk to me," she said, "I'm only keeping it in because it's hot and I like to keep the hair out of my face."

"Not because I said it looks nice on you?" he teased, leaning forward slightly. Rhea could feel her ears flush.

"Why would I do anything just because you think it looks nice?" she grumbled as Khalon got up to follow her.

19

Poseidon rubbed the top of his head as he ducked into the entrance of the large cabin home where the meeting was taking place. He had traveled to Sylva, the land of woodland creatures and most of the humans in Asynithis, in order to find information about the woman that tried to kill them a few nights ago. Poseidon remembered seeing Rhea tuck the reaper's cloak underneath her cloak as he came in. If whoever is killing the Gods are using reaper's cloaks and if the Mortiferis were involved... He couldn't bear to finish the thought.

He had found out that the woman's name was Everly and was someone who was very involved in the politics of Sylva. Sylva was a very politically heavy country as they didn't have a royal family. So many of the creatures in Sylva were old, and lived forever with their trees or lakes or creeks that they were attached to, that it didn't really make sense to have one royal family. They also had a lot of humans living in this country and humans seemed to prefer the idea of democracy. A man at a local store had pointed Poseidon in this direction telling him:

"If you want to know more about Everly, I suggest going to that meeting that's happening over there." So, that's how Poseidon ended up in this cramped cabin.

Moving around the cabin wall, red hair marred with gray caught his sight. He swiveled, following the figure with his eyes. They were wearing green leggings and a leaf shaped top, but the figure was unmistakable. Even from behind, her muscular build was out of place in this crowd. Poseidon pushed past various creatures and caught up to his sister.

"Neith?" he whispered, putting a hand on her shoulder. She turned around, and met his eyes. Her emerald green eyes met his hazel ones in bewilderment. She stared for a moment and then leaned towards him slightly.

"What are you doing here?" she asked. Poseidon laughed slightly.

"I could ask you the same question," he pointed out. She pursed her lips, deciding whether she should tell him her reasoning or not.

"I'm in disguise," she merely said. "Don't call me by that name. Here my name is a human one. Amy."

"Amy?" he asked, not able to hide the distaste he had for the name. "Why Amy?" Neith stood up straighter.

"I felt that it was a classic human name," she said, defensively.

"A classic human name would be something like Olivia or Hannah or something," Poseidon countered. She scoffed at him.

"How little you know of humans," she muttered. Poseidon made a face and then looked away from her.

"I'm guessing you're on a mission for An," Poseidon said after a while. She didn't look at him, but her body stiffening gave away enough.

"What are *you* here for?" Neith asked.

"Well, *Amy*," Poseidon said, giving emphasis on her ridiculous name, "I'm here following up on a lead."

"A lead?"

"A human came to these meetings. I'm just trying to find out more information about her," Poseidon explained. Neith stared at him and then she ducked her head as she started to laugh.

"What?" Poseidon asked. Neith gave him a knowing look.

"You don't know what this meeting is for, do you?" she asked, pointedly, a smirk growing on her lips. Poseidon stared at her as he tried to figure out what she meant by that.

"Is it something weird? I heard it's a political meeting that she went to all the time," Poseidon muttered. Neith pointed at her nose and nodded, but started to laugh once again.

"You're in for a wild ride, Brother," she said, laughing. Just as she finished, a human came up on the makeshift stage. A huge applause followed her entrance and she smiled at the crowd. She had chocolate long brown hair that was tied up in a ponytail and she was almost as pale as Neith was. Holding up her hands to quiet the gathered crowd, she addressed them.

"Unfortunately, I won't be speaking today," she said, which was followed by groans and boos. Her face mimicked the sadness that the crowd seemed to feel. Looking around at the faces of the creatures, Poseidon felt wary about what was happening in the building.

"But," she said, with newfound enthusiasm, "Our favored candidate is here to give a speech!" A huge applause was given. *Right*, Poseidon thought, *it is that time where Sylva would be having elections.* To Poseidon's surprise, stepping onto the stage was a dwarf. Dwarves weren't really known for their leadership, so the sight was a marvel to Poseidon. The dwarf stroked his long strawberry blonde beard as he walked towards the center of the stage. Poseidon hadn't seen a dwarf in a while and had forgotten just how short they were. Actually, Poseidon was the tallest person in this building and standing out during a semi secret mission didn't seem like the best idea. He backed up so that he would be against the wall as Neith gave him a knowing look.

"Please welcome Martin Flintcoat!" the first woman proclaimed as the crowd went wild. He put up his stubby hands, pushing the air as if telling the audience to step back, but his intention was to quiet them.

"Thank you, thank you," he said to the crowd. Poseidon didn't know what Neith meant. This seemed like a normal political rally to him. He raised an eyebrow at her as she started to silently laugh, looking back at him.

"Wait for it," she mouthed to him.

"As you all know," Flintcoat started to say as the crowd became silent, "Before the humans had taken over our world, elves ruled Asynithis." Poseidon's eyes widened as Neith burst into silent laughter again. *Oh no.*

"Asynithis was flourishing under the rule of the elves and now that we have all separated from being under their rule, we don't have enough jobs," the crowd yelled out their agreements, "no direction!" *Oh f—.*

"I have been in talks with King Adamar and if you vote for me, I'll be sure to bring Asynithis back to its former elven glory!" Flintcoat exclaimed.

"Told you," Neith mouthed, smugly, as she turned back around to listen to the rest of Flintcoat's speech. Poseidon stared up at the ceiling as if the wooden logs up there would help. *The assassin was a gods-damn elf apologist.*

20

After asking an injured soldier on the road for directions to the battlefield, Rhea and Khalon could see in the horizon the smoke billowing over small white tents. Rhea looked over at Khalon, feeling the anxious energy coming from him. She lightly put a hand on his arm. He had been staring at her weirdly all morning and it had been making her feel uneasy. But she just chalked it up to him being anxious in seeing his dad for the first time since he banished Khalon and made him give his life as a sacrifice.

"Your dad doesn't hate you," she said, guessing at what he was thinking. Khalon snorted, withdrawing his arm away from her unconsciously as he marched forward.

"You don't know my dad," Khalon said. Then quietly, "I don't even know him, really." Rhea didn't know what to say to that, opting to move forward in silence.

"Rhea," Khalon said her name now with ease.

"Yes?"

"The war with the beastoids is wrong, I think," Khalon said slowly. Rhea's heart dropped as she realized where his thoughts were going. He looked over at her, the sun hitting his black eyes making them a chocolate brown.

"I don't think you should accept me as a sacrifice in order to help my father in this war," he finally said. There was fear hidden in his eyes, though his face remained as stoic as ever. Rhea chewed on the inside of her cheek. *I don't want you to die.*

"I can't reject a sacrifice that's already been accepted," Rhea lied, refusing to look at him.

"You haven't really accepted me yet," Khalon replied. "You haven't given him your answer."

"Me coming to the battlefield is answer enough," she huffed. Why would he say this to her? She had already felt bad making him a temple servant, and had already thought about letting him go. But after seeing that he had the spirit of the dragon in him, she couldn't just let him leave her protection. It didn't matter if it was another cage to him or not.

"Your dad will kill you," she said after a long while of just the sound of their footsteps.

"He might not," Khalon said, hopeful. "If I tell him I'll never step into Draconia again, he might not." Rhea didn't say anything. She knew what the draconian royal family was like. The Red Dragon family had been in power for years, killing anyone who showed signs of having the spirit of the dragon. It was how they kept their reign. She had stupidly believed that King Vien must have had the spirit of the dragon within him since the beginning of his reign because she hadn't seen him kill anyone with signs of it. But now she knew it was because the spirit of the dragon was within Khalon the whole time. Considering he had no trouble killing those that were only speaking about Khalon, she felt that King Vien wouldn't hesitate in killing his own son, no matter who birthed him. King Vien was too far gone.

"Let's go," she finally said, ending the conversation. She

saw Khalon give her an exasperated look in her peripheral vision, but she didn't acknowledge it. Without her protection, Khalon would die. She wasn't going to let him die.

The draconian camp was on the border of the Longwei Desert, a small forest sprouting in the same area. They were beyond the trees, repairing their armor and sharpening their weapons. Most of the tents were white, but the red tent in the distance was where the king resided, Rhea assumed. She started forward but Khalon pulled her back, his grip tight on her arm.

"Do you think I should wear the reaper's cloak?" he asked, his eyes searching hers. She knew what he was afraid of: the soldiers clamoring towards him either in praise or anger. Either way would be bad for him. Rhea pulled his hand off of her arm, shaking her head.

"No, they should know Khalon, Prince of Draconia, was here," she said, marching forward. Khalon hesitated and then followed after her. They walked through the camp, Rhea leading the way. She felt eyes watching her, horrified, but most were looking at Khalon as he followed her. They recognized his face; it was hard not to. How many draconians did you see with scales in the shape of a claw mark creeping onto the side of their face? However, Rhea surveyed the faces of those around them, and they looked anxious. As if just seeing Khalon, recognizing him, would get them killed.

As they got closer to the red tent, two soldiers stopped Rhea, barring her with their swords crossed in front.

"Excuse me," she said, trying to get past them. They moved when she moved, refusing to let her get any closer to the king's tent. She stared at them in disbelief, her body starting to heat up with anger.

"State your business," one of the soldiers stated, gruffly. Her lips tightened into a line as her jaw clenched. She could see the horror in their faces at seeing her, but they still stood their ground.

"I am the God of Death, here to see the king," Rhea said through her teeth, holding her head up high. Despite her more humble beliefs of her being a God, she still hated being questioned. She looked at the two soldiers who still refused to move.

"I am literally here with his sacrifice," she said, gesturing to Khalon behind her.

"The son of the king," the other soldier said, his voice quivering slightly, "needs to be dead for you to see his highness." Rhea's eyebrows raised slightly as she looked at them. Then, she felt herself starting to laugh.

"The king dares to tell *me* what to do with my own sacrifice?" she heard herself say. Her blood was starting to boil as she balled her hands up in fists.

"If you haven't accepted his highness' sacrifice, then you cannot meet with the king," the first soldier declared. Rhea laughed again.

"The King of Draconia believes that he can order the God of Death around," Rhea said, nodding her head bitterly as she felt herself standing up straighter.

"Then, *his highness*," her voice dripped with sarcasm, "should be okay with me killing his whole army as punishment." As she said this, she felt the voices of the underworld rise up into her as she spoke one word. She turned to the rest of the army, her eyes glancing at their frightened faces. Her own face relaxed.

"Die," she said, the souls whispering the word after her. She watched as the soldiers around her started to slowly drop to the ground, wordless screams bearing their faces. The soldiers that were in front of her dropped their weapons, as they felt their bodies start to waste away. Slowly, the soldiers started to look like corpses, gray and gaunt. Khalon looked around, finally frightened of her. He looked at her as she looked past him, not wanting to see his horror.

"Rhea," he said, desperately, "Stop this." He grabbed onto her shoulders but she closed her eyes, still feeling the souls coursing through her, eating the lives of the soldiers in front of her.

"Stop it!" he cried, his hands reaching up to her face. His thumb resting on her cheek, the slight pressure on her face building as his anxiety rose. She kept her eyes squeezed shut and felt a lump in her throat swell up, knowing how terrified he must be of her.

"That's enough," a voice boomed from behind. Her eyes fluttered open, looking up at Khalon whose eyes were fixed on the person behind her. His hands still rested on the sides of her face but were slowly dropping down towards her shoulders. They balled up into fists. She felt the voices of the underworld quiet as the soldiers gasped for air, regaining their color and weight back to their bodies. Turning her head and body slightly, she looked into the face of King Vien.

"He looks like you," she said. King Vien's face softened, staring at hers. She knew what he probably saw.

"Dal," he uttered. Then he shook his head, bowing it as he gestured for her to come inside of his tent. Walking forward, she tugged at Khalon's arm, bringing him forward as well. Inside of the tent looked like a strategy meeting. There were figures on top of a map that looked like a battlefield. The draconian men that were inside were Ministers of Draconia. Owning parts of land and in charge of different aspects of Draconia, they were also considered advisors to the king. Their heads were bowed as Rhea entered.

"Leave us," Vien spoke, causing the Ministers to leave the tent as quickly as they could. She could see that they also were affected by her previous command and they wanted to be out of her presence as quickly as possible. The king walked over to the chair that sat at the back of the tent, gesturing for her to follow him. He sat down, groaning as he did, and stared lazily at her. The disrespect was high. She felt herself bristle in annoyance.

"You have come to aid us in battle then?" he asked, pouring himself a glass of tea. He gestured towards it, his face asking her if she wanted any. She held up her hand and shook her head. Instead of drinking the tea, however, he drank a glass of dark red, almost black wine. Rhea frowned at it.

"You believe yourself to be better than the God of Death?" Rhea asked, ignoring his question. He swallowed his wine, staring her in the eyes but then looking away quickly. He couldn't look at her without seeing his dead lover.

"You are just a girl," he muttered, "But I can see that you possess greater power than I." His face contorted angrily as he put down the glass. Though Khalon and King Vien had the same face, the facial expressions they made were different.

"My *body* is a girl, *child*," Rhea snapped, "My soul is older than your first ancestor." His eyes glanced up at her angrily as he picked up the wine glass once more, pointing at her.

"Have you or have you *not* accepted my son as sacrifice?" Vien drank more of his wine. It sloshed out a bit, causing some of the deep red liquid to drip down his chin. He wiped it off as Rhea stared at it. It was as if a ton of bricks suddenly hit her in the head. *That's how they've kept it up all these years.* She had always wondered how they were able to fake having the spirit of the dragon within them. *No wonder why every King of Draconia has gone insane. Blood lust.* Smiling at him, she walked forward a bit. He shrunk in his seat, seeing the unfamiliar facial expression on his beloved.

"I don't accept your son as sacrifice," Rhea said, feeling

Khalon stiffen behind her in surprise. Vien's eyes narrowed at her as he glanced over at his son who stood behind.

"Fine," Vien said, "Leave him here." Rhea shook her head as she continued to walk forward, grabbing the glass from Vien's hands. His eyes widened in surprise, and she could see that little bit of fear start to creep through. Her smile widened more.

"No, Khalon will be able to go where he wishes," Rhea said, swirling the liquid around in the cup.

"Your highness," Khalon interjected. Rhea glared at him. "I'll leave Draconia and I'll never come back. I promise." Vien's face contorted as he stood up out of his highly decorated chair.

"You think leaving Draconia fixes your treasonous actions?" Vien growled, "No. The God of Death won't take you? Then you will get the traitor's death that you deserve." Rhea sighed and then stepped in front of Vien, partially blocking his view of Khalon.

"No, sorry," she said. "You will not kill Khalon." He looked down at her, his eyes flashing.

"You have no jurisdiction over how I rule Draconia," he hissed. Rhea shrugged, dipping her finger into the wine. She watched as Vien's black eyes widened as she then put her finger into her mouth, tasting the bitterness of blood.

"Except, King Vien," she said, smacking her lips at the taste, "I know your secret." Her eyes hardened as she then threw the glass to the ground, shattering it, causing the "wine" to splatter everywhere.

"I will make sure that your whole country knows what your family has been doing for a millennium. Dragon's blood?" she scoffed as he stared at the blood that was pooled on the ground. He looked scared, desperate. She could feel Khalon staring at her in shock.

"You kill Khalon," she whispered, stepping closer to Vien,

"I'll kill you. And make sure to ruin your family's name in the process." Smiling, she then turned away, beckoning Khalon to follow her. Khalon stared at her, a mixture of emotions on his face. But he followed her anyways, taking a look at his father who had dropped to the ground, staring helplessly at the Dragon's blood that had started to seep into the dirt. Rhea turned around, stopping at the entrance of the king's tent. Khalon stopped behind her.

"Oh," she said, looking back at Vien. His eyes wandered and then made eye contact with hers.

"As a gesture of good grace," she continued, "if you continue on this path of trying to make the beastoids disappear, you'll end up dying." She pointed towards her head, indicating that she could see his impending doom, and then smiled slightly at his expression, leaving the tent.

21

Khalon watched his father's expression fall as he heard Rhea's premonition. He stared at him for a moment as his father looked up. Vien's eyes searched Khalon's identical ones as Rhea exited the tent.

"Where did I go wrong?" he asked, before crawling towards the pool of blood. He dipped his finger and brought the blood towards his tongue. It was as if he couldn't help himself. What had happened to his father, Khalon couldn't begin to understand. But dragon's blood? He couldn't imagine his father lying to the masses in order to keep power. And where did he even get the blood from?

"This isn't you, dad," he said, calling him the name that he hadn't called him in a while. Khalon started to walk out of the tent, but gave his father one last look. Vien looked up at him, his eyes glassy. Neither of them exchanged any words, but Khalon liked to believe that Vien apologized to him for everything. It was a simple wish, a wish that Khalon would never fully get granted.

He ran to catch up to Rhea. He quickly grabbed her by the

arm and whipped her around. She pulled her arm out from his grip and stared up at him, indignantly. Every time she tried to look angry, she just looked funny doing it, but Khalon couldn't find amusement in her expression this time. Her hair was still pulled back by that silly makeshift ribbon, he noticed as he felt his anger building.

"What are you *doing*?" Khalon said. Rhea rolled her eyes and continued to walk out of the camp.

"What do you mean, Khalon? You mean *saving* you?" Khalon caught up to her, walking backwards so he could face her.

"Saving me? You just humiliated me in front of my father and the whole Draconian army," he pointed out. Rhea's face scrunched up in disbelief.

"Humiliated you? *Humiliated* you? Are you *kidding* me?" she cried out, her mouth open. She stared past him, searching the horizon for something to say to Khalon, and decided to just walk forward past him.

"Yes, you humiliated me. I wanted to solve it for myself. I— I didn't need you to threaten my father and my whole family along with him," Khalon fumed.

"Do you *hear* yourself right now?" Rhea stormed, whipping herself around so she could face him. Khalon stopped in his tracks.

"Your *father* was going to kill you. *I* released you from all duties. You aren't my temple servant anymore. You don't *have* to leave Draconia if you don't want to. You won't die," she listed out all of the benefits that she had given Khalon. If he was honest to himself, he knew that she helped him gain his freedom. A freedom that he had never had before in his life. But...

"You became a monster, Rhea," he said, his voice dipping into a whisper. He remembered the voices that had come out of her when she was killing all those people. He closed his eyes, remembering the same sound that he had been hearing in his dreams recently. Rhea stared at him, her face going through a roller coaster of emotions. But for a second, Khalon thought she looked hurt.

"A monster," she whispered to herself, nodding. She looked up at Khalon.

"You made everyone around us start to die and you threatened the king like it was nothing. You even enjoyed toying with him the way that you did in there," Khalon said, gesturing to the area around them. *And you've been disappearing every night,* Khalon almost said but couldn't bring himself to.

"You're suddenly going to get all self righteous about killing people, Khalon? Really? Champion of the Ring of Fire? Haven't you been killing people since you were, what did you say? Ten years old? How many people have *you* killed, Khalon? Maybe think about that before calling me a monster," Rhea snapped. Khalon stared at her.

"I might've killed people, but I did it to survive. And the way that you were killing those soldiers, it wasn't survival and it was unnatural," Khalon said, anger building in his chest. Rhea looked like she was going to say something and then shook her head, slightly. She took a deep breath and then faced Khalon, fire burning in her eyes.

"I made everyone start to die around us because that's what I do. That's who I *am*, Khalon. I *am* Death. I'm the one you see for your last judgment when you die," she said, taking her finger and poking Khalon with it, angrily. She looked up at him, her eyes expressing the betrayal she felt.

"And I did it for you, you know." Khalon shook his head, scoffing at her words.

"If you believe that you made nearly a whole army die for

me, then you're sorely mistaken, your *holiness*," Khalon whispered as he leaned down to her eye level.

"No, you're just—" she started to protest.

"You almost made them die for your own *pride*," he whispered. He felt her shake from anger as he straightened back up. "And you saved me for your pride as well. You couldn't have my father having more power over me than you."

"*That's* how you think of me," she whispered, her face contorted into an expression Khalon had never seen before.

"I *know* that's how you are," he said, "That's how *all* you Gods are." Rhea turned to walk away but then she turned back, glaring up at him.

"Maybe I *did* try to kill a whole army because my pride was bruised. King Vien was being highly disrespectful and fear is a powerful tool, Khalon," she admitted. "But saving you? I have been wracking my brain for the past few days trying to figure out how to not accept you as a sacrifice but also let you live. I *wanted* you to live and not in a prison of my own making. Saving you to one up King Vien was *not* my goal, though an added bonus, it was not due to my pride. It was due to—" She choked on her words, tears starting to form in her eyes. Khalon's face slightly softened.

"Yes, Gods are prideful. We demand respect. But we are also feared, for a very good reason," she said, softly. "At least you realized that today. I'm not an ordinary girl, Khalon. I'm not a girl at all, though I might look it. I am a God. And if you were scared of me today, then that's because you finally saw me for what I truly am."

"You're not a sadistic creature that revels in death, Rhea," Khalon started to argue but the look in Rhea's eyes back in the tent made him stop. She *did* enjoy it, toying with the king; holding his death and his secret over his head. Maybe what

Rhea said was right. Maybe he hadn't truly seen her until that day.

Rhea searched his eyes, waiting for him to continue. When she realized that he wasn't going to, she pulled the makeshift hair band out of her hair, opting to tuck the copper locks behind her elven ears instead.

"You're free to go and do whatever it is that you want to do, Khalon," Rhea said. Khalon stared at her. Her face was expressionless. The same face that she gave to those who looked at her in horror. Khalon wondered if that was the expression that adorned his face now.

"I don't know what to do," he whispered. Rhea shrugged.

"That's the freedom of choice, I guess," she said, her voice without any of it's usual upbeat tone. It was just as icy as her face. She stared at Khalon for a moment longer, her eyes softening for a moment, before disappearing into the shadows.

"Rhea," he breathed as the last of her faded away. He stared at the empty space that Rhea was standing in before. Groaning, he put his hands on his head and squatted down so that he was close to the ground. Closing his eyes, he cursed himself for even starting that argument.

"Why are you so terrible with words?" he asked himself, replaying the conversation in his head. It wasn't that she humiliated him. He didn't really know how he felt about the whole situation. But he saw her face, how her skin had started to suddenly come alive as she sucked the life out of the others around her. He remembered how her eyes twinkled when she was holding his father's life in her hands, toying with him and his cup of blood. Those things made him feel scared, terrified even. It was a side of her that he had yet to see. And he kept remembering the voices that he heard in his dreams. It sounded exactly like...

No, it wasn't that she humiliated him. It was that she

scared him. And he foolishly never thought that she would. She was right. This whole time he had been seeing her as just another girl, when in reality she was a God that has been walking around on this world since the moment it was created. She was past, present, and future. And he was just a draconian.

He picked himself up off the ground after a while and went to look for transportation. Despite Rhea saying he had the benefit of still staying in Draconia, he knew that he did not. His father, despite Rhea's threats, wouldn't let him live. And even if he did, he knew his brother Khai wouldn't as well. He had heard the rumors of those rallying for him to become King of Draconia someday, threatening his half brother's position. And now that he knew he truly had the spirit of the dragon within him, he just couldn't stay and risk the life that Rhea had given him. Why would he want to stay in a place that held only bad memories anyways? No, he wouldn't stay in Draconia.

There were some answers that he wanted to seek out for himself and for other reasons, which he was unable to admit were about Rhea. He had been having dreams where this voice that sounded like a thousand voices was talking to another about the deaths of Gods. And every time he had awoken in the middle of the night, Rhea was gone and in the morning, it was like she never left, sleeping as peacefully as can be. He needed to know if they were connected and the Seer was the only one who could provide him answers. Apparently, she was in Ustrina, a country near Draconia. Khalon resolved to walk to the nearest hover train station, deciding to take the journey to Ustrina.

————

Ustrina was a country very different from Draconia. Khalon watched as the city of Invenire blurred past him. He was able to get onto a hover train by using the jewels that he stole from the dragon eyes that were embedded in the stone street in Furvus. Invenire was filled with buildings made from clay and stone. Ustrina was a country composed mainly of deserts, with some rainforests in various areas. The capital, however, was in the middle of a desert. Surrounding the large city were tall walls protecting it from sandstorms and enemies. Unlike Draconia that refused to have hover cars whipping about within the capital city, opting for other ways to travel like biking or a scooter, Ustrina had many hover cars, covered in sand, whipping about the air field. Khalon got off of the train, taking in the new sights. He had never been to Ustrina before. It was breathtaking, Khalon felt. It really was a whole new world to him. He noticed curiously that many of the women wore loose scarves around their heads and the people in general wore light airy clothing on their bodies to combat the heat of the sun.

Though, for some, the heat didn't matter much to the citizens living there. Many of the creatures of Ustrina had descended from creatures like the dragon who went into hiding. There was the Inkanyamba clan that still survived within the walls of Invenire, though the Phoenix clan had run most of them out into the rainforests of the land. The other creatures were witches. Many witches were born or had moved to Ustrina due to the great magic of the land, so they said, which Khalon could now confirm the rumors with his own body. He could feel the magic radiating off of the ground and into his body, energizing him.

He looked around in wonder for a moment longer. Then, he reminded himself the reason as to why he was here. The Seer. Khalon surveyed his surroundings to ask for directions to see the reincarnated clairvoyant.

"Excuse me," he asked a witch, stopping her on her walk. She looked up at him annoyed.

"Do you know how to get to the Seer?" he asked. She scoffed at him, walking around him.

"You can't just go and see the Seer," she said, "You have to request her." Khalon walked alongside her, keeping up with her long strides.

"How do you request to see her?" he asked.

"You have to go to the palace and request her," she said, matter-of-fact as if everyone knew this.

"The Seer lives in the palace?" he asked, his heart sinking. She smirked at his facial expression, probably finding his ignorance amusing.

"Anyone can see the Seer, draconian," she said, "But, she has a long waiting list. If you're patient, you might be able to see her in a month's time." Waving goodbye, she continued on her way. Khalon sighed. He didn't have a month. He needed to know about the Mortiferis, but more importantly, about who was behind them.

Putting his hand over his eyes, he gazed up at the Ustrinian palace. It was made of light brown clay and had jade domed roofs adorning it. He ran to catch up to the witch.

"Why is the Seer in the palace? Does she advise the King of Ustrina or something?" Khalon asked. The witch smirked a little, her eyes twinkling.

"The Queen of Witches reincarnated herself into the youngest daughter of King Tafari, Princess Esi," the witch responded. She twinkled her fingers as Khalon stopped in his tracks, the airy clothes of hers flowing behind her. Princess Esi, Khalon thought. He had heard the rumors about her. She was born to a concubine, a human, of all creatures. It continued with his theory that the Gods and other spirits were being reincarnated into human mixed or human bodies. But that wasn't the only part of the rumor that had made it cross borders. While many kings took on concubines, it was almost unheard of to have a child with one. Every king has a witch that assists them and one of the many duties that a witch has is to make sure that a child is never created with a concubine. Khalon was one that wasn't immediately destroyed in the womb. Princess Esi was another. The other curious thing about Esi's conception is that immediately after she was born, King Tafari ordered her mother to be killed. It was a rumor that definitely made Khalon's ears itch when he heard it being told to another in the Ring.

He looked up at the palace and started towards it. Waiting list or not, he knew what would make the Seer want to see him immediately. They had a shared story, a similar past. And just as he was curious about her, he was sure that she was probably equally as curious about him.

22

Freya paced in front of her temple. The Love God's temple was adorned with roses, growing up the side of it. She stopped, standing with her hands on her hips as she watched her temple servants flitting about, tending to the vast garden that spread in front of it.

"So the election is coming up in the next month or so," she said, after much thought to the temple servant next to her. Dela was the temple servant that Freya liked the most. She was a fairy, like most of Freya's temple servants, but she didn't put on any airs for Freya, just because she was a God. Dela didn't care one way or another what Freya was and always kept Freya in check which she appreciated. Dela nodded her head.

"Yes, and they want you to," she checked her clipboard, "to sponsor a candidate that you like the most at the next debate." Freya groaned.

"Is it because I'm the only major God in Sylva?" Freya asked, looking down at Dela. Dela was short, like all fairies. Freya couldn't help but wish she didn't have human genes within her soul's body. She always felt like a giant walking around all these fairies. Sighing, she pulled her freshly braided hair into a ponytail.

"Honestly, couldn't Ganesha do it? She *is* the God of Knowledge and what not. Wouldn't her opinion matter more than mine?" Freya asked, sauntering back over to her chair. Her temple chair was huge, much bigger than she was, which was a common characteristic of the chairs in all the Gods' temples. It was made of rose quartz and was shaped in a giant heart. She felt that it was cheesy and a bit of an eye sore, but there wasn't much one could do about a chair that was made hundreds of years ago.

"Well, the people of Sylva mostly pray to you, Freya, not to Ganesha. It makes more sense to want your support rather than your brother's," Dela said, following Freya to her chair. She stood idly next to it, looking even smaller. "And since you are much older than the last election, they want your sponsorship now as it will mean more." Dela guessed Freya's next comment. Freya slumped down in her chair.

"*Fine*," she said, putting out her hand, "Give me the list of candidates." Dela gave Freya the clipboard and Freya looked down the list. She paused as she saw one name.

"That dwarf Martin Flintcoat is running for President of Sylva?" she asked, looking at Dela in disbelief. Dela merely shrugged and then nodded. Freya frowned.

"Isn't he the one who—"

"He's an elf apologist, your holiness," Dela finished. Freya's frown deepened. She noticed that there was a growing collective that was for the old ways of medieval times.

"Does he have a good chance at winning?" Freya asked after a long moment of silence.

"He has a thirty percent approval rating."

"The people of *Sylva* of all places want an *elf* apologist to be President? Don't they understand the ramifications if that were to happen?" Freya asked. Dela shrugged again. Freya made a little sound of annoyance as she flipped through the other candidates. She would have to be dead before she dared to see the elves take over Asynithis once more. It was bad when the humans made the magical creatures go into hiding, but it was a much worse time when elves ruled over the world. And, in Freya's opinion, the elves hadn't changed all that much in their way of thinking.

"Also, your brother is wandering around different small towns of Sylva asking about a human girl," Dela said after a long silence of Freya flipping through pages. Freya rolled her eyes.

"Which brother? My brothers do a lot of things involving all kinds of creatures. I don't really need to hear about it unless it concerns one of my temple servants," Freya said, waving Dela away. Dela remained put. She tucked her straight black hair behind her little ears.

"It's Poseidon, your holiness. And he's asking about a girl who might know how to kill the Gods," Dela continued. Freya looked over at Dela, curious.

"Well, if he's wondering about who might know how to kill Gods, he probably should ask our other brother that he insists on traveling around with," Freya muttered, looking back at the clipboard in her hands.

"I hope you're not talking about Tezcatlipoca, himself," a lazy voice erupted from beside Freya. She looked over in shock at the wet Poseidon standing next to her. He hit the side of his head, trying to get water out of his ear. The curls on the top of his head glistened from the water beads clinging to it. He was traveling through water again and Freya couldn't help but feel a pang of jealousy at the extra power that he had over her.

"You *don't* suspect Rhea is behind it?" Freya asked, leaning on the armrest of her chair as she looked down at Poseidon. He shrugged.

"If you're saying that because of what Ganesha said, shouldn't you also be suspecting our brother of this terrible deed as well, since she seems pretty knowledgeable about the Mortiferis in the first place," Poseidon countered. Freya shifted in her seat. He had a point but she wasn't about to let him know that.

"Ganesha is the God of Knowledge. I'd be surprised if she didn't know," she bristled. Poseidon chuckled slightly.

"What are you doing in Sylva anyways? A human girl has something to do with the God killer?" Poseidon laughed a little at her nickname for the murderer.

"Yeah," he said after a while, "Manungal had to carry out a promise for the Draconian King and brought along her draconian temple servant. And I had said I would investigate the girl who tried to kill them with a Mortiferis tooth." Freya's eyes widened as she stood up from her chair. She beckoned Poseidon to follow her and motioned for Dela not to. They walked quietly into the maze that was her garden.

"Do you have the tooth?" she asked. Poseidon shook his head.

"No," he said. She looked at him sharply as he took a step back from her gaze.

"Don't tell me you let Rhea take it."

"What if I did?" he asked, indignant. Freya sighed.

"Don't be surprised if the tooth ends up going missing," she merely said. Poseidon gave her a quizzical look and then sighed himself.

"Freya," he blew, "I *really* don't think that Morana is behind this." But Freya noticed his tone seemed off. She glanced at him, knowingly.

"Rhea's body's soul probably isn't. But our brother?" Freya raised her eyebrows as they turned a corner in the maze.

"If Arawn truly is behind this, as you think, then why would she order the human to attack her temple servant?" Freya pondered on it and shrugged.

"I'm not sure, Poseidon, but I will say that I don't trust our brother. He's always been an angry soul. Him reincarnating after so many years is curious to say the least." Poseidon nodded along with what Freya was saying. She could tell that he agreed with her, but she also knew that the Sea God always had a soft spot for the God of Death.

"She cares about the temple servant," Poseidon said after a while. "Even if it *is* the God of Death's soul controlling what is happening, she wouldn't order anyone to try and kill him." Freya looked at him for a while, surprised at this information.

"When you say she cares..." Poseidon nodded.

"It's very tangible. You'll be able to see it all over the draconian when you meet him," he muttered.

"But our brother never... not after—"

"I know," Poseidon interrupted. Freya stared at him in shock for a moment, but then promptly composed herself. She didn't think the God of Death had a love bone anywhere in the depths of his soul after what had happened.

"*By* the way," Poseidon said looking around the garden, "Do you only accept fairies as temple servants these days or...?" Freya could feel herself get a headache from her brother.

"Tree nymphs don't like to leave their trees, water nymphs don't like to leave their bodies of water, and dwarves could really care less about me. Fairies are practically my children and I love being around them. Ugh, I don't know why I didn't choose a fully fairy body this time around," Freya groaned looking down at herself. She just felt too tall, though less tall standing next to Poseidon's human body.

"You know why. Because of the state that Asynithis is going through, we have to make a statement," Poseidon said. Freya knew he was right. Picking humans showed the magical creatures that the Gods didn't agree with how they were running things, that the Gods could give the world back to the humans if they so chose to. Poseidon paused.

"Only female fairies though?" He raised an eyebrow.

"You know that men go crazy in my presence when I am in a woman's body. It would just be annoying to have male fairies here all the time," Freya said, dismissing Poseidon's questions.

"Wouldn't female fairies also act the same way?" Poseidon pointed out. Freya sighed, dramatically.

"Yes, of course. But, women are better at hiding it in my presence than men are." Poseidon sucked on his teeth as he looked around.

"That's too bad," he said. "Male fairies are *so much* better to look at." Freya rolled her eyes, perking up a bit at the sight of Dela walking towards her so that she could leave this conversation.

"Yes, Dela?" she asked, meeting Dela in her path.

"The Prince of Aureum is here," she said, pointing back at the temple. "He's waiting for you." Poseidon chuckled.

"Speaking of men who go crazy in your presence," he said under his breath. Freya looked visibly annoyed as she smacked Poseidon's arm. She walked back to her temple, already knowing which Prince of Aureum it was going to be. *Those damn elves...*

Standing on the steps of her temple stood Prince Elion. His white wavy hair was pulled back into a ponytail, showing his pointed ears, and he was wearing elven armor. He looked back at her, his blue eyes lighting up at the sight of her. She had to admit that he looked quite handsome standing there in that uniform. She walked past him as Poseidon stayed back, leaning against a limestone column.

"To what do I owe this pleasure?" Freya said, gingerly sitting on the edge of her tacky chair.

"Your holiness," Elion said, bowing deeply. He looked like a puppy eager for some praise. Freya held up a hand.

"Freya, please," she said, smiling. Why was he here? And how long did she have to look at that elven face for? She felt her finger start to tap the edge of her seat.

"Freya," he said shyly, "I have something important I need to tell you." Freya looked at him as Poseidon watched, amused.

"Well? Out with it," she said, impatiently. Elion's eyes glanced around warily.

"The Gods are being killed, permanently," he whispered. Freya stared at him for a long while, annoyance clouding her face.

"Yes," she said after a while, "Yes, we're aware." Elion looked surprised that she already knew and looked over at Poseidon who was also nodding. She wasn't sure if Elion was even aware that it was the Sea God standing next to him.

"Is that it?" she asked. Elion shook his head, nervously wringing out his hands. She leaned forward slightly. He was way too nervous for someone who had just heard about the Gods being killed.

"My—my brother," he stammered. He took a deep breath as he stared into Freya's eyes. She saw him melt at her gaze and for some reason, whatever look she had pointed in his direction gave him some kind of newly found confidence.

"My brother is conspiring with a shadowy figure to kill them all. My brother is behind it," he said. After a while, he clarified, "Adamar, the new King of Aureum." Freya and Poseidon shared a shocked glance.

23

Khalon thought that Princess Esi would want to see him right away because of their shared background. He couldn't be more wrong, to no one's surprise but his own.

Khalon looked up at the palace as he walked backwards from the side door that was just slammed in his face. He wasn't one to use his status in order to get into places, mostly because he never had the chance to. But the minute the opportunity presented itself, he stupidly said, "Hi, I'm Prince Khalon of Draconia," as the guard laughed in his face and then shut the door, nearly hitting his nose. *I guess being a bastard prince isn't worth much here either,* Khalon thought. He stared at the door for a long period of time, an idea forming in his head. He remembered what Poseidon said when he first met him in the flames of hellfire, *"The Seer is spouting off some nonsense."* Khalon's eyes lit up. *That's right,* he thought, *the Seer would know about what is happening to the Gods.* Maybe, if anything, she'd want to figure out how Khalon knew what was happening. The Seer wasn't like An. She didn't know everything besides the visions that she would get. Curiously, Khalon wondered if the dreams he had been having the past few days were similar to the visions the Seer has. With newfound confidence, Khalon walked up to the door that was just slammed in his face. Knocking on it, the large door opened to reveal the guards that had just laughed at him.

"Back again, draconian?" one guard said, his face hiding a smile. Khalon felt his ears turn red.

"Please tell the Seer—"

"Like I said," the guard stepped forward, making Khalon step back slightly. It wasn't that Khalon was afraid of the guard, it was more that he valued his own personal space. "If you want to see her highness, you must sign up like everyone else. Princess Esi doesn't discriminate."

"Just please tell the Seer that it has to do with the Mortiferis," Khalon finished, his eyes pleading with the guard. The guard stared at him, confusion clouding his face.

"You mean the bedtime story? It's about the bedtime story?" he asked, looking at the other guard. The guard next to him shrugged his giant shoulders.

"I've never heard of it."

"You've never heard about the bedtime story with the Mortiferis monsters??" the guard asked in disbelief.

"You're old, you know," the other guard retorted.

"Old??? Why I—"

"Please just tell her. I promise you that she'll want to meet with me," Khalon interrupted, straightening up a bit. The first guard stared at Khalon, stroking his white curly beard. His dark hand contrasted the whiteness of his hair. It was almost as white as an elf's, thought Khalon but he could smell that the guard was not mixed with elf whatsoever. He was a descendant of the Phoenix.

"Fine," the guard finally said, "Wait here." He shut the door again in Khalon's face, though a lot softer this time and without the echo of his laughter ringing in Khalon's ears. Khalon stared up at the palace once again, hoping that the Seer would see him. After a few minutes, the door opened. Instead of the guard, stood a young girl, a little younger than Khalon, with curly black hair that fell in ringlets around her face. Her eyes were white as if the color of her irises were sucked out of her. She stared in Khalon's general direction.

"The Prince of Draconia?" she asked, her voice smaller than Khalon expected. Her eyes surveyed the area in front of her. Khalon's eyes widened. The Seer was blind.

"Yes, I'm here," Khalon said, quickly, mentally kicking himself for referring to himself as the Prince of Draconia. *How embarrassing to be addressed like that.* She stared at his chest, hearing his voice. The veins underneath her brown skin glistened red, the sign of a royal Phoenix. Other Phoenixes looked like the guard that was standing in front of him. They looked curiously like humans, but they still had the ability to regenerate and heal. The Phoenixes that had the royal family blood coursing through them retained all the abilities of the creature of old. They can regenerate themselves, fly, and use the fire that made their blood glow to heal others or destroy.

"Please," Esi said, "Follow me." Khalon ducked his head as he entered the side of the palace. The tunnel that she led him down was dark, with almost no light showing the pathway. There were dim electric lights on the sides of the stone wall and the glow of her veins also lit up the path in red, but Khalon's eyes weren't adjusting to the darkness enough, almost tripping over his own feet. She paused and gave him a warning of caution before continuing down their path. Eventually, the tunnel opened up revealing a room barely lit with a crystal ball on a table in front of them. She beckoned Khalon forward, making her way to the chair in front of the table.

"Is the crystal ball for show or do you actually use it for visions?" Khalon asked, gesturing to the ornament. Esi smiled slightly.

"Humans adore it," she said, "I can't bring myself to tell them the truth." Her white eyes were unnerving to look at as they somehow made eye contact with his.

"You said that you had questions regarding the Mortiferis," she said softly, her fingers tracing something on the table.

"Yes," Khalon said nervously. She paused her tracing, waiting for him to go on.

"What are you doing anyways?" he stalled, pointing at her fingers. She looked confused and then Khalon remembered that she couldn't see what he was talking about.

"Sorry," he said, "I mean with your hands."

"Oh," she said, looking down, "I trace what I see. It helps me calm myself."

"Oh," he responded. She smiled again at his general direction.

"The Mortiferis?" she asked. Khalon clenched his jaw and then relaxed it.

"I think I'm connected to them, somehow," he said slowly. She stared at him, shock filling her face.

"Go on," she said, gesturing towards him.

"For the past few days, I've been having dreams. I see this elf with long white hair and he cowers in fear from me, even though he tries to hide it. I've seen things that have already passed. I saw, I think, Belenus die. Wither away into nothing. I saw myself being attacked. I have had dreams of Poseidon and murdering all of his temple servants. It's not like I'm watching someone else do these things, *I* am the one doing it." Khalon remembered his dreams, trying to keep himself from shaking.

"When I wake up from my dreams, Rhea, the God of Death, she's gone," Khalon whispered. "She disappears at night. I don't know where she goes and she doesn't remember where she disappears to either. I thought maybe that... I don't know." Esi stared at him, processing his words.

"There's another thing," he said. Her white eyes were focused on him. "In my dreams, I hear a thousand voices coming out of my mouth, at one time. And... I've heard that same voice coming from Rhea. Just once, but it...terrified me."

"You do not have witch's blood within you," she more said than asked. Khalon shook his head and barely uttered the word "No."

"I don't understand why you are able to see visions that only I can," she said slowly. She nodded her head, as if confirming something to herself.

"I have the same visions, though more fractured than yours. And I can see them before they have happened," she said, taking a shaky breath. "It sounds like you have been traveling with her a lot recently. You are connected to her and her doings. I have seen her fate as well." She closed her white eyes, sitting extremely still. Khalon held his breath. Her doings...

"You think she's behind the Mortiferis," Khalon said quietly, not wanting to believe it. Esi shrugged.

"I am not one to talk in riddles, as I think the future of Asynithis is in peril," she said. She looked slightly scared.

"The Mortiferis are going to take over," she said, "Unless the Saviors come from Earth." Her white eyes looked into Khalon's once more.

"Earth?" he asked. She stared at him.

"Be careful about Rhea," she said, "She will either save you or destroy us all."

"Could she save everyone? Save Asynithis?" Esi shook her head, staring now at the crystal ball, probably out of habit.

"She will save you, if she can, but she cannot undo what has already been done."

"What can I do?" Khalon asked, his voice breaking slightly. Esi smiled sadly at him.

"This is Rhea's journey," she whispered, "Only she can go against the God of Death."

24

Rhea woke up in a cold sweat. She was staying in the home of a creature that she just took the soul of. He was an old man and was pushing past his time. Luckily, he had lived a good life and was greeted with the face of his loved one that had passed earlier. It was a peaceful transition and not one marred by horror. Rhea was sick of people looking at her in horror. Even the person who could truly see her face had given her that look... She shook Khalon's face out of her mind.

Wiping the sweat from her forehead, she tried to remember her dream. Rhea didn't normally dream as the God of Death's soul kept her from doing so. But, recently she had been having dreams. The other dream she had the other night was of Khalon, a dream of insecurity. And just now, she had the feeling that she had a dream before she woke up, but a dream that she couldn't recall. The only thing that she could remember was Ganesha. And Ganesha's face was marred with a different kind of horror. A desperate and terrified look of horror before... She shuddered. The face that she was remembering was one of agony and then slowly morphing into one with the blood of a God. Silver. Silver blood dripping down Ganesha's face. Rhea sat up in the dead man's bed, putting her head in her hands.

She didn't even know how she had gotten into the man's bed in the first place. The last thing she remembered was taking his soul down into the underworld. Retracing her steps, she remembered that Francine had given her an update about how the underworld's progress had been going since Rhea left to the surface. Rhea recalled that this was the longest she had gone without doing her duties and that was as far as she could remember. Struggling to get out of bed, she instinctively reached into her pocket for the Mortiferis tooth that she had kept hidden there. Her hand felt around, finding nothing. Her eyes widened as she continued to feel around and eventually turned the pocket inside out. The tooth was gone. Her heart dropped. *No, it can't be...* she thought to herself. It was impossible. There was no way. But the sleepless nights, the reaper's cloak, the...dream... *No, it was just a nightmare. Ganesha is fine.*

Rhea stood up and opened up the door to the underworld, the ground shaking as she did. She hurried down the steps, the torches lighting up as she walked down them. The underworld was just as she had left it. It was busy, with reapers rushing through, either holding souls in their containers or leaving to go up onto the surface. Rhea ran towards the room with the strings of fate, opening the door to a surprised Francine, Farrah, and Felicity. Felicity's face frowned as she looked at Rhea's face, guessing at what Rhea was feeling. She rushed over, dropping her scissors as Farrah picked them up to cover for her.

"Rhea, sweetie, what's wrong?" she asked, putting an arm around her. Rhea felt her face contort, a lump appearing in her throat. She swallowed it the best that she could.

"Felicity, was I acting weird earlier?" she asked, searching Felicity's green eyes. Felicity frowned, staring at her.

"What do you mean?" she asked. Rhea stared over at Francine.

"Francine," she pleaded. Francine looked up in thought.

"You were a little odd, I guess. You just got quiet and said you had to go. I just figured you had to meet Poseidon as you were talking about that earlier," Francine said.

"No, but did I sound like—Did I sound like... *him*?" Rhea asked, almost whispering. Francine and Farrah shared a look as Felicity made Rhea sit down in a corner.

"Are you talking about the God of Death?" Farrah asked, a lock of blonde hair falling into her face. She took a pin out of her pocket and pinned it back. Rhea hesitantly nodded. *It couldn't be...*

"When he talks through you, he sounds just like you," Felicity said, her eyebrows furrowed. "It's hard to tell when he *is* talking if he's determined to keep it a secret."

"But you *can* tell," Rhea pointed out. They were able to tell when she was younger. When Rhea was around five years old, the God of Death's soul kept trying to integrate with hers. It wasn't abnormal. All other Gods lived with their body's souls in perfect harmony. They weren't exactly one, but their thoughts and memories were all intertwined, for the most part. If Rhea wanted to tap into the God of Death's memory, it was incredibly draining to do so and she still wasn't sure that she could access it all, even if she wanted to. On top of that, she had never heard the God of Death's thoughts, unless he was trying to take control of something within her body, for example, her mouth. He was always watching through her mind, but she was never able to converse with him and when she tried to, there was a giant wall that was impossible to get through. But, during the time where the God of Death was seemingly trying to integrate with her, she kept blacking out. Big chunks of her memory were missing. She remembered sixteen-year-old Felicity realizing what was happening to her. Rhea remembered Felicity telling Francine, "He doesn't want to integrate with her. He just wants her gone."

"We can tell sometimes, yeah," Francine answered Rhea. Her natural hair was out, framing her face. "But, we were only really able to tell during that time because you were telling us you didn't remember doing something that you did. And you did that a lot. That's how we were able to figure it out. Not really because he was acting differently."

"Why are you asking us about this, Rhea?" Farrah asked. "You haven't told us that you've been blacking out."

"I—I had a weird dream," Rhea said. The Fates gave each other another look.

"I *know* I don't dream," Rhea answered hastily before they could ask the obvious question. "But, I think I had a dream, or a nightmare. And I also don't remember leaving the underworld. I woke up in the bed of a person I just took the soul of."

"It's possible that if he is taking over that he might have been doing it while you yourself thought you were asleep," Farrah mused. Francine nodded, but the eyes that glanced at Felicity looked scared.

"And if you've become aware of the possibility, then you might've been slightly conscious while he took over recently," Francine paused, "*If* he's been taking over."

"Why is it that our souls don't integrate, like other Gods?" Rhea asked. She had asked them this before, after learning about the integration. But they hadn't really given her a clear answer then either. The Fates exchanged looks once again.

"I'm old enough that I think I should know the whole story," Rhea said. Felicity rubbed Rhea's shoulders.

"The God of Death has only reincarnated a handful of

times over the past millennium. The first time was when all the Celestials first came to Asynithis, physically. Before the War happened, Asynithis was a bit of a godless world. Humans were their own Gods and had no care to what happened to Asynithis, whether they destroyed it or not. The Gods woke the magical creatures up from their long hidden sleep in order to bring Asynithis back to the glory it once was. And one of the ways that they did that, in order to spread their message, was by putting their own selves into the bodies of humans. They found that integrating the two souls was the best course of action, as it still kept the body's human emotions with the memories that the Gods had. The God of Death also did this, but because he *is* death, he was slowly killing his host," Felicity said, her eyes glassy as she remembered a past that her own soul went through.

"He fell in love with another human girl, during the War," Farrah took over. "The War was just starting and humans wanted to use the Gods against the magical creatures that were trying to take back their home. They were desperate, of course. And they used their machines to torture the Gods into using their powers to help them. It was a horrible situation. The God of Death wasn't someone that they could easily control, due to the nature of his power. They couldn't use their machines to get him to kill millions of people. That's just not how that works, you see. So," Farrah shuddered from the memory.

"They tortured her instead. The girl that he had fallen in love with," Francine said, her jaw clenched tight. A face flashed across Rhea's mind. A crooked smile and chocolate brown eyes. Eyes like Khalon's. Her curly brown hair fell into her face as the light set her aglow. Rhea's chest started to hurt and she rubbed it for a little.

"Yes," Rhea breathed, "I remember her." Francine looked

concerned as she gave another look to Farrah. Felicity just kept rubbing Rhea's back.

"But the God of Death cannot love," Rhea choked out, feeling the pain of her past. Felicity shook her head.

"No, he can. He just chose not to. Not after what happened to Tallulah. She was the first creature he ever loved, and will probably be the last," Felicity said. Rhea knew that she was not the last.

"We all know what happened after that," Farrah said. Rhea knew the story. The first God of Death cried tears of blood for days, creating the pond that was out by her temple. And then he finished the War for the magical creatures, against the word of the God of All. Billions of humans died. They were almost extinct if it weren't for the God of All stepping in. She knew that much of her past. Memories of Tallulah screaming out in pain flashed through her memory. Her blood was everywhere, clouding her vision with red. Rhea's eyes felt hot as she stared at the Fates. They were watching her, as if waiting for something.

"Morrigan was the first name that I went by," Rhea stated, remembering. Farrah nodded, but her face contorted into concern.

"I didn't love anyone else but her," Rhea said, unable to figure out how she could've forgotten Tallulah. Her hand in hers, walking along the river. Whenever she was with her, the whole world was brighter. She felt like she could do anything.

"Even human myths knew that the God of Death didn't love others that often," Felicity nodded. "Since then, when the God of Death would reincarnate, he would kill the host body's soul. It would be just him. And that's dangerous within Asynithis because a God just being a God is terrifying, Rhea. They do not have emotions like we do. And it's possible that the God of Death wouldn't have even loved

Tallulah if it wasn't for the human soul that he had within her—"

"How could you say that?" Rhea erupted, standing up to face Felicity. Felicity cowered from Rhea's anger as fire flashed in her eyes. "How could you say that I wasn't in love with her?" Rhea couldn't control what was coming out of her mouth. She knew who was speaking through her.

"Your holiness," Francine barely uttered. Rhea's eyes glared at her.

"You *belong* to me. The only reason that you three reincarnate is *because* of me, do you understand? You would not have creature bodies if it weren't for me," Rhea boomed. The three Fates bowed their heads.

"We didn't mean to offend," Farrah apologized.

"Offend? You dared to utter her name and then tell me to my face that I didn't love her. That it was my host soul's feelings and not mine. You do not understand what a God feels," Rhea hissed. The Fates stayed quiet.

"This time," Rhea growled, "You won't be able to stop me." The anger started to slowly melt away as Rhea put a hand to her head. Felicity caught her and lowered her back onto the chair.

"I'm sorry," Rhea gasped, "He kind of just came out."

"It wasn't right for us to talk about her. She's a sore subject," Farrah muttered. Francine frowned.

"It's odd that he was so close by though. He normally is dormant," Francine said. "Lately, I've noticed that he is not."

"Could what happened before be happening again?" asked Felicity, her tone going slightly higher than normal.

"She hasn't been killing humans," Farrah pointed out. "It's not the same as what happened last time."

"Unless it isn't humans that he's angry with anymore," Rhea said, quietly. The Fates stared at her.

"What do you mean Rhea?" they asked in unison. Surprised by speaking at the same time, they stared at each other and smiled slightly at the coincidence.

"The God of Death has only reincarnated a handful of times. And he only reincarnates to get his own agenda done, right? At least, that's what it seems like. And I think..." Rhea took a deep breath, "I think he's been angry with the other Gods." They stared at her in disbelief.

"You think you're the God killer," Francine realized, sitting down next to the table where the strings were being pulled and then cut by the scissors floating. Rhea nodded.

"Why would he be trying to kill the Gods?" Felicity said, obviously not believing what Rhea was saying.

"He's been angry around them," Rhea said, "I can feel it. I argue with Poseidon a lot more than I usually do. I just feel irritated by him. I feel irritated by Freya and all the other Gods as well. Those meetings are *torture*, and I used to think maybe it was just An but I think it's all of them."

"Rhea, I don't think you're killing the Gods. That doesn't make sense to me. The God of Death is vengeful, for sure, but he wouldn't kill the Gods just because of the death of her," Farrah scoffed.

"I don't think this is about Tallulah," Rhea muttered. She wasn't sure exactly what it was about. But she had a sinking feeling that at night, she was at least planning the murders. She had a sneaking suspicion since the night that Khalon fought that assassin and she found the reaper's cloak.

"An is here," Farrah muttered, her eyes looking glassy. Rhea grabbed onto Felicity's hands before she got up.

"Please tell me that you guys can do what you did when I was five. Please tell me you can put him to sleep again," Rhea whispered. Felicity's face contorted into an unrecognizable facial expression.

"Rhea," she said, "I don't know if we'll be able to do that again. His soul gets stronger the longer you live. When you were younger, it was easier, but now, I'm not sure." Her voice drifted off as the door opened. Standing there was An. His shaggy black hair fell into his eyes and he blew them out of his face. Rhea had a sinking feeling in her chest.

"I need to see the strings," An said, walking towards Rhea. Rhea stood up and hesitantly walked over to the cabinet that held the golden strings. Inside, another string was cut and had turned white. Ganesha's face covered in silver blood flickered through Rhea's mind. She closed her eyes.

"It has happened again," An said to her but she could barely hear him. "It was Ganesha." Rhea felt her legs give out from underneath her.

25

Essarae screamed as her legs were held back by the servants. Her white hair stuck to her sweaty heart-shaped, tan face. Adamar, the King of Aureum, backed away from the crack in the door of Essarae's bed chambers, and continued nervously pacing. Edwyrd clapped a giant hand onto Adamar's shoulder as he looked up at him.

"It'll be fine, brother," Edwyrd said, giving him a toothy smile. "The first of us to have a child. It's exciting." Adamar stared at Edwyrd, knowing what he had done to his unborn child. He gulped down the unexpected guilt that came on and then nodded, smiling nervously.

"We are all looking forward to meeting your son, the future King of Aureum," Ardryll said, his face blank. Though, Adamar thought, Ardryll's face always had a lack of emotion in it, unless Lord Crispin was around.

Hours after it began, the screams subsided and the door opened slightly. The servant looked nervous, as she stuck only her head out of the doorway.

"Your highness," she said, her voice shaking. She knew, as all the other servants did, the nature of Adamar. She also knew her position when it came to him. She was human, he was an elf. And elves didn't care for humans or any other creature for that matter. And Adamar especially despised any creature that wasn't an elf.

"What is it?" Adamar said, trying to keep his voice even. *Was it...?* "Please tell me Essarae is—"

"No, no," the servant interrupted, "The queen is perfectly fine. But it's... Please come inside, your highness." She opened the door a little bit more, and Adamar could feel his brothers, well the two that were around anyways as Elion had mysteriously disappeared, try to peer into the bedchamber. Adamar slipped through the doorway and promptly closed the door, Edwyrd giving him a thumbs up before it shut. The servant, whose blonde hair was tied into a complicated single braid down her back, nervously led him to the bed where Essarae was lying, smiling at him. She was holding the baby. Their son. The future king.

"Your highness," the servant said, stepping in front of his view of his baby.

"What's wrong?" he asked, irritated. "Everything looks perfectly fine." Her eyes nervously looked up as she tried to think.

"The baby... I don't think the baby is an elf," she whispered, her eyes looking frantic. "Or at least, it's not a *full* elf." A cold chill went through Adamar's body. *That damn Love God...*

"What?" he asked after a while.

"The baby... he doesn't look like—"

"Let me see him for myself," Adamar said, pushing the servant to the side. The birth-witch stood over Essarae and the baby, wiping something off of his face.

"Oh Adamar," Essarae said, her eyes glazed over, "Isn't he

absolutely beautiful?" She sat up a little more as Adamar stared at the child in shock. In all ways, the baby looked like an elf. His ears were pointed and he had delicate features that resembled his mother and father. But, his hair was incredibly black, not the brilliant white of an elf's. Adamar felt his body freeze.

"His hair," he whispered. Essarae put a couple of fingers through it.

"It's so thick, isn't it? Much like my mother's hair," she said, her voice in almost a dreamlike state.

"Essarae," he said, sitting down on the bed next to her. She looked at him, but he didn't really feel that she was really seeing him.

"Essarae, do you see what is wrong with our baby?" he asked. Essarae frowned, looking back down at their child.

"What ever do you mean, Adamar?" she asked, her voice almost childlike. "He's absolutely darling, don't you think?" Her gray eyes looked back up at him. Adamar looked frantically at the birth witch who stood there, frozen by his anger.

"Why is he like this? Explain the meaning of it," he ordered. The birth-witch looked at the baby, frowning. She was an experienced witch. Her gray black hair was pulled back into a low bun at the nape of her neck.

"He has an energy about him that I have only felt once before, your highness," she muttered. Adamar stared at her, expectantly.

"I don't know if you know this, sir, but I was there for the birth of the God of Death," she said, her voice quivering slightly. "The energy that comes from your son..." She shook her head as if it wasn't possible.

"He's mine," a million voices whispered into the air. The birth witch's face contorted into fear as Adamar felt his body freeze. He slowly turned around to look into the shadowy face.

"You said that you would help my wife birth an heir,"

Adamar's voice quivered uncharacteristically. The hooded figure stood still.

"I *did* give your wife an heir," the voices said, echoing with one another. The cloaked figure moved around the room, as if it were floating, coming closer to Essarae and the baby. Adamar instinctively moved so that he was closer to his wife. The voices laughed.

"Adamar, please don't pretend to care for her now," the voices chastised. "It's too late for that."

"What did you do to my son?" Adamar surprisingly demanded. The figure stilled once more.

"Than is the heir to the Mortiferis," the voices whispered. Essarae's eyes lit up at the name.

"Than," she cooed.

"The child is the only person who can control them, as he is a child of mine and theirs," the voices said, echoing around the room.

"What do you mean he's the only one who can control them?" Adamar asked, his voice shaking. The figure's shadowy face moved to look at him. Adamar stared into blackness, it was as black as the hair on his son.

"I took your sacrifice's body, Adamar, but the soul of Than is part Mortiferis and a piece of mine," the voices cooed. The figure moved around the room once more, but towards the other side of the bed.

"The Mortiferis cannot be controlled. I could only put them to sleep for a little while," the voices echoed. "They are awake now."

"What's going on?" Essarae asked, suddenly concerned. Her eyes still looked glazed over, but there was a bit of a panicked expression on her beautiful face.

"It's fine," Adamar said, his hand finding hers and patting it. She went back to staring lovingly at the child in her arms.

"Asynthis will be destroyed, to a point," the voices slithered around the room. "I have only brought a few of them here with me, but they will do the job." The figure suddenly turned to an empty spot in the room.

"Don't think that this soul will be able to stop me," the voices hissed at the empty space. A chill went down Adamar's spine as the figure turned back towards him.

"The Gods will be no more, and the world will be yours to rebuild. It is what you wanted," the figure said.

"But what about my son? How do I explain my son?" Adamar asked, angrily gesturing towards the...*thing* that his wife held..

"Have you ever heard the humans' tale of a singular God?" the voices said, dying down to barely a whisper. Adamar stared at the figure with a mixture of fear and annoyance.

"The Christian God," the blonde servant uttered. The figure turned towards her as her face turned into a wordless scream.

"Yes-s-s," the voices drew out, "Such an interesting story, isn't it? Than is my Jesus. Tell them that. He will bring in a new Asynithis."

"How will he know to tell the Mortiferis to stop?" Adamar asked, knowing he couldn't tell the elves that his son was supposedly the son of the God of Death.

"He will do my bidding on Asynithis. I am a part of him. He will know," the voices echoed as the figure disappeared into the shadows. Adamar stared into the empty space for a moment, knowing what he had to do now. What happened could not leave this room. He got up and walked towards one of the armored statues. He had made sure there was one in every room of the palace when he was made king. The witch quickly turned herself into a thousand butterflies, fluttering around him and then out of the window. He blew his white hair out of his face quickly. If the birth-witch could keep the secret of where the God of Death came from, he was sure she wouldn't utter a word to anyone about what happened here.

"Please, your highness, we won't tell anyone," the blonde servant pleaded as she stepped in front of the others. Adamar brandished the sword and spilled their human blood all over the room. Essarae didn't bat an eye. With spots of blood dotting his clothes and face, Adamar walked out of the room and quickly closed the door behind him. His brothers' eyes widened for a moment at the sight.

"He didn't survive," Adamar said, still holding the bloodied sword in his hands. "Tell everyone that my son didn't survive." Edwyrd stared at him and then nodded. Ardryll wasn't fazed by Adamar's violence. Adamar knew they both would just think that the murders of the servants were just a moment of anger. He looked back at the room and thought to himself that he made a good decision in making sure all the servants were human in the palace. They would've been harder to kill if they were elves.

———

Khalon woke up, sweat covering his face as he wiped it with the back of his arm. *"Don't think that this soul will be able to stop me,"* the voices had said to him in his dream. It was like the faces that were ever changing around Rhea's face except there was a shadowy darkness that encased her sleeping face. He remembered what the Seer had told him. *Only she can go against the God of Death.* The God of Death knew that Rhea would be the only person who could stop him. Except... What was it that the figure said? Khalon tried to remember his dream, a vein bulging out of his forehead as he thought hard in concentration. He looked around his surroundings. Princess Esi had allowed him to stay in a spare room in her quarters of the palace, except her quarters were seemingly just under it. It reminded him of his cell back in the Ring, though there weren't any windows, barred or otherwise, to look out of. The ceiling above him started to shake as he heard distant screams. Esi wandered into the room, her white eyes seemed to glow as much as her veins did.

"It's happening," she muttered. Khalon remembered. *They are awake now.* The Mortiferis that the God of Death had brought to Asynithis have been awoken.

"There's one in every capital city," Esi said, her voice sounding faraway. Her white eyes searched the area around her, as if she could see what was happening.

"His goal is to kill the royal families of each country," Khalon said, realization sinking in. "Then, he'll go after the Gods." Esi nodded.

"You don't need to help me," Esi muttered, "I will always be okay. My soul will always move on, as that is its destiny. But my sister." She pointed towards the ceiling. "My sister needs help. She cannot hear." Khalon stared at her for a moment.

"She can't hear?" he asked. He now knew why King Tafari let Esi be born and why he killed her mother afterwards.

"I'm sure she would've awoken from the vibrations," Esi mused, "But I'm worried about her. You are a Champion from the Ring, yes?" Yes, but that didn't mean he knew how to fight a Mortiferis. Or save anyone from a global disaster. All he knew was how to fight a man with a sword. That was literally it. He ran his head over his growing hair. He needed to buzz it again. He hated how he looked like a chia pet when his hair grew in. It just grew out of his head and seemed to never fall.

"Yeah, yeah," Khalon shook his head, getting rid of the thought. *This was not the time.* He grabbed Esi's arm and pulled her with him. "Let's go."

"You can leave me," Esi said. Khalon scoffed.

"I'm not leaving anyone."

26

Freya felt herself being shook out of her slumber. Opening one eye, she looked up at Elion. Groaning, she sat up.

"Yes, every God's dream is to be woken up by a pale elf," she was starting to say when Elion quietly shushed her. His hair was in his face slightly, and he was wearing a white nightgown, common for elves to wear but plain ridiculous in Freya's eyes. She scrunched her nose and looked out the window of her bedroom in the temple. Her chair slightly covered her view, but she could see a part of... She didn't know how to describe it. It was something out of a nightmare. Past the monster, from what Freya could see, were what looked like to be white ashes.

"What *is* that?" she more mouthed than whispered. Elion shrugged as he was trying to get his elven armor on. It was white, of course, and was made of some stretchy material. Freya had asked about it once a long time ago and was told that the humans created it for the elves. The elves loved to take human creations, but they would never accept humans as one of them. She knew this, and despised the elves for it. Freya

quickly got out of bed as she saw the horrific creature disappear from the window's view, just wandering in the gardens of
her temple.

"Where's Poseidon?" she hissed. Elion shrugged to that as
well, putting on the heavier armor over the body suit. He tied
his wavy white hair into a ponytail as he searched for his
sword.

"Do you know *anything*?" Freya muttered in annoyance as
she looked for her own armor. Luckily, when Freya was
younger, Neith would come and fit Freya into armored outfits.
"Just in case," she always said. She also gave Freya's body some
training so that her body would react to Freya's well trained
mind. Her armor was draconian. Even though draconians were
sometimes just as bad as the elves, she knew they had better
armor. What armor was better than dragon skin? She pulled
her long braided hair into a ponytail, the gold beads adorning
her hair fell against the back of her armor. She noticed as Elion
stared at her for a long while. Freya couldn't help but roll her
eyes.

"Please pick your drooling mouth off of the floor. We have
— whatever that is — to fight," she whispered, stalking
towards the door of her room. Her bedroom's door opened into
the front of the temple, so she had to be sure that the monster
wouldn't see them right away. Pressing her face against the
window, she stared as the back of the monster was turned
towards her, still wandering through her garden. She wasn't
sure what it was waiting for.

"It came from the capital," Elion said from behind her,
making Freya nearly jump out of her skin.

"Please, Elion, shut the fuck up," she whispered. She
needed to think and also *where the fuck was Poseidon?*

"Why am I the Love God of all things?" she felt herself

whisper as Elion looked at her in shock. Shaking her head, she started to open the door when Elion grabbed onto the handle.

"We're just going to go out there?" Elion asked. Freya stared at him incredulously.

"You would rather we stay in here?" she asked. She could see that Elion was caught off guard by her sudden change in personality. She rolled her eyes. She couldn't be bothered with the superficiality of manners at the moment as she was pretty sure that the monster came for her. She knew it would eventually be making its way back to the temple.

"Do you see those white ashes over there?" she asked. The direction towards the capital was covered in dust, like nothing existed past the border of where her temple lay. The town of Viridis, as Sylva didn't really have any major cities, looked to have been disintegrated.

"Viridis is gone, do you understand me?" Freya said, putting her fingers to his eyes and then back to hers. Elion looked confused.

"Are you an idiot? Why the hell did you come here if you're going to stall me? Is this part of your brother's plan?" Freya whispered angrily. Elion's light blue eyes widened and he shook his head.

"No, no," he said, taking his hand away. "I'm here to protect you. I want to make sure you're okay. I-I don't want you to die." Freya scoffed as she looked through the crack of her door.

"Thanks kid, but I think I've been in more battles than you ever will be in a lifetime," she muttered. Suddenly, a sound that sounded like a thousand screams was heard coming from the monster. Freya and Elion dropped to the ground, covering their ears. It was as if her eardrum was about to shatter. Tears started to form in her eyes as she listened to the horrific cries of what sounded like creatures dying. Just as soon as she heard the scream, the door to her bedroom opened.

"Dela," Freya breathed, her head looking backwards at an upside down Dela.

"C'mon, Freya," she said, pulling Freya to her feet. The monster was still screaming its thousands of heartbreaking screams as Freya and Elion ran out from her bedroom. Freya looked back as she watched her temple servants stand in front of the creature, trying to fight it off. The monster unhinged its jaw, revealing rows and rows of teeth, biting one of her temple servants in half. The rest of her body turned into gray dust. Freya suddenly couldn't feel her legs, as they felt like jelly, and Dela desperately tried to keep her moving. She turned back to face where she was going. Another temple servant was dragging Poseidon towards the same direction. Freya breathed a sigh of relief. At least Poseidon was still alive. Dela pushed her into the woods behind the temple. Freya couldn't help but notice that the moon was full tonight. It looked dimmer than usual, but Freya tried to shake the thought out of her head. As Freya started to run, she noticed that Dela had stopped walking.

"Let's go, Dela," Freya said, her voice reaching a pitch that it hadn't before. Dela backed up, her long black hair was braided into a singular braid. She always had it like that before she went to bed.

"We'll keep it distracted," Dela said, defiantly keeping her chin held high. Freya looked at her incredulously.

"Don't be ridiculous, Dela, c'mon," Freya said, closing her eyes and then beckoning Dela to come to her.

"It was an honor serving you, your holiness," Dela said, her face not betraying the fear that she probably felt.

"Dela, that *thing* is a Mortiferis. If it kills you, you'll cease to exist. Your soul will never find the underworld. You *will* disappear, forever," Poseidon confirmed Freya's worst fears. *That was a Mortiferis.* That was the monster that has destroyed realm after realm.

"I promised to protect you as much as I can, your holiness," Dela said. She looked down at the ground and then back up at Freya, "I'm sorry." Then she ran full force back to the temple. Freya heard a guttural cry come out of her mouth as Elion held her back. The other temple servant shakily backed up away from Poseidon as he tried to reason with her. She also ran back to the temple and Freya heard the monster scream, except the scream had a few more horrific sounds added to it. The sounds of her temple servants.

"Let's go," Poseidon said, pulling Freya to her feet. This wasn't the time to mourn the lives of creatures. They had to save themselves. Freya wiped her face and tried to keep standing, though her legs felt like they were going to give at any second.

"You *still* think Rhea isn't behind this?" she hissed to Poseidon. He scrunched his eyebrows. He knew what Freya was referring to. They had seen the God of Death kill in a similar way. Using the voices of those who had passed. The Mortiferis seemed to just use their screams.

"Let's just go, Freya, please," Poseidon said, grabbing her hand. She hastily grabbed Elion's hand before Poseidon turned them all into water, traveling through the water that was always in the air. Freya felt herself start to freeze as Poseidon released them from being water molecules at the shores of the Argenti Sea. Elion fell to the ground, coughing up water that was in his lungs. He held himself up with one arm as he just continued to throw up water over and over again.

"Sorry," Poseidon said, rubbing Elion's back, "It's hard for creatures who aren't used to it to travel through water."

"How did we—" he threw up again, "—even do that?" His voice was hoarse.

"Uh," Poseidon tried to think, "Well, I can travel using any kind of water. Like... magic, I guess. Yeah, I'm using a sort of magic, let's say. And the air has water in it, even without you realizing it actually. It might not feel like there's water in the air, but there is. And so, even though it's definitely a harder way to travel, that's how we got here."

"You, An, and Rhea have the fastest way to travel through the world and I have no way to travel like that. I have to take the normal creature way," Freya complained, staring into the dark murky waters of the Argenti Sea. The image of the moon rippled as the waves came to shore. The moon was definitely dimmer than normal. Freya's eyes burned.

"All I have is the power to make creatures fall in love with me," Freya muttered, kicking a rock into the sea, "Or help someone have a child."

"Hey," Poseidon said, putting an arm around her shoulders. "You know, everyone has their own place in life. Are my powers awesome? Yes. Do I rule over everything that's under water and it's all at my control? Yes. But you know, it's tiring sometimes. Plus, without your powers of love, this young man would've never come and told us about his brother's despicable plan." Freya shrugged Poseidon's arm off of her in annoyance.

"Just for the record," Elion said, his voice cracking as he held up a hand. He was still on the ground, poised as if he were about to throw up again. "Who said I was in love with Freya? I'm not in love with Freya. I just want to, you know, do a good thing and—" He ended up throwing up again.

"Gods," Freya said, putting a hand to her temple, "I so wish it was Edwyrd who I bewitched. He would've been so much more helpful in this situation." Poseidon nodded.

Out of the corner of her eye, she watched someone start to come over to them. She quickly took out her sword and pointed it in the direction of the woman. Elion tried to do the same, but he was still weakened and on the ground, so it wasn't really much help. The woman was completely naked, but fish scales still clung to parts of her body. She had long black hair, typical of mermaids in Argentiunda, and her cheekbones were high, making her features sharper somehow. Her eyes were almond shaped and her teeth were shifting from sharpened to normal human-like teeth.

"Your holiness," the mermaid said, bowing slightly. She glared up at Freya and Elion. Freya crossed her arms and looked around as she watched Elion's ears turn red and his eyes frantically become downcast. Absent-mindedly, she noticed that what used to be Poseidon's temple behind them had been turned into whitened ash.

"It looks like you guys took care of the bodies," Poseidon said, motioning for the woman to lift her head. "Thank you for that."

"We know what is happening," she said, her voice still distorted from switching from a creature that could survive in water to the one standing in front of them now.

"Are they in the waters as well?" Poseidon asked. She shook her head.

"No," she said, "The Mortiferis cannot survive in water. Besides, the elven king wouldn't be interested in ruling Argentiunda anyways. He can't breathe down here." She smirked slightly.

"Is that my brother's plan?" Elion asked. The mermaid looked Elion up and down and scrunched her face up in distaste. At least Freya wasn't the only one who disliked elves.

"We have ways of spying on you surface dwellers, yes," she said. "We believe that is his plan."

"Apsara," Posiedon said, making her turn her gaze onto him, "Will the people of Argentiunda be able to house us under the sea? For protection?" Apsara bowed her head slightly.

"Of course, your holiness," she said. "It will be hard for you and your friends as your bodies cannot breathe under water. But our witches have a concoction that has worked for you before." She gestured towards someone's head that was in the water. Gills moved on their necks and their black hair was slicked back from the water.

"It only worked for a couple of hours last time," Poseidon said. Freya frowned.

"Can't you breathe underwater, Poseidon?" she asked. His face reddened a bit.

"I can breathe longer than an average human or creature that lives on the surface. But I can't breathe in water as I used to, no," he said.

"Because of the body that you chose?" she asked. He shrugged.

"That seems to be the case." Apsara motioned for the creature in the water to come closer. She swam closer to the shore, revealing part of her tail that flashed blue.

"The concoction is stronger than before. It should also help with the pressure," she said. Apsara turned towards Freya, "Our cities are deep under the water. No light hits it, the pressure is a lot for your airy bodies." Freya nodded slowly.

"So, we might die under there," Freya said.

"At least we'll reincarnate if we die down there. Up here, we won't," Poseidon shrugged as he grabbed the concoction from the mermaid's hands.

"I'm not going to reincarnate if we die," Freya muttered. She was just going to stay in the other realm of Gods. She wasn't *ever* going to come back to this hellscape. Poseidon drank the concoction and another mermaid appeared alongside the one that gave him the liquid. She held up two more bottles of it. Freya hesitated and looked over at Elion who gave her a "Are we really doing this" look.

"Bottoms up," she said, throwing the other bottle to Elion. He caught it, although barely. She twisted off the cap of the bottle and downed the contents. It burned her throat as she swallowed it. She watched Elion do the same and suddenly she felt so much pain in her lower body.

"What is happening?" she asked, her voice distorting, as she watched Poseidon grow gills on the side of his face. His legs were starting to be melded together and he fell to the ground as she watched her dark legs pull themselves together into one leg. Her feet turned webbed as she fell headfirst into the water. They looked like mermaids but without any scales, and it was almost enough to make her stomach turn. Apsara seemed to have a similar gut reaction as she stared at the weird looking mermaids that they turned into.

"We need to change the concoction more," she muttered as she swiftly turned herself back into a mermaid. Her scales were black that were golden at the bottom of each scale. Elion crawled his way to the tide so that he was next to Freya. He was even more disgusting looking as a mermaid than an elf. Freya ducked her head into the sea, following the three other mermaids. They were incredibly fast and she felt like a child trying to walk for the first time.

"You just have to move your legs as if they're one leg instead of two," Poseidon said, swimming easily up to her. She could hear his voice clearly under water. Their voice boxes must've changed to accommodate the difference between the air and seawater. She tried to move her legs as if they were bound together or as one and she felt herself push forward through the sea.

"Please," Apsara shouted from the front of the group,

"Hurry up. The sharks will be coming at the smell of your creature flesh." Sharks?

"If not the sharks, then the cetus," the other mermaid laughed. Cetus? Freya had heard of the term before but she had never seen one. All she knew about it was that it was a horrific sea monster.

"Don't worry, the cetus won't come near the Sea God," Apsara reassured them. But the sharks would?

"Sharks are kind of rebellious creatures. They come from my own heart, you know," Poseidon whispered, nodding and winking at Freya. He was insane, Freya thought. Who created creatures in order to devour you and not listen to you? Wait a minute...

"Do you think that Rhea—"

"I don't want to talk about Rhea unless she's here to defend herself," Poseidon interrupted, actually using the name that she had chosen this time. Freya's eyes widened and she looked forward, trying to concentrate on swimming.

"We are now going to move towards Amnis Lux," Apsara said, pointing her webbed hand towards the darkness. The mermaids dipped downwards, moving their tails hard, almost blowing Freya backwards. They started swimming into the darkness at a fast speed.

"It's harder trying to angle yourself upside down like that," Poseidon said, trying to demonstrate it. His two legs that turned into one flailed around until he had himself angled down.

"Okay, so then just—" his face started to turn red as he flailed around until his tail started to cooperate with his movement. His tail moved hard as he pushed himself forward. Freya took a deep breath of water and then angled herself downwards, as Elion did the same. He struggled with it for a while as Freya seemed to get the hang of it pretty quickly. They continued to swim into the abyss as the water around them got darker and darker. The pressure didn't seem to get to them during the downwards dive, however, which was something that Freya was worried about.

As they got closer to the city of Amnis Lux, lights from the ocean floor could be seen. It was incredibly bright for the eyes that adjusted to the darkness, but it was a beautiful city. In all of Freya's lifetimes, she had never seen the cities underneath the water. The buildings were made of rocks and what looked to be coral-like material. The palace of Amnis Lux was made entirely of gold and was in triangular shapes. Many of the buildings were shaped much like a triangle but looked like squished cylinders on top of squished cylinders. There were points at the top of each building and the city was full of mermaids and other sea creatures swimming around.

"It's beautiful," Freya breathed. And probably the biggest city she had ever seen. It was something out of a fairytale. Apsara smiled brightly.

"You wouldn't see buildings like this up on the surface," she said, proudly, swimming towards the palace.

"Are you okay with staying down here for a little now?" Poseidon said, almost equally as proud as Apsara about their city. Freya looked at the different mermaids with different colored tails, resembling the many different fish that lived in the sea.

"Since they're so naturally fashionable," Freya smiled, "I guess I'm okay with it."

"As long as we don't die," Elion added. Freya rolled her eyes.

27

Than is the heir to the Mortiferis... The child is the only person who can control them... The Gods will be no more... Rhea slowly opened her eyes, hearing the many voices echo around in her brain. *Don't think that this soul will be able to stop me.* She sat up from the ground that she was lying on, holding her head. She didn't remember coming up to the surface and her conversation with An felt like lifetimes ago, even though she knew it was only the day before. It felt like her body was about to split in two. She heard what the God of Death said, but this time in her own voice. *Than is the heir to the Mortiferis.* So, Rhea thought, *the baby elf, Adamar's kid, is the heir to the monsters.* The kid is also the only person who can control them which means... Her eyes widened. The God of Death can't control them. *He was right.* Her body's soul wasn't going to be able to stop him as he made sure that she wouldn't have known about what was going on until it was too late. Her hand hit the ground, hard, as she hung her head. She was an idiot.

"Rhea," she heard Farrah's voice cut through her inner

monologue, "Something's going on." Rhea felt a fluttering in her chest, and not the good kind. It was the kind that made it hard to breathe and made one feel lightheaded.

"Coming," Rhea said to herself out of habit. Moving her hands away from her body, she brought the door to the underworld to the surface. The ground shook and Rhea pushed herself off of the ground, defeated. There wasn't anything that she could do.

When she got into the underworld, the lobby was in chaos. The rotting corpses of reapers were running around not knowing whether to go up or to stay in the lobby. Some reapers were coming down without any souls in their containers.

"What's going on?" Rhea asked as she ran towards the Fates. Francine took her hand and led her into the room with the strings of life.

"Rhea," Francine said, "Something is happening up on the surface." Rhea put a hand to her forehead, rubbing it.

"Yes," she said, "The God of Death, he released a few Mortiferis onto the world." Francine gave Rhea a look.

"I think it's a bit more than a few," she said. A knock came from the door and Felicity opened it slightly to the face of a reaper. Part of the reaper's face was just its skull while the rest was slowly rotting off.

"Ma'am," the reaper said. Felicity's face fell from hearing that.

"You know, I don't think I'm that old to be called a 'Ma'am' yet, Sarah," she muttered.

"Apologies, ma'am," Sarah, the reaper, said. Felicity went to correct the reaper again but before she could, Rhea stepped in.

"What is it? We're having a meeting," Rhea said, a bit harshly. The one eye that the reaper still had blinked.

"Oh yes," she said, "Um, Viridis has fallen. It's gone." Rhea stared at her.

"Sorry?"

"Oh sorry," Sarah said, the skin on her mouth falling off of her skull. She pushed it back into place. Speaking a little louder and slower, she said, "The...town...of...Viridis...is...gone. Turned...to...ash...poof!" She made a little explosion movement with her hands. Rhea stared at her. She remembered why Sarah was a reaper.

"Don't talk to me like that," Rhea said. Sarah cowered a bit, probably from the fire burning in Rhea's eyes.

"Viridis has turned into ash," Rhea repeated as Sarah nodded. She remembered the wall from back in the inn when that human girl seemingly tried to kill Khalon. It had disintegrated completely into ash.

"It was the Mortiferis," Rhea said, "He must've sent them to different parts of Asynithis."

"What about the souls?" Francine asked, stepping towards the reaper. Sarah looked at the ground. "We could ask the souls what happened." Rhea had a gnawing feeling in the back of her head as she looked at half of Sarah's guilty face.

"There aren't any souls, are there?" Rhea whispered. Farrah looked at Rhea in shock.

"There can't be no souls," Farrah argued, crossing her arms, as the reaper nodded her head.

"When we got there, the bodies had no souls in them. And when we searched the area for if the souls turned into ghosties, there were none of those either," Sarah answered.

"They don't just make bodies disappear," Rhea explained, "They destroy the soul as well. It makes sense as to why the Gods' souls can be destroyed. Gone forever."

"So all those creatures," Farrah said, her eyes wide, "Gone. They can't pass on or be punished or... they just disappeared?"

"We've never seen anything like this before," Francine said. She looked over at Rhea, motioning her to come. Rhea walked over to her as they walked towards the ebony cabinet that held the golden strings for the Gods.

"That's not all," Francine whispered.

"Thank you for that information, Sarah. Please tell the other reapers to not panic. We're just in a crisis is all," Felicity said politely, as she closed the door on her. Francine opened the cabinet, revealing many white and broken strings.

"Some of the Gods were reincarnating, I think because they were sensing what was happening. They were all killed," Francine said as Rhea looked at all the strings in horror.

"You mean, I sent monsters to kill little, defenseless babies," Rhea whispered after a while.

"It wasn't you..."

"But it was, Francine. He is me and I am him. And whether I was conscious or not of it, I should've recognized it far in advance. Honestly, I should've recognized it once King Elkhazel died," Rhea ranted, backing away from the strings. The Fates looked confused, unsure what Rhea was talking about. But Rhea knew. She had some kind of deal with Adamar that he would be king and it wouldn't be questioned. She had felt it when she saw him, and that's why she had lied about his soul being equivalent to Elkhazel's. At the time, she thought it was to just save Elion's life. But now...

"Rhea," Felicity said as Rhea shied away from her touch.

"Please," was all Rhea could muster up as tears started to stain her face. She wiped them away quickly. The Fates shared another look with one another.

"We need to know if An is one of them," Farrah finally said. Rhea glared up at her. She had to touch each string in order to figure out whose essence was on them.

"Wouldn't you be able to know? You *are* in charge of these strings," Rhea angrily gestured around the room.

"We can't when it comes to the Gods," Farrah said, "You know the God of All is a bit more secretive about what happens to you all." Rhea sighed as she moved her legs forward towards the ebony cabinet. There was some part of her that wanted, no, *needed* to know whether An was among the ones who had lost their lives forever. Rhea started to touch the whitened strings, feeling each Gods' last moments. Hotei, who reincarnated in a mixed shojo's body and the God of Alcohol, was dead. Bastet, the God of the Moon, was dead. The God of the Sun had also passed and so did Ceridwen, the God of Rebirth. The world was about to look a bit dimmer with both the souls of the sun and moon having been destroyed. Neith was still alive, thankfully, but Alator's string was flickering in color. An was still alive, to Rhea's gut reaction of disappointment. Poseidon and Freya were as well. The rest were nearly dead, or about to be.

"An is still alive," Rhea said, unable to hide her disappointment. Francine raised an eyebrow.

"I'm guessing the God of Death doesn't like that," Francine said. Rhea shook her head.

"No," she said, "He doesn't."

"These are the dark days," Farrah whispered, barely under her breath. A knock on the door echoed around the room. Felicity opened it to reveal another reaper. It was a complete skeleton. His end was coming soon, Rhea absentmindedly thought as one of his ribs clattered to the ground.

"The city of Furvus is about to fall, it looks like," the reaper said. Rhea's eyes widened. *Khalon.*

"It also looks like Alator's temple is being attacked as well." Rhea looked back at Alator's flickering string.

"I gotta go," Rhea said, pushing past the skeleton as another one of his bones fell to the floor. She needed to get to

Furvus. To save Khalon but Alator as well. She wasn't sure what she'd be able to do, since the Mortiferis apparently don't listen to her. But, she had to do something.

She ran up the stairs, willing the doors to open up in Furvus near Khalon. When the ground opened up, she was in the throne room. A boy, younger than her, was staring at her. They were about the same height. He was a draconian. It was clear by the fact that he had many red scales covering his skin. He wore a traditional Draconian outfit, which was made out of blue silk. His hair was a brown color and his eyes were lighter, but there were some elements of Khalon in his face. Once Rhea noticed the similarity, it hit her like a wall.

"Khalon's brother?" she asked as his jaw dropped at her appearance. He held a hand to his chest, still in shock.

"Khai," he said.

"Right," Rhea said, utterly annoyed by where she ended up. She was trying to go save Khalon in Furvus, because obviously he would've... unless...

"Khalon isn't here in this city, is he?" Rhea asked Khai, whose eyes were still wide in shock. He cleared his throat at the sound of Khalon's name and straightened up a little. He still wasn't taller than her, to his obvious disappointment.

"Khalon was banished from Draconia," Khai said, his voice a little forceful.

"Why? Because he has the spirit of the dragon within him?" Rhea asked, a little sarcastically. Khai cleared his throat once again.

"It's because he has committed treason," he said matter-of-factly. His face wasn't frozen into horror like most beings upon seeing Rhea's face was.

"You're the God of Death, aren't you?" he more said than asked. Rhea raised an eyebrow.

"How did you figure?"

"You're wearing a black cloak that is supposed to shroud your face. Curiously though," he said, stepping a little closer to Rhea. She stepped back. "I can see your face through it. I guess my knowledge master was wrong." Rhea frowned. First of all, knowledge masters were telling lies about her powers? Chalking it up to the reaper's cloak? The reaper's cloak mimics her own powers. But also... He could see her? Was it because the God of Death's soul was partly in a different being so now her powers were fading slightly?

"You're kind of ugly, to be honest," Khai said, leaning back. A little smile was playing on his lips. Rhea's eyes narrowed.

"You don't *need* to be honest, you know," she muttered. She wondered if Khalon thought she was ugly too. The palace around them shook suddenly.

"Do you know what's going on out there?" Rhea asked him. He shrugged.

"Someone is attacking the palace, my mother said. She's out there trying to help the military fight it," his eyes dulled a bit.

"You don't want to be out there fighting that," Rhea advised, guessing at what his disappointment was. He shrugged.

"Well," Rhea said, "It was nice meeting you Prince Khai — I guess — but I have to go save the God of War. Hopefully you survive the attack of the Mortiferis." Khai grabbed onto her cloak. She looked down at it and then back up at him, and he slowly released her.

"Sorry, you're not going to help the city? I thought that's why you were here."

"No," Rhea said. "If the Gods die, that would be a worse situation, don't you think?" Rhea sniffed around him quickly.

"Besides," she said, "The dragon blood coursing through your veins should protect you." Smiling, she disappeared into the shadows as Khai looked horrified at what Rhea knew. She watched from the shadows as he morphed easily into a red half dragon half humanoid looking creature and stalked out of the throne room. The powers of the dragon that was unnaturally coursing through him should help him against the Mortiferis, somehow. For Khalon's sake, she hoped Khai survived it.

She flitted through the shadows, heading towards the top of Dragon Mountain, where Alator's temple was. When she jumped out from the darkness, surrounding her was ash. Half eaten bodies, with the rest either in piles of ash or just grayed out corpses, marred the sacred ground. Alator's temple was half destroyed as well. She heard him yell out and whipped her head around to see a Mortiferis disintegrate Alator's sword.

"You mother—"

"Alator!!" Rhea shouted, throwing something at the monstrous creature. It had many horns on it and looked like a mish mash of the most grotesque, nightmare creatures that have ever existed. A pang throbbed in the temples of Rhea's head as a memory invaded her mind.

———

"Why would you create these?" a booming voice was heard ringing around Rhea's head.

"Why can you create beings but I cannot? I'm the one who takes care of their souls," a childlike voice said.

"You are death, though, brother. You cannot create life," the loud voice continued.

"I just wanted to create beings that understood me and worshiped me," Rhea recognized the voice as her own.

"What you created aren't controlled by you," the voice morphed into An's speaking voice.

"I don't want creatures that are controlled. I want them to have free will," Rhea said, quietly.

"These creatures don't have a thought in their head. Because you have created them, all they can do is destroy. What you've done is very dangerous to the worlds that I've created," An sounded exasperated. A spiritual hand was waved and the nightmares that Rhea created were thrown to a far off world. One that An had experimented on long, long ago, against the will of hers.

"What will become of them?" Rhea asked.

"Hopefully, it takes them forever before they come to our newer realms," An had dismissed the topic.

———

Rhea shook her head as she stared at the creature that she created. Her heart ached at the loneliness that she felt at the time. And a part of her knew that An must have known it was her that was orchestrating the killings this whole time. She watched as Alator cut off his arm as the Mortiferis bit it, turning part of the arm gray. It fell to the ground with a thud. Alator screamed as he ran his new sword into the Mortiferis' chest but it was to no avail, as Rhea knew. The Mortiferis didn't have life within them. They were just shells. They were death. She tried throwing something at it again, and the Mortiferis turned to look at her. She couldn't see its eyes, if it even had eyes, and it unhinged its jaw revealing rows of teeth as it screamed at her. Her legs froze as she stared at it, her heart breaking at the sight. It seemed to stare at her, as its mouth closed. Then, it turned around to face Alator once again. A part of her felt that the monster recognized her.

"Rhea!" she heard Alator scream desperately. She knew he needed her help but there wasn't anything that she could do for him. Prayers were filling her head. Creatures were calling out for the God of Death, and Rhea could feel his satisfaction deep within her. *Rhea,* a voice cut out through the other prayers. Her heart stilled as she heard it. A sense of relief washed over her. He was alive. *Rhea,* Khalon's voice said again, a bit more desperate. She stared as Alator screamed her name once more, as the Mortiferis unhinged its jaw and bit down on his screaming head. His neck turned to ash while the rest of his body turned gray and fell to the ground with a thud. Rhea bit back the tears that threatened to spill onto her face as she slipped away into the shadows, following Khalon's voice.

There wasn't anything I could do, she tried to convince herself. *I can't control the Mortiferis. There's nothing that I could do.* Rhea's eyes opened as she stepped out of the shadows, standing in front of Khalon. His face looked down at her and it was like she had come home. His half-moon shaped eyes softened as he looked upon her, but his face and jaw looked tight. His large hands grabbed onto Rhea's shoulders as he whipped her around and tried to move her as she stared into the face of another Mortiferis. *Great,* she thought.

28

"Where's your sister?" Khalon called, turning his head slightly towards Esi so she could hear him.

"Her bedroom should be... I'm not sure..." Esi mumbled to herself as she wandered throughout the halls of the palace of Invenire. Khalon could feel the walls rumble but the floor still seemed steady enough. He heard screams coming from outside of the palace.

"Esi," he said, "We need to get to her soon." Every bone in his body was warning him that this wasn't the safest place to be.

"I'm not allowed up here usually. I'm trying to remember where she might be," Esi said, her tone indicating that she was frustrated. Her white eyes looked around the room.

"Do you think she would've stayed in her room, if she felt what was going on?" Khalon asked. Esi took a deep breath at the thought and shook her head.

"No, she probably would be trying to go and fight. She might be arguing with our father right now," Esi sighed.

Khalon stared at Esi for a long while as she shifted uncomfortably from the gaze that she couldn't see.

"Okay," Khalon said, "Where would your father be?" Her face lit up.

"Oh, that's easy," she said. "The throne room." *Of course,* Khalon thought. All the kings in Asynithis seemed to love to bask in their ego by hanging out in the throne room. Khalon pivoted, grabbing Esi's arm as he walked past her. Her footsteps quickened as she tried to catch up with his long strides. It would be easy to find a throne room in a palace. *You just look for the biggest, most annoyingly grand room and you'll find it,* Khalon thought to himself, looking into each room they passed. They ran down the stairs and Esi's head turned suddenly.

"This way," she said, pulling Khalon's arm towards the direction that she wanted to go. "I hear my father."

"Great hearing," Khalon muttered, dragging Esi down the long hallways of the palace that eventually opened up into an airy throne room. The throne room had ornate columns, painted gold and black. The ceiling rose in the middle and it looked like steps going down towards the corners of each room. Despite the black decorations, the room was very well lit. King Tafari was standing on the last step that led towards his towering throne making gestures with his hands angrily. A girl that was around the same age as Khalon stood in front of the king. Her brown hair was in twists that were in a circular bun on the top of her head. Her hands that were gesturing back just as forcefully were darker than Esi's. She wore armor that had spikes on the shoulders and was a dark deep red that almost looked black, making it glisten red in the light. Almost like Khalon's scales. The back of her neck's veins glowed red, indicating that she was a royal Phoenix. King Tafari looked up at the intrusion and his face softened a little bit.

"Esi," he said, gesturing towards her as well as signing

what he was saying. The girl turned around to look at them. Khalon took a step back at seeing her face. She wasn't just a Phoenix, but an Inkanyamba as well. It looked like her pupils took over the whole of her iris, and her eyes were large and round. Her teeth, when she parted her mouth slightly, were all pointed. Her hands moved while she frowned.

"Oh," Esi said as she signed back, "She's saying that I shouldn't stop her and that she has to protect our people."

"How are you even able to see what she's saying?" Khalon asked, bewildered. Esi giggled.

"I am able to see what she signs a second before she signs it, in my head. It was something that I tried hard to develop in order to be able to communicate with her," Esi explained. "It takes up a lot of my sight, if you understand what I mean." She said that more quietly, even though her sister wouldn't have been able to hear. Khalon understood what Esi was trying to convey. Because she focused her energy on trying to predict what her sister would say to her, she lacks in other areas of her future telling. Khalon stepped forward towards the girl as she signed something towards her sister. A servant appeared beside her. She was shorter than the girl.

"This draconian won't be able to stop me either," the servant said, her tone a bit annoyed. Her face didn't betray any emotion but when Khalon looked at the girl, she definitely looked annoyed.

"What do you think I'm trying to stop you from, Princess...?" Khalon asked. The servant signed towards the girl but the girl interrupted, signing back. It seemed like she could read lips.

"Kamaria," the servant said, in the same annoyed tone. Khalon swallowed.

"So? What do you think I'm trying to stop you from?" he asked.

"*Please* stop this child," King Tafari exclaimed from behind her. The servant interpreted what the king said to Kamaria's distaste. She looked over at her father and signed something to which he started signing back, angrily again.

"She said that she's grown now and needs to protect this country as their future queen. To which my father is saying that she isn't going to be Queen of Ustrina and to stop trying to force his hand," Esi whispered to Khalon. King Tafari just had a baby boy with Queen Sade, his new Phoenix wife. A miracle baby, he was called and he was going to inherit the country.

"Princess Kamaria," Khalon said, stepping forward. As the servant signed to her, she turned around to look at him, unnerving him with her eyes.

"Whatever is out there isn't something that you or anyone could fight. I probably wouldn't be able to fight it and I'm a Champion," Khalon said. She scoffed as she signed back.

"A Champion? That means nothing here. You don't know how to fight like I do. I have been in real battle, with multiple opponents. You have only been in one to one fights. Don't come here acting like you know how to fight more than I," Kamaria said through the servant. Khalon stared at the servant's expressionless face as her tone changed from annoyed to angry.

"Also," the servant said, sounding more frustrated, "Look at me when I'm talking, not at her. She is just my voice." Khalon quickly looked at Kamaria as she glared at him.

"Okay, you're right in that I haven't been in actual battle which you obviously probably have been. But," Khalon continued, "that monster that's down there, it's called the Mortiferis. It isn't destroying the city just because it wants to kill the people. It's destroying the city to get to you and your family, and unfortunately, your army and people are in its way."

"What do you mean that it is a Mortiferis?" King Tafari

boomed, walking down the steps of his throne he wandered over next to his daughter. Despite being over five hundred years old, he didn't look a day over thirty.

"The Mortiferis are here and they've been killing the Gods," Khalon quickly explained, "And it looks like they're being used to get rid of all the royal families on Asynithis as well." Tafari stared at him, hard.

"Is what he says true, Esi?" he asked. Esi nodded slowly as he glared at her.

"Why did you not tell me?" his voice echoed around the throne room.

"The God of All warned me not to speak of my vision," Esi whispered. Tafari angrily whipped around to head back to his throne.

"Get Queen Sade and Prince Sipho. We need to leave this country," Tafari ordered his servants. They quickly slipped out of the room as another servant brought his armor.

"You are right when you say that the Mortiferis cannot be easily fought," Tafari mused, shrugging into his chest armor. "But, my daughter is right. We cannot just let our people suffer for our sake without trying to defend them. I will buy you time." Kamaria shook her head and signed desperately. Tafari's face softened as he signed back. He looked up at Esi as she started to speak.

"Father, if the Mortiferis takes you, we won't be able to get your ashes and—"

"I know, Esi," he said. "I know." Khalon had heard of the tradition that the Phoenix do. The king takes his ashes once he has died and it is then mixed into a drink for the heir to consume. The heir then has the essence of the king from before, and all of his memories.

"If Sipho is going to be king, he needs the memories of all

the kings before," Kamaria was signing, her servant's voice desperate.

"It was halted before, you know, after the elves invaded. He will be the first memory to many other kings after him," Tafari said.

"I will fight with you," Kamaria signed. Tafari shook his head as he took his daughter's head into his hands, for a moment before signing as he spoke.

"Kamaria, you are a great fighter. You have fought alongside me for thirty years," Khalon's jaw dropped at the mention of her age. He had forgotten that Phoenixes live long and grow slowly. "I am grateful for you but this is a suicide mission. I will die in this battle. And you have hundreds of years left to live. Your purpose is to bring peace to the Phoenixes and the Inkanyambas. You cannot die yet." Kamaria's eyes filled with tears as she looked away.

"Take care of these two," Tafari said to Khalon as two members of his military came to the throne room. Khalon nodded as he left the room with Kamaria glancing at Khalon warily.

"More like I should take care of you two," Kamaria sassed. Khalon tightened his lips.

"Let's go," he said, pulling Esi along. Kamaria grabbed Esi's arm and ripped it from Khalon's to which Khalon rolled his eyes over. He then led the way out of the throne room as the palace shook once more.

"If it's one Mortiferis, why does everything keep shaking?" Kamaria called out through her servant.

"I don't know!" Khalon called back, trying to find a window they could jump out of.

"Parts of buildings are being destroyed. The shaking is from buildings falling," Esi responded. Kamaria rolled her eyes but Esi was blissfully unaware of her sister's gesture. Khalon used the hilt of his sword to break a window and motioned for everyone to go through it.

"We should've waited for Sipho," Kamaria signed. The servant interpreted as she tried to push Kamaria towards the window.

"Father has a perfect plan for Sipho," Esi responded, "He'll be fine." Her eyes moved quickly and then they stilled.

"It's all part of what needs to happen," she whispered, almost sadly. Khalon could tell, by the tone of Esi's voice, that their brother was not going to be fine at all.

"C'mon," Khalon motioned. There was something not right in the air. "We need to get moving." Kamaria helped Esi through the window and then hopped out herself. The ground wasn't too far below them. The servant looked scared for a moment, as her head looked out the window at the city of Invenire being destroyed before them, and then composed herself. She pulled the rest of her body out of the palace. Khalon looked behind him, a bad feeling gnawing at the back of his neck, and he jumped out of the window, landing on his feet.

"We need to go," he yelled out. The city was partly in flames and partly in gray ash. The back of the palace faced the south side of the city, and beyond that was a wall. People were screaming, but there was one sound that cut through Khalon's brain. It was the sound of horror.

"Keep close," Khalon called out as Kamaria grabbed Esi's hand. They ran after him, Kamaria holding a sword in her left hand and Esi's hand in her right. The servant was right behind Khalon, in the middle between Khalon and Kamaria. Witches were in the streets muttering spells to protect themselves and others were actively attacking something that was coming towards them, fast. Khalon picked up the pace, hoping that Esi would be able to keep up. They weaved through the city, others coming behind them to stop whatever monster was heading towards their way. Once they hit the wall, Kamaria put out her hands. Fire came from them, turning the stone wall red. She looked like she was muttering something under her breath as storm clouds started to roll in. She burned through the wall, creating a bit of an entryway. Khalon gestured for them to go. As he pushed Esi through, he saw Kamaria's black eyes widen. He turned around and his eyes took in what had frightened her.

It was what had to be a Mortiferis. It was something out of Khalon's deepest fears, huge and terrifying. It didn't look to have any eyes, but its mouth revealed rows and rows of giant, pointed teeth. He held onto his sword with both hands, his knuckles turning white.

"Khalon!" He heard Esi cry out. The Mortiferis seemed to recognize something in Esi's voice. It started to barrel towards them. *Rhea*, Khalon thought to himself, hoping that she could hear his prayer. As it got closer, Khalon's thoughts grew more desperate. He closed his eyes. He didn't know if he would be able to kill a Mortiferis. It destroys everything it touches. He could feel the spirit of the dragon stirring within him, begging to be let out to protect them. He opened his eyes to survey the monster. It looked like it had been hit multiple times, but it was still moving. Mostly because it wasn't alive, Khalon suddenly thought. He prayed to Rhea once more to save him and suddenly, a shadow appeared in front of him. Stepping out of it was the familiar round face of Rhea's. Her bronze eyes glanced at him, and her hood was down — probably from the speed in which she was traveling — revealing her shoulder length copper brown hair. The carousel of faces that encased her own were more faded than usual.

Khalon never felt happier to see her, and by the way her eyes were lighting up, he knew she felt the same. He quickly broke out of what he was feeling as the Mortiferis came faster towards them. Grabbing her shoulders, he whipped her around. She stared at the Mortiferis, but from her profile, Khalon could see that she wasn't afraid.

"Hold my hand," she said. Khalon grabbed it and then reached back to grab Kamaria's hand. They all linked hands and then disappeared into the shadows right as the Mortiferis almost bit his head off.

29

Elion's eyes were wide as they swam through the city of Amnis Lux. It was something out of a fairytale, even though he was highly aware that he himself was a fairytale in the eyes of humans old. But not everyone got to see the wonders of the nation of Argentiunda. Mostly because not everyone was able to breathe underwater. Apsara swam through a doorway leading into something that looked similar to a pub, except everything was covered in algae and small sprouts of coral. A small man sat on a chair behind the bar. His hair was bright red and it floated around his head, like a giant crown of sorts. He held a bottle and drank the water that the liquid permeated. The man was a shojo, a sea spirit. Elion had heard stories about them from humans that worked in the palace in Aureum. Their human countries used to be where Draconia was now. Apsara swam towards him and situated herself on a barstool as Elion noticed that there were many mermaids in the establishment eating heads of fish with their hands. He was shocked by the scene of it all.

"Umeshu," Apsara greeted. He slurped the water that held

his alcohol and smiled slightly. His cheeks were red from the liquid.

"Guardian of the Argentinundan Royal Family," Umeshu exclaimed, spreading his arms out. His arms were partially covered in red hair. "To what do I owe this pleasure?" Apsara rolled her eyes.

"Could you get some drinks for my friends here? Also, do you have any extra lodging?" Apsara asked. Umeshu rubbed his face slowly as he thought.

"I miiiight," he drew out the word. Apsara sighed and pulled a small bag from the pack slung across her shoulders. She dropped it and it slowly sank to the bar's surface. Umeshu grinned at Apsara and slyly grabbed the bag, looking at its contents. His eyes widened at the amount of sand dollars that were in the bag and then put it underneath the top of the bar.

"Okay," Umeshu said, "I have some available lodging upstairs. Don't know how these humans and an elf will survive the night." Apsara sat up straight, glancing at the faces of Poseidon and Freya. Elion was trying not to stare at Freya too much. He didn't want his cheeks to betray his thoughts when he looked at her in mermaid form.

"Excuse you," Freya swam into Elion's vision and he averted his gaze immediately. "I am not fully human. I am half fairy on my mother's side, for your information."

"This is also the God of the Sea and the God of Love," Apsara muttered, coughing as she did. Poseidon waved a partially webbed hand as Umeshu's face deepened in redness.

"Oh it's no trouble," Poseidon said, grabbing a seat next to Apsara. "I quite like being called a human, you know. They're pretty ingenious."

"If they die from drowning on my watch, it's not my fault," Umeshu muttered to Apsara, taking another gulp of the water around him in order to breathe in his alcohol.

"You are free from the guilt of our deaths," Poseidon said as Umeshu handed him a poorly shaped bottle. He took the cap off of it, letting the alcohol start to rise through the water. He quickly slurped at it.

"We're dying anyways," Freya shrugged, taking a seat next to Poseidon. Elion was the only one left treading water as he looked at the three sitting comfortably on the bar stools. He went and sat next to Freya, trying to hide his face. It was hard sitting next to her in mermaid form. Freya didn't have scales, but instead her skin had hardened into a shell-like armor covering her body in skin so black it was almost blue. But it still showed the shape of her exactly. It was enough for Elion to feel embarrassed at his own thoughts.

"Dying?" Umeshu exclaimed as Poseidon tried to slurp all his alcohol before it floated to the ceiling. He put a hand to his face again as he thought.

"Oh yes," he said, "I heard you surface people were all dying by some monster. Who was it in here that heard about it? Dinh! Dinh, come over here." A merman looked up from his fish head and stared at the shojo.

"What?" he called from where he was sitting, clearly not wanting to get up and swim over to where Umeshu was.

"Come. Over. Here," Umeshu gestured more urgently. Dinh sighed loudly and then swam over to the bar.

"Yes?" he asked.

"Tell these folks what you heard about what was happening to them surface people up there," Umeshu gestured towards them. Dinh lazily looked over at them, an expression of disgust appearing on his face as he took in their sight.

"These *are* surface people," he pointed out. It must be weird for him to see mermaid-looking creatures without any scales, Elion mused.

"Yes, yes, but you're in the presence of—"

"Umeshu, if you say another word I'll rip your throat out," Apsara threatened. Umeshu stared at her and then took a big gulp of another bottle of alcohol that he just opened up.

"Right," Umeshu cleared his throat, "Anyways, these lovely folks would just like to know what's going on."

"Well, I was on the coast of Sylva, swimming about. I like to human watch. They're interesting creatures, no offense," Dinh said, putting a hand up towards Freya and Poseidon.

"For the record, I'm only half—"

"Offense not taken," Poseidon interrupted Freya's beginning speech. She frowned. Her button nose was the cutest when she frowned. Elion quickly shook the thought out of his head.

"Anyways, that's when I saw them disappearing. They were turning into ash, some of them. Others were able to escape but there was this creature that..." Dinh's voice slowly lulled. His eyes were glazed over and it was clear that he didn't want to talk about it. "Anyways, it just seems like there isn't a way for you surface people to survive if there's monsters like that."

"Interesting stuff, isn't it?" Umeshu said, his eyes wide like he just heard the greatest piece of gossip in his life. "A monster that even surface people can't beat. We got a ton of monsters here, thanks for that by the way." Dinh looked confused at Umeshu's sarcastic gratitude towards Poseidon. After a moment, Umeshu waved him away.

"That would be all Dinh, thank you," he said.

"Stupid orangutan," Dinh muttered to Umeshu's unconcealed shock. It was as if a lightbulb popped up in Elion's brain. Of course, that is what the shojo looked like to him. An orangutan under water.

"That is a *slur* to us shojos, Dinh. A slur!" Umeshu said, standing up and shaking his fist. "If I hear something like that out of you again, you're banned from this establishment."

"You banned me for the same thing last week," Dinh argued. Umeshu paused at that as he tried to think.

"Did I?" he asked. He sat down again as his hand went to his face. "Did I? ...Oh yes!" His eyes lit up. "Right, I was drunk that night but I *did* ban you. This is the eightieth time you've been banned, Dinh." Dinh shrugged as he swam back to his seat with his friends.

"Sorry about the sea monsters," Poseidon belatedly apologized. Umeshu shrugged.

"It's whatever," he said, "Keeps things interesting." Apsara glared at him and then swam away from her seat.

"I must get back to my post," Apsara said, "But, Umeshu won't say a word about your whereabouts and he will give you good lodging." She glared at Umeshu as she said this, which he cowered from.

"Right, of course," he muttered. He took out three large, ancient keys for three separate rooms. "The finest rooms for the finest creatures, of course." Freya smiled slightly but she looked disgusted at having to stay in this building.

"Rooms are upstairs," Umeshu said, pointing towards the roof. "Really comfortable coral, truly."

"Thanks," Freya muttered. Elion couldn't tell if she was being sarcastic or not. They swam up the stairs and looked inside the rooms. Elion's room was lit by a glowing ball of algae. All the furniture was made of white coral and it looked nice enough. There wasn't too much green algae sticking to the furniture, just to the walls.

"Come into my room, so we can discuss," Poseidon said, suddenly appearing next to Elion. Elion jumped slightly at his appearance and nodded. They all gathered in Poseidon's room and sat on the coral furniture as Poseidon closed the door.

"There's something that Apsara said that has bothered me," Poseidon started. Freya nodded, her human leg tail moving slightly so that she could stay where she was.

"The elven king cannot breathe underwater," Freya repeated, "It bothered me, too. Especially with what has been going on in Sylva." Poseidon's eyes widened as Elion tried to follow along.

"You knew what was happening in Sylva?" Poseidon asked, almost accusingly. Freya made a face.

"I *barely* knew, but yes. I recognized the severity of it when I saw the candidates for election," she muttered.

"Sorry," Elion interrupted, "Am I the only one confused here?" Freya snickered at Elion's words, a webbed hand covering her mouth.

"*You* would be, wouldn't you?" Freya slightly teased, but there was venom behind her voice.

"Sylva was becoming a bed for elf apologists," Poseidon explained. "The girl that I was looking for, the human girl who came to kill Rhea and Khalon, she was a known and outspoken elf apologist." Elion's face contorted into more confusion. He held up a webbed hand. His pale skin looked even paler underwater.

"I'm sorry," he said, "What is an elf apologist?" The two Gods stared at Elion. He cleared his throat. "I-I get that my brother is trying to take over the world but what does that have to do with elves as a whole?" Freya gave Poseidon a knowing look as he waved her look away.

"Aureum really doesn't teach you guys what happened, do they?" Poseidon said. Elion shrugged.

"While I think it's terrible for my brother to try and take over Asynithis, it's not anything new. The humans did it once and we don't fault them for it," Elion argued.

"The humans did it *once*, yes, but before them it was the

elves. And where did they get the formula of genocide? Also from the elves," Freya muttered angrily. "This would be the second time for you all, if Adamar manages to get it done. Although, by getting rid of the Gods, he has an easier time of it."

"What do you mean 'the second time'?" Elion asked quietly.

"An was a bit more hands off at the beginning," Poseidon explained. "He wanted to watch and observe what the creatures he created on this world would do. It's not anything new. In a different world, similar to this one but in a different realm, he tried to see what it was like if he was in complete control. It bored him. So the Gods weren't on Asynithis, we answered small prayers but didn't for bigger ones. During this time, the elves had some belief that they were superior to the other races of Asynithis. They slowly took over, in the guise that they wanted to teach other races the knowledge that they had come to know. Instead, as we all know, the elves tend to take from other races to build up their own society."

"That's not true," Elion countered, "We have created everything that modern society uses. Hover cars were created by the great elf inventor Ettrian Theralei, and *everyone* uses those." Freya looked up as she thought about what Elion said.

"No, I'm pretty sure his human servant invented it one day. He was always using his humans to think of things, wasn't he?" Freya said, nonchalantly, as she looked over at Poseidon.

"Yes, Ettrian worked his servants very hard for the sake of science," Poseidon agreed. "But, that is just in more recent times. How to make fire was figured out by the first dwarves, but elves said it was them that figured it out. And it goes on for the rest of Asynithis history." Elion stared at the two of them, his heart pounding. *No, it couldn't be true*, he thought. He knew elves had a bit of a purist way of thinking. Elves couldn't marry outside of their race due to the beautiful signature white hair of elves being marred with color. He knew that particularly his brother very much had disdain for the other races of Asynithis, especially humans. But then...

"If humans copied elven strategies when they took over, why do elves hate them so?" Elion asked, sitting up a little straighter.

"Because they were able to take over Asynithis for much longer than the elves ever did. Plus, who likes being copied?" Freya laughed.

"At first the humans were all in agreement, they wanted to get rid of magical creatures. At the beginning of their evolution, they were treated much like how the beastoids are treated now. Once they rid the world of magical creatures, at least so they thought, they turned on each other, valuing what the elves hold so dear," Poseidon said. Elion didn't need an explanation for what elves valued. He knew and Poseidon knew he knew.

"So, my brother wants to bring back the old days," Elion muttered. Poseidon nodded.

"It seems as though there is a growing coalition that wants the old days to come back. The draconian was wrong. It *was* an organization, though not really one that wanted the Gods gone, per say," Poseidon said. Freya frowned at what he said.

"With the Gods gone, they can take over a bit more easier now. No one to ever stop them, like how we stopped the humans after a while," Freya whispered. "And of *course* some humans are embracing it, despite the fact that they will still be on the bottom of the totem pole."

"Those who remember the history hate elves. It is why Argentiunda is not very fond of them. Though elves didn't stand a chance in the water, on land, they were very brutal to Argentiundans," Poseidon said.

"Adamar taking over the world is only secondary to what is currently happening, though," Freya pointed out. "The Mortiferis is a bigger threat. Have you seen them before, Poseidon? You have been around from the beginning." Elion knew the religious tellings of the Gods. First the God of All suddenly came into existence and made the world. When he became lonely, he created a brother who filled the world with seas. When the God of All began to make creatures, he taught the God of Sea to make them as well and they had a great time creating the world. Eventually, the creatures were multiplying too fast and it was destroying the world, so the God of All then created the third brother, the God of Death. Creatures started to experience death and there was balance in the world.

"I *have* seen them before," Poseidon quietly said, his eyebrows furrowed as he thought. He looked like he was in a lot of pain, sifting through all the memories that the God of Sea had.

"What happened to them? How were you able to get rid of them?" Freya asked. Poseidon held up a hand as his face turned red slightly, veins popping out on his forehead.

"Sorry," he said, breathlessly, "This isn't really information I'm privy to. He has this memory hidden, deep down." Freya nodded her head.

"I understand," she said. "Take your time." He stared at the ground as he concentrated while Elion shifted his makeshift tail uncomfortably.

"Yes, I have seen them. It was when the God of Death was... young," he struggled to speak. It was against what the God of Sea wanted, it seemed. "He just wanted to... he wanted to..." Poseidon looked like he was in pain and then suddenly, his head lifted up and his hazel eyes looked like waves were crashing in them.

"The God of Death wanted to create, like the God of All and

I," Poseidon's voice seemed calmer and deeper somehow. Freya's eyes looked slightly frightened but she averted them quickly when he made eye contact.

"He created the Mortiferis. They were haphazard looking, as they look now, but the main thing is that they did not have a soul or a thought in their heads. They were created from death, and were death. They could destroy anything that they touched, including us. The Gods had no control over them," Poseidon continued. "The God of Death wanted them to have free will, similar to the creatures God of All created. However, those creatures could not hurt God of All, could not touch him. These creatures could. It was a long time ago, after God of All experimented with his hundredth planet. When the Mortiferis were found out, and it was found that they could not die as they already were and they could not be controlled, God of All sent them to the first planet he experimented on. It was *realms* away from here."

"So we're not the only planet that has life?" Elion asked. Freya looked at him like he was stupid.

"Of course you're not. There are many planets in this universe that have life. But, there are many realms as well. Parallel universes, as it were. We jump from each to each. Currently, we're focused on this one," Freya shrugged. Her eyes slowly looked down to the ground. "Or, we were."

"The more that God of All created new realms, new worlds to experiment on, the more massive of a responsibility the God of Death had. It must've strained him," Poseidon said, his voice slowly drifting and fading. He looked like he was in pain again and then he relaxed.

"So it was the God of Death that orchestrated this whole thing," Freya pointed out. "And that's why you sought her out when you were attacked."

"And it was him that must've manipulated my brother into

going along with it," Elion said. Freya raised a disbelieving eyebrow.

"You know the nature of Adamar. All of us Gods know as well. If the God of Death did any manipulation, which I doubt she did, it didn't take much," her nose scrunched up as she said it and Elion looked down at the ground. He knew who Adamar was, how inherently evil. It really wouldn't have taken much to convince him to rid the world of the Gods and bring Asynithis to its former elven glory. Elion sighed.

"He said that even you guys can't touch the Mortiferis. So how are we supposed to fight them?" he asked, dejectedly. Freya and Poseidon exchanged a glance.

"We don't know," Poseidon answered.

30

Rhea dropped Khalon's hands as they shifted out of the shadows into the forests of Caedoxia, causing the others to stumble out of the darkness. It was dark now and being in Caedoxia wasn't what Rhea was planning, especially since the sanction against them had recently been decreed in the last couple of years. The vampires of Caedoxia weren't able to feed on creatures without consent and only were able to feed within the borders of Caedoxia, the country that most vampires chose to live in. A lot of them were starving. And with — Rhea looked around — at least two part humans, including herself, it would be hard navigating through the forests without encountering one.

"We're in Caedoxia," she whispered slightly so that only Khalon could hear. Part of his body was still in the shadows and the other was still coming back into his physical form. He looked down in her general direction in surprise by what she said. Traveling in the shadows was delaying his eyesight.

"We're *what*?" he asked, his slight irritation obvious.

"It's hard to run around in the shadows with — what —

four other creatures?" Rhea said, matching Khalon's irritation. He rubbed his head in thought. Rhea noticed that his hair had gotten slightly longer. It wasn't really a good look on him as it seemed to grow out in all different directions.

"By the way, are you going to cut your hair anytime soon?" she asked, unintentionally picking at an insecurity in Khalon in order to change the subject. Although, she had to admit she preferred him with the almost buzz cut look that he had usually. He turned his head and stared at her incredulously.

"I'm sorry I haven't gotten a haircut during the *end of the world*," he muttered. "It didn't really *cross my mind*. Besides, I highly doubt that my hair has gotten *that* much longer in the past couple of days since the last time I've seen you."

"Well, I mean, I could notice it so obviously..." Rhea muttered under her breath.

"Are we in Caedoxia?" a girl with unnerving white eyes asked, her head turning towards Rhea. She recognized her soul as the reincarnated Seer, otherwise known as the Queen of Witches. Rhea sighed as the topic that she was trying to avoid was brought back up again.

"Oh, the Seer is here," Rhea said, more to herself than anything, but responded with: "Yes, unfortunately."

"I'm half human, I'm unsure if you know, and I don't really feel *safe* here," the Seer said, scrunching up part of her face on the word "safe."

"I am also part human, so I understand your worry," Rhea muttered. It was a well known fact that ever since the humans had taken over Asynithis, a vampire's favorite meal was a good full blooded human. Considering they barely get that now, part human would have to suffice.

"It's hard for her to travel in the shadows with extra people," Khalon explained. In a quieter voice, but not really that quiet, Khalon leaned in and asked Rhea, "*Where* were you trying to take us?" She threw her hands up in frustration.

"I don't know. I was just trying to bring everyone to safety. I wasn't really thinking about the destination," Rhea said, frustrated. Khalon straightened back up and nodded to himself, as if he had thought that the whole time.

"This is the God of Death," the Seer said. Rhea stared at her for a moment, a feeling of fear washing over her.

"Yes, and you are the Seer," Rhea said, her voice like ice. She didn't want to know what her future held, but she had a feeling the Seer was going to tell her anyway.

"Esi," she said, smiling slightly. Then her white eyes glazed over as her legs buckled from underneath her. Khalon made a move to catch her, but he was too late. She sat there, her legs underneath her as she used her finger to draw in the dirt. Her voice came out distorted as they all looked upon her in horror.

"*White, Gold, Red, Gray, Green, Blue.*
Six eggs that were sent away.
She whispered, 'Be loyal and stay true'
Before she began to decay.
They were all sent to a different world that had mortals who *didn't believe.*
The Mortiferis caused havoc and burned,
But don't worry, the Saviors didn't forever leave.
Seven lives they will live before they come back.
In return for our suffering they'll give their lives when the *demons attack.*" It looked like she had drawn six egg shapes, but then she started drawing within them. The Phoenix, who Rhea assumed was the Princess Kamaria considering the Seer was Princess Esi, signed desperately as she sat down next to her sister.

"She's not done yet," Rhea translated. Khalon looked at her, surprised.

"You know sign language?" he asked. She gave him a look.

"Of course I know it. I've been alive longer than this world has," she muttered. Kamaria signed for them to shut up.

"Six eggs were sent away
But six will come to stay
For when the heir arrives, all will bow
For no one can resist
The Gods' ancient vow.
Everchanging eyes, who see all
Only he can stop the Mortiferis
And reverse death's fall," Esi continued, her voice still sounding far away and distorted. She stared straight ahead as she drew a symbol that looked something like an eye but it had complicated lines within it.

"She keeps mentioning eggs," Rhea whispered. Khalon nodded.

"She had told me when I met her that the Mortiferis will take over unless the Saviors from Earth come, whatever that means," Khalon whispered back. A part of Rhea stilled. She wished Khalon hadn't told her that.

"Terra is a different realm from here," Rhea answered. "Like ours but as she said, it has mortals that don't believe. Specifically, it's just a world of humans." Khalon didn't look fazed by the information. Esi took a giant breath as she continued speaking.

"The one who can pierce through
With the rays of the sun
She can breathe life into
Mortiferis' and Death's one.
But beware the holy burning of this child.
She might be God's gift
But her mind dares to become wild." Esi drew a symbol in the next egg shape with her long nails that looked like an elaborate

sun. God's gift? Rhea felt the God of Death stirring inside of her. Whoever she was, she was created by An. They all were. Either already have been, or will be, and she knew that the God of Death was going to try and stop him.

"The King of the Seas,
The uniter of ocean floors,
He will cure the disease
That plagues creatures beyond shores.
He will lead the creatures of water
Back to the seas of Asynithis
And help stop the slaughter
Of creature blood since." The third symbol she drew was in the shape of a raindrop but held what looked like to be a wave with a fish's tail. Created by the God of Sea? Rhea wondered if each of these eggs were something that was a collaboration between the Gods left. *No,* Rhea thought, *I can't listen to this.*

"Tell her to stop talking, I can't be listening to this vision," Rhea said. Kamaria signed at her, a bit frustrated and angry.

"I can't tell her to stop. Once she starts, she cannot stop," Kamaria signed. Her servant interpreted with a blank face for Khalon. Rhea sat down in front of Esi and grabbed the hand that was drawing.

"Esi, you understand who I am and what is inside of me. I can't be hearing this fortune or I will try to stop it from happening," Rhea pleaded. Esi's eyes stared right at her.

"Asynithis will awaken
Once the Mother takes a step.
The world will be retaken
Once the Mother has wept.
For she has all life
Coursing through her veins.
And the world will grow despite
The ash that remains," Esi continued. Her other hand drew

the next symbol which was a tree with vines circling it. An arm reached out from the tree. Esi was already filling in the next two symbols: a swirl intertwined with another swirl with two eyes peeking through and a square with four flames connected by a dark spot.

"Khalon, I can't be here," Rhea said, about to disappear into the shadows, but he grabbed her arm to stop her.

"I think you're supposed to hear this," Khalon said quietly. "It's odd timing. The moment she met you, she had this vision. And she told me she doesn't normally talk in riddles." Rhea stared at him as Esi's curly hair rose around her face, as if some kind of electric current was moving through her.

"Born of wind and born of fire,
Ice in her veins and darkness in his
Apart, they bring strength and can inspire.
But beware those demon twins,
For we'll all be dead
Unless they're torn.
For Darkness on Darkness
Is the most deadly thing.
They'll side with the Mortiferis
And become Dark Queen and King.

White, Gold, Red, Gray, Green, Blue.
Six eggs that were sent away.
She whispered, "Be loyal and stay true.
Before she began to decay.
One chance to save our world
Or our world will forevermore be gray." Lightning flashed across the dark sky and Esi's white eyes seemed to glow at the end of her words. Then, she passed out, her eyes closed as Kamaria screamed out. She crawled to her sister's head to

make sure that she was okay. Khalon started to step forward but then stopped, his eyes on the horizon.

"What is it?" Rhea asked as he put a finger to his lips. His eyes searched the darkness until he found what he was looking for.

"So, I'm guessing you're out of steam traveling in the shadows, right?" Khalon leaned in to ask Rhea. Rhea felt her heart pound as she tried to quiet her head.

"Yeah, I don't think I'd be able to get very far with all these people," Rhea muttered. She stared at the spot where Khalon was looking, but couldn't see anything. *He must be able to tap into his dragon eyes now*, Rhea thought to herself.

"Is it a vampire?" Rhea asked. Khalon nodded as he squinted.

"It's not just a vampire," Rhea confirmed. Khalon nodded again.

"I don't think we'll be able to outrun them either," Khalon muttered. *Great*, Rhea thought. She looked at their group as she tried to think of a plan.

"It's fine though," Khalon said, "You can take down a whole army, I'm sure you can take down a vampire and a werewolf." *A werewolf?*

"So-o-o," Rhea said, drawing out the word. Khalon raised an eyebrow. She swallowed. "Here's the thing... My powers, *I think*, have been weakened." His head fully turned to look at her.

"What do you mean you think your powers have been weakened?" he angrily whispered at her. She frowned at his tone.

"Well, see, the thing is, and it was quite a surprise for me as well to have come across this information," Rhea began. Khalon motioned for her to keep talking. She cleared her throat. "So it turns out that the God of Death's soul has been taking over my body at night and planned this attack on the Gods and Asynithis as a whole with King Adamar, the King of Aureum—"

"Yes, I already know all that," Khalon said, frustrated with the repeated information. Rhea tried to hide her shock.

"Oh okay," she said, thinking about how to speed it up. "Well, apparently the God of Death—"

"Put part of his soul into Adamar's kid. Yeah, I already know," Khalon finished. Rhea glared up at him.

"Well, if you already know, *Khalon*, why are you asking me why my powers are weakened?"

"It's weakened because of that?" he asked. Rhea stared at him for a while.

"Don't talk to me anymore," she said.

"I mean, you don't think you can kill a vampire and a were-wolf?" Khalon asked. Rhea shrugged.

"I don't think I'm in control of the underworld anymore really," she said. "It's a miracle I can still travel in the shadows, honestly."

"Because part of his soul is missing from yours?" Khalon asked. Rhea nodded her head furiously.

"Yes," Rhea exclaimed, "That's why people can now see my precious face." She pointed at her face. Khalon scoffed.

"Only I can see your face," he said.

"Oh yeah?" she asked, stepping closer to him. "Tell that to your brother."

"You saw Khai?" Khalon's face couldn't hide his surprise.

"Okay, guys," the servant's voice cut through as Kamaria signed quickly. "There's a werewolf and a vampire about thirty yards from us. I feel like we should do something about it. Also, yes, we can all see her face." Khalon stared at Kamaria in shock.

"*Everyone* can see her face now?"

"Can you please just get your sword out?" Rhea said,

annoyed. She already heard that she was ugly from Khai. She didn't want to be reminded that everyone could see her and think the same thing. Khalon pulled his sword out from his vest, whipping it out so that the blade came out. Kamaria held her sword with two hands as she stood up, standing in front of her sister. Her servant took Kamaria's place of holding Esi's head.

"Thank you, Aponi," Kamaria signed. The servant nodded. She stared at Esi's face as she ran a hand above it, over and over. A witch, Rhea realized. She was surprised that she couldn't sense it before. But, she tried to turn her attention to the vampire and werewolf standing before them. The vampire was incredibly tall and his face was gaunt. It looked like he was starving while the werewolf stood slightly behind him. It was clear that the wolf was still a pup. It was a human looking face that had morphed into a wolf. He was almost as tall as the vampire and he stood on all fours. His ribs were visible through his thin fur.

"Humans," the vampire said, as the werewolf sniffed the air. "Or partly at least."

"We don't consent to you feeding on us," Khalon said. The vampire smiled, making his skin tighter across his face.

"In Caedoxia, we don't punish those that feed without consent. We are a starving people, as you can see," the vampire gestured to him and his partner. The werewolf smashed its teeth. "Not enough food."

"C'mon," Khalon whispered towards Rhea, "You can't take on a couple of almost dead creatures?"

"Don't talk to me," Rhea whispered back.

"You don't want to fight a draconian and a phoenix," Khalon said, holding his head high. "Besides, we have the God of Death here." The vampire laughed as he looked at Rhea.

"The Gods have no jurisdiction here. They left us long ago," the vampire smiled, but there was a touch of bitterness in his voice.

"Anyways, I've heard all the Gods are dead," the vampire shrugged as he stepped closer. Khalon and Kamaria tightened the hold on their swords.

"The God of Death isn't," Khalon said through his teeth.

"She's about to be," the vampire smiled as he and the werewolf lunged forward. Khalon stepped in front of the vampire who was about to sink its teeth into Rhea's neck. His sword hit the vampire's jaw and the vampire took a step back, surveying the situation. Kamaria had stepped in front of the werewolf, her sword cutting into the werewolf's stomach. It howled in pain. Rhea looked around Khalon to watch the vampire's expression.

"I don't need a human's blood for sustenance, especially one marred by elven blood," the vampire snarled. "A draconian would do just fine." The vampire moved quickly, its figure blurred. Rhea watched as Khalon's skin hardened into scales as his eyes watched the blurred movement. Her eyes closed as she tried to concentrate on the souls of the underworld. Bringing up their voices, she felt their voices echo around inside of her as her eyes opened.

"Die," she whispered, the voices repeating her words, as the vampire stopped moving suddenly. His eyes glanced at her desperately as Kamaria cut the werewolf in half. The two halves fell to the ground with a thud as Kamaria wiped the black blood off of her face. She scowled. The vampire's face slowly turned to gray as his eyes became lifeless. He dropped to the ground as he stared helplessly up at Rhea as she walked closer to him.

"I *am* God," she said, a thousand voices coming out of her mouth as the vampire breathed his last breath. Suddenly, it felt like she was kicked in the chest as she doubled over, trying to catch her breath.

"Rhea!" she heard Khalon cry out, grabbing her before she fell to the ground.

"That took a lot of energy out of me," she whispered, smiling up at him weakly. Khalon stared as the vampire's corpse started to disintegrate into ashes while the wind eroded his body away.

"You created the Mortiferis didn't you," he whispered. Her eyebrows raised slightly. He was more quick-witted than she had thought. Slowly, she nodded her head, trying to stand up. Khalon supported her.

"The God of Death did. Long ago," she said, surprised by her honesty.

"Esi is okay," Aponi said, her hands finally stilled at her side. Kamaria glared at Khalon and Rhea as she walked over to her sister to check on her. Esi looked like she was sleeping, as her breath deepened.

"She'll wake up soon," Aponi assured Kamaria, signing as she talked. Kamaria thanked her and petted her little sister's hair.

"It's the God of Death who does that, right?" Khalon asked after a moment of silence. Rhea nodded her head.

"My powers come from him. It's not this body or this body's soul that does it," she muttered. "I was afraid he wasn't going to respond to my words." Suddenly, Rhea felt a whoosh of air pass by her. There was a part of her that sank at the realization of who was coming. Stepping out of the wind was a young boy with shaggy dark hair, holding the arm of an older woman with short red-gray hair. Her eyes were swollen, as if she had been crying.

"An," Rhea greeted him coldly. "Neith."

"Rhea," An responded in the same manner. He looked

around at the broken corpse and pile of ash that lay on the ground. "I see you've had an eventful evening."

"Every evening is eventful in Caedoxia," Rhea said, her voice still like ice. Khalon looked between them, his eyes following their faces as they talked.

"So this is the God of All?" Khalon asked, staring at An. An didn't seem shocked by his surprise. He understood it was hard to feel any kind of reverence for a kid.

"God of All and Goddess of War and Weaving," Rhea introduced them, gesturing towards An and Neith. Kamaria's eyes grew wide at the mention of how Neith was the Goddess of War. She bowed her head slightly. Neith nodded in acknowledgment and gestured for her to straighten up.

"A great warrior," Neith praised Kamaria as Kamaria read her lips. Aponi interpreted her words for her, but Kamaria was already blushing at the highest compliment.

"I saw Alator pass," Rhea said, a bit apologetic. "I'm sorry I couldn't help him."

"Didn't help him? Or *chose* not to?" Neith's eyes flashed as she stepped towards Rhea. "An told me everything." An held up a hand.

"We are not here to fight," An said, his voice as monotone as ever. Rhea couldn't help but roll her eyes. "Rhea cannot help what has been hidden from her. It is not her that your anger belongs to." Neith scowled as she stood next to An.

"Why are you here?" Rhea asked. An stared at her, his eyes as dull as ever.

"The prophecy," An said. "We have much to discuss."

"How did you even *hear* about the prophecy? She literally just said it," Rhea said exasperatedly, gesturing towards the sleeping Esi.

"I know all," An said in a matter-of-fact tone. "Poseidon and Freya are still alive in Amnis Lux." Rhea wasn't surprised to hear that they were alive, but rather that they were able to hide in Argentiunda. She shook the thought out of her head. She shouldn't use the word hide. It made it seem like she was trying to find them.

"All the rest of the capital cities were destroyed, except Furvus and, of course, Amnis Lux," Khalon's face came alive at what An had to say, probably thinking about his little brother. "Most of the royal families and governments are destroyed. Including the oligarchy here in Caedoxia."

"Okay, why are you telling me this?" Rhea said, not able to help her annoyance.

"We must meet up with the rest of our remaining family," An said, his voice betraying a hint of sadness. Rhea stilled, staring at him.

"I can't," she whispered. He looked at her, his eyes coming alive a little, something that happened when the God of All was a little closer to the surface.

"You must."

31

It was unnerving for Khalon to gaze upon the God of All for the first time. He was just a lanky kid with shaggy black hair and gray eyes that almost looked glazed over at all times. It was as if his eyes held so much knowledge and memories that it couldn't quite come alive. It was the only part of An that aged him, Khalon thought to himself as he noticed that An's eyes reminded him of Esi's. At the thought of the Seer, he glanced over at Esi's sleeping body and found that his eyes continued to wander until they ended up on Rhea's face. Her eyes were squinted slightly, like she was in pain, and her face was twisted up into frustration. The more Khalon looked at her, the more she seemed to dazzle him, in a way. He missed her; he could admit that to himself.

"You must," An said. Something in his eyes made Khalon want to look away. It wasn't a request that was given to Rhea, it was an order. Her face fell. Khalon knew that she was the reason this was happening to Asynithis. He also knew that she wanted to do everything she could to stop it, even if it meant isolating herself from everyone that she cared about. His gaze lingered on her for a moment longer before he tore himself away from her. He couldn't think about how Rhea felt. His body was itching for some kind of action that he could take in order to save his world.

"How would we even be able to get to Amnis Lux?" Khalon asked An. "It's completely underwater and some of us aren't really water friendly." Khalon gestured towards himself, Kamaria, and Esi. They were all fire based creatures and water wasn't really their friend. An glanced at them, his eyes surveying the three creatures.

"You all do not need to come," he said. "Just the Seer." Rhea's head popped up to look at him incredulously.

"We can't just leave them. Especially in Caedoxia," Rhea argued. An looked down at the corpse that lay near his feet.

"They seem to be able to protect themselves just fine," An pointed out. Rhea's mouth stayed agape.

"An—" Rhea started.

"They don't need to come," An demanded. Rhea's eyes searched his face, but there was nothing she could say. Khalon could see her try to open her mouth, but nothing would come out. This was the power of the God of All. Khalon felt himself get irritated. He had never seen Rhea be at a loss for words.

"I'm not going to let Rhea go by herself," Khalon said, standing tall. Kamaria signed angrily the same thing, but for Esi. He knew his size didn't intimidate the boy that held the God that created the whole of Asynithis and perhaps other worlds. He was the God of All, but Khalon couldn't help posturing himself in order to be intimidating. An stared at him, blankly. It felt like he could see his past, present, and future. Again, he felt himself reminded of Esi's gaze.

"Fine," An finally said. "They can come. But the waters will kill the fire inside of you." Khalon knew what An was insinuating. If the fire inside of him dies, his body would end up withering away and An wasn't going to keep that from happening. Rhea's eyes looked frightened as she stared at him, desperately.

"I can hold all their fires," Aponi said, standing up from the ground. The moon illuminated her long, dark hair.

"If they are gone too long, the fires could consume you. Especially three," An warned. Aponi shrugged.

"My powers can handle it," she assured. An shrugged back, as if saying that it was her funeral.

"Fine," he muttered, waving a hand towards all of them. Khalon felt his stomach turn as his body became lighter. He looked down at himself and it was as if he was starting to disappear. Desperately, he looked towards Rhea who smiled slightly at him.

"It's like traveling in the shadows," she said. "Except, An travels through wind and light." Her smile and eyes were the last thing that Khalon could see before she disappeared into the air. Suddenly, he felt this rushing feeling, and everything around him blurred into multiple colors and flashes of light. They were traveling incredibly fast. And just when they started, the wind spat him out and the ground came rushing towards him. Khalon stuck his arms out, and they barely caught him, his head hitting the floor. He felt the contents of his stomach start to rise up as he gasped for air. It felt like he was holding his breath but also breathing too much at the same time.

"Air travel is a bit taxing on the body," Rhea muttered, pityingly, as she rubbed his back. Khalon let the bile come out. It wasn't a lot, but he could feel the air leaving his body. He turned his head slightly and watched as the waves came closer and closer to him. The sight of the water made him feel sick, and just as he realized how he felt, he turned back around to throw up once again.

"Creatures," Rhea said, a bit annoyed. "Such fragile bodies."

"There is beauty in fragility," An answered, defending his creations. "It is why so many of us fall in love with them." Khalon felt Rhea's body stiffen.

"Let's go," she said, stepping away from Khalon as he tried to push himself to sit up. His head felt dizzy and the sound of Kamaria emptying the contents of her stomach as well wasn't helping with his own nausea. She was having a harder time than him, though, from what Khalon could tell. Esi was perfectly fine. The Goddess of War, Neith, was stalking up and down the shoreline, her hands on her hips as she stared out into the sea.

"The Argentiundans must know you're here," she boomed. Her voice was strong, but still held a feminine charm to it.

"They will be here shortly," An said. Khalon wasn't sure how they were going to be able to stay under the water for long. Just as he was thinking this, a mermaid pulled herself out of the sea. Shells were intertwined into her long, brown hair as she stared at the creatures. When her dark eyes found An's, she bowed slightly.

"Your holiness," she said.

"Princess Luni," An greeted. Her tail flipped out of the water, flashing gold scales. Khalon's eyes couldn't take in enough of the sight. He had never seen a mermaid before.

"My brother is awaiting your presence. He has found the ones that you were looking for as well. They're staying at a shojo pub," she said. An nodded.

"Will you be able to take these creatures to the palace as well?" Her eyes that looked like ebony jewels gazed over at them.

"Once their fires are put somewhere safely, we can. We've developed a new potion. It seems to be working for the others," she answered, her eyes finding An's once again. An glanced over at Aponi who seemed starstruck at seeing a mermaid. She quickly composed herself as her ears turned red. Gathering her arms and hugging them to herself, she muttered some words under her breath. Khalon felt his breath get caught in his throat as something started to be pulled from him. It wasn't painful, but it was an uncomfortable feeling.

"You won't be able to use the spirit of the dragon in the waters," An said as Khalon felt something seem to punch at his chest. He couldn't speak. His eyes looked over at Kamaria's, whose black eyes looked desperately at Aponi. She looked like she wanted to rip her throat out. Slowly, fingers intertwined with his own and squeezed his palm gently. Bewildered, he looked over at Rhea looking up at him, the tips of her eyebrows raised. She looked like she was in pain watching him. And then, Khalon felt the last of his essence come out of his body. Aponi looked like she glowed slightly as the fires settled with her. Her face showed her discomfort.

"Are you sure you'll be able to hold the fires within you for at least the night?" An asked, looking slightly concerned for the witch. Aponi nodded her head.

"Of course," she answered. An stared at her slightly and then nodded once.

"Let us go," he said. Two other mermaids popped out of the water, small bottles in hand. Princess Luni motioned for them to drink it and as Khalon did, he felt his body start to burn. It was incredibly painful as his body contorted into something that would be able to survive in the water. His legs melded together, and his face felt like it was cut open as gills appeared at his cheeks. Luni's gills moved at her neck and Khalon wished his were at his neck as well. Gills on your cheek? He felt like it would look so strange. He stared at Rhea as her body contorted. If she was in pain, she didn't show it.

Her hand had dropped his and as he looked at hers, it was webbed. Khalon felt his balance become compromised as his feet turned webbed as well, and dropped into the ocean, trying to hold his breath. He realized, as his face hit the salty sea, that he could still somehow breathe as the water moved through his gills, down his throat, and into his lungs.

"Come," Luni said, her voice echoing in the water around them. They followed Luni into the depths of the Argenti Sea, the city of Amnis Lux illuminating the dark, deep waters. Khalon stopped in admiration, letting the others swim ahead of him. It was a city that he had never seen before. Many different sea creatures were swimming throughout it and it was lit up by algae. The architecture was breathtakingly unique. It truly was a beautiful city.

Luni, with the two other mermaids, swam up to the golden structure that was in the middle of the city. It was made of triangular points that were connected to each other with long rectangular hallways. She swam through a door, motioning for the others to follow her. Rhea's copper brown hair was surrounding her head like a large halo. On her back were black markings that went down her spine. It looked like a tattoo and was in letterings that Khalon had never seen before. He had heard about the Celestial language, but this was the first time he had ever seen it. Khalon felt the air leave his lungs once again as she stopped and looked at him. She was beautiful. Khalon didn't know how he had ever thought she looked like a shih tzu.

"What?" Rhea asked, her face confused as to why he was just staring at her. Khalon shook his head, taking the thought out of his mind, and they swam into the palace together. The palace doors opened up into the opulent throne room. Sitting on a chair made of gold, shells, and sand dollars, sat the current King of Argentiunda, the brother of Princess Luni.

"King Maleko," An said. His gills were on his neck and Khalon couldn't help but feel envious of it. Khalon already had scars and scales on his face, gills just had to be making his face look even more weird. Maleko bowed his head.

"God of All," he said. His hair was brown, wavy, and long, moving slightly with the water. His skin was as dark as Khalon's and his arms were marred with black markings, similar to Rhea's, but it was in different shapes rather than letters.

"The guests that you required are here," Maleko said, gesturing towards the creatures that were swimming in. Khalon's eyes widened as he recognized Poseidon's face. His brightened, a smile breaking out across his face.

"It's been a while since I've seen you two," Poseidon said, swimming right up to Rhea and Khalon. Khalon noticed the other two that were next to him. One was the most beautiful creature that Khalon had ever laid eyes on, and the other was a pure elf. Rhea tried to hide her smile as Khalon hugged Poseidon back.

"I'm surprised to see you still standing draconian," Poseidon teased. "Although, I've heard some news that your brother was able to defeat a Mortiferis so I guess I shouldn't be too surprised." Khalon stiffened. Khai?

"What have you heard about Khai?" Khalon asked, swimming closer towards Poseidon. Poseidon backed up.

"Oh, well, it just happened but—"

"Later," An ordered. Poseidon's mouth shut. "We must discuss more important matters." Khalon stared at An incredulously. His brother fighting a Mortiferis, let alone defeating it, *was* a pretty important matter.

"King Maleko," An addressed the Argentiundan King, "I must tell you that tonight, many royal families have fallen. The capital cities of every country have effectively been destroyed.

Part of the Aureum army is already in movement towards the last royal family that is still persisting, which is in Draconia. The rest of the Aureum army have begun invading their neighboring countries. Princess Kamaria and Princess Esi are the only ones left of the Ustrina royal family. It is undeniable that the elves will take over Asynithis once more." Kamaria cried out at Rhea's translation. Prince Sipho and their father were dead. The memories of the Royal Phoenixes were gone. But Khalon was preoccupied with a different piece of information. The Aureum army was coming for his brother.

"What does that have to do with me?" Maleko asked, shifting in his throne. "The elves couldn't take over Argentiunda before. They won't be able to this time either." An shook his head, turning towards Esi. Esi had awoken while transforming into... whatever creatures they were supposed to be. She swam up, her white eyes glowing.

"Just the part about Argentiunda," An said, his voice barely above a whisper. Esi nodded, her curly hair surrounding her head.

"*The King of the Seas,*
The uniter of ocean floors,
He will cure the disease
That plagues creatures beyond shores.
He will lead the creatures of water
Back to the seas of Asynithis
And help stop the slaughter

Of creature blood since," her white eyes dimmed and her voice faded as she got to the end of that part of the prophecy. Khalon winced as he remembered the whole thing. None of it made any sense to him.

"What is this?" Maleko said, swimming up from his throne. His eyes flashed angrily at An. "*I* am the King of the Seas. What disease does this child speak of? We have never suffered from plagues like you surface creatures have."

"This is part of a larger prophecy, Maleko," An said, calmly. "The elves have the means to turn your people into surface creatures. It's a sickness that Adamar will develop with the elven witches in order to weaken the power of the seas."

"Elves cannot be witches," Maleko scoffed. "Witch powers can only be developed in humans and within our people. Elves cannot—"

"Elves can," An interrupted. "They can. And they are realizing that now. They will bring your people to the surface. You must be ready. It *will* be a genocide."

"Can you not stop them, God of All?" Maleko said the term sarcastically. An either didn't notice or didn't care and shook his head, almost sadly.

"We will be gone soon," An said. Poseidon stared at him sharply.

"What do you mean?" Poseidon asked. An shook his head, not wanting to continue the conversation.

"Draconia hasn't fallen, like you said," the girl who stood next to the elf swam up. "How do you know that Aureum will prevail over Asynithis? How do you know that we will cease to exist?" *We?* It hit Khalon that she was one of the Gods as well. Neith swam back and forth, holding her head and her eyes made Khalon feel that he should stay far, very far, away from her.

"War is one sided right now, Freya," she said. "Alator is dead." The girl called Freya stopped moving her tail.

"Alator is..."

"Dead, yes," the Goddess of War finished her sentence.

"I'm sorry Neith. I really couldn't—"

"Save it, Rhea," Neith growled. Rhea looked away.

"How did Khai save Furvus?" Khalon asked, changing the subject.

"Furvus is not saved. It has fallen. But, he will protect the rest of it from Aureum," An answered.

"Okay, but how?"

"Dragon's blood," Rhea answered. She shrugged as Khalon looked at her, incredulously. "Apparently, your brother has fallen for the same addictive substance as the rest of his 'great' line."

"What do you mean?" Khalon asked, slowly.

"Khai has all the powers that you have, as long as he is drinking dragon's blood. Although, that means that there's a dragon somewhere underneath the city of Furvus. I probably would bet that he's protecting that dragon more than the city. It's the last one left, I believe," Rhea mused. She looked upwards as she thought. "Or, it might not be the last one. I can't remember."

"A dragon's power can destroy a Mortiferis?" Rhea looked at An, annoyed.

"The fire from a dragon can, yes," An answered. "It is not the most effective way to destroy a Mortiferis, but a lot of it can break down the body enough that it won't move."

"Mortiferis *can* heal their bodies," Rhea said, almost proudly. Khalon knew it wasn't her that was proud as he looked into the fire that was in her eyes.

"Yes," An looked exhausted, "But it slows them down enough."

"So Khai used the power of a dragon in order to stop the Mortiferis from completely destroying the city of Furvus," Khalon confirmed. An nodded.

"Yes," he said.

"And I could do that too then," Khalon said. An nodded again.

"You could," he answered. Khalon shook his head as he looked at Rhea.

"I have to go help him," Khalon said. Rhea scoffed.

"He doesn't like you. He thinks you committed treason," Rhea said. "And he knows the truth about the spirit of the dragon now, so he knows it wasn't treason that was committed."

"I can't let Draconia fall," Khalon said. "I can't let Aureum take it."

"He won't let you have the throne," Rhea pointed out. Khalon couldn't believe what he was hearing.

"I don't *want* the throne, Rhea," he said. "I just want to keep him safe. If he died, I would never forgive myself. No matter what is between us, he's still my little brother." Rhea looked like she wanted to say something, but then her eyes focused on something behind Khalon.

"I will come with you," Rhea said, her eyes focusing back on Khalon. His heart skipped a beat. "Draconia is the only thing protecting Ustrina from Aureum. If Aureum takes Draconia, they'll take Ustrina." Khalon felt his face fall as he realized that Rhea was translating for Kamaria. He turned to look at her.

"Yes, you can come with me. I'll need your experience in battle," he said. Kamaria smiled slightly. An stared at the two of them.

"You can do as you please. But it will be to no avail," An said. "Only those from the prophecy can save Asynithis." Khalon looked back at the lanky kid that held so much power within him.

"No offense, An," he said, "But you said you're dying. So you don't know what might happen after that." Touching Rhea's arm lightly as she looked away from him, Khalon nodded towards Kamaria. She signed something towards Rhea.

"We'll watch over her," Rhea said as she signed back, referring to Esi. Kamaria touched her forehead against Esi's and then swam over to Khalon. Khalon glanced back at Rhea for the last time. He knew that whatever happened next, he might never see her again. She stared back at him, realizing the same thing. The Gods were all going to die, according to An. And that included her.

"Don't look at me," was all she said. But Khalon knew what it meant.

"Don't talk to me," Khalon said back, with a smile. Rhea smiled slightly back, but her eyes looked sad. Khalon knew she understood what he meant but he wished he could hug her or hold her before they parted. But, he swam out of the palace without doing either, Kamaria in tow. He wanted to pray for Rhea's safety, but there was no one to pray to anymore. All he could do was make sure his brother and his country were all right. And he knew just how to do it. Whether Khai would accept it or not was another matter. Swallowing hard, he swam towards the surface.

32

Rhea watched as Khalon swam away. A part of her burned as she watched the back of him leave. Kamaria followed closely behind him. She looked back to glance at her little sister, but Khalon didn't look back at all. Rhea knew this might be the last time she'd see him.

"You love him," Rhea was surprised by the voice suddenly next to her. She scoffed.

"I don't love him, Freya," Rhea muttered. Though it made Rhea think. Did she? Freya laughed, but without emotion.

"Your soul betrays you, Rhea. But I would be careful. It is not the God of Death that loves him, you know. It is you, yourself. It's written all over him. Your love encases him," Freya warned. Rhea felt herself stiffen. If the God of Death didn't love him, there was no way to protect him from herself.

"Poseidon thought it was our brother who loved the draconian," Freya guffawed at the thought. "But, I knew it wouldn't have been. He's fond of him, for sure. But I think that's you influencing him. You're the one who's in charge most of the time, aren't you?" Freya stared at Rhea for a long while as Rhea shifted slightly through the water.

"Our souls can't come together as one because—" Freya held up a webbed hand.

"I know why," she dismissed. "But this is the first time that the body's soul is in charge mostly. He must've been saving his energy for something else."

"This is unimportant," An interrupted before Rhea could tell Freya exactly why the God of Death has been saving his energy. An looked over at Maleko and bowed slightly.

"King Maleko, is there a room that I can go in with my brothers and sister?" An asked. Maleko nodded, almost dejectedly. He was still processing what An had said before about a witch's plague.

"Luni," Maleko ordered. Luni nodded and motioned for them to follow her. She led them into a room made entirely of pink coral and bowed before closing the doors.

"Should an elf be listening in on this?" Freya asked, crossing her arms. The elf next to her looked slightly insulted.

"I told you what I heard about my brother. I'm not friendly with him and I don't agree with what he's doing," he muttered. At the mention of "brother", Rhea recognized the elf. Elion, King Elkhazel's youngest son and the only one who was worthy of King Elkhazel's soul.

"He is a good elf," Rhea pointed out. Elion silently thanked her.

"I wouldn't trust what *you* have to say," Freya said, pointedly.

"You just told her that she is in charge of the body more than our brother, Freya," Poseidon argued, exasperated.

"Did you not hear what An said earlier? We're all going to die and it's her fault," Freya said, her voice becoming shrill. "She designed the end of the world and the end of the Celestials and we're supposed to listen to anything that she has to say?"

"We have lived long enough anyways," Poseidon whispered. Freya looked at him incredulously as she turned away. Neith just continued to glare at Rhea.

"I'm sorry that I have caused all of this. I'm sorry that I created those monsters long ago and, just, I'm sorry. I'm sure we can live through this though," Rhea said.

"I want to hear it from our brother, Rhea. Not from you," Freya muttered, her eyes flashing at Rhea. Rhea felt herself shrink.

"We won't live through this," An said to Rhea. "Did you not listen to the prophecy?"

"Prophecies can be rewritten," Rhea pointed out.

"No," An said. "This one cannot. We, the Gods, will not live through this. These are our last days."

"What prophecy?" Poseidon asked. An turned towards Esi who's white eyes moved around quickly as she recalled it. Her eyes started to glow.

"Please tell them," An said. Esi repeated the prophecy that was said to Rhea earlier and Rhea felt the same feeling that she had then; that she needed to run as far away as she could. Poseidon's head was bowed as he listened and Elion's eyes just got wider and wider. Freya's face was contorted in concentration and then defeat by the end of the prophecy.

"It says nothing of the death of all Gods," Freya pointed out, though her voice betrayed her.

"One chance to save our world or our world will forevermore be gray," Poseidon repeated the ending. "If these saviors are the only ones who can save Asynithis and this realm, then that must mean that we're long gone and powerless." An nodded.

"Yes, they are the only ones who can save this realm and all other realms. Only they can destroy the Mortiferis once and for all," An said. He narrowed his eyes as he thought. Rhea could tell he was looking into the future.

"There are many outcomes that could happen," Rhea said. An nodded.

"If they fail, the realm that Terra is in could become in peril as well," An said.

"Earth," Freya clarified.

"Earth? Is this the 'different world where mortals didn't believe' line that she talked about?" Elion asked, referring to Esi. An nodded once again.

"How are we going to send... eggs? They are made in eggs?" Freya asked.

"The reflections," Rhea said, the answer dawning on her. "Any reflection can take someone to a different realm, if they do it right. But, I can jump to different realms pretty easily through reflection. I've done it a lot. So, who's to say that once those eggs are sent, that someone can't go after them and destroy them?" *Someone like me*, Rhea thought. An stared at her, life coming into his eyes.

"We will close the portals once the eggs are sent. I can do that, but it will take every last bit of strength that I have left," An said. "They won't open back up until they are ready." *Every last bit of strength?* Rhea stared quizzically at An as Freya shook her head.

"This won't work. The portals don't follow linear time. We might send the eggs back but it might be in the 1900's in Earth's time and hundreds of years into our future," Freya pointed out. "It would be too late by then."

"Asynithis would be fine," An assured.

"Seven lives they will live before they come back," Esi repeated one of the lines from the prophecy. "It's already been foretold that it will be a long while before they come to save Asynithis."

"The Mortiferis destroyed every capital city and wiped out nearly all the royal families and leaders of Asynithis in one night," Freya pointed out. "They can destroy Asynithis in a few days, if there are more of them."

"There isn't," Rhea interrupted. Freya gave her a look of distaste. "There are only a few. Enough to get rid of the capital cities but not enough for a whole army. I only brought enough to get rid of the Gods. Not enough to destroy the whole world." At least, Rhea hoped she didn't.

"They didn't come on their own," An confirmed. "The rest of them are a few realms away. It was almost time anyway." Rhea could feel that An was trying to comfort her, in a way.

"So, only these saviors can save Asynithis," Freya repeated. An nodded.

"Seems like there are a lot of ways that it could go wrong," Poseidon pointed out. An nodded again.

"They will be tested. But by the end, they will be strong enough to save their home world and the one they grew up on."

"That's why there's seven lives that they have to live," Esi joked. Rhea stared hard at An. There was something that An had said that was still bothering her.

"How are we supposed to create these Saviors of Asynithis?" Rhea asked. An turned towards Poseidon. Rhea could tell that An already knew. Somehow, he knew everything, as if he was the one who planned it in the first place. A part of her, the God of Death, stirred in annoyance.

"I will need your help, Poseidon," An said. "You're the only other God here that can create souls and energy." That comment cut Rhea deeply. She tried to shrug off the feeling as An turned towards Neith.

"Neith, you will need to protect us while we create the eggs. I have a feeling that someone might try to attack us while the eggs are being created," An said. Neith nodded in obedience.

"Is that someone Rhea?" Freya point blank asked. An stared at Rhea and nodded slightly.

"They *are* your creations, Rhea. I understand how you would feel a fierce urge to protect them from doom," An stated. Rhea scoffed.

"I understand that they're evil creatures. I'm not going to try to stop you. But I know I can't make any promises, especially when I'm asleep," Rhea barely whispered the last part of her sentence.

"They're not evil. They just... are," An said. Rhea felt even more annoyance bubble up inside of her. Who was An to tell her about *her* creations?

"The battle for Draconia's capital is important," An continued. "We have to create the eggs and send them at the highest point of Asynithis. The highest point is at the top of Dragon Mountain, in Draconia. It is also very close to the capital. It will be used as a distraction."

"Creatures will be dying during that battle," Rhea pointed out. Namely one draconian that she didn't want to meet their end yet. "Don't call it a distraction." An shrugged, almost apologetically.

"I still don't think this is a good idea," Freya muttered.

"It's the only one that we have," Poseidon pointed out. "Hopefully, these 'Saviors' know what they're doing."

"I have a plan that has been put into motion," An reassured them. "Besides, if everything does get destroyed, we won't be around to see it."

"A sick joke, An," Poseidon said after a while. An's face broke into an uncharacteristic smile.

"It's the end of the world, Poseidon. If we can't joke now, when can we?" he asked. Freya rolled her eyes, but smiled slightly too. An told them to meet him up on the shores of the Argenti Sea in the morning. Then they will all travel to Dragon Mountain once the battle has begun. Before exiting the room, Rhea grabbed An's arm. He looked down at the gesture and Rhea quickly let him go as he looked up at her.

"Yes?" he asked.

"An," Rhea started. She paused.

"Yes?" he asked a bit more forcefully.

"What do you mean it will take every last bit of strength for you to close the portals?" Rhea asked after a while. An stared at her for a while, and sighed a sigh that seemed to have been bottled up for centuries.

"Brother, I knew you were going to do this someday," An said after a moment of silence. "And every time that I have created something, I have used bits of my soul, like you have done for Than, Adamar's new child. That includes all of us Gods as well. I have been planning for the end, since you've created the Mortiferis. And my energy is almost up."

"What do you mean?" Rhea pressed. An looked at her as he tried to think of what to say.

"Well," he said, his eyebrows furrowed at the top of his forehead, "It means that creating these eggs will be the last thing that I can really do before I... decay, as she put it in the prophecy."

"You'll decay," Rhea repeated, the words not really sinking in. This was something that she had always wanted. An dead. But the idea that it would've happened soon anyways... She killed her family for no reason.

"We would've all disappeared with you anyways," Rhea muttered, reality sinking in. An nodded, a bit pityingly.

"Yes," he said. "Although, your soul is living within something you created. You might not wither away. And Poseidon might not either, though it might take up the rest of his energy as well, helping me."

"Thanks for answering me, An," Rhea said, acknowledging that he didn't have to say anything. He nodded slightly and then started to swim away. He paused at the coral door frame.

"Rhea," he said, "There *is* something that you can do. It will stop the Mortiferis for a while. Think about what I said today and you'll find the answer in time." Rhea stopped herself from rolling her eyes.

"Thanks," she said, biting back the sarcasm. Why An couldn't just tell her was something she couldn't understand. Granted, if the God of Death heard it... well, if the God of Death heard it who cares? It wasn't like he could stop her within her own body. Besides, it was probably something only he could do anyways.

But still, his words made her think. And she could feel the God of Death thinking along with her. What was it that *she* could do to stop the Mortiferis for a while? She replayed the conversation over and over in her head until she eventually found the answer. Her soul could stop the Mortiferis. Her soul, the part that was connected to the God of Death, might be so overwhelming to the monsters that perhaps, her energy might be able to stop them.

33

Adamar quickly walked down the hallway as he wiped the sweat rolling off of his forehead. He didn't understand how Furvus was still standing. Turning a corner, he could feel the shadow behind him. He needed to get into his private quarters as fast as possible. Opening the doors, he felt the shadow follow him in and then the cloaked figure stepped out of the shadows. It grew taller as it stood before him.

"The Mortiferis didn't destroy the city of Furvus or kill the royal family of Draconia. To my knowledge, two of the princes are still alive!" Adamar whisper-shouted angrily. He stared into the emotionless shadowy face, exasperated, but fear still crawled through his skin.

"You forget your place," the voices slithered over Adamar's body as he froze, "I do not take orders from you." Adamar involuntarily shivered.

"Of course," Adamar muttered. "I am only worried about battling the Draconian army. They are... *arguably*... better at battle than us." Adamar sounded like he was choking, admitting that Draconia could be better than Aureum at anything.

"Use the Mortiferis," the figure whispered. Adamar felt his body freeze at the mention of the Mortiferis. He had seen them as his army carried them back, sleeping, locking them up into the basement of the palace.

"U-use them?" Adamar stammered. The figure floated around the room.

"The Mortiferis can be awakened, if you use the child," the voices said, repeating themselves.

"Than?" Adamar asked, his blood slightly starting to boil at the mention of his "son". His wife, Essarae, was obsessed with the child. She refused to be apart from it as if she knew that if she stepped away from the baby, Adamar would immediately try to kill it. He shrugged inwardly. He had to admit that she knew him very well.

"Yes," the figure stated. "Find a witch that will bring your minds together. It won't last for long, you would only be able to give a singular command. Use the Mortiferis to defeat Draconia. And let them get to Dragon Mountain."

"What's on Dragon Mountain?" Adamar asked.

"Hope," was all the figure said, in disgust, before disappearing. Adamar stared at the empty space. He needed to find the most powerful witch of all of Aureum.

———

Rhea woke up on the shores of the Argenti Sea. Her body was covered in her black cloak and she wasn't wet at all, indicating that she had been out of the water for a while. She sat up, the sand sticking to her hair and back, as she looked out into the sea. The sun was starting to rise. Holding her head, she tried to remember where she was and what was just done. *Let them get to Dragon Mountain*, she heard echo in her mind as she tried to get past the impenetrable wall that was the mind of the God of Death. She felt the God of Death curse her within.

"I'm sorry I'm trying to stop you," she said out loud, sarcastically. Them. She tried to think of what the God of Death might be referring to. Of course it had to be the Mortiferis. *To defeat Draconia*, she was able to get that thought out past the wall. Her eyes widened. Khalon.

"You're going to use the Mortiferis to defeat the Draconian army," she muttered to herself. "Khalon is there." *What does that matter to me?* It was the first time she could hear his thoughts, not echoing as hers but as his alone.

"I can't let you do this," she whispered, standing up. She had to go to Khalon to warn him. *It's already been done.*

34

Khalon pulled himself up onto the shores of the Argenti Sea, his body morphing back into his bipedal self. His legs pulled themselves apart as he tried not to scream from the pain. He had trained to dull his nerves when he was younger, but the pain of one's limbs going from one to two was a feeling he couldn't describe. Kamaria wasn't far behind. His clothes were folded neatly next to Aponi who was sleeping against the base of a tree. Khalon felt his face burn as he quickly ran towards his clothes, throwing back Kamaria's. They dressed facing away from one another. If Kamaria felt equally as embarrassed, Khalon didn't notice. He leaned down and shook Aponi's shoulder who's eyes sprung open. Khalon took a step back, surprised by her reaction. She stared at him and Kamaria for a moment as the rest of her slowly woke up.

"Oh," she said, standing up. "You guys are done?" Khalon shook his head.

"No, but I need to help my brother in Draconia," Khalon

said. Aponi stared past him as Kamaria signed to her. Khalon turned around to look at Kamaria.

"And I am going to give him my expert help in battle since he's never been in one," Aponi said as Kamaria smirked smugly at Khalon. He rolled his eyes.

"Yeah, we'll see who takes out more elves," he said in a joking tone, but inside his heart was pounding. He hated taking the lives of others, and he could feel the fear creeping into his chest.

"Well, before that," Aponi said, dusting the grass off of her colorful pants, "You probably will need your fires back." Khalon completely forgot that the fire was out of his body. If he and Kamaria were going to go into battle, then they would need their fires in order to adequately defend themselves. Aponi spread her arms and her face scrunched up in pain as she started to glow. Khalon felt the breath get pulled out from his lungs as something replaced it. Unlike before, it wasn't painful but rather a slightly uncomfortable feeling as the fire settled back into his body. He felt himself get stronger as he stood up straighter. Yes, the fire is what makes a being a draconian. He watched as Kamaria's eyes were closed as she took back her fire. Her face looked peaceful.

"Did my hair turn white again?" Aponi's voice cut in suddenly as Khalon looked at her. He took a step back.

"Y-yes," he felt himself stammer and immediately kicked himself mentally for doing so. Aponi's hair was as white as snow, like an elf's, when before it was as black as can be. Aponi sighed deeply.

"Not again," she muttered.

"Why is your hair white?" Khalon asked, his eyebrows raised.

"It happens sometimes if I use too much magic," she grumbled, kicking at the ground. She sighed loudly, again. Her face changed as she interpreted Kamaria's words.

"It'll come back," she said as Kamaria. Then her face dropped again as she talked for herself. "I know, but I look like an elf like this." Her lower lip jutted out as she pouted for a little and then shook her head to show her usual blank face.

"What will happen to Esi's fire?" Khalon asked. Aponi stared at him.

"When Esi steps out of the Argenti Sea, I'll feel it. I'll be able to give her the fire then, no matter where I am."

"So, Draconia?" Kamaria signed at Khalon. Khalon nodded.

"I need to talk to my brother," he said.

"Prince Khai," Kamaria signed. She made a face as she did. He had the feeling that they had met each other before.

"But getting there will be a problem," Khalon muttered out loud. Kamaria's eyes twinkled.

"Or will it," she signed, a smile budding on her lips. She pointed a finger to the sky while a burst of fire came out of it. Khalon tried to hide his jealousy at how well Phoenixes were able to use their power. Draconians could only use fire if they themselves had the spirit of the dragon within them. And even then, the power didn't come at will through any part of their body like a Phoenix.

The fire sparkled into the sky like a mini firework and the sparks fell to the ground like rain glittering in the moonlight. Kamaria's smile grew bigger as she closed her eyes. Khalon looked up into the sky as he heard wings flapping in the distance. Blocking the moon was a giant creature that looked like it had bat wings attached to it. It's face was long and it looked as if it had a beak and was covered in gray scales. It lowered itself onto the beach as the sand blew around them. Khalon tried to shield his eyes from the mini sandstorm as

Kamaria looked up in wonder. Her black, round eyes looked even darker as she admired the beast.

"A Kongamato," she signed, happily. Khalon looked at the creature, curiously. Most beasts of old had died out or evolved into something that would fit into the old human world. He never thought he would see a creature like a Kongamato or even a dragon, though he knew one existed somewhere.

"All Inkanyambas have a Kongamato. My extended family granted me one when twenty years had passed," she signed. "I couldn't get one earlier because as half Phoenix, I grow very slowly. Mentally and physically." Khalon nodded, but was still too shocked to speak. The beast measured him with beady eyes.

"Go up on the Kongamato with her highness," Aponi said, pushing Khalon forward. He swallowed his fear and followed Kamaria up onto the Kongamato by stepping on the edge of its wing and pulling himself up onto the back. He tried to still his body to not show that he was shaking.

"What about you, Aponi?" he asked, looking behind him. He knew there wasn't enough room on the creature.

"Oh don't worry," Aponi said. "I have my own way of flying." She then turned herself into a human sized white bird, almost in the blink of an eye. Khalon's eyes widened.

"What is happening," he said to himself.

"Flying should be a piece of cake for you, dragon," Aponi said for Kamaria. His eyes almost fell out of his head. Even as a bird, Aponi can speak.

"I'm a thunderbird," Aponi said, recognizing his shock and confusion. "We shapeshift."

"Impundulu," Kamaria signed. Aponi nodded after interpreting.

"We have different names in different cultures, but they all mean the same thing. Lightning bird, thunderbird. We're all the same."

"They're not usually witches though, are they?" Khalon said, insecure about his facts.

"I killed my witch," Aponi said, her voice gruff. "Absorbed her powers." Khalon nodded slowly.

"Right," he said. "*Right*," he said, again, but more quietly. He was traveling with a murderer. *Would've been good to know earlier*, he thought. Aponi started flapping her wings as she flew into the sky. Kamaria patted one of Khalon's legs, trying to be comforting but instead frightening Khalon more by the action, before directing the Kongamato to follow after Aponi. He bit his lip back to keep from screaming the whole way, but once they were up in the clouds, gazing down at the patches of land beneath them, he felt a sense of calm wash over him. He wished Rhea could see what he was seeing. He didn't know when he had started feeling some sort of attachment towards her. But he could feel it growing by the second.

The Kongamato flew with surprising speed. He could see the countries blur past underneath him and more surprisingly, Aponi was able to keep up with the Kongamato. He watched as the city of Furvus came into view. Smoke was rising from the city and part of it was in ashes. The Kongamato slowly lowered itself as Khalon took in the sight. His city was partially destroyed. The streets were quiet and empty but the palace still had their lights on. Khalon hopped off of the Kongamato before it was able to settle onto the ground. Aponi shape-shifted back into her human self as she landed, as Kamaria followed behind Khalon.

"We have to warn my brother, but not only that," Khalon said, taking a deep breath, "We have to convince him."

"Convince him of what?" Aponi asked.

"We have to convince him to let the beastoids join in with us," Khalon said. Kamaria crossed her arms and made a face before signing at him, angrily.

"You killed the beastoids for wanting their own independent country and now you want to team up with them? What makes you think they'll follow suit?" Kamaria signed.

"I know," Khalon said. "I know that we killed a lot of them but if they want their own independent country, being under Aureum won't give them that."

"It might be better than teaming up with the enemy," Kamaria signed back. Khalon chewed on the inside of his lip. If Kamaria felt this way, would the beastoids?

"We have to at least try," Khalon said after a while. Kamaria stared at him with her bottomless black eyes and then nodded once. She will go along with the plan, even if she thought it was futile.

"They *are* better at battle," she signed. Khalon nodded.

"Yeah, because they do what you do," Khalon said. "And most draconians don't know their signs. I only know a few because a..." How could he describe Liam? "...a co-worker of mine knew some signs." She chuckled.

"We had them make up their own signs," Kamaria signed, smiling at the memory. "They wanted to unite with one another and they couldn't speak to different species. The best way was to create their own sign language. A few people I know helped them develop it. Only they and the beastoids know their signs."

"Do you know them, since you know the people who helped develop it?" Khalon asked. Kamaria's smile faded.

"If I did, I wouldn't tell you," she signed, glaring at him. Khalon put his hands up defensively.

"All right, all right," he said, turning back around to face the palace. He motioned for them to follow him as he walked up towards the looming building. It was guarded by the brain dead guards that would guard the Ring. They weren't able to communicate much or reason at all, so trying to tell them that he was supposed to be in the palace wasn't going to go over very well.

"I'll go take a look around the palace to see if there's another way in," Aponi said, understanding that Khalon had only been in the palace a few times in his life. Khalon nodded as Aponi transformed herself into a white bird and flew up towards the top of the palace. Khalon and Kamaria watched as she circled it multiple times before landing.

"There's an open window," she said, "But someone is sleeping on the bed there. If we move quietly, we may be able to get past her and to the throne room."

"Is Khai in the throne room?" Khalon asked, his heart falling into his stomach. Aponi nodded.

"Yes," she said. "He *is* king now. And he's surrounded by military personnel it seems."

"What do you mean he's king now?" Khalon asked, slowly. Aponi stared at him, her eyes softening as her face grew sympathetic.

"Your brother was sitting on the throne," she said. "It must mean that your father is—"

"No—"

"—dead," Aponi still finished her sentence, though quietly.

"There's no way," Khalon said, almost accusingly. "He also has the powers of the dragon. He drinks the same substance. There's no way that he's..." His voice trailed off. He couldn't say the words. His father couldn't be dead. That day could not be the last time he saw his father. Aponi and Kamaria exchanged glances.

"I could be wrong," Aponi said, shrugging one shoulder.

"But your brother is at least acting king now." Khalon stared up at the palace windows.

"Let's go," he said. Aponi sighed deeply and transformed back into a bird. She carried Kamaria, slowly, up through the window first and then came back for Khalon. Her talons dug into the vulnerable parts of Khalon's vest as he glared at the gesture. This vest was something his father gave to him, though indirectly.

"Why...are...you...so...heavy?" she huffed as she flapped her wings harder in order to get higher up the palace wall.

"I'm not that heavy," Khalon muttered, crossing his arms. She flew higher trying to get Khalon through the window, but instead Khalon's middle hit the edge of the window while the rest of him hit the wooden side of the palace.

"Ow," Khalon whispered angrily as he pulled himself through the window.

"Sorry," Aponi said. "That's my bad." Khalon glared at her as she swiftly flew in through the large window and transformed back into her human self.

"Why didn't you transform into a bird when we were fighting that Mortiferis?"

"What was I going to do? Carry everyone over the wall? I could barely carry you," Aponi pointed out. Khalon opened his mouth to say something else when Kamaria put a finger to her lips and pointed to the sleeping woman in the bed. Khalon closed his mouth as he stared at the woman. Queen Aoife. *Damn*, Khalon thought to himself. *She* lived but his father didn't? *What a nightmare.*

They quietly scurried across the room and opened the sliding door into the hallway. Piling into the thin hallway, they quickly walked down it. Khalon was surprised guards weren't outside of Queen Aoife's quarters. Maybe Khai didn't really care for his mother like he thought.

"So how are we going to get into the throne room?" Aponi whispered as they peeked around the corner.

"Just walk in," Kamaria signed.

"I don't think we can just walk in," Khalon whispered back. Kamaria laughed a little.

"I can," she signed, before standing up straight. She walked around the corner as Khalon and Aponi tried to stop her. Aponi sighed and then made her face go blank before walking behind Kamaria. Khalon didn't know whether he should wait or if he should follow. Spinning around, he decided to follow after them. Kamaria stared at him like he was an idiot. In hindsight, it might've been the wrong move.

The guards outside of the throne room stared at Khalon, recognizing him. Khalon forgot that he was 1. Banished from Draconia and 2. Was a Champion in the Ring of Fire and had shown he had the spirit of the dragon within him in that same arena.

"This is the Princess of Ustrina, her royal highness Princess Kamaria," Aponi said, stepping in front of the two. One of the guards narrowed his eyes. "She requests to speak to the new King of Draconia."

"You already know that the king has changed?" the guard asked. Kamaria signed as Aponi interpreted.

"We have spies everywhere," Aponi said for Kamaria. "Let us speak to your king. It is a matter of great importance." The guard leaned back as his eyes fixated on Khalon.

"I don't know if you know this, your highness, but you have what one would call a traitor in your midst," the guard said, gesturing towards Khalon.

"He is important to our mission," Kamaria signed. "And your king will have your head if he doesn't hear this message." The guard stared at Kamaria, obviously weighing the fact that he didn't know Khai very well or his nature.

"Fine," the guard said. "But if he didn't want to see you, you tell him I fought you from coming in. He'll believe that a Champion bested me." He knew enough about Khai to recognize that he was young, at least, Khalon mused. He motioned for the other guard to step back, who did so, warily. Kamaria walked through first, sliding the doors open as Khai looked up from his seat. His eyes stared straight into Khalon's.

"What is the meaning of this?" he demanded. Khalon could see something in Khai's eyes that wasn't there before. A bit of an orange glare came from his light brown eyes. It reminded him of Rhea's eyes. The Ministers of Draconia were lined up on either side of the throne, facing one another and creating a bit of an aisle from the entrance to the seat.

"This is her highness Princess Kamaria of Ustrina," Aponi introduced. Khai stared at the Princess.

"I heard that Ustrina's royal family was killed," he said, pulling a piece of paper out from a box. He read over it again and nodded. "Yes, our ambassadors stated that the royal family was murdered by the Mortiferis that attacked Invenire."

"Your sources are wrong," Kamaria signed. "And we've literally met before." Khai looked away from her.

"Sorry, the name Kamaria? Not familiar." Kamaria rolled her eyes dramatically. Yeah, they had definitely crossed paths before, Khalon concluded.

"Don't you at least know the sign of a Royal Phoenix?" She looked annoyed and Aponi's voice held the same annoyance that was on Kamaria's face.

"Their veins, your highness," one of the Ministers said to Khai. Khai's eyebrows furrowed as he stared at Kamaria's face. "They glow red." He and Kamaria glared at each other for a long while before he nodded, waving the Minister away.

"I apologize for any offense," Khai said. Khalon stared at his brother. It was the first time he had seen him for a long while. He was older than before, and looked a bit lankier, obviously going through the steps of beginning adolescence.

"What is this about, Princess Kamaria? Or should I say Queen of Ustrina?" Khai said. Kamaria stared at him, her face unwavering.

"I am not Queen," she signed. "The people will decide what to do about who will lead. My sister could become Queen as well." Khai nodded, acknowledging the information. He looked down at his papers.

"Why do you have my brother in your ranks?" Khai asked, his eyes slightly glancing up at Khalon for a moment and then flickering to Kamaria. There was a sense of calmness about his demeanor instead of the high energy that Khalon was used to.

"Your brother has a message for you, from the God of All," Kamaria signed. She took a step back and looked pointedly at Khalon. Khalon and Khai stared at each other for a long while before Khalon stepped forward.

"Khai," he began and then shook his head. "Your highness, the ones who sent the Mortiferis to each capital city of Asynithis were the elves of Aureum. They have the Mortiferis under their control and they used these monsters in order to rid the world of royal families."

"They obviously did not succeed in that," Khai joked. The Ministers laughed in obligation.

"Yes, they didn't succeed. But their army is coming to Furvus to take down the city and you. They mean to take over Draconia," Khalon said. This sent a flurry of conversation to echo around in the throne room. Khai frowned as his Ministers discussed this information with one another.

"The Aureum army will probably be using human creations. Creations we don't have," Khalon pointed out. "And we don't know if they'll use the Mortiferis or not, but—"

"We do know," a voice interrupted Khalon. The voice preceded the body appearing, but stepping out from the shadows was Rhea. Her hair was tied back in a ponytail and her hood was off of her head. She glanced over at Khalon. Khalon couldn't help a smile appearing on his lips at the sight of her.

"They are using a witch to connect Adamar and his son's minds in order to control the Mortiferis. They *will* use the Mortiferis during this battle," she said. Khai's eyes widened at her appearance.

"God of Death," he said. Khalon noticed that Khai looked small in his father's throne. "We will be fine if they use a Mortiferis. I destroyed one." An eruption of agreement came from the Ministers.

"You destroyed *one*, yes. But you can't destroy three or even seven at a time," Rhea pointed out. "Let alone a whole army of them." That was news to Khalon.

"Did you bring a whole army here?" he whispered. Rhea shrugged, her eyes not leaving Khai's. But as Khalon looked at her he could tell that she was lying. *She's trying to scare him.* Khai watched the exchange and then straightened up in his seat.

"How do you know that Aureum will bring with them the Mortiferis?" Khai asked.

"Because I told them to," Rhea said, nonchalantly. She then made a face and corrected herself: "Well, not *me* but the other soul that resides in my body is the one who told — you know what? Never mind. It's too complicated to explain." Khai stared at her and then looked at his Ministers. For a moment, he looked helpless. And how could he not? He had only been king for barely a night.

"The Draconian army is strong, there's no doubt," Khalon said, stepping forward. "But, we will need help. And the beast-

oids are powerful in battle, Khai — I mean — your highness."
Khai shook his head.

"No, we can't have the beastoids join us in battle. We are at
war with the beastoids," Khai countered.

"That's our father's war, not yours," Khalon said quietly.
Khai stared at him.

"The beastoids *are* very good in battle, your highness.
Better than we are, admittedly," one of the Ministers piped up.
Khai stared at him in thought.

"The beastoids wouldn't agree to team up with us," Khai
said after a while.

"I told you so," Kamaria signed at Khalon while Aponi
whispered the translation. Kamaria smirked as Khalon rolled
his eyes.

"They will in order to defend their home and if you negotiate with them," Rhea said.

"Negotiate?" Khai asked.

"Give them their own country," she said. "If they help you
keep Aureum from invading Draconia, they can have their own
country."

"That's a tall order. And you of all creatures know what
they've done to us," Khai argued. *Done to us?* Khalon looked
over at Rhea as she nodded.

"Perhaps," she said. "But what other choice do you have?"
Khalon shook the thought out of his head. He'd find out eventually what happened.

"They're coming soon, Khai," Khalon said, desperately.
"They'll be here in a few hours. *You're* king, Khai. You need to
make a decision, and soon." Khai stared at Khalon, his expression unreadable. Finally, he motioned for a Minister to come
closer.

"Make contact with the beastoids, and go as fast as you
can," Khai said. "We don't have a lot of time." The Minister

nodded and swiftly left the throne room. Khai made eye contact with Khalon.

"Let's hope that their help is worth it," Khai said. Khalon nodded, smiling at his brother.

"It will be."

35

Freya woke up suddenly as she felt herself start to choke. *That damn concoction,* she thought to herself as she swam out of her room. Knocking on Poseidon's door, she held her breath for as long as she could. Poseidon opened the door and Freya pointed to her wrist indicating that time was up. He nodded and gestured for her to go. Freya quickly swam out of the palace towards the shore nearby. As Freya swam, Poseidon knocked on Elion's door. Elion opened it as an uncomfortable feeling started to settle into his chest.

"We have to go," Poseidon said. "The potion is fading."

"What about the others?" Elion asked. Poseidon shrugged.

"I saw Thanatos leave earlier. An will get the others," Poseidon said. Elion's face scrunched up at the name. *Who the heck was Thanatos,* he thought to himself. But, he nodded anyway and followed Poseidon up. Poseidon threw a stone at An's door and shrugged when Elion's face questioned it.

"I don't want to waste time," he muttered. Quickly, they swam to the shore.

Freya paced back and forth, dressed in her armor once

again. She watched as Elion and Poseidon surfaced from the water and turned around as they changed back into their bipedal figures. Elion screamed out in pain at the transition, but Poseidon stayed quiet, numb from his past multiple transitions. Freya turned back around after some time had passed.

"Where's Rhea?" Freya asked. Poseidon shrugged.

"Yama left earlier last night," Poseidon said. He squinted at the sun that just rose. "I think she left recently."

"To where?" Elion asked. Freya sighed.

"Where do you think? To help that draconian from herself probably," she turned towards Poseidon. "An?"

"He's coming."

"Can you believe all this nonsense? This savior talk?" Freya said, gesturing towards the sea. She sat down in the sand in frustration. "I mean, we're all just going to die?"

"We've been alive for long enough," Poseidon said. "We've created thousands of worlds together. At some point, Gods have to disappear as well." Freya scoffed.

"You might've lived long enough but I *am* younger than you," Freya pointed out. Poseidon laughed.

"Barely. Once creatures started to fall in love with each other, you just appeared out of An's chest. It was disturbing, to say the least," Poseidon recalled the memory. Freya frowned.

"We're all just extensions of An," Freya muttered. Poseidon nodded.

"Yes, though, *well*, not all of us," Poseidon said his thoughts out loud, referring to himself and the God of Death. Freya knew he was right. It was complicated, how they all came to be. But An purposefully made his two brothers while the rest just popped out of him as creatures continued to live, in order to divvy up An's work. She was An and An was her. There was no separating the two of them.

"When do you think Aureum will invade Draconia?" Freya asked as she looked up at the changing sky.

"Probably in a few hours," Elion muttered. "My brother likes to strike in the morning. It's advice that Edwyrd had given him one time. Something about how people have just woken up and need more time to wake. I think it's just because Edwyrd doesn't like fighting at night, to be honest." Elion stopped as he thought about his brother. Freya could tell on his face that he was wondering where Edwyrd aligned.

"He's probably leading the strike," Freya said. "Adamar isn't one to be found on a battlefield." Elion looked away. He didn't want to talk about the sins of his family. Freya, Elion, and Poseidon sat down by each other on the beach as they waited for An. These were their final moments, and they all knew it.

"Elion," Freya said after a while. "You should go back to your brother." He looked at her like she said the most ridiculous thing.

"What?"

"You don't need to die with us, Elion. You have your whole life to live," she said. "You should be with your family."

"You just told me that my family is evil. Why would I want to be with them?" he asked, his face contorting into disgust. Freya felt her face soften as she looked out into the sea.

"They're still your family," she said, watching the waves come into shore. "You don't get to choose them. But you love them anyway." *Like Rhea*, she thought but couldn't bring herself to say out loud. It wasn't that Rhea was evil, Freya had realized. It was more that there was a sense of duty there. The underworld had gotten to be too much for her, with all those worlds. They had to be destroyed or the Gods might continue to make more and more worlds. A selfish decision, but not one that she could fault, really.

"I'm not leaving," Elion said with childish stubbornness. "I will protect you." Before Freya could insist that she really, truly, does not need any protecting, especially protection by a child no less, An's head popped out of the water.

"Oh, you're here?" she asked. The sun was high.

"It's time," he said as he pulled himself out of the water. The Seer and Neith weren't far behind. Freya looked away, politely, as they all got dressed. Neith grabbed her arm afterwards and helped her up from the sand.

"You remembered your armor," Neith said, almost proud. Freya rolled her eyes slightly and smiled. She pushed Neith lightly.

"I remember all your teachings, Neith. Even from lifetimes ago," she said. Neith smiled back.

"You're worthy of the name Freya," Neith said. It was a big "to do" that Freya had chosen that name, when technically that was a name that Neith could've chosen as well. But she didn't, so Freya didn't understand what all the fuss was. It was the humans' fault for putting them together when they were actually separate Gods.

"We must get to Dragon Mountain. Esi?" An asked, turning towards her. She had pulled her curls up to the top of her head. *She must foresee a battle*, Freya thought.

"The battle between Draconia and Aureum has begun," she said, her eyes moving back and forth as if she was watching something. They were unnerving, those eyes that see all. The daughter of An.

"Then we must go," An said, waving his hand. Before Freya had time to protest traveling by light, the sun flashed in her eyes and suddenly they were standing on top of the snowy peak of Dragon Mountain.

"You would think since it's named Dragon Mountain it'd be warmer," she said, holding her arms around her body. She felt someone touch her arm. Turning towards the action, Elion was staring straight ahead, holding himself up by holding onto her. She rolled her eyes.

"Are we there? Why is it so cold? Also, am I the only one who can't see anything?" Elion asked.

"Don't worry," Esi said, "I can't see either."

"Oh," Elion said, smiling at the voice not realizing it was the blind Seer talking. "I'm glad I'm not the only one."

"She's already blind, Elion," Freya pointed out. Elion paused.

"Oh." An laughed. Freya jumped at the noise. An wasn't the type who laughed often and Freya had seen him smile and laugh far too much in the last few hours. Disturbing, to say the least.

"Don't worry," An said. "It's just from traveling by light. It'll pass soon." He turned towards the empty, snowy peak.

"So," Freya said. "Where are we supposed to create these eggs?" As Freya said this, An turned his palms towards the ground. Taking a deep breath, he slowly raised his arms as the ground around them started to rumble.

"Oh, he's going to create it now. That's great," Freya muttered sarcastically under her breath. The stone jutted out of the ground and came together in a makeshift hut. An moved his hands and the hut got bigger and taller. Suddenly, the ground stopped shaking.

"Should be done now," An said, his face scrunched together in thought. They moved towards the stone building and An opened the door.

"Neith," An said. Neith nodded and stood right outside of the door.

"She's not coming in?" Elion asked. Freya shook her head, almost sadly.

"She's ordered to stay outside of the lab, in case something comes to attack us. She's our first line of defense as the Goddess of War, you see," Freya explained. She looked back at the door that closed, worried about her sister.

"She'll be fine," Poseidon reassured as he threw an arm around her shoulders. Freya shrugged the gesture off. She knew he was lying. They were all dying today. *But it's in order to save this world and the next,* Freya thought to herself, trying to believe her words. The stone building looked rugged on the outside, but the inside had all the makings of a top notch lab. Freya looked around in wonder. She never could understand how An was able to create just from a thought.

"Poseidon," An said. Poseidon left Freya's side and wandered over to An. An pointed at an incubator and started to talk to him about how they should create the beings that were to become the Saviors of Asynithis.

"Do we just sit here and wait?" Elion asked. Freya shrugged as she leaned on her sword.

"We're the second line of defense. We have to protect Poseidon and An, but mostly An," Freya said. Elion stared at her for a moment, and dropped his voice to a lower decibel.

"Are you sure you want to give your life up for this?" Elion asked. "Couldn't you just hop to a different world? I could kill your Celestial body right now, if you want." Freya raised her eyebrows at the intensity that was being thrown her way. She stared up at the ceiling as she thought about what Elion said.

"Honestly, do I want to die? No, who wants to die?" Freya asked, a dry chuckle escaping her lips. "But, I do believe in An's vision, in the future that he foresees. And if that future doesn't hold me in it, I'm okay with that."

"I don't understand." Freya turned her head to look into Elion's eyes. *Such a young creature,* she thought.

"You wouldn't. My life was given by An. It is his to take as well," she merely muttered. Elion's eyes still betrayed his confusion, but he nodded once as if he understood what she meant.

"What about Esi?" Elion asked. Freya frowned as she thought about who Esi was. Then it dawned on her.

"Oh right," she said. "The Seer. Yes, the Seer is pretty important. An will probably be consulting her about the prophecy to make sure the eggs are just right." Just as Freya was saying this, An was asking Esi about the eggs.

"What colors were the eggs again?" Esi was sitting near An as she recalled the prophecy.

"White, Gold, Red, Gray, Green, Blue. Six eggs that were sent away," Esi recited. An nodded.

"So each egg is a different color. And each color represents a child," An mused.

"They probably should be human," Poseidon said, concentrating. An nodded.

"Yes, but humans that can hold enormous power within them," An responded. Poseidon stared at An, confused.

"If they need powers like the Gods, that'll be difficult to create. We couldn't create bodies for ourselves either. It's too much power," Poseidon pointed out. An shrugged as he pushed up his sleeves.

"We just have to make them stronger humans then. They'll be true Celestials, unlike these bodies," An said. Just as An started to get to work, with Poseidon breathing down his neck, Freya heard a sound come from outside the lab.

"Did you hear that?" she asked Elion. Elion nodded, his eyes wide. Freya stood up straight and walked towards the door. Outside, she could hear a muffled scream and some movement.

"Neith needs our help," Freya said, turning towards Elion. She turned around to look at An who's back was turned towards her.

"I'm going outside," Freya said. An turned so that his profile was showing.

"It's a Mortiferis," he said, turning back around. "Stall it for as long as you can." *You mean stall it until it takes my life,* Freya thought. She took a deep breath and then hit the button so that the door opened. Elion followed after her. An watched Freya's back as the door closed swiftly behind her.

"You should go," An said to Poseidon who was forming a fetus in the incubator. Poseidon stared at him.

"Are you sure you can do this by yourself?" he asked. An knew what Poseidon was thinking. An could tell that he didn't look well to Poseidon. It took a lot of energy for him to create this lab, but he knew he had enough to finish making the Saviors.

"I'll be fine," An replied. It wasn't the answer that Poseidon was looking for, but An rarely gave him the answers he wanted to hear. Poseidon hesitated for a moment and then adjusted his clothes. He wished he was wearing armor. Or at least a jacket, since it was colder than the underworld outside. Poseidon pressed the button, taking one last look at An who was bent over in concentration. This was the end, he knew, but he wasn't about to go without a fight. The door opened and Poseidon watched as Freya stabbed the Mortiferis with her sword, the monster screaming the sound of thousands. It took everything in Poseidon's power not to cover his ears. He felt his hand start to shake as he stepped out of the lab, the door closing quickly behind him.

Freya bent over from the sound, as she was too close to it. As the Mortiferis opened its mouth, Elion stepped in front of her, brandishing his sword at the Mortiferis' face. Poseidon watched in amazement as the Mortiferis hesitated, its face looking at Elion for a moment. Then, instead of eating Elion as Poseidon had noticed that the Mortiferis usually do, it hit him with its arm, which sent Elion flying. He hit the ground with a sickening thud. Poseidon stared at the mangled elf, who lay there. But he could see that Elion was still breathing. *It spared him*, Poseidon thought to himself, turning to look at the Mortiferis in wonder. *Why did it spare him?*

He didn't have much time to think as Freya dodged the Mortiferis' mouth and ran towards Poseidon. Her eyes looked desperate.

"Neith? Where's Neith?" Poseidon called out. Freya glanced over to the left of Poseidon. He slowly turned his head and there was the bottom half of Neith, her corpse gray and ash covered her. She was gone.

"We don't have a chance," Freya called out. Poseidon stared at the Mortiferis, his heart pounding. If he wasn't here, his life might be spared but... He shook his head. He couldn't think like that. Even if he could remain after An had left, he had to make sure that Asynithis could be saved. He made some of his favorite creatures on Asynithis. He couldn't just let it all be destroyed. Raising his arms, he was able to make the snow rise, blowing the Mortiferis backwards.

"The Mortiferis spared the elf," Poseidon said to Freya. "I've never seen one of these creatures do that before."

"Rhea must've changed how it thinks," Freya responded. She looked like she was about to cry. "I thought that child was going to die. Because of me."

"He'll live," Poseidon said, throwing more snow at the Mortiferis. It screamed angrily. "I don't think we have much time."

"We just need to stall," Freya said. "We won't survive, I know. But we have to make sure that An has enough time." Poseidon nodded. He ran quickly and grabbed Neith's sword, steadying himself. Freya eyed him.

"I think it'd be better if you just continued with the snow thing," Freya muttered.

"You don't think I know how to fight?" Poseidon asked, flabbergasted. Freya rolled her eyes.

"I *know* you don't know how to fi— just put down the sword," Freya shouted as Poseidon swung at the Mortiferis, clearly missing. He ran backwards as the Mortiferis lunged forward, dropping the sword and throwing more snow to blow the Mortiferis back.

"Bad day," Poseidon said as an excuse. Freya nodded sarcastically.

"Right," she said, her tone sarcastic. Poseidon looked around. They were running out of blocks of snow that he could throw.

"The time is now," Poseidon said. Freya took a deep breath, and lunged forward with her sword, knowing it was futile.

An listened to the commotion outside asking Esi what was going on.

"Neith is dead, but the monster spared the elf," Esi said, her white eyes looking around as if she were at the scene. An felt his chest ache. He knew someone had left but he wasn't sure who. Sweat beads were forming on his head as he started putting the fetuses in the eggs.

"So all that's left is Poseidon and Freya," he whispered. Esi's eyes glanced at the direction that he was in.

"They don't have much time. There's not enough snow for Poseidon to use," Esi said, her voice shaking a little. An sighed. He didn't want this child to die as well.

"You won't die, Esi, this isn't your end," An said. Esi smiled slightly.

"I know," she whispered. "I've seen bits and pieces of my

future." An put the last fetus into an egg, the egg closing up. They were highly decorated eggs with drawings and symbols all over it. They all looked like they'd been carved out of stone.

"The last of the Celestials," An whispered, his chest aching more. Esi's eyes widened and he could see tears forming in them. She closed them.

"Freya," she whispered. "She's left us." An closed his eyes. He needed to hurry. Poseidon wasn't going to last much longer, especially since he never felt the need to learn how to wield a sword.

"Recite the prophecy, quickly. I need to make sure I got each of the Saviors right," An ordered. Esi's eyes glowed as she quickly recited the prophecy once again. An sighed, his arms holding him up as they leaned against the lab table. It was done.

"Never tell anyone what is really in these eggs, Esi," An said. Esi stared in his direction.

"I won't, God of All," she said. He took a deep breath, and then raised the six eggs, making them float in the air. He turned towards Esi, who's eyes widened as her jaw clenched. Poseidon was gone.

"You must go," he said. Esi looked at him, her face looked haggard and older than her young age. She nodded as An waved his hands, turning her into air. He sent her away, though he knew he wouldn't be able to send her far. As he did, he watched as the walls around him started to disintegrate. Standing in front of him was the monster that he banished long, long ago.

"I'm sorry," An said to it, hoping that his brother might get the message. "For everything." The Mortiferis screamed, the screams of Poseidon, Neith, and Freya intermixed in them. An closed his eyes, tears welling in them for the first time. He pressed a button underneath the table, turning the table into a giant mirror. Quickly, he threw the eggs through them, sending them to Terra.

"You won't be able to go after them," An said towards the Mortiferis, who stared, in what An thought was shock, at the mirror. An breathed in and then released all the energy in his body in order to close the portals. Looking down at his hands, he watched as they started to gray and disintegrate in the wind. He looked up at the teeth of the Mortiferis that was about to end him. He smiled slightly.

"Be loyal and stay true," he said, keeping the prophecy's integrity in tack. And then he faced the dark throat of the Mortiferis.

36

"They said no," Khai said to Khalon. They had been waiting in the throne room for a couple of hours for the beastoids' response about joining in battle with one another.

"Did you tell them the apocalypse is here?" Rhea asked, standing up from her seat. The Ministers from earlier had all left and it was just Rhea, Khalon, Khai, Kamaria, and Aponi still there.

"Yes, and they said they would never team up with murderous racists like us," Khai muttered. He scoffed at the ground and looked incredibly angry. Rhea didn't want to be there when he exploded.

"Did you tell them the offer of their own country?" Rhea asked. Khai gave a dry chuckle.

"The Ministers and I all agree that we should not offer them their own country," Khai said. "That's too much."

"That's the only way they would join in," Rhea sighed, annoyed. Draconia was going to be taken over and once

Draconia falls, all the countries that Draconia blocks would be taken over as well. And they were all more worried about politics. Rhea angrily walked away from Khai. He was a child. No wonder why the God of Death wanted to rule the world so that there was no... She stopped herself. These weren't her thoughts. She had to keep him out of her head. She beckoned Khalon towards her. Khalon hesitated, staring at his brother, but then followed Rhea to the corner of the throne room. Kamaria tried to talk some sense into the young King.

"We need to make sure they don't get to Dragon Mountain," Rhea said. Khalon's thick eyebrows furrowed together.

"Dragon Mountain? What's happening on Dragon Mountain?" he asked, leaning against the wall. Rhea tried not to stare at his arm. She was thinking about him? At a time like this? She shook her head.

"They're creating the Saviors on Dragon Mountain once the battle starts. We have to make sure no one goes that way," Rhea thought for a moment, "At least, for a while." Khalon nodded in acknowledgment.

"Okay," he said. "I don't know how to convince my brother." Rhea shook her head in disgust.

"Your brother is a child who was raised by a power hungry witch. He won't budge," Rhea sneered. Khalon shook his head in disagreement as he stood up straight. He looked back at his little brother.

"He will. We just have to give them something else that works for both Draconia and the beastoids," Khalon said.

"We don't have much time, Khalon," Rhea said, touching his arm slightly. He looked down at the gesture and then smiled.

"I got this," he said, though Rhea had a sinking feeling that Khalon didn't in fact "got" it. He walked towards Kamaria and

Khai who were in a heated argument. Kamaria looked like she wanted to hit him over the head and Khai looked like he wanted to burn her to bits.

"Instead of giving them their own country, why don't we just give them sovereignty. They live where they already have been living and will have their own Minister or two to represent them in the palace but ultimately they get to make their own rules and laws to live by on that land. They'll still be a part of Draconia but they will live on their own terms. Win win, don't you think?" Kamaria frowned at Khalon's suggestion.

"Sovereignty is not the same as having their own country," Kamaria signed. Khalon nodded.

"I agree but Khai..."

"We don't need them," Khai said, stubbornly. Khalon pleaded with his eyes.

"Khai, we *need* them," he said.

"They won't agree to sovereignty. They'd be stupid to," Kamaria pointed out.

"*I* am the one who is king, not you. *I'm* the one who saved Draconia and *I'll* make sure Draconia doesn't fall," Khai exploded, standing up from his chair. His skin flickered between turning into scales and skin. Khalon's frown deepened.

"You've been drinking dragon blood," he said. Khai scoffed.

"So what if I have? You got to be blessed with the spirit of the dragon but not all of us have to suffer. I have the same powers now. Perhaps even more potent because I am consuming it all the time—" Khalon didn't want to hear another word of him convincing himself of his decisions.

"What about the dragon? Is it in pain?" Khalon asked. Rhea watched as his face contorted into agony.

"It's alive," Khai muttered. He looked away, walking back to his throne.

"Your mother forced you to do this?" Khalon assumed, his face relaxing once again. Khai turned to glare at Khalon before sitting down.

"Do not speak of the ill," he said. Khalon's eyes widened.

"Queen Aoife is ill?" he asked. Khai turned away, not wanting to discuss further.

"I'll protect Draconia. Like I did before, without you," he hissed. Khalon stood still for a moment longer. Rhea could see his blood boiling within him.

"I can't believe you want to ask the beastoids for help after what they did to our father," Khai muttered, almost under his breath. Khalon stared at him, his heart stopping.

"What?" Khai stared at his brother and shook his head, frustrated.

"It's nothing."

"Fine," Khalon said, turning away. He gave Rhea a look that read that he would want to talk to her about this later, but Rhea didn't meet his eyes. She waited for a moment longer, exchanging concerned looks with Kamaria, and then followed after Khalon. Before they could walk out of the throne room, a draconian wearing full armor made from dragon skin entered.

"They're here," he said. Khai stood up slightly, his face going through a mixture of emotions. But quickly his face hardened, an expression that Rhea had seen on Khalon's many times. It was a mask to hide the fear that bubbled deep within.

"Let's go," Khai said. He quickly morphed into a humanoid dragon, covering himself in red scales. It was stronger than any armor. Khalon glared as his brother stalked out of the room, following after him. Kamaria hopped up out of the chair she had just sat in and beckoned for Aponi to follow her. They were about to go into battle.

Rhea's throat closed up as she ran to catch up with Khalon. She tapped him on the arm and his head swiveled around. His expression was hard and he looked angry, but his eyes softened when he saw her.

"I... I don't know how to use a sword," she said. Khalon stared at her, dumb-founded.

"You don't know how to use a sword?" he asked. Rhea shifted uncomfortably.

"Is it *that* much of a shock that I don't know how to use a sword?" she asked. Khalon nodded his head, his eyes still wide. Rhea sighed.

"I just never learned. I'm not the only one. An and Poseidon never learned as well. We don't really need to. It's not like we ever go into battle," she muttered. "Plus, I can kill people just by saying so, so it's not like I really need to know how to wield a sword." Khalon twisted his mouth in concern as he continued to walk straight ahead.

"Rhea, your powers have weakened," Khalon pointed out. Rhea puffed out her cheeks in frustration.

"Yup," she admitted. "But hopefully I'll be fine. Give me a sword just in case." Khalon stared at her as she continued walking. She couldn't tell what he was thinking, but she knew he was concerned. He needed to let go of her anyways, she thought. She wasn't going to live for much longer.

"I'll find a sword for you," he said. "But you need to answer a question for me." Rhea looked at Khalon's face, and though it was as stony as usual, she could guess what the question was.

"It was that day, when I told him his future," Rhea answered. Khalon didn't dare to look at her.

"He continued with the battle and didn't heed my warning. He's been dead for a while, Khalon. But his soul..." Rhea wasn't sure how she could put this. "His soul is missing. It disappeared when he died. We don't know where it went." His eyes widened as he heard about his father's soul, but that wasn't what he cared about most. Khalon never had much hope about the afterlife.

He was quiet, after Rhea spoke, and he looked up at the sky momentarily before continuing to walk. He didn't say another word. The father that he always wanted to have loved him, was gone. There was no chance for them to ever fix their relationship. Rhea felt the pain that was brewing underneath Khalon's skin and quickly looked away. She should've told him. At some point, she should've told him.

They then walked out of the palace and towards the edge of Furvus. Rhea squinted her eyes and could see that over the hill that belonged to No Man's Land was an army of elves. Their white hair was covered by a helmet and they wore white armor. It was said to be as strong as draconian armor, but Rhea knew that it wasn't quite there.

"Unicorns," Khalon said, astonished. His eyes were wide like a kid's and she chuckled at his reaction.

"Elves and unicorns go hand in hand," she said. "They breed them." Khalon nodded as they caught up to the rest of the draconian army. Both armies were just standing there, waiting. For what, Rhea didn't know. Khalon ran up to a tent and dipped inside as Kamaria adjusted her armor next to Rhea.

"Esi?" she signed. Rhea shrugged.

"She's with An. An won't let his daughter die though," Rhea reassured. Kamaria frowned.

"Daughter?" she asked. Rhea felt her face heat up.

"Oh, uh, the Seer is An's daughter. It's why she has his eyes. The eyes that can see all," she explained. Kamaria stared at her for a moment and then turned away. She pointed a finger to the sky, fire erupting from it and exploding into little sparks. Rhea held her breath. She had heard the Princess of Ustrina was granted a Kongamato but had never seen one in this lifetime. They were hidden away with other Inkanyambas in the rainforests of Ustrina. Normally Kongamatos were called by lightning, as Inkanyambas can control the weather. But, Kamaria had an affinity for fire more, and trained it to come by it.

Rhea looked up as she heard the wings flapping loudly. The wind started to pick up and she put a hand over her eyes to look at the beast. It was what she remembered, deep in her memory. It lowered itself; its beady eyes keeping a watchful eye on her. The other draconians scattered in fear from the beast. They had never seen a creature like it before. Kamaria hopped on.

"I've taken care of the reinforcements," Kamaria signed to Rhea. "Let the bastard know." Rhea winced at the word "bastard" but nodded. Kamaria flew up to the sky as Rhea looked over at Aureum's army. If they were fazed by the Kongamato, they didn't show it. Khalon stepped out of the tent holding a sword made from the blood of a dragon. It was similar to what Khalon had, but it was smaller. And at closer look, it was a synthetic material, not a true white glass. He paused for a second, seeing the Kongamato, but then walked over to Rhea.

"You've seen it before," Rhea deduced. Khalon rubbed the back of his head.

"Yeah, we rode it when we came here. Also, Aponi here can turn into a bird," he said. Aponi shrugged as he said this and jumped while transitioning into a white bird. Rhea pursed her lips. The witch's essence was so strong coming off of her, she didn't even realize that Aponi was a lightning bird.

"She killed her witch, didn't she?" Rhea asked. Khalon nodded, surprised that Rhea knew.

"Here," he said, handing her the sword. "Hopefully it keeps you safe rather than putting you in even more danger."

"Excuse you, I'm *millions* of years older than you. I *think* I can manage a sword," she said, ripping it out of Khalon's hands. A smile played on his lips and Rhea ducked her head. She couldn't look at him for too long. It made what she was going to do so much harder. She heard the general of Draconia's army calling out directions to their men. The soldiers in the back were riding on horses called Chollima. She had heard that they were able to run faster than any other horse, and were difficult to tame. It was why the Draconian army had little. The Chollimas grunted and flapped their wings as the general continued shouting. Khalon adjusted the armor that he had put on while he was in the tent, and started walking towards the front of the line. Rhea grabbed his arm, quickly.

"Before I forget, Kamaria said that she has taken care of the reinforcements," Rhea said. Khalon frowned.

"Whatever that means," he muttered. He then grabbed Rhea, pulling her towards the battlefield. "Stay close to me, okay? I want to keep an eye on you." She nodded, staring up at him. *Will he be sad?* She wondered. *Will he be okay once I'm gone?* Rhea shook her head. She didn't even know if he liked her like that. Gripping her sword, she concentrated on her weakened power. Hopefully, she'll still be able to use it, despite how distant the God of Death felt. *It won't work*, she heard him think.

"You can't stop me," she said aloud. Khalon glanced at her confused and then shrugged it off. The ground shook as the unicorns took off down the hill. The Chollimas took to the sky and the Griffins in the Aureum army followed after them. The battle had started. Khalon stood his ground and morphed himself into a black scaled dragon. His scales flashed red in the rising sun, and he bashed his teeth together as his gold eyes surveyed the army. Rhea could hear the sounds of sword on sword, of flesh being ripped apart. She heard screams and watched as the elves came towards her. She concentrated and slowly took the life of those around her. It was all over-whelming.

Khalon was fighting with every part of him. He breathed fire and watched as Kamaria sent down inflamed arrows onto the army below her. Wings made of fire were surrounding her, and the sky slowly turned gray. The power of an Inkanyamba and a Phoenix. He felt his sword cut through the opponents around him like water. He had no time to think, only to act. Making sure he kept an eye on Rhea, he got rid of anyone that was around them, while she also helped. But he could tell that she was looking more and more tired.

"Are you okay?" he was able to say. She looked up at him.

"It's happening," she said, her eyes glassy. He frowned as the sky got darker. In the distance, the reinforcements that Kamaria was talking about were coming over the horizon, flying on Kongamatos. Khalon smiled at Rhea.

"Kamaria got the Inkanyambas to come," he said as he fought back an elf. Rhea's white face looked grayer by the second. She looked towards the Aureum army.

"Not that," she breathed out. "Them." Khalon looked towards what Rhea's eyes were fixated on and he felt his heart almost stop. There were Mortiferis. Many of them. Perhaps more than twenty. A lot more than Rhea had thought.

"He pulled them out before An closed the portals," she muttered, smiling slightly. But her eyes looked angry. Khalon stared at the Mortiferis as he watched his brother ride his Chollima closer to the army of monsters.

"Khai!" Khalon cried out, but he knew it wasn't worth it. Khai couldn't hear him. Rhea looked up, her eyes looked like they were about to spill over with tears.

"What is it?" he asked. Blinking back the tears that threatened to leave her eyes, she grabbed his face as he morphed back to his humanoid self. Her thumb stroked the claw mark of scales that were on part of his cheek, as she wouldn't meet his eyes.

"My family is gone," she choked. "But, I'll make sure that you and your family are okay."

"What are you—"

"I think I might love you Khalon Draconia," Rhea whispered. Khalon frowned. Why was she saying this? "Me, Rhea. *I love you.*"

"Rhea, why are you talking like you're about to die?" he asked. She looked down and then bit her lip. He had never seen her look more scared.

"I think I'll always love you," she whispered, stepping up on her tiptoes. She kissed him quickly on the lips and before Khalon could do anything, she turned away and her body disappeared into the shadows.

"Rhea?" Khalon cried out as he watched her pop back out of the shadows, but closer to the Mortiferis.

"Rhea!" Khalon shouted as he tried to run towards her. He cut down some elves, trying to get to her. She looked back, her eyes meeting his. He thought she mouthed that she was sorry, and then suddenly, she arched her back, her arms out as if she had been pushed backwards. A burst of energy came from her body as the Mortiferis descended on her. It knocked them down, one by one, and Khalon watched as they hit the ground. He waited with baited breath to see if they would rise, but they stayed down. His eyes searched the bodies for Rhea's, desperately looking for her. *She sacrificed herself*, Khalon thought as he ran towards her. *Why would she sacrifice herself?*

The battle continued around them, as if nothing happened,

the elves only pausing for a moment as their secret weapon was cut down. Khalon couldn't understand how the world didn't stop spinning. Kamaria's Kongamato landed nearby where Khalon was and she jumped off of the beast, running at full speed towards Rhea. Khalon saw her, her copper hair splayed out around her face. Her eyes that used to hold fire in them were just brown now. They stared up into nothing as Khalon grabbed her head.

"Rhea," he whispered, his eyes burning. Kamaria caught up to him as Aponi landed next to Rhea's body.

"You can't be sitting here like this," Kamaria signed.

"I didn't get to tell her," Khalon said, his voice the smallest he had ever heard it. Kamaria glanced at Aponi.

"I didn't get to tell her," Khalon repeated, tears starting to spill over. Teardrops hit Rhea's face, the salty liquid staining her pale skin. *I didn't get to tell her that I love her too.* It felt as if someone ripped Khalon's lungs out. He couldn't breathe. He pushed the hair off of her face as he held her head close to his chest.

"Khalon," Aponi said, a hand on his shoulder. He could barely feel it.

"The Mortiferis aren't dead," Aponi said, a little louder. The words hit his ears but he wasn't able to process it. "They're sleeping." As she said this, Rhea's body started to fade into the shadows, taking with her the bodies of the Mortiferis. Khalon tried to grasp at her body, desperately, as she faded. He called out her name as the last of her body disappeared, her eyes still fixated on the sky.

Khalon tried to pray to anyone for help. He tried to pray to An or Poseidon. But it felt different. The thoughts weren't going anywhere.

"We need to go," Aponi ordered as Kamaria helped Khalon to his feet. He stared at the spot that Rhea once was. The Gods of Asynithis were gone. He could feel it. But if Rhea could disappear into the shadows, maybe she wasn't dead. It was the only hope that Khalon had as Kamaria dragged him up onto the Kongamato.

I love you, Rhea, Khalon prayed, hoping that she would be able to get the message. *I'll find you.*

ACKNOWLEDGMENTS

Thank you to my loving fiancé for listening to each chapter as I read it aloud in order to figure out if I actually like what I wrote or not. Also for listening to me ramble on about how scared and nervous I was about releasing this book into the world. You are the absolute best partner in life and I appreciate your unwavering support and advice!

Thank you to my dad for getting me into the habit of reading all of the time. You taking me to the library every couple of weeks so I could bring home a giant stack of books to read is one of my favorite memories. Without you, I don't think I would've ever become a writer. You have always believed in me and loved whatever I would write, even if it was terrible. You gave me this giant imagination that I have and I can never thank you enough for it!

Thank you to my 엄마 for always pushing me to be the best that I can be. You have always told me that I can be anyone I want to be, as long as I work hard. Because of you, if I want to do something, I'll do it. No matter how hard or difficult it might be. This book was one of those accomplishments. I have you to thank for my strong will-power and positive outlook on life. Thank you, 엄마!

And lastly, thank you to my wonderful book cover illustrator and best friend, Laurel Mosher. Thank you for dealing with my fickleness during this process and for creating such a beautiful cover. Even in high school, you have always been excited to read my stories, and I really appreciated your editing advice that you gave while reading my story. Thank you for always encouraging me! You're the best!

ABOUT THE AUTHOR

Bianca K. Gray is the author of her first novel *The Celestials*. She graduated from the University of Virginia with a Bachelor Degree in English. Bianca also received a Master Degree from the same institution in English Education. A former 8th grade English teacher, Bianca has always had a love of literature that she wants others to discover and cultivate within themselves. She currently resides in the *sometimes* sunny San Francisco, CA with her fiancé, rambunctious shih-tzu, and the most adorable kitty cat.

instagram.com/biancakgray.author